Taylor Gray grew up wg far too much romance ─── it research. She spends h─── a notebook and wishin─── ─── er characters thought. She lives in a house overtaken by plants and pictures with her husband, son and cat.

facebook.com/TaylorGrayAuthor
instagram.com/taylorgrayauthor

Also by Taylor Gray

The Autumn Falls series

Autumn Falls

Silver Sky

Redemption River

Starlight Mountain

Midnight Promise

AUTUMN FALLS

TAYLOR GRAY

One More Chapter
a division of HarperCollins*Publishers* Ltd
1 London Bridge Street
London SE1 9GF
www.harpercollins.co.uk
HarperCollins*Publishers*
Macken House, 39/40 Mayor Street Upper,
Dublin 1, D01 C9W8, Ireland
This paperback edition 2025

1

First published in Great Britain in ebook format
by HarperCollins*Publishers* 2025
Copyright © Taylor Gray 2025
Taylor Gray asserts the moral right to be identified
as the author of this work
A catalogue record of this book is available from the British Library
ISBN: 978-0-00-879754-6

This novel is entirely a work of fiction. The names, characters and incidents portrayed in it are the work of the author's imagination. Any resemblance to actual persons, living or dead, events or localities is entirely coincidental.

Printed and bound in the UK using 100% Renewable Electricity
by CPI Group (UK) Ltd

All rights reserved. No part of this publication may be reproduced, stored in a retrieval system, or transmitted, in any form or by any means, electronic, mechanical, photocopying, recording or otherwise, without the prior permission of the publishers.
Without limiting the exclusive rights of any author, contributor or the publisher of this publication, any unauthorised use of this publication to train generative artificial intelligence (AI) technologies is expressly prohibited. HarperCollins also exercise their rights under Article 4(3) of the Digital Single Market Directive 2019/790 and expressly reserve this publication from the text and data mining exception.

For Charlotte L

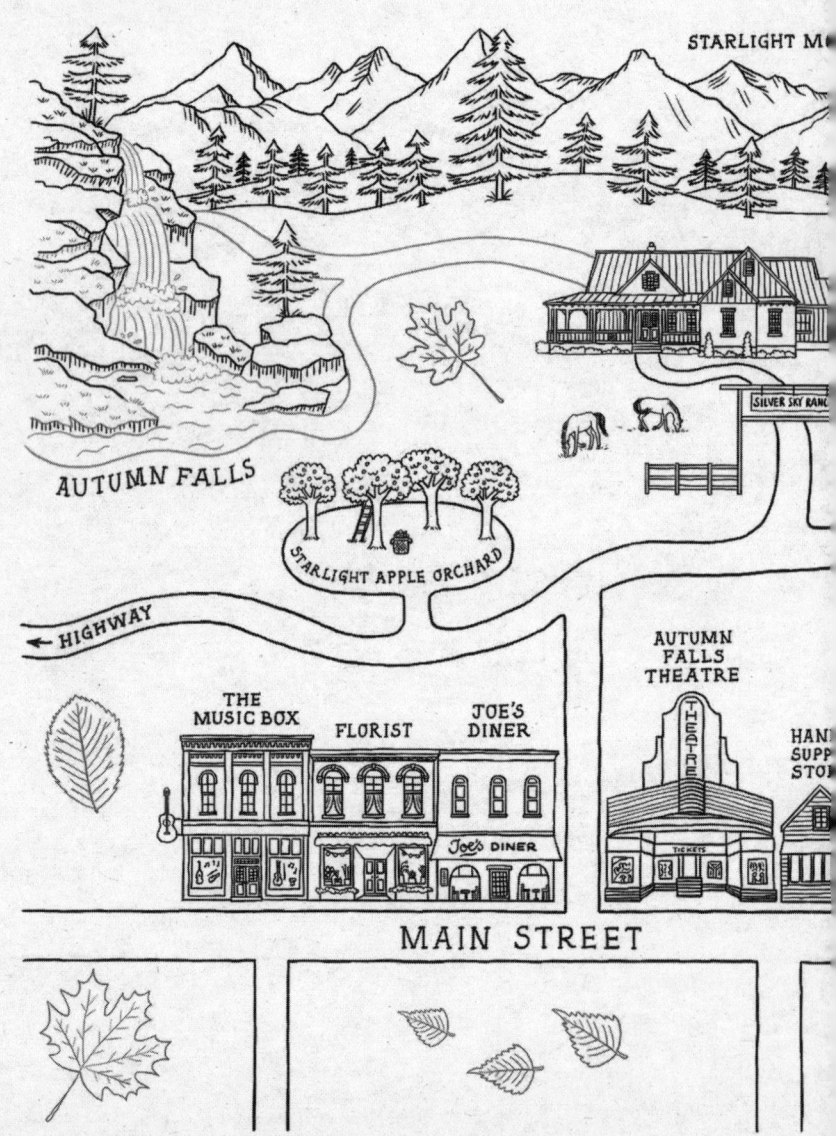

Playlist

Sugar Talking - Sabrina Carpenter
this is what autumn feels like - JVKE
Northern Attitude - Noah Kahan, Hozier
Flowers - Miley Cyrus
gold rush - Taylor Swift
Sweater Weather - The Neighbourhood
'tis the damn season - Taylor Swift
Falling - Harry Styles
Blackbird - The Beatles
the grudge - Olivia Rodrigo
Scott Street - Phoebe Bridgers
Vodka Cranberry - Conan Gray
Man I Need - Olivia Dean
Sexy to Someone - Clairo
Wagon Wheel - Old Crow Medicine Show
I Love You, I'm Sorry - Gracie Abrams
US - James Bay
Silver Springs - Fleetwood Mac
Skinny Love - Bon Iver
Cleopatra - The Lumineers
You & I - One Direction
we fell in love in october - girl in red
Wildest Dreams - Taylor Swift

Prologue

"Tell me you won't miss this."

Bella and Logan stood side by side at the edge of the waterfall, the sun glistening off the endless cascades of water, the pool beneath them inky blue in the early evening light.

"I won't miss it," Bella replied.

Logan rolled his eyes. He knew her well enough to know when she was lying. "Yes, you will."

She took a step closer to the edge, thought back to the first time she'd stood there, toes curled over the rock, Logan beckoning from the crystal-clear pool below. It had taken all her courage to dive, the sound of the waterfall rushing in her ears, but it had felt as close to flying as she ever could have imagined before she'd plunged into the icy mountain water. When she came up laughing, Logan's eyes glinted like he'd shown her treasure.

"Okay, I admit, I'll miss it."

She watched his mouth tilt up in victory before adding, "Not as much as you're going to miss me, though."

"I'm not going to miss you!" He made a face like the idea was ridiculous, his dark brows drawn together in a frown.

"Yes, you are!" She laughed and went to bash him on the chest for trying to deny it, but on reflex he caught her hand with his—too much time spent sparring with his brothers.

The touch was so unexpected that it seemed to catch them both off-guard. She looked up and saw Logan's laughing blue gaze become suddenly serious. Felt her heart tighten in her chest as something passed between them that had always been otherwise ignored, contained, unspoken. She watched his throat as he swallowed, as his hand held hers a fraction too long and a look came over his face that she'd never seen before. *Don't do it, Bella,* a voice said in her head. *You're going. You're out of here. Look away.*

So, she forced herself to look away, anywhere. And her eye caught on the signet ring glinting in the sunlight on his finger.

"What is *that*?" she asked, incredulous.

Logan winced and immediately dropped her hand. The moment thankfully diverted, back to friends, her thrumming heart the only giveaway the look had ever happened.

"My dad gave it to me," he said, slipping the ring off and passing it to her. "It's been in the family for years. Handed down from father to eldest son for generations. You know, 'Here, the ranch is yours now.' Or will be."

"But you don't want it, do you?" She frowned, studying

the insignia of the Silver Sky ranch engraved on the surface before passing it back.

"Yes." He put the ring back on, looked at it. "No." He paused. "I don't know." He tipped his head up toward trees above them. She knew his expressions so well, the sharpness of his jaw, the depth of his sigh.

The waterfall roared behind them, the sun flickering through the pine trees danced on their skin.

She could say, "It's not too late to come to New York with me," but she knew that he never would.

The wind rustled the trees above them scattering pine needles. One must have landed in her hair because he reached forward and untangled it gently, chucking it absently to the ground as he kept his eyes on hers. "I will really miss you."

When he said it, she felt the aching pull to do what she would never do and reach up and trace the side of his face with her hand. And maybe he would wrap his arms around her and she could stay there forever.

But she could never stay. Just as much as he could never leave.

Their paths led in different directions.

Fearing he might step closer, that his hand might reach over to touch her and then she'd never leave, with all her willpower she backed away, one step, then two. Then when she knew her feet were close enough to the edge, she turned and she dived, flying down, down into the deep, dark pool of the waterfall. Slicing through the glassy surface, the shock of the cold leaving her breathless.

When she came up for air, she looked to see Logan

standing at the lip of the rock, watching, the sun behind him so she couldn't see the expression on his face, her heart thumping with a mixture of relief and something dangerously close to regret.

Chapter One

Logan reclined back in his chair and checked his watch.

The interviewer could sense he was losing him. "Last question." He glanced down at his notes and back up with a mischievous glint in his eye. "Carter Media's one of the major independent contenders in the global music industry, there are always rumors of offers on the table. What are the chances of you selling up?"

Logan raised a brow at the stupidity of the question. "Zero."

"Haha. Seriously. You're one of six siblings. You've been incredibly successful first in the boy band, Silver Sky, now as head of Carter Media. Do you ever think about slowing down? Starting your own family? For the listeners, Logan has just shaken his head."

"I'm pretty happy as I am, thanks." Logan remained impassive while internally rolling his eyes.

"So, life's good?"

He angled his head, wry smile on his lips. "Life's great."

The interviewer knew that was the best he was going to get. "Good to hear it," he said. "Any final words of advice for fellow entrepreneurs?"

Logan didn't need to think about it. "Work harder and smarter than everyone else…"

Before he could add any more final words of wisdom, there was a quick rap on the door and Marianne, Logan's PA, said, "Sorry to interrupt. Logan—it's urgent."

Logan frowned.

Sensing something was seriously amiss from the look on Marianne's face, the interviewer gathered up his papers and said, "Thanks for talking to me, Logan." They had a quick distracted handshake. "Always a pleasure."

Marianne stood restlessly in the doorway, ushering him out.

When the door closed and she started walking toward him, Logan said, "What's going on?"

"It's your brother," she said.

"Which one?" Logan asked, immediately alert. *What had happened now? What disaster needed clearing up?*

"It's Jack, Logan. He was in an accident—car crash. He's dead."

Jack, Logan, he's dead.

Jack, Logan…

He kept replaying it as he sat on the plane to Autumn

Falls. The way Marianne's lip had pulled in a subtle gesture of sympathy, the buzzing silence in his head.

It was hard to comprehend that he was flying home for his brother's funeral. It still felt so unreal.

He glanced back to the newspaper in his hand, the aircraft bouncing through turbulence, his heart tightening at the sight of Jack's face lighting up the front cover, the infamous dimple in his cheek, the lazily laughing eyes. Everyone knew, if you wanted a good time, you went to Jack.

Logan steeled himself to turn the page to where the pictures continued, the most recent showed Jack on the red carpet at an awards ceremony, taken just weeks ago. He was the big Hollywood star, now. Or had been.

Logan had to squeeze his eyes shut for a moment at the idea that he'd never see Jack again. It was like every few minutes his brain still had to catch up with the reality. He felt the sudden claustrophobic tightness of the plane, the lack of escape, the sound of his heart in his ears. But he pushed it down, unscrewed the cap of his water and took a cooling sip.

On the opposite page were photos of Logan and his brothers. All of them young, on stage in Silver Sky, Jack with his arm punching the air, grinning wide. Images that Logan had barely glanced at in years. Toothy, youthful faces full of hope and promise and excitement, guitars around their necks, sweat on their brows, eyes shining bright, it was like looking at wax figures, paused in time, wondering who they all could have been had they taken a different path.

Of course, the article had matched the pictures of them

as boys with who they were now. There was Noah getting into his SUV in Autumn Falls looking furious at the camera intrusion; Brodie at the airport, hand raised in open greeting—relaxed and confident when it came to the press.

Logan's jaw clenched to see shots of his baby sister, Willow, coming out of the Cornelia Street Ballet studios, head cocked defensively, he imagined her confronting the faceless lenses with a, "Really? You think this is helping? My brother's just *died*!"

There were no recent pictures of Ethan, of course—it seemed even the press couldn't find him—just an old shot of him out on maneuvers in desert camo gear, looking blank-eyed and ruthless.

And then there was Logan himself, striding stony-faced past reporters outside his New York office. Memories of having the camera shoved in his face had made him surge with an anger, he was surprised to discover, he could barely suppress. Transporting him instantly back to his time in the band and the suffocating relentlessness of the paparazzi—camped outside every hotel they stayed at, confining them to their rooms, the grasping hands snatching at their clothes, running after them in the street, nails scratching their skin. The tapped phones. The undercover journalists masquerading as room-service waiters. The honeytrap kiss-and-tell stories. The lies conjured up by their manager on slow news days, stories that sowed the first seeds of mistrust between them and had his mom crying on the phone and his dad retreating further into resentment.

Then at the bottom of the page was the photo Logan had been avoiding. There was Bella outside the front door of her apartment, cap pulled low, face hidden. The lights of the hounding camera flashes reflected in her sunglasses. He'd be lying if the photos of her didn't make him uneasy. She looked terrified. She may not be his favorite person in the world, but seeing her there in black and white he felt some, perhaps misplaced, duty to protect her through this mess. At the same time, he remembered Jack sobbing on the phone, "She's left me, Logan. She's gone!" and reminded himself that Bella was more than capable of looking after herself.

Chapter Two

Logan pushed the newspaper away and stared out the window as the pilot announced ten minutes to landing. It was going to be tough, seeing his family—seeing his mother, especially—so upset. He didn't know if Bella was coming to the funeral, she hadn't returned Marianne's messages. He still hadn't been able to track down Ethan. He could feel his control on things slipping. Just being back in Autumn Falls was going to be uncomfortable enough.

It was a welcome surprise when he landed, therefore, to see not the Mercedes he'd ordered waiting, but his brother, Brodie, arms crossed, red Wayfarer sunglasses on, leaning against his little silver Aston Martin.

"What are you doing here?" Logan asked with a bemused smile as Brodie stepped forward and clapped him into a hug. It never mattered with Brodie whether you'd seen him yesterday or two years ago, he was exactly the same.

"Because I thought you might want to see a friendly

face," Brodie replied, and Logan found himself momentarily choked.

Never had he been *more* relieved to see a friendly face. Especially Brodie's, who was born smiling, his mouth always turned up at the corners, his eyes crinkling like he was forever waiting for the joke. He was just one of those people that made you feel better just being with him.

"Thanks," Logan managed and Brodie tightened the hug, "It'll be okay."

Logan stepped back. He nodded. "I know." He glanced away for a second to tamp down the feelings, took in the surroundings. The pine-covered hills behind the concrete runways, the scrubby grass around them, the familiar, green-roofed terminal buildings. He felt momentarily like an animal sensing a trap.

Brodie narrowed his eyes as he assessed Logan and said, "You look…" He searched for the politest word.

"I don't need to hear it." Logan went around to sling his bag in the trunk. He felt completely out of place in his shirt and suit pants, fresh from the office, especially compared to Brodie who was forever coolly casual, like life was one long vacation.

"I was gonna say you look stressed." Brodie smirked, yanking open the car door.

"Yeah well, you try organizing this circus." Logan got his sunglasses out of his top pocket, slipped them on. Even they felt plain and businesslike compared to Brodie's bright red ones.

Brodie blew out a breath as if to say, no thank you.

"Dad's already threatened a couple of reporters with his shotgun," he said over the top of the car.

"He hasn't?" Logan groaned, tipping his head up to the sky as he opened the passenger door and folded himself into the tiny sports car.

"Oh, he has." Brodie nodded, starting the engine. "Just like old times."

Closing his eyes for a second, Logan shook his head. "This is actually a nightmare."

Brodie threw back a half-smile. "People Jack knew have been arriving all day. The press are having a field day. Just to warn you, they're everywhere."

Logan thought of Bella again.

"Ready?" Brodie asked.

Logan nodded. "You know me, I'm always ready."

Brodie laughed.

They drove out onto the main airport road, passed camped-out photographers. Cameras flashed. Names called. Logan's body went rigid, his heart pounded. He thought he was done with all this.

It was only when they hit the highway that he could relax. Or as much as he could relax with Brodie driving, at one point having to steady himself with a hand on the dash, earning him a white-toothed grin from his younger brother.

The concrete airport scenery gave way to the wide-open country, the waft of pine through the window, the sun hitting the acres of pasture, the mountains majestic in the distance, the Redemption River winding casually alongside. Logan stared out at the long, straight road ahead. There was no bumper-to-bumper traffic, no horns, no shouts or bustling sidewalks, just space and sky, and in his head he started counting the days till he could get back to New York.

He undid his cuffs and rolled his sleeves up past his elbow, raked a hand through his hair.

Beside him, Brodie hummed along to the radio, nodding his head, tapping the beat on the steering wheel. He was like their mom, always singing.

The reminder of her led Logan to ask, "How's Mom?"

Brodie glanced over, "Devastated. Putting on a brave face."

Logan's chest tightened at the idea. "And Dad?"

"Who knows!" Brodie took his hands off the wheel to shrug.

Logan gestured for him to put them back. Then thought about his dad, wondered what he was feeling. Emmett Carter was not one to show emotion.

"How are *you*?" Brodie asked.

The emphasis on him Logan read to mean because he was closest to Jack. The eldest two brothers, they were, as their mom always said, thick as thieves. "I'm okay," he said, because he'd never say anything different. "I think it'll make more sense when this is over. When the public side of things has died down."

Brodie nodded but didn't look convinced.

Logan stared blankly back out at the view, at the lush grass and the wildflowers tipping into the kaleidoscope of summer. He thought how the person he would most likely message about how surreal it all felt was Jack. Just a couple of quick, snatched messages that would be enough to make him smirk and then get on with his day. All the shorthand and inside jokes that came from knowing someone a lifetime gone in an instant. "Did you talk to Jack much recently?" he asked.

"No. Not for a while. I should have done but—" Brodie glanced across, guiltily "—there just wasn't time."

"I know." Logan sighed. "Sounds stupid now, doesn't it? Not enough time."

Brodie shrugged sadly. "Everyone's busy."

"Yeah." The road stretched out endlessly ahead of them. Busy was a terrible excuse. Since he'd learned about Jack's death, he'd been regretting all those missed opportunities to see each other. Neither of them had made it back for Christmas—Logan because of work, Jack because he was filming somewhere abroad. He thought how often they canceled their plans last minute because something more urgent came up. And because Jack posted constantly on Instagram, Logan felt like he knew what he was doing, most of the time anyway, and there was always a running thread of casual messages between them.

Why hadn't they tried harder? Why hadn't he insisted they meet?

The photo of Bella in the newspaper flashed into his mind, he immediately closed his eyes to get rid of it. When he opened them again, the horizon miraged and he saw up ahead the first sign for Autumn Falls.

Brodie glanced his way, said wryly, "Home, sweet home."

Chapter Three

Bella stood in the hallway of the little cabin on the Starlight Apple Orchard that had been her family home since she was sixteen. Her mom, her stepdad and her friend, Claudette, hovered around her. It was the morning of Jack Carter's funeral.

"You don't have to go you know?" said her stepdad, John-Luke, who was as dressed up as he could manage in navy pants and a black sweater.

"I do," Bella replied, steadfast. She felt stiff and uncomfortable in the kind of sharply tailored clothes that she used to wear when she'd worked at *Vogue*, but she'd bought the outfit because it felt like armor and she needed that kind of protection today. She nodded toward the closed curtains of the front window that hid the waiting paparazzi. "They'll be worse if I don't." She'd already had to deal with them waiting outside her apartment in New York, being jostled and pushed she tried her best to brace for each knock as she walked out of her front door. Then at the airport, blinding camera flashes, endless, goading comments to get her riled up, hands banging on the car roof.

Claudette went to peek out at the waiting photographers. "I could say you're ill."

Bella gave her a look like that might possibly make things worse and Claudette winced in agreement.

Her mom leaned over and enveloped her in a hug that smelled comfortingly of almond moisturizer and soap. Bella would have stayed there all day, but she made herself pull away. "It'll be okay. I think it might even help to go."

No one looked convinced.

But then John-Luke said matter-of-factly, "Right, then. As we planned, your mom and I will drive out from the garage. You and Claudette go out the back and leave in Claudette's car through the delivery gates. We'll send you a text when we're ready."

Claudette nodded. "Got it."

Bella hated that her family all had to be involved in dodging the press intrusion, but was eternally grateful all the same. She slipped on her sunglasses and walked with Claudette through the house.

Her heart pounded with every step she took, her eyes barely registering the beautiful rows of blossom-laden trees, her palms sweating as she got in the car and Claudette drove them out the back gates where, of course, more press were waiting, not fooled for a minute by the decoy of her parents leaving out the front and pushing their cameras against the car window, shutters firing a million frames per second.

Bella covered her face with her hands until they were clear.

While she hated it, she could deal with the press intrusion again for this short time—during her short marriage to the infamous Jack Carter, she'd dealt with it daily, and since the divorce had been forced to get used to being vilified and blamed for ending the nation's fairy-tale romance. It was seeing the Carter family again that put her most on edge. Made her have to deep-breathe, suddenly queasy. It had been so long since she'd seen them. What would they think about her, how would they act when they saw her?

The road leading to the churchyard was packed with reporters, security guards keeping them all in check. Bella kept her eyes fixed ahead as they drove past, didn't want to look at the cameras, focused instead on the line of limos inside the gates and a veritable soup of celebrities making their way up to the church. Then, once they were safely through the gates themselves and parked, she had to steel herself for a moment before opening the door. Her body was working against her—fighting to stay in the car. Sweat bristled on her skin. Her fingers shook.

Claudette looked a little worried when she said, "Are you going to get out the car?"

Bella nodded. "Of course. Sorry." She forced herself to open the door. It would be okay.

The barrage of photographers audibly increased the moment she appeared on the path up to the red brick church with its white tower. Her mom and John-Luke tried their best to shield her. Bella kept her head down, sunglasses fixed in place, she certainly wasn't going to give the cameras her eyes. She tried for cool, calm strides but her heart raced and her legs started to shake, making her realize she wasn't used to walking in high heels any longer. The noise of the cameras was overwhelming, rapid firing, like gunshots. She didn't look up until she'd reached the church.

And there they were. The Carters.

She had been dreading this moment. So much slander and speculation had been written about her over the years, everyone had an opinion about her and Jack's marriage, but the overriding public opinion was always that it was her fault. She ruined it, then she went after the money. The papers, she had come to understand, could write what they liked. A good story was always preferable to the truth. There were only a few people's opinions she really cared about and most of them were standing in front of her now.

Jack's parents, Martha and Emmett Carter, and beside them, Noah, Brodie and Willow. She could barely look at them.

When Emmett saw her, he immediately looked away and Bella felt the disapproval curl inside her. She didn't know whether to carry on, to say hello to Martha or whether to do so would be seen as an intrusion. She wanted to shrink back but felt John-Luke put his hand gently on her arm and it gave her the courage to take the step forward. At the same time Martha did the same, stepping to greet her with a polite upward tilt of her mouth, not quite a smile but not a frown. A detached acknowledgment that allowed Bella to say, "I'm so sorry."

And for Martha to nod and say, "Thank you," before turning away.

Noah came forward then, gentle eyes lit with good nature, and said, "Good to see you, Bella."

"You, too, Noah." He was so comfortingly familiar that she wanted to clutch him to her like an old, dear friend.

It was only Brodie who hugged her, as handsome as ever and smelling of expensive cologne, but his movements felt as similarly detached as Martha's had, the only difference being that his actions and expressions denoted years of media training.

Poor Willow, ashen-faced and clearly devastated, just shook her head, unable to say anything before she crumpled against Noah.

Bella stepped back feeling suddenly like a fraud, like she shouldn't have come, because when she thought about Jack's death, she just felt blank.

The church door opened. "Okay, we can—"

Logan.

Dark hair, sharp blue eyes, broad, solid shoulders. He struck an immediately formidable presence in his tailored black suit and crisp white shirt. It was the moment she'd feared the most. Her pulse pounded in her ears. She tried to keep her chin high. There was a pause as he saw her, a fleeting glance of surprise replaced quickly with what she could only describe as disgust. But he covered it like a professional, one blink and any trace of feeling was gone.

He gave her the briefest of nods, then turned to his family, "We can go in."

It was the first time she'd wanted to cry.

Chapter Four

The funeral service went on around Bella. Like she was underwater, there but not there. It was a sea of unfamiliar faces. People she'd never met before in her life, and half of them Jack probably hadn't met, either. If they'd really known him, they would never have come, she thought bleakly. A couple of well-known actors spoke, entertained with tales of Jack's antics on film sets. Willow read a poem, her voice quietly composed until suddenly it wasn't and the words cracked as she spoke them. It was awful, her heartbreaking sorrow laid out bare in front of them all. Brodie jumped up to stand next to her in support, holding her to him while she finished the reading.

Logan was the last to speak. He stood at the lectern, back straight, jaw sharp, no need for the cue cards he'd started out with.

"Jack Carter wasn't just my brother, he was my best friend." His words were eloquent, his expression calm and professional, but she was surprised to still be able to sense the struggle in his eyes, knew that he would see it as a crippling failure, Jack dying on his watch.

His words however were too much for Bella, the immortalizing of a great man who she knew wasn't great at all. So, she tried to close her ears, change her focus onto something else. And her gaze rested on the siblings in the front row, the backs of their heads only vaguely changed since she'd known them. Noah's hair was longer, but Brodie's was still the messy blond mop it had always been —if more artfully disheveled now—and Willow's remained a wild tangle of curls.

She thought about the first time she saw them in New York, after they'd won the talent show and got the record deal.

It still all seemed like a surreal dream, felt like only the day before that Logan had called her to say, "Ethan sent off an audition tape, we only did it to try and give Mom something to smile about while she was in the hospital. We didn't for a second think we'd get an audition, and then, well—" he'd laughed, bewildered "—it's kind of gone *insane*!"

Overnight stars, the brothers had been whisked away on press junkets and tie-in tours. It was months before they could find a window to see Bella, and by that time, she'd started doing work experience at *Vogue* as well as studying fashion. She'd sauntered into the record company thinking she was it in the pencil skirt and sky-high stilettos she'd borrowed from the *Vogue* fashion cupboard and been ushered up to the fourth-floor recording studio after saying demurely, "Logan Carter's expecting me."

As soon as the elevator doors opened and she saw Logan strolling down the hallway toward her, faded jeans and white T-shirt, a crooked grin on his lips, all pretense of maturity was gone and she was tottering to meet him, shaking her fists with excitement, unable to wipe the smile of disbelief from her face at how plush and expensive it all was. "This is *so* incredible!"

Logan, equally bemused and amazed by it all was about to hug her, then paused, and taking in her outfit said, "You look too fancy to hug."

She waved it away. "Don't be silly." Then taking in his newly cut, styled hair said, "You look too famous to hug." But it wasn't just the looks, it was the confidence that radiated from him. She felt suddenly like he was a famous person and she was just another of his adoring fans.

He laughed the comment away and wrapping his arm around her waist, almost lifted her off the ground. When she smelled the washing powder his mom used, her apprehension vanished as he went from famous stranger to exactly the same Logan.

"The others are all in there," he said, pointing to a studio full of equipment. The next half an hour went by in a blur. All the brothers bantering and as boisterous as puppies. At one point, almost bowled over by an exuberant Ethan wanting to show her something, Bella felt Logan's steadying hand on the base of her spine. It was always there, the memory of that protective touch flittering comfortingly—reassuringly—over her skin.

It was Jack who dragged Ethan away in a brotherly stronghold. "Get over here, we've got work to do!"

Laughing as he wrestled him down onto the stool in front of the keyboard, he then looked up at Logan and said in a faux-official voice, "Time is money, dude," as if it was a phrase that they'd been told a million times by a manager.

Logan turned to Bella and said, "Yeah, we'd better get back to work, sorry."

"That's fine!" she said, hiding her sudden disappointment. Realizing then how much she had missed them—Logan especially—friendly faces in a city of anonymous ones. "I've got to get back, too."

But then Logan walked her back to the elevator, and when he hugged her, tighter and more genuine, she couldn't help herself from admitting, "I've really missed you all."

And he had said against her neck, "Me too." Almost breathing her in with a sigh. "I'm exhausted. I didn't realize how much I'd missed normality until just now!"

In the look they shared it was like they both suddenly saw languid days lying in the summer sun, hikes through the mountains, fishing, running, messing about. The freedom of youth, friendship and anonymity.

Then suddenly, smiling quietly to himself, he'd taken her by the hand and marched her back to the studio where all his brothers waited, looking suddenly as tired and deflated as Logan. "Do you think we should just take the afternoon off?"

Over an intercom, she heard someone, a record exec, shout, "Do you know how much this place costs!"

Bella saw Jack shrug his shoulders with a glint in his eye in response, his eyes goading Logan to go ahead. The others watched wide-eyed. The air buzzed with hope. Bella knew full well that Logan was the only one of them with the authority to shut the afternoon down, to cancel the schedule and throw the whole machine into disarray. She squeezed his hand mischievously.

He looked at her, boyishly handsome suddenly as his face split in a grin. Then he turned back to Jack and said, "I think we should have the afternoon off."

Ethan whooped. The boys couldn't get out of there fast enough, the record exec hollering at them down the corridor as they all ran like schoolkids.

They headed down to the basement garage, calling dibs on who was going where with who. Ethan wanted to see the Statue of Liberty, Jack wanted to go to a bar. Brodie pulled open the door of a tinted window SUV and said, "I'm going to the beach."

Noah made a face like the idea was crazy. "Which one?"

Brodie shrugged, slipped on his sunglasses and said, "The closest. I don't care."

Logan, however, led Bella around to where a huge black motorcycle sat gleaming under the garage lights.

"What is that?" she laughed, her hand running along the leather seat.

"It's my new toy," he grinned, hair disheveled where he'd raked a hand through it.

"You coming to the beach, Logan?" Ethan called.

Logan shook his head and said to Bella, "Want to see New York?"

Brodie shouted, "Bella, beach with us or bike with Logan?"

"I'm meant to go back to work," Bella said looking guiltily out toward the exit.

Jack shouted, "Come with us, Bella!"

But Logan ignored them all, straddling the bike, he revved the engine, thrust a helmet at her and, eyes sparkling as if there was no choice at all, said, "Just get on the back, Bella."

Unable ever to resist him when he looked at her like that, she hitched up her skirt to the most dignified length she could and jumped on the back while all the boys in the SUV booed. She could just hear Logan's deep rumbling laugh as he kicked the bike into life.

It was easy to forget the fun and naivety of those early days, before the band stopped taking breaks, before half an hour wasn't enough for their guards to drop, before they started to believe their own hype. Before the cracks appeared and the money grew and grew while the dream turned sour. Before the five of them were chewed up and spat out into the world. Older, harder and each to their own.

Before Bella was sitting on a hard church pew. Standing by a grave and watching as a coffin was lowered into the ground. Walking with Claudette back to her car hoping to slip away without anyone noticing.

But as they crossed the tarmac, a sleek black Porsche parked in front of them bleeped as it unlocked. Bella paused. She was pretty sure she knew whose car it was. She caught Claudette glance over warily as she stiffened. "Are you okay?" she asked.

"Fine," Bella replied, turning around. As expected, there

was Logan, dark gaze hooded, striding toward them, emotionless, steely faced.

Claudette squeezed Bella's hand. "You don't have to talk to him."

"Yes, I do," she replied with a sigh, and squeezing her hand back, she let go and went to meet him midway.

Logan stopped about a foot away from her, put his hands in his suit pockets and, with his head turned toward the goings-on of the departing mourners, said, "I didn't think you'd come."

Despite her better judgment, she felt herself bristle at the fact he wouldn't look at her, the dismissal in his tone. "I thought it would create more drama if I didn't."

His head swung back. "There I was thinking you'd come to pay your respects."

She held his gaze, refused to cower, but said nothing.

He huffed a laugh, no humor on his face. "To be expected, I suppose."

It was her turn to look away in annoyance. "I'm leaving now so—"

He cut her off. "You're not coming to the wake?"

Bella shook her head. "No."

He frowned, blue eyes narrowing in disdain. "I think it would seem strange if you didn't," he replied. There was an edge to his voice nowadays, as if he was used to people doing exactly what he said.

Bella really didn't want to go to the wake. She could feel her heart fluttering like a caged bird in her chest, but she didn't want him to sense her vulnerability. She'd barely come to terms with her own mistakes, she wouldn't have the truth of them crushed by the giant fist of Logan Carter. So, she lifted her chin a little and pushed her shoulders back. Self-protection made her say, "I really don't think it's necessary. The press have gotten the shot they want."

His lip curled in disbelief. "I'm not talking about the press, Bella!"

She had to look away, she knew exactly what he was talking about, but she couldn't face being pressured into going to the wake, couldn't take any more of the pretense. It was easier to act aloof.

There was a beat of silence as he seemed to process his own incredulity, allow the rumors about her to align with the actuality. Then he sighed as if it wasn't worth the effort. "Look, Bella, he was my brother. You may not have loved him, but I did. And my family did. I don't want anything to ruin this day for any of them." She looked back when she heard the hint of a plea in his voice. "You owe him that, at least."

She felt herself flinch. What she did and didn't owe Jack was a messy question, but what she found herself fighting was what she owed Logan. She couldn't overlook the fact that he really knew nothing about, or had never accepted, what Jack was really like, that he was mourning a beloved brother. And at this close distance, he looked tired, weary of it all. She imagined him propping up the rest of the family and felt a dangerous flicker of sympathy. Against her better judgment, she said, "Fine." Then immediately regretted it when Logan gave a curt, satisfied nod, no trace of the previous emotion on his face, just an understanding that, as always, he'd got what he wanted.

Chapter Five

The wake was held at the Silver H Polo Club. Like the Carter family ranch, the grounds sat under the shadow of Starlight Mountain and the brothers had spent their youth playing Friday Night Lights games on the lush green pitch. At one point, Logan had been earmarked for Team USA potential, but that was all ancient history now. The club still held all the memories however, racing around the warm-up track with Jack at his heels. Logan stared out the window for a moment, at the acres of grass and the gray mountains beyond. Heard in his mind the crack of the mallet, the thundering hooves and the cheers of the crowd. There was nothing that beat the rush of a game of polo, not a stage in front of a hundred thousand people, not money, not signing a deal, nothing.

He tore his gaze from the window. Found himself suddenly disorientated to be there at his brother's wake.

The whole drive over he'd been distracted by his conversation with Bella. When he'd caught her trying to slip away from the funeral, the bland disregard he'd been determined to uphold had morphed into annoyance. Her cool, detached façade had grated more than he'd expected, fueling the anger he already felt about her for causing dividing lines between him and Jack. He couldn't help the frisson of superiority he'd felt when, pushed, she had agreed to come to the wake. To do what was right for a change rather than what suited her.

As soon as he felt it however, he was ashamed of the pettiness. He was better than that, surely? He surveyed the crowd of mourners, aware that it was being back home that was throwing him off-kilter. The last few days had drained him. Once again, having, to face his dad's stony, judgmental silence, which had only grown over time and made even worse now by grief. He'd muttered something the previous day about Ethan's whereabouts, *"All that money and you still can't find him,"* directing his hard gaze at Logan, seemingly holding him alone responsible for his youngest brother's absence. Logan had doubled his efforts to locate Ethan. But whatever channels he tried, he still couldn't get in touch with him. He was either buried deep in some black-op mission somewhere or was just deliberately not replying. Trained to be invisible, Ethan had cut himself off from their world a long time ago. The worst was the heartbreaking sadness on his mom's face when she'd looked Logan straight in the eye the night before and said, "Why does it take this—this tragedy—to bring us together? What's happened to us?" As if Logan might have the answers.

Luckily, Brodie had taken the role of host for all Jack's celebrity friends; he still hung around in those circles. And the new pastor, Jacob, who his mom had reservations about because he was so young, was currently trying to coax his dad into conversation, which earned him a medal in Logan's eyes. So, after working his way respectfully through familiar faces from Autumn Falls, people Logan recognized but shamefully couldn't remember the names of, who wanted to offer their condolences, he went over to stand with his mom, Willow and Noah for a breather. Except, to his dismay, their conversation happened to be about Bella.

"I'm just not sure what to say to her," said his mom, absently holding a glass of sparkling water and looking over at where Bella stood with her friend, Claudette.

When he'd seen her at the church, Logan had been surprised by how different she looked. Of course, she was older than when he'd last seen her, but she looked somehow detached, impenetrable. Even her clothes, the sharply tailored coffee-colored suit and black shirt, were businesslike and impersonal. If the old Bella was still in there, he couldn't see her.

His mom went on, "Every time I spoke to Jack about her it would always be about new demands she was making or the fallout from some newspaper story. I just don't know what to think. How can I talk normally to her when I know how hurt he was?" She glanced at Logan, her eyes wide with confusion. "And the divorce proceedings were so bitter and seemed to go on for so long…"

Logan felt his jaw clench to see her so bewildered. "I know," he said, putting his arm around her. "He said the same to me."

The phone calls Logan did manage to have with Jack would always be about Bella—how her lawyers were fleecing him, how badly she'd used him, how, when stories of her being unfaithful broke in the press it was like she was trampling on him again.

"He was heartbroken," Willow added.

Noah made a face. Not massively noticeable, just a twitch.

"What?" Logan asked.

"Nothing," Noah replied as if he hadn't done anything.

Logan itched to know what his brother was thinking, but knew you could never push Noah to speak, not if you wanted an answer. When he watched Noah glance back in Bella's direction, he could sense an uncertainty in him about her where Logan didn't want there to be one. He wanted this to be black and white, end it, move on. So later, when Noah headed to the bar, Logan went with him.

"Do you know half these people, Logan?" Noah asked, looking out at the crowded room.

Logan stood beside him, hands resting on the glossy wooden bar top. Noah claimed to have half an inch of height over Logan, but Logan wasn't convinced. What he did have was a deep tan from long days on the ranch and the kind of muscle strength that couldn't be got from the city gym. He shook his head. "Barely."

Noah huffed a laugh. Turned to one of the bar staff and asked for an OJ.

"No champagne?" Logan raised a brow. The champagne was how he was planning to get through the afternoon. He'd pick his car up in the morning.

"We've got an auction tomorrow—couple of hundred cattle. Some of us still have work to do later." Noah ran a finger around the restrictive collar of his shirt. He wasn't a suit guy. "And *someone* decided the funeral *had* to be this Friday."

Logan winced because it was him who had rushed it through. "I wanted to get the press off our backs."

At that, Noah glanced toward where Bella was sitting with her mom and stepdad, underneath an oil painting of a winning thoroughbred, seemingly waiting out the day with detached politeness. "How's she doing?"

Logan narrowed his eyes. "She's a master at this."

"I don't know, Logan," Noah replied, less certain.

"Well, she did love it once. And, what do they say—you reap what you sow." He watched her tuck a loose strand of hair that had fallen from her neatly swept-back ponytail behind her ear. "She's sown enough to keep her busy for a while."

Noah didn't reply, which made Logan play back what he'd just said into the silence and realize, to his annoyance, that he sounded petty again. To counter the feeling, he added, "What was that face you made earlier, about Jack and her?"

Noah shrugged, dark hair falling over his brow, "I just…" He paused. He clearly had more to say but chose not to and turned back to slug half of his juice.

"What?"

"Nothing."

"Just spit it out, Noah," Logan said, frustrated, unable to stop his eyes from going back to where Bella was, following her around the room when she stood up and headed toward his mom to presumably offer her condolences.

Noah drained his OJ in a couple of gulps, put the glass down on the bar top and said, "I just don't buy the whole heartbroken thing. I mean Jack, heartbroken? Really?"

Logan felt himself tense at the words. His eyes narrowing and his heart rate doubling as he watched Bella speaking to his mom.

When Bella and Jack had first got together, the nation had gone wild for their whirlwind, fairy-tale romance. While Logan hadn't been thrilled about it, he knew there was nothing to warrant him being jealous—he was the first to admit that he and Bella had only ever been friends, and whatever undercurrents there might or might not have been, she was never his to lay claim to. Still, there had been a certain reluctance to answer whenever he saw Jack's name flash up on his phone screen, knowing that he'd be regaled with stories about where they were vacationing, what parties they'd been to, what house they were buying.

But then when it was announced that they had split up, Logan willingly listened for hours to Jack's acrimony. And while he did it because that was what he always did—he looked out for his brothers—he also knew that deep down, it ignited a part of him that was glad the relationship had failed. He hated that about himself, so he'd always doubled down on the advice and the sympathy, talking Jack calmly through his tears and frustration. So, he knew for a fact that the split had left Jack ragged. Logan had never seen Jack cry until that moment, and Jack had put up with some pretty tough love from their dad but always came bouncing back with his infamously who-cares smirk. When Bella left, Jack just couldn't cope. He lost weight, he didn't sleep. He might not have been perfect, but in the last year she'd wrecked him, and that Logan couldn't forgive her for. "Believe me," he said to Noah, more tersely than he intended, "he was heartbroken."

Noah didn't say anything for a moment, just turned his empty glass around where he leaned on the bar.

They both watched as Bella shook his mom's hand with polite respect then turned to merge back into the crowd.

"I liked Bella," Noah said, pushing himself upright. "I've always liked her. And I've never thought the picture Jack painted fit." Then he walked away, all cowboy swagger, back toward the rest of their family.

Logan's blood pulsed at the words, his head suddenly a roaring mass of confusion. He looked again at Bella, and for a moment she came into focus differently, her long hair seemed to be tied less neatly than he'd thought, her eyes more tired, and was her head bent in defeat or dismissal as John-Luke said something? Was her mom's hand laid reassuringly on her shoulder?

Like a clock going back, Logan could picture her when she was sixteen sitting at the Carter family table for Sunday brunch. Everyone giving their egg order to his mom, Martha, as she stood at the stove. "How do you like yours, Bella?"

"However they come!" Bella replied, as if a tailored order was an unbelievable luxury. She'd arrived in Autumn Falls that summer from England, after her mom had married John-Luke. She'd gone on to add, "I'm not really a breakfast person. My mom's always worked shifts at the hospital so she's not around for breakfast very often. And my dad—well, I'm not sure he knew where the kitchen was when they were together and even less so now." She said it flippantly, but Logan knew that the reason she'd come to the States was because her dad had refused her request to live with him full-time. There was always some reason or other as to why he couldn't have her with him. Logan had heard him on the phone and it was always *next year* or *after the summer*, or when he'd settled into his new job, or things had calmed down with his new girlfriend, it was always the same promise—*Soon, Bella, soon*. She'd never admit the reason out loud, but Logan had garnered enough to know that her dad had the room but didn't want the responsibility, and Bella felt the rejection like a bullet through the heart.

Martha came over with a plate stacked with pancakes and a bowl of scrambled eggs for those who'd requested them. "How are you getting on with John-Luke?" she asked Bella.

Bella shrugged. "He's okay, I guess."

Martha had nodded like she understood the complexity of having a stepdad, or just that she had heard stories in town about how reluctant Bella was to settle into her new family life. "I've known him since school. He's a good man."

Again, Bella had shrugged, noncommittal. Their relationship had always been fractious. John-Luke trying, Bella rejecting.

And yet now, here in the polo club, John-Luke was standing by Bella's side like a bodyguard.

Logan willed her to look over and meet his gaze so he could get a grasp of what was going on, see something to confirm the fact that he should just let her walk away and forget about her.

But she didn't look up, if anything she looked further down, heading, he realized, with her entourage, to the exit. Before he could do anything—not that he knew what that would be, talk to her perhaps?—Question her?—his own father blocked his view. Emmett had come to the bar to refresh his water. Logan found himself immediately standing up straighter, like an army officer had him under inspection. A stern-faced man at the best of times, wearing a suit, Emmett was doubly forbidding.

Caught off-guard by thoughts of Bella, Logan found himself saying, "Everything all right, Dad?"

Emmett, never one for platitudes or figures of speech, raised a dark, graying eyebrow. "What do you think, Logan?"

Logan tried to subtly ground himself, took a slug of his own drink and said, "Yeah, of course, stupid question."

Emmett grimly surveyed the mass of people and muttered, "It's a circus." Then he shook his head, picked up his water and added, almost as an afterthought, like the words wouldn't act as an irrevocable punch to Logan's gut, "Could have predicted this from the moment you left for that audition."

Chapter Six

Logan spent the weekend with his family. He had his own house north of Main Street but stayed in his old bedroom on the ranch. His dad and Noah left for the auction at the crack of dawn and Logan made sure he was up with them, asked his dad if there was anything that needed doing while he was gone. His dad locked him with a hard, blank stare and said, "You forgotten how the place runs?"

Of course Logan hadn't forgotten. It was etched in his brain. He'd spent the first eighteen years of his life following his dad's orders, he'd asked in case there was something specific and they both knew that. Logan looked into his dad's gray eyes and would have held that stare for as long as it took but knew he had to be the first to look away.

It was Noah striding back through the kitchen on the pretense of forgetting something who said under his breath, "Fence line on the north pasture needs fixing."

When they'd gone, Martha poured him a cup of coffee, her face pale and tired, and said, "You know what he's like, Logan. It's his way of coping."

Really? Logan thought. We're still saying that? But he nodded. "I know." He smiled at his mom who, usually so confidently assured, was looking unbearably vulnerable. It was a reminder of when she'd been ill, all the vibrant energy dimmed inside her, her lips wobbling on the verge of tears as she smiled back. This wasn't the time to say that it would be nice, if just once, the old man dialed back the guilt for them all having left.

It didn't take Logan long to fix the fence, he filled the rest of the morning with yard work. Kept himself close to the horses; Star, a chestnut mare belonging to his sister, poked her head over the barn door when he went past and one look in her big brown eyes made him want to put his head on her neck and disappear forever in the smell and warmth of her.

Brodie sauntered outside at one point. Leaning against the barn door where Logan was mucking out, he said, "What are you doing?" with a bemused frown on his face when he took in Logan's sweat-stained T-shirt. "This is what Dad hires people for."

Logan paused, wiped his brow. Why was he doing it? Because he'd rather shovel muck than sit engulfed in the guilt and sadness of the house, unable to breathe. "You here to help?"

"No way," Brodie grimaced. "I'm thinking about going fishing, up by the lake, where Jack liked. You want to come?"

Logan would love to go fishing, sit and think about his brother, remember the times as kids when they'd camp out by the lake all night, cooking fish they'd caught over the fire, but he shook his head, "No, not today." There was something about his dad coming home, asking what they'd done all day and him saying fishing, or even that he'd caught up with office work, that he couldn't allow to happen. With everything else going on, he could feel it brewing inside him—the danger that he'd rear up and retaliate in the face of the look his dad would give him, like they were all disappointingly soft, city boys who didn't know what hard work was.

Brodie, in contrast, didn't have such qualms and, shaking his head as if Logan was a fool, said, "Dad won't care that you've done this, you know that?"

Not wanting his intentions to have been so transparent, especially not to his younger brother, Logan reached for his water bottle and said, "I don't care what he thinks."

Brodie snorted. "Yeah, right," and left before Logan, who had a mouthful of lukewarm water, could reply.

He worked till his body ached, stopping only when he heard his dad and Noah return—Noah's dog, a black and white Border collie named Rocky, barking excitedly to be back—and Logan realized he was starving.

They ate in near silence. Logan, Brodie, Noah, Willow and their parents, all sitting around the giant wooden table that used to be a hive of life when they were younger. Now they were all near strangers. And their brother was gone. And none of them knew what to do or say.

"How was the auction?" Logan asked, because the silence was too smothering.

"Like any other auction." His dad didn't look up.

Brodie caught Logan's eye and raised his eyebrows, like *I told you so*.

Noah said, "It was busy," trying to smooth things over.

Over the other side of the table, Willow put her fork down and, clearly trying to make conversation, said, "How long are you staying, Logan?"

Logan glanced at his plate. "I have to leave tomorrow." He was desperate to get away. One of his deals was imploding and it was a good excuse, even if just to himself, that he was needed back in the office.

"So soon?" His mom took a shaky breath at the fact, but she didn't ask him to stay longer, none of them asked anything of each other anymore.

They fell into silence again, the only noise the scraping of cutlery on plates and the dog, Rocky, snoring softly in the corner. Then suddenly, Emmett balled up his napkin and chucking it down on the table, pushed his chair back and stood up. "I've got work to do."

Martha said, "But we're all together."

Emmett cast his eye disparagingly around the table and muttered, "No we're not."

Chapter Seven

Most of the press photographers left after the funeral. They had the pictures they wanted. But still Bella wore a baseball cap pulled low, sunglasses and the plainest clothes she had—a black T-shirt and a button-up denim skirt—when she walked out of the house that evening. Her mom said it was a bad idea, but she needed some fresh air, couldn't stay cooped up at the orchard any longer and she promised she'd stick to the back streets. But then, when she got near Main Street there was something about the light and the snatches of view of the shops, the tantalizing familiarity of it, that lured her closer.

She stepped out onto the wide, bright sidewalk and felt an immediate calm at the well-known sights—the cut-out guitar hanging from the awning of The Music Box, the buckets of flowers spilling out the front of the florist, Joe's Diner with its arched windows, and the old chrome theater sign. It made her lean against the brick wall and remember the shock she'd first felt when her mother fell in love with an American and they suddenly picked up and moved from London to Autumn Falls. Just the memory of being sixteen and arriving in the small town, surrounded by fields and mountains and a million cattle and roads that stretched on to infinity, put the first smile on her face since arriving back. She started walking, pausing to glance in The Music Box, where she had persuaded the owner, an old music roadie called Dusty, to take her on when he was hiring because, while she had no passion for music, she was desperate for money and flat-out refused to pick apples at the orchard. In retrospect, she should have realized that, given her complete lack of musical credentials, she only got the job because John-Luke pulled some strings. It made her shudder now at the memory of what a brat she was back then—fuming still from her parents' hideous, bitter divorce and the subsequent rejection by her dad. She was terrible at the job, hopeless at remembering the specifications of various instruments, but then one day, in walked Logan and Jack Carter. She could see it so vividly. They came in to pick up a restrung guitar, all cocky swagger and lazy smiles when they saw her behind the counter.

Jack, the more conventionally good-looking of the two—blond, chiseled, cute dimples—leaned up against the register, smiling eyes assessing, while Logan said, "You new around here?"

And she replied with her sharp British accent, "What gave it away?"

Jack barked a laugh, while Logan's cheeks pinked ever so slightly, and Bella decided to take pity on him. "Yeah, I'm new. Arrived last week."

Jack leaned further forward, braced against the glass counter, all cocksure and self-assured, and said, "You need someone to show you around?"

Bella raised a brow. "I don't think there's that much to see."

It was Logan's turn to laugh, hands in the back pockets of his jeans, thick black lashes hooding his eyes. "There's a few hidden gems," he said, detached but interested enough to add with a crooked half-smile. "You just need to know where to look."

Walking down Main Street now, Bella felt the tug of sadness that she and Logan were nothing but strangers now, he wouldn't laugh at anything she said anymore. He used to laugh all the time. Even at jokes he knew were defense mechanisms, but he let her have them anyway. Like when she told him she was going to New York as soon as she could and he said, "I envy you, knowing what you want."

And she said, "Yeah, you envy me having a dad who doesn't want me and a mom with a new boyfriend who lives in a house where everything smells of apples!"

He'd laughed rather than offering platitudes she wouldn't believe and said, "I like the smell of apples."

Bella kept walking. She thought about the funeral, seeing Logan talking to his dad. She'd recognized the stiff formality, the capitulation in his body language and expression. She could almost see the way his brain scrambled for something to say, or rather, the right thing to say, while Emmett stood stony and unapproachable waiting for whatever he'd ordered at the bar. The whole exchange looked so uncomfortably familiar that she almost felt sorry for Logan that things had changed so little over time.

She passed the diner, and when she did, the owner Loriana turned her back as Bella approached. Was it deliberate or by chance? She felt her muscles tense at the likely possibility of being branded the outcast. Could she hear whispers? Were people avoiding her? Up ahead, Starlight Mountain loomed ominously on the horizon, black shadows of the clouds gliding over its surface. Outside the deli, someone had left a newspaper on the table. When she passed, an image of Jack stared up at her in black and white —tousled hair, satisfied half-smile—his eyes following her knowingly as she hurried past. Someone bashed her shoulder; she glanced back but they didn't turn. The cars seemed louder. Her jaw clenched, her heart was beating too fast.

Then suddenly she heard her name. "Bella! Bella! Over here!"

She looked up on instinct and was blinded by a flash. She stepped back, disorientated, the photographer, who had just walked out of the grocery store and clearly couldn't believe his luck, kept clicking, a barrage of lights in her face. She was out of practice, wincing, trying to shield her eyes from the brightness. People in the street had stopped to look. Someone had their phone out taking a picture. Panic started fizzing in the corners of her vision. Her breaths shallowed.

Then suddenly a black Porsche screeched to a halt and she heard Logan's voice say, "Get in."

Chapter Eight

Logan didn't want Bella in his car. Didn't want her perfume infusing the interior, didn't want to notice the length of her legs as she angled them away from him, her bare arms as she crossed them protectively around herself. He was still simmering from his dad storming out of the kitchen and leaving an emotional mess behind him. His mom welling up, Willow crying into her napkin, Noah going silently to stand at the window while Brodie sat at the table, his elbow resting on the wood, his forehead in his hand. Logan had pieced it all back together, he'd stopped Brodie from leaving that evening, persuaded him to let things cool down, stay the night, have breakfast and they could leave together. He'd sat with his arm around Willow and tried to focus on practical things. It transpired that his mom had been worrying because she wanted to go to Jack's house in LA but his dad refused to fly, so Logan agreed to go with her even though she tried to tell him he didn't have the time—which he didn't—and in the end, Willow said she'd go, to his hidden relief.

He'd gone for a drive to get some space—he didn't have the brain capacity for Bella, let alone the annoyance he'd felt seeing her so vulnerable in the street.

As the car purred away from Main Street, she looked fixedly ahead, trying to catch her breath. He said, "It's okay, you can relax."

She pulled her sunglasses off and shot him a sidelong look. "No, I can't."

Their eyes met for a second. Mistrust and disdain prickled between them yet infuriatingly it fueled something more in him that he didn't want to acknowledge. He turned back to the road.

She stared resolutely out the window. "They're everywhere."

"Well, what do you expect?"

"I don't know, I don't care, I just don't want them in my life again." She took her cap off and ran her fingers through her hair. He noticed her hand was shaking.

He refused to feel sympathy for her. After today, he would never have to see her again. That would be it. Line drawn. Except part of him wanted her to suffer, wanted her to feel the hurt that Jack had felt, acknowledge that she'd played her part in it all. He wanted her at least to admit her regret.

Or was he fooling himself? Was it really all about him? Did he just want to reach over and let his fingers tangle through her hair? See if she still smelled like she used to? Of soft, warm sunshine. His hands clenched on the wheel. *Stop*,

Logan. To see if her skin, with its light summer tan, felt as smooth. His teeth clenched. He craved a glance.

She said, "Where were you heading?"

"Nowhere," he replied, looking determinedly straight ahead. "I had to get away from my dad."

"Like old times," she said wryly.

He laughed then regretted it, annoyed that he'd relaxed his guard.

They drove on in silence. For Logan, a thousand things he wanted to say shot noiselessly between them. He wanted to rip open what felt like a shield around her and see through to who she really was.

Without looking his way, Bella said, "Could you drop me at the orchard, please?"

"Yes."

It was like they'd never met. Like nothing had ever happened.

His fingers tapped the steering wheel, he felt frustration rise in his chest. As they passed under the streetlights, he could see their reflections in the windshield. Bella and him, reappearing and disappearing as the light changed.

He wanted answers about what had happened between her and Jack, how it had gone so wrong, what she'd been playing at. He wanted to put everything behind him. He wanted to know how she'd been so rigidly detached the entire day. So he found himself saying, because he couldn't seem to help himself, "Do you not feel anything about what's happened?"

She flinched, clearly taken aback by the comment.

"Of course I feel things," she replied curtly, glancing only momentarily his way then back to the window.

It wasn't enough.

Logan felt his blood throbbing in his temple. "It certainly doesn't seem like it."

She just shook her head, not deigning to answer.

The space in the car felt smaller, closer, inescapable.

He was determined to break that façade. "Did you ever actually love him?"

A sharp intake of breath, but again no reply.

Logan sighed, as if dealing with a petulant child. "Look I don't know what went on between the two of you—"

She cut him off straight away. "No, Logan, you don't."

Which annoyed him even more, so he carried on as if she hadn't spoken, "But I know that he was devastated when you left."

Her jaw tightened as if deliberately holding back a retort.

He knew he should stop. "And then all the stalling with the divorce. What was that all about? I don't know why you didn't just take the money and run. Surely, he'd suffered enough, hadn't he?" He shook his head, emphasizing his disapproval.

She glanced back, eyes narrowed, and said with a slowly dawning clarity, "Are you trying to blame me somehow for his death?"

Logan made a face, as if she was misinterpreting what he was saying even though it was exactly what he was implying. "No. I'm just saying he was in a really bad place when you left, and I can't help thinking that he never recovered from it."

She inclined her head, perfectly arched eyebrows drawing together, but again she said nothing.

For the rest of the journey, he felt her simmering in fury next to him. The anger radiating off her prickled through him in pure satisfaction. It felt good to see her riled. Less like a statue. He wanted his brother's death to mean something, to be felt by her as Logan felt it, with all the guilt and confusion included. Seeing her hands clenched in her lap made him have to hold in a smile of petty triumph as he drove along the wide, open road to the orchard, bristling silence humming between them all the way to the front gates.

She'd unclipped her seatbelt and had the car door open the moment he pulled to a stop, stepping out without a backward glance.

"Well, it was great to see you," he called as she slammed the door, feeling a rush at the haughty lift of her chin.

He watched her walk away. He was about to throw the car into reverse when he saw her pause, then turn back. He cocked his head, intrigued, as she came closer, her face set with determination as she yanked open the Porsche door.

"I filed for divorce a year ago. It was him who wouldn't sign. And if you think I was holding out for the money then you're wrong because there wasn't any."

Logan scoffed. "Of course there was money. He was—" But the look on her face made him stop. Was it pity? Was she *pitying* him?

"He spent everything. Jack was in debt up to eyes."

Logan could feel his own bewilderment on his face and tried to school his features enough to pull together a response, but before he could, she said coolly, "I suggest you get your facts straight before you start throwing out accusations, Logan," and slammed the car door.

He sat in stunned silence, watching her figure retreat up the path to the red front door of the orchard, his heart thundering in his ears. Was it a joke? How could there be no money? He kept seeing her eyes, felt the sting of that pity deep in his stomach. When the front door closed behind her, Logan leaned his head on the steering wheel, eyes closed. When he took a breath, he realized he could still smell her perfume in the car and knew he'd already been back in Autumn Falls too long.

Chapter Nine

Bella's mom, Heather, was waiting for her when she came in, eyes filled with worry, her hand clutching her phone as if the whole town had been calling to let her know what had happened on Main Street.

"Are you okay?" she asked, standing up and coming over as Bella walked into the living room.

The house felt like a sanctuary. So different to when she'd been a kid and seen it only as the consolation prize, a stopgap until her dad would welcome her back—she'd been so blindsided by his empty promises. The mid-century modern furniture that Bella had once thought ugly, the sweet apple smell that she'd complained pervaded everything, the crocheted blankets she'd thought old-fashioned, all of it now felt like the warm hug of safety.

"Not really," Bella said, her voice trembling as she spoke.

Her mom immediately wrapped her arms tight around

her, pulling her close into a hug and softly stroking her hair as she cried. "It'll be all right, Bella."

Bella nodded into her mom's shoulder, buried her face in the fabric of her sweater, felt like a teenager not a grown woman, her legs shaky, her breath in gasps.

"It's okay," her mom soothed. "It's over. You're free of it now."

But even as Bella pulled away, wiping her eyes with a Kleenex from the box on the coffee table and nodding in agreement, she remembered the look of furious confusion in Logan's eyes as she'd slammed the door of his Porsche and knew she wasn't free.

Chapter Ten

The extent of his brother's debts soon became apparent. Logan dealt with the immediate issues and paid Jack's staff all outstanding wages, but there was money owed every which way he looked, from hotel rooms and casinos to taxes and legal fees. What puzzled him was that he'd invested for all of them in Carter Media when Silver Sky split, there was money there if Jack had wanted it, he just had to ask.

Logan, however, couldn't shake the memory of Bella's expression as she'd leaned into the Porsche. It haunted him, appearing when he was in meetings, lying in bed at night, staring absently at his computer screen. All he could see was her mocking pity and it simmered in his veins. So, when Willow phoned to say Jack's house was almost bare and they hadn't stayed long—their mom was too upset by how impersonal it was, like a hotel—Logan realized he had to go and see it himself. Lay some ghosts to rest.

Jack's house was up in the Hollywood Hills. Logan

drove the winding roads in a hired black Mercedes. He was unfamiliar with the route because they always met at the private members club that Jack had a stake in with a couple of other actors. And when he arrived, he had to double-check the address, shocked by the huge new concrete walls towering impenetrably around the house like a prison.

He keyed in the code and the gates drew slowly back. The big white mansion waiting, starkly imposing, as he pulled up. He could feel Bella's eyes, watching and waiting. His skin prickled as he walked inside.

Get yourself together, Logan. It's only a house.

Inside it was exactly as Willow said, stark and impersonal. There were spaces on the walls where art—he vaguely remembered large, expensive canvases—had once hung.

His gaze swept over the shelves bare of anything except the odd vase or sculpture, a photograph of Jack laughing and joking with a bunch of celebrity friends. Logan found himself smiling, the bright enthusiasm on his brother's face infectious. It made him proud and sad and sorry that all that life and energy had gone.

He backed into the hallway, then taking the stairs two at a time he went in search of more. More of his brother. But the second floor was the same as the first. Nothing, just impersonal cream rooms with neatly made beds and glistening bathrooms. The only way he could tell the master suite was Jack's room were the clothes hanging in the walk-in closet. But as he slid open the closet doors he had to pause, it wasn't just Jack's clothes hanging in there, Bella's were there, too. He recognized sweaters she'd owned, and dresses. His hand ran down the cool silk fabric of one on its hanger, then he scrunched it tight as he felt the unsettling confusion of why any of her belongings would still be there.

He went over to stand by the window, hands braced on the sill, staring out at the once-manicured, now overgrown, lawn, the flowerbeds left to wilt and the green-tinged pool, feeling irritatedly in the dark and out of control, feelings he was not good with.

As he looked out at the sad, unloved view, his eye caught on the pool house, a white building at the far end of the garden with a slate roof and Venetian columns. He couldn't see much from where he stood at the window, but what he could see looked like stuff, like belongings.

Logan stalked through the house, out through the garden, no tentative fear this time as he pulled open the pool-house door.

The smell hit him first, the rotten sweetness of stale alcohol and cigarettes, but what he saw wasn't much better. The sleek gray corner sofa was now doubling as a bed with rumpled sheets and a pillow. The coffee table was littered with debris: dirty plates, a smattering of white powder, a half-drunk bottle of vodka. The TV screen had shattered, like someone had taken a swing at it. In the bathroom, Logan yanked open the little cupboard and found rows of prescription bottles. Before he could take it all in, he had the bin in his hands and swiped everything in, every trace of Jack's lifestyle. He couldn't bear the idea of his mom ever seeing it. And it was only when it was done and bagged up that he paused, wiping his forehead as he realized he'd started to sweat. Feeling himself getting angrier with Bella. She had known about this.

But there was no time to pause, because then Logan's attention was caught by a picture on a shelf by the window, crowded in among various awards and trophies—a prized Golden Globe but never, to Jack's chagrin, an Oscar. He'd jokingly blamed his past in the band for people not taking him seriously enough. Swallowing down a sudden nervous trepidation, Logan walked over to the framed photograph and picked it up. The color had faded because of the direct sunlight, but Bella and Jack's smiling faces were still crystal clear.

He stared at it for a moment, then, resting the frame on his knee, he clicked the silver clips off the back and flicked out the layers until he was holding the glossy print. Almost unable to believe what he was doing, breath tight in his chest, he unfolded it and smoothed it out. Now, there were the three of them, standing, side by side, Jack, Bella, Logan, smiling at the camera on a hot summer polo day. His brother had folded him back.

Just looking at the picture, Logan could remember the heat, the sweat trickling down his back, the smell of the freshly cut grass, the unadulterated joy of a rare tour break back in Autumn Falls. He remembered lying on his back with his hands clasped behind his head, sunglasses on, staring up at the sky, his brothers all thankfully there with him, so he could relax.

Brodie was soaking up the sun, glass in one hand, the other casually stroking the grass beneath him. Ethan, whom Logan had had to track down in some grimy club the night before where the press were having a field day, was quietly snoring as he slept off a hangover. A couple of bruises on his face from a fight that he couldn't remember but which a British tabloid had the exclusive on from the opponent, and Logan was in the process of negotiating an interview in exchange for them burying the story. Noah was somewhere else with his girlfriend, Livvy. Jack had his legs stretched out in front of him, propped up on his elbows, saying, "This is the life! Can you—" but then he'd paused, his attention diverted elsewhere. Logan remembered sitting up to see Bella walking toward them. "Hey, guys!" she smiled, looking all chic and *Vogue* but flopping down on the rug just like the same old her.

Logan had invited her but wasn't sure if she'd come. It was only when he saw her that he realized how much he wanted her to be there, she was more than a breath of fresh air, she was a touchstone to real life. At that point, it was a couple of years since the early exotic days of fame, and the sheen was definitely wearing off. They had been at loggerheads with their management. There were issues over creative control, royalties, management style, everything. Jack could barely be in the same room as Dexter, their manager. Noah was homesick and constantly on the phone to his girlfriend. Ethan spent half the time with his nose pressed up to the window of the hotel, jittery and restless like a caged animal, then he'd sneak out at night without telling anyone, looking for whatever fun or trouble he could find. Even Brodie, permanently buoyant, had taken to zoning out on the PlayStation any chance he got. So, they'd made the decision—wise or not—to sack their management. Instead, Logan would manage them himself.

When everyone had said hello, and Jack had jumped up to pour her a glass of champagne, Bella looked around at them all and said, "So, you said we were celebrating?"

"Yes, we are!" Jack slapped Logan jokingly on the back. "This guy's the new big boss."

Bella snorted a laugh at the idea and the corners of Ethan's lips tilted up as he snoozed.

Logan made an exasperated face. "We're managing ourselves. I'm just the frontman."

Jack winked. "Sure thing."

Bella shook her head at Jack winding him up and said, "Well, I think it's brilliant. To a new era for Silver Sky!"

Brodie whooped and raised his glass. "Yeah! To us!"

From where he was lying on the ground, Ethan opened one eye and raised his empty hand to join the toast.

Logan smiled along with them but was secretly terrified by the task he'd taken on. Terrified about exactly what Jack had just implied—that he was the boss, that now it was his job alone to keep them in check.

Bella gave him a nudge. "You okay?"

He frowned, as if *of course*. "Fine, yeah, can't wait. It's a great move for us."

Bella raised a brow like she could see straight through him to the daunted little boy playing businessman underneath. As the others chatted and laughed, she leaned over and said quietly in his ear, "You'll smash it, Logan, you always do."

He cocked his head, trying to stay impassive, but felt a tremor of relief inside at her belief in him.

Bella lay back on her elbows, glossy brown hair hanging loose, looking endearingly between them all. "We should do a shoot together!" she said, sitting back up as she warmed to the idea. "Something to mark the change. What do you think?"

Jack said, "Definitely!"

Bella grinned. "I can talk to my editor." She looked around at the club. "We could do it here with like a preppy, polo vibe." She clapped her hands. "What do you think?" The others were nodding in agreement, but Logan remembered noticing that she was directing the question at him. It was the first real moment that he'd felt in charge, and, perhaps to his shame in retrospect, he'd liked it.

"Yeah, sounds like a great idea," he said, and watched her eyes glimmer with excitement.

Someone whistled in the background, and they all looked around.

"Oh, no. We're on in a minute and I've got to get changed." Jack shot up from the rug, grabbing the gym bag on the ground next to him. "You coming, Logan?"

Logan nodded.

"I didn't know you were playing." Bella watched Jack go.

"It's just a practice match," Logan replied, starting to stand up. "We're both pretty rusty." He tried to sound casual, but he'd been dreaming of playing this game since it was mentioned. It was a special type of agony watching all the guys here at peak fitness, peak skill. Growing up, Logan had worked the ranch then trained every spare moment he got. He knew his ponies better than he knew himself. Knew exactly the second they tired. Knew which one exploded with speed, which one could turn on a dime.

But that was another life, he thought, looking around at his brothers lounging around with champagne, Bella typing an excited email about the *Vogue* shoot, his parents over by the stands chatting with friends—relations with his dad having broken down further since, having refused any of the money the boys made, he'd discovered Logan had been incrementally paying off the ownership loan for the ranch.

Logan had tried not to think of what could have been—there was no point, the juggernaut they were on was unstoppable, he couldn't get off, even if he wanted to. As if to prove the fact, his phone rang as he was going to get changed. It was the record company with the first of a million things that he had to do in his new role. Phone pressed against his ear, Logan went to stand in the shade, trying to firefight as best he could. When Jack came back, ready to play, he frowned when he saw him still in his jeans and said, "You're supposed to be getting ready for the game."

Logan shook his head, pointing to the phone. Jack rolled his eyes, then shrugged and shouted, "Brodie, you're going to have to play instead of Logan."

Which made Brodie grimace and Bella look over with concern to where Logan wished he could wrap up the call. But problems and logistics kept coming. He gestured that he'd be five minutes, but then he heard Jack say, "Hey, Bella, do you want to come and meet my horse?" and she stood up and wandered off with him as Brodie jogged to get changed, and watching them go, glued to the phone, Logan remembered thinking, even then, that his other life was disappearing faster than he could keep track.

Sitting now on the arm of the gray sofa in Jack's pool house, Logan stared down at the picture of the three of them, the sharp fold line separating him from the other two. He remembered it being taken, a casual shot by Brodie after the game, Jack the triumphant winner dressed in their club uniform, Bella between them. Logan in his jeans and shirt trying his hardest to smile because he couldn't shake the feeling that he had missed out that day and there was a creeping suspicion that it was only the beginning.

While all the brothers grew up playing polo—they'd all first sat on a horse at about three years old—it was Jack who was Logan's main competition, the one he could always see just over his shoulder. Only a year younger than him, Jack was gifted, with the same natural sporting talent, and he pushed and pushed to overtake. Logan could hear the breath of Jack's horse when they took the circuit, always striving to outdo him but never quite getting there. In Logan's mind he was useful for Jack, he pushed him to be better. What made a person work harder than having someone to beat? Not that Logan would ever let Jack beat him.

Logan put the photograph in his pocket, trying to ignore his heart pounding in his ears, and walked around the rest of the pool house. On the desk, he wasn't surprised to see stacks of bills, there were probably divorce papers in there as well. He bent down and picked up clothes from the floor, folding a T-shirt and placing it over the back of a chair just to try and get some sort of order from the chaos. Jack's old teddy bear sat on the shelf by the window. He picked it up to take back for his mom.

Then, sitting in an ashtray next to the bear, to his horror he saw a signet ring. He picked it up refusing to believe it was the same one that Logan had been gifted by their dad, passed down through the generations and lost—much to Emmett Carter's disgust—when the band were on tour in Europe. But just holding the ring in his hand, he knew, without having to study the familiar engraving and the dented metal of the band, that it was the same one.

Staring at the ring, Logan struggled to get air in his lungs. He didn't want to think about why Jack had it. When he'd taken it from him. Why he'd taken it. He remembered both the pride and loathing he'd felt when it had been given to him by his father. He remembered Jack being in the room at the time, the almost imperceptible look of conspiratorial sympathy he'd given him to undercut the significance of the tradition simply because they were eighteen-year-old boys who wanted to get out and see the world, not be chained to the ranch all their lives. But had all that been a lie? Had Jack, so often overlooked by their dad—the cool, self-possessed one who glared back with a smirk on his face when he got a verbal lashing—been the one to want to feel the pride, want the privilege of being able to loathe a birthright?

Logan could barely even look at the ring now. He closed his eyes for a second, and slipped it in his pocket along with the photo.

He thought of the moment a few years later, when Jack had explained how Bella had interviewed him for his new film and they'd got chatting, and one thing had led to another. Logan had watched him trying to suppress his enthusiasm. Eyes downcast for a moment, Jack had looked up at him, almost pleadingly earnest, and said, "All that matters is that you're okay with it, Logan." He had then reached over and gripped Logan's forearm. "I promise, I wouldn't do anything to hurt you *ever*. If you don't want it to happen, just say the word." Maybe he'd meant it. Or maybe he was just a really good actor.

Logan had to get out of the suffocating, airlessness of the pool house. He didn't want to have seen these things. He didn't want his brother to have slyly, insidiously taken the things that meant the most to Logan, simply to prove that he could.

Holding the teddy bear in one hand, with the ring and the photograph in his pocket, he picked up the bin bag and strode out of the pool house back through the garden and the main house. He couldn't get out of the front door and into the car fast enough, his hand trembling as he gripped the wheel, his foot almost revving on the accelerator as the front gate slid open with painful slowness. He was so desperate to leave that he didn't think about photographers, how precious an image might be of the older Carter brother leaving the late, younger one's house. So, when the cameras flashed, Logan was caught off-guard, face raw and exposed, exactly the photo they'd been hoping for.

Chapter Eleven

Bella stayed in Autumn Falls for longer than she'd anticipated after the funeral, reluctant to tear herself away from the protective bubble of home, especially this time of year, waking up to birdsong and the hum of bees, and the warm air scented with apple blossom. Exhaustion had settled over her and she seemed to sleep most of her free time, trying not to think of anything, or anyone, but sometimes the memories got the better of her. When that happened, she took herself down to the Autumn Falls Theater, where Claudette worked.

To start with, Claudette welcomed her in. "Look at you, hot-shot New Yorker, wanting to help out in my lowly Autumn Falls Theater!"

Bella had laughed and Claudette seemed pleased to see it. Less so when Bella looked around in surprise at the jam-packed room with space for barely more than a big worktable and a couple of mannequins and said, "Is this it?"

"Yes!" Claudette replied defensively. "We can't all have a room of seamstresses at our fingertips. It's back to basics, Bella—get sewing."

Claudette had an intern, Alice, who was eighteen and giggled nervously every time Claudette spoke.

Bella and Claudette had gone from Autumn Falls to art school together in New York. Claudette had shared in all the giggling fun at Silver Sky concerts, the backstage passes, the celebrity spotting, the carefree dancing in VIP lounges at festivals. She knew her history. Bella had left *Vogue* when she'd married Jack, but when they'd split and she was back in New York and in desperate need of a job, it was Claudette who had suggested she apply for the assistant position in the costume department of a theater in Soho that she'd heard about, encouraged her to believe that she could get back out there. Bella had been shaking like a leaf at the interview but immediately clicked with her soon-to-be boss and had been working there for the last year, loving the reclaimed feeling of purpose. Those extra days spent in Autumn Falls were the first vacation time she'd taken.

But as the days went by and Bella was still in Autumn Falls, helping pin and sew, Claudette said, "You need to go back to your life. You're hiding."

"I'm having a break!" Bella defended.

Claudette eyed her mistrustfully. "Looks like hiding to me." Then picking up her bag, said, "I'm going to get coffee."

Bella sat at the desk, convincing herself that she was taking a well-deserved break. That her heart didn't thunder every time she walked out in the open, she wasn't glancing over her shoulder, that she didn't panic every time she thought of her empty New York apartment and the irrational fear of bumping into Logan. She told herself she wasn't spending most of the day killing time, waiting till she could curl back up in bed.

Her phone buzzed, echoing around the empty room and making her jump.

It was a message from Claudette. *"This doesn't look good."*

Underneath, she had forwarded a photograph from a gossip website. Bella tensed as she opened it, expecting to see an awful snap of herself or some new, salacious story. What she didn't expect to see was Logan.

Her hand went to her mouth. The shot was taken through a windshield. She'd never seen him look like that. His hair scruffily pushed back, his hand raised, mouth grimacing, eyes blazing in shocked fury.

She zoomed in to study every detail, tried to steady the nervous thrum of her heart. She knew exactly where he was, she'd recognize those concrete walls anywhere. She noticed her hand tremble as she skim-read the article: "… *found at his brother's house, caught in the midst of grief."* A chill ran through her. That wasn't grief. Logan wouldn't let anyone see his grief. That was confusion, anger, it was vulnerability. And he wouldn't be happy about it.

It was only the next evening, when there was a long impatient ring on the orchard buzzer, that she realized she should have been waiting for him to come and find her—of course he knew where she was staying—instead she was half-asleep on the sofa.

She jumped up, rubbing sleep from her face and retying

her hair. She was almost certain it was Logan, but the sight of the Porsche out the window confirmed the fact. She stopped and stood for a moment, gathering herself. Her mom was working a night shift, John-Luke was at The Music Box where his band practiced. She wondered if Logan knew she was alone, as well. She drank some water. The buzzer buzzed again. She pulled a long cardigan over her T-shirt and shorts and went out into the hallway to answer the door.

Logan waited on the step with his back to her and she felt herself tense at the size of him, the broadness of his back, the height. He wore dark pants and a shirt, like he could head into the office if he needed to. She recognized the way his hair just brushed the collar at the back. And when he turned around, she recognized the hardness in his eyes from the website picture.

"What are you doing here?" She stood slightly behind the door, shielding herself.

He was glancing down at his phone—why waste a second when you could be working?—but spoke as he raised his head to look her in the eye. "Hello to you, too."

She seemed to have a heightened awareness of his every move, the way he slipped his phone in his pocket, the glance over his shoulder to check they weren't being watched.

"It's late, Logan, I don't want to do this now." She stepped back further. He was too imposing. She wanted this conversation to be somewhere neutral, emotionless. Not when she was in the safe cocoon of the orchard house wearing an old T-shirt, gym shorts and a cardigan, and about to go to bed.

A truck cruised down the road, lights illuminating the dusk. Logan glanced around at the sound then turning back said, "Can I come in?"

"No. I don't want you here." She stood with her shoulder firmly against the door. "We can meet another time."

He raised a brow as if no one had ever said no to him. "Just let me in."

"Don't tell me what to do, Logan."

He inhaled a frustrated breath through his nose. "I don't need any more photographs being taken of me."

She looked behind him at the road. They were too visible standing there.

"Oh, for goodness' sake." She covered her face with her hands for a second, then pushed her hair back from her face. "Fine, come in."

As he stepped into the hall, the bare floorboards creaking, she knew it was a bad idea. She closed the door and went to stand between him and the hallway, leaning against the stair post, allowing him no further inside the house than the entryway.

Neither of them spoke for a moment. The silence put her further on edge.

"I went to the house," he said in the end, hands in his pockets, his expression calm and controlled where she felt off-kilter and on the back foot.

She nodded. "So I saw."

"Why didn't you warn us how bad he was, with the pills and—" he shook his head "—everything else."

She'd wondered how he'd start. "It wasn't my responsibility, Logan, to tell you about your brother."

"That's bull." He took a step forward and she pressed herself back into the wooden stair post. "One phone call about the state he was in and I could have done something. That was all you needed to do."

She narrowed her eyes in disbelief at what he was saying. "How was I supposed to know you didn't know?" Her hand went to her chest and underneath it she could feel her heart pounding. "You talked to him all the time."

"And you lived with him! If I had known how bad things were," he spoke with tight restraint, "I could have tried to save him."

"He didn't want anyone to save him, Logan," she snapped back. "Least of all you!"

Silence.

Logan's eyes darkened. His brows drawn together.

Bella swallowed. She looked down at the patterns in the wood on the floor. Her skin prickled. Her muscles tensed. She didn't want him here anymore, invading her space, making her feel small.

Logan just watched her. His jaw clenched, breathing in slowly through his nose.

"I think you should leave," she said, walking quickly past him toward the front door.

He shook his head, his hand grabbing hold of her arm to stop her. "I want to know what happened between the two of you."

She flinched at his grip. Eyes alert to his fingers pressing into her skin. "And I want you to let go of my arm," she said as steadily as she could. They were close enough for her to see the flecks of gray in his narrowed blue eyes. "Now."

She saw the moment his brain took over from his instinct and he relaxed his hold. He had the sense to look chastened at being caught out of control. "I apologize."

She pulled her arm tightly into her side. "You need to leave."

He took a step forward. "I'm not leaving here, Bella, till I get some answers."

They were so close that she could see the different flecks of blue in his eyes and the darkness of his lashes; the nearness of him made all the tiny hairs on her body stand on end. She felt the air shift around her, and when she tried to swallow she felt her breath hitch in her throat. She saw the moment he noticed, when his brain sensed how vulnerable she was to his proximity, and she saw a sneer of satisfaction play on his lips.

It was enough to make her stalk past him to the door, haul it open and spit, "Go."

While her legs were shaking, Logan walked smoothly around her out the front door, not looking back as he took the front steps quickly and strode back up the path the way he'd come.

She shut the door and stood for a second, hand over her mouth, eyes squeezed tight, heart thumping in her ears. How could he? He'd come into her space and tainted it. How dare he?

How dare he make her out to be the villain?

How dare she have let him?

It was enough. She couldn't live like this any longer, always on tenterhooks in fear of Logan Carter's disgust.

Her hand threw open the door before she could stop it.

He was standing by the front gate, back on his phone.

"Come back here!" She was trembling now. Blood pounding in her ears. She saw him pause as he lifted his head from his screen. "Don't you dare do this." She jogged quickly up the path so they were level.

His lip curled as he said dryly, "You just told me to leave."

"You want to know what went on?" she spat, injustice infusing her body at the look he gave her. "You think *I* broke *him*?" Her breath shook as she inhaled.

"Yes, quite frankly!"

Don't do it, Bella.

"*He* broke *me*, Logan."

He scoffed at the words.

"Don't you dare dismiss me." She jabbed him in the solid wall of his chest. "That's always been your problem, you never listen to what you don't want to hear. *He* broke *me*, Logan!" Her voice rising to a shout as she repeated, "*Jack* broke *me. Me!*"

"Calm down!" he ordered, his voice laced with warning.

"I said, don't tell me what to do!" she shot back.

A car drove past, slowing at the sight of them arguing so publicly on the sidewalk.

Logan had his arm around her shoulders faster than she could get the words out, hightailing her back into the house away from the prying eyes of the street, kicking the door shut behind him. "What are you doing, shouting in the street?"

She ripped herself from his hold as soon as they were inside. Logan was speaking but she wasn't listening. What *was* she doing? She'd snapped in full view of whoever was walking past. She covered her eyes with her hand, trying to get her thoughts into some kind of order.

When she heard him say flatly, "It was between the two of you. I should never have come," she looked up.

Brushing hair that had fallen across her face to one side, she said, "But it wasn't the two of us, Logan. It was never just the two of us. Because there was always you."

Chapter Twelve

Logan paused, hand on the door latch.

Bella stood still, heart thumping, now only wanting him to leave with the truth, whether he believed it or not.

He didn't turn. "I don't know what you're talking about. There was never anything between us."

"No," she laughed, humorless and cool. "I'm well aware of that, Logan. But it wasn't that simple." She clutched her arms around her body. "You're a fool if you think it was."

There was a pause that seemed to tick on forever. She looked away at a tapestry of the mountain view on the wall. At her shoes carelessly discarded on the floor.

His voice broke the silence. "Tell me, then." He turned around to face her. "Tell me what happened."

"You're going to listen?"

The nod was imperceptible.

"Well, in a nutshell, he just wanted what you had, Logan." She made a vague attempt at a smile, like it was a dumb joke. Of course he didn't laugh, because it wasn't funny. "And me, I just wanted someone to love me, I think. My dad had just died." She could still remember the blank terror of it, a hollow that had opened up inside her. "I was a mess. And there was Jack, all charming and funny, and I suppose he reminded me of the old days. He reminded me a bit of you, but the version who had time for me." She pushed her hair out of her eyes, tiredness suddenly creeping over her. "But he wasn't like you at all."

Logan didn't say anything, just watched her as he stood broad-shouldered and impenetrable.

Her breath shook when she inhaled. It was harder than she'd expected to dredge up everything that she'd never said out loud before. "You were gone by that stage, Logan. You didn't reply to messages, you didn't even call me when my dad died. You chose everything else except me. You chose the record label, you chose building that business. The band finished and you moved onto the next thing, forgot about everything else. It was always just another thing. Another version of glory, another thing that came way before I ever would. And I couldn't work out what had happened. Where you'd gone. You were meant to be my friend."

Infuriatingly, she felt a tear slide down her cheek, falling from her chin onto her arm. She saw Logan move slightly, as though he was going to come nearer, but then stay where he was.

She swallowed, reached up a hand to wipe away any more tears, pulled herself back together. "I just got left behind, Logan. You left me behind." His eyes were hollows in the darkness. "You know, the more famous you got, the more involved you were in the business. When you'd invite me to stuff, it was your brothers who talked to me when you got dragged off by some head honcho or other, it was them I hung out with when you were hours late in some meeting or other when you'd said we'd go for dinner. It was embarrassing, it started to feel like they were taking pity on me—and I know they were my friends, and have always been my friends, but I was coming for you, Logan. You were who I wanted to see more than anyone, you were my best friend, you were..." She sighed up at the ceiling. "I don't know, I guess to me, you were my family. You were who I had, who I trusted, who I relied on. And it started to feel like you didn't see me as anything more than someone on your to-do list to call once in a while."

"That's not true," his voice surprised her.

She glanced up, brow raised in defiance. "There's only so many unanswered messages a person can take before they get the message, Logan."

He shook his head.

"I know friendships come to an end, but I didn't think ours would. I hate how naïve I was." She looked down at her bare feet, looked anywhere but at him. "And then my dad died, and I didn't cope very well with that. At all."

"You could have said all this to me at the time."

"No, I couldn't."

"Why not?"

"Because you were busy, Logan!" She had to laugh, looking up at his taut, emotionless expression. "You wouldn't have listened. You're only vaguely listening now, and that's only because you're the one who wants answers."

She watched him take a breath in, look away from her and exhale slowly. "I would have listened."

"You had too much to do. You always have too much to do. Too many people to look out for."

"So, it's my fault?" he cut in sharply. "That's not the way I remember it, Bella. From my perspective it felt like yes, we all drifted apart I'm not denying that. But then you *chose* Jack, you chose the fame, you chose the lifestyle."

"Chose him over what, Logan?" she shot back. "Like you said, we were never together!"

The words hung like an echo.

He closed his eyes, shook his head. "I didn't mean it like that."

She looked down at the floor. She knew that wasn't what he'd meant, she'd said it to get a reaction—the days when that unspoken spark had flickered between them seemed so long ago it was like two different people in another life. So far, beyond the odd shake of his head, Logan had showed no visible sign of being moved by anything she'd said. Whereas Bella felt like she was peeling her skin off and standing naked before him.

She needed to put some distance between them.

Turning away, she walked down the hallway into the kitchen. Throwing open the window for some fresh air. The sweet scent of the orchard in the evening filled the room.

She'd poured herself a glass of water and was standing by the half-open window when she heard him come into the room. She felt his movements like the two of them were connected together by thread.

She could see him behind her in the reflection of the glass. His eyes dark hollows in the window.

"So, go on, then," he said coolly, "explain how I'm somehow responsible for your disastrous marriage."

She bristled at his take on the past. Wanted to grasp him by the shoulders and shake him into seeing what she was saying. "Don't patronize me."

"Come off it, Bella. We all saw the life the two of you led, we all saw the papers, the interviews. Fine, maybe it went sour, but you had a great time together. From the outside, it looked very much like the life you wanted."

Why was she doing this? She leaned forward and pressed her forehead against the cool window for a second then turned around to look at him. "There are photos of you in the band that make it look like it was the life you wanted, Logan. Everyone can make a picture tell a story."

He shrugged. "I was fine in the band."

"Oh, please." She rolled her eyes.

"We're not here to talk about me." Logan raised his chin. "We're here to talk about you and Jack."

Bella glanced up at the ceiling. "Fine." He was so difficult to argue with. "Yes, it was always nice to hear from Jack. He kept in touch with me after the band split up, and then when he agreed to do an interview for *Vogue*, he requested me to interview him. At the time it was what I needed." The memory of that period sat like a knot in her stomach. A tangle of confusion. "When Dad died—" she still got frustratedly choked when she said it out loud "—it was really sudden and I was just floored." She looked at the floor not at Logan. "I think I'd always held out for some kind of reconciliation. I thought there would always be time for him to be, I don't know, impressed by me?" She rolled her eyes at how stupid it sounded. "For him to realize he wanted to make a place for me in his life. But then—" she shrugged "—he was gone, and I was just left there, with life completely normal around me, and not quite able to grasp onto anything. It was so confusing, to feel so much about someone who didn't feel enough for me. So, I don't know, being with Jack—he was charming, attentive—it was like a connection back to a time when I had been *really* happy."

Logan raised a brow as if she'd just contradicted herself.

Bella raised hers back, as if to say, life isn't black and white. "And then, well, it was a whirlwind. At the beginning they were really good times. It *was* like the fairy tale the papers made out it was. And I think we got—or I got—really swept up in that. I didn't have to think about anything. Of course, we should *never* have gotten married. It was a stupid, spur-of-the-moment, Vegas mistake." She laughed when she said it, trying to make it lesser, but it didn't work. The words caught at the end, she wasn't ready to laugh about it yet. "By the time I'd realized how destructive it all was, I was stuck. I couldn't get away."

She turned around to the little table where she'd put her glass of water, took a sip to buy herself some time. Then she slid into the chair by the table, turning half his way as she said, "That world, Logan…" She shook her head. "It's so easy to get caught up in it. I was lost and I was lonely, and to begin with Jack treated me like I was precious, and I fell for that. He made me feel like I was someone again." She stared at the water in her glass.

Logan laughed like he didn't believe it.

She glanced up, stared him straight in the eye.

He stared back, defiant for a beat or two, then looked away out the window.

"It was fun for maybe six months, a year." She'd waited so long to admit all of this to somebody. To tell Logan. Not even to make him understand, but just to make him hear it. "But he wasn't in it for me, Logan. Jack didn't love me. I don't even know if he liked me."

Logan's head swung back, eyebrows drawn. "Of course he loved you."

Bella smiled sadly. "Your problem, Logan, is that you think everyone's like you. That no one's playing a different game."

Chapter Thirteen

Bella ran her finger up the side of her glass, catching a stray drip of water before it puddled on the table. "You remember the day you broke your collarbone, Logan?"

He glanced up, and she took his expression to mean that he could hardly forget it.

They were in Autumn Falls for a charity polo game. It was the first time Bella had arrived home with Jack, married. She remembered feeling awkwardly conspicuous walking into the club. Jack, however, had no such concerns, swaggering in as confident as ever with his sunglasses on, in his navy-and-white uniform. They were mobbed almost the moment they arrived. As a couple, they'd become a brand overnight, everyone wanting a piece of them. It wasn't about Silver Sky anymore, the band was dead, Jack was the man of the moment—his latest movie was raking it in at the box office—and his fame had gone stratospheric.

She remembered the moment she saw Logan in the

distance liaising with the grooms. He didn't turn at the commotion, but she knew he knew that they were there.

"You wouldn't even look at me," she said, her gaze still trained on the glass of water in front of her.

In the end, however, he had to look, politeness dictated it, the groom he was talking to had nodded in their direction to let him know they'd arrived. And when he turned, and she saw the familiarity of his features, Bella had felt herself relax, known that whatever had happened up to that point didn't matter, because there was her friend. As their eyes met, she realized that the feeling of wanting him to smile her way was worth more than her pride ever would be, so she had smiled softly, openly, his way.

But he'd looked straight past her, pretending he'd seen nothing at all.

"But when it came to Jack," she said, looking up now to see Logan brace himself for an uncomfortable truth that he didn't want to hear, "you were happy to go all out."

The crowd had parted to let Logan stride over to greet them. The brothers together was always gold in the eyes of the press. As he came closer, Logan had kept his gaze very deliberately on Jack, almost refusing to acknowledge Bella's existence. But in contrast, Jack had very pointedly slung his arm possessively over Bella's shoulder, tugging her in tight to his side causing her to stumble in her high heels on the grass. She remembered so clearly the feeling of bemusement, because the gesture wasn't a natural one for their relationship, it was always more equal than that, never such a public display of ownership. Then she caught the look that passed between the brothers and in that split-second came the moment of clarity that all Jack wanted was to see Logan's envy, and that she had made a monumental mistake.

After that, the build up to the game passed in a blur. Bella spoke politely with the Carters—Emmett as monosyllabic as ever, Martha trying her best to smooth any awkwardness over—but Bella was too distracted to concentrate. She avoided her mom and John-Luke, knew that with one look her mom would see straight through to a problem. Instead, she sat next to Noah in the stands, he was never one for probing questions.

The match itself didn't hold any importance. It was meant to be a fun day out in the name of a good cause. The Carter brothers had made a hefty donation. For the teams, the youth squad were mixed in with veterans and current A players. To add a bit of friendly competition, Logan and Jack were placed on opposing sides.

Logan was always a player recognized for his strategy and control, yet also, when necessary, his ruthless determination. His respect on the pitch was uncontested. But that day, eyebrows were raised. He played with a fire inside him—the control he was so famous for was nowhere to be seen. Of all the horses he rode in the game, he favored a particularly devilish black Argentinian who happily responded to the fight. And when he bought her on, the pair were unstoppable.

Jack, however, was in training for an action movie and was fitter and stronger than he'd ever been. Usually the more aggressive of the two on the field, Logan's maverick play seemed to dial Jack down, made him watch and wait.

Made him strategize where normally he'd race headlong into the fray.

Bella watched from the stands, hands clenched, heart in her throat. She could see it coming, she could see suddenly everything she'd thought was concrete and immoveable in Logan disappear as he charged the pitch to ride off his brother.

It wasn't a play that was going to win the match. Logan should have let it go.

Sitting beside her in the stand, Noah sucked in a breath as he watched Logan charge up alongside Jack. "*What* is he doing?"

Other players seemed to pause in shock, spectators winced, Bella put her hands together, fingers laced under the chin, praying for him to slow down, the umpire bellowed. But in a heartbeat, Logan maneuvered the fiery black pony with such innate skill, played with such ability, that she heard people laugh for doubting him. While she berated herself for thinking that Logan might not be one hundred per cent in control, might have let his emotions get the better of him.

But then, obviously so high from the victory, so sure of himself and exhilarated, Logan didn't see the young player who had stopped in his path to gawp in admiration.

The sweating black pony reared and Logan fell.

The crack when he hit the ground echoing around the stands.

Noah was out of his seat sprinting down the steps and onto the pitch. Bella raced after him, pausing when she saw his parents and officials racing over to join the medics and

Logan raise a hand to show he was alive, aware that it wasn't her place to be there in the surrounding crowd.

She'd stopped on the sidelines, and it was only then that she saw Jack watching the medics in action, up on his horse, stick across his thighs, the ghost of a smile playing on his lips.

In the orchard kitchen now, Bella looked up at Logan whose hand had reached to touch his collarbone. She had heard that the torn ligaments, shattered bone and dislocated shoulder took months to heal and created a permanent weak point, putting an end to any hopes of playing professionally again.

"I think I understood then that I was just the prize," she told him. "You would fight Jack, you would race him, you would show him what it meant. But you never would have fought for me. You were meant to be my friend, but you never would have put your emotions on the line for me. Even now, I'm dispensable."

Logan's expression was thunderous.

She stood up, could feel herself getting hot and annoyed. It all still made her fists clench and adrenaline shoot through her system. "I knew then that I'd made a mistake but I was too proud to admit it. I was a mess. I just blocked it out by partying, drinking, whatever. Any possible way to drown out the feelings I had about my life, my dad, the mistakes I'd made. I'd pretty much cut myself off from Mom and John-Luke. I guess I was lonely." Pulling her hair up she suddenly felt the need to get it away from her face and her skin. She needed some space from herself. But she didn't have a hairband so she let it go and it fell back in whatever haphazard style it was in from earlier.

"But I'll tell you something, Logan. I didn't deserve the life I got. I didn't deserve him. You want to know who your brother was, he's in that house. All Jack wanted was to be at the top, to be the best, to be the most adored. I didn't fit that." She was angry now. Hated having to explain it, relive it in her head. "But he couldn't let me go, could he? Because I was the prize." She stared Logan straight in the eye as she spoke. "After that he changed. Pretty quickly, actually." She could feel her bottom lip start to tremble. It was so frustrating. She didn't want to look weak in front of Logan. "To be honest, I think he might have hated me." The sad shame of it made her defend herself with a resigned smile.

Logan looked down at the floor.

Was any of it going in? Was he listening? Was he hearing.

He raked a hand through his hair and sighed. "I don't understand why you stayed."

"Oh, Logan." She shook her head despairingly. "I tried to leave. Lots of times. He said he'd change. He begged me, said he'd do all sorts of awful things to himself if I left. So I stayed for a bit longer." She felt the press of tears again and couldn't stop them this time. "I don't want to be crying," she said, grabbing a square of paper towel and wiping frustratedly at her tears. "I just want you to hear my side."

Logan watched her, the muscles in his face taut and serious. Then he nodded and she wasn't sure if it was to urge her on or in understanding.

She went on anyway, because she had to get to the end.

"I didn't leave, because you get used to living a certain way, being treated a certain way." She wiped again at her eyes, then bunched the paper towel up in her hand. "Ways of behavior, feelings, they become normal. And it's only when you're out of them that you realize how not right they were." She braced herself against the kitchen island, could see her reflection in the glass of the picture frame behind Logan. She didn't want to look at him, but more so, she didn't want to look at herself. She looked down at the wooden countertop. "The more famous Jack got, the more paranoid he got. The worse he got, the smaller I got. When I tried to leave then, he wouldn't let me. I couldn't get away. I couldn't get out of the compound. You've seen the walls, Logan." She felt her chest tightening at the memories but she made herself carry on, tell him everything that had happened, the violence and fear of it all. She couldn't remember everything but she did her best. Movements and expressions existed like snapshots in her head, but the feelings were pin-sharp. The air sucking out of the space. The crack of the back of a hand. The normality of the furniture around her. The mug she drank coffee out of rolling and smashed on the floor. She could hear her own voice. Begging. She remembered the isolation, the feeling that it was her and only her and no one would help her. The fear that he would kill her.

She had to pause. Mask the rising panic with a sip of water. Breathe. "It wasn't just being physically trapped. I was afraid of him." She saw herself a shell of a person. A husk. Nothing there anymore that she would recognize now. "And then, well—" she blew out a breath, shook her head to gloss over it "—I don't know, I woke up, I suppose. Some survival instinct must have kicked in. In the end, my mom and John-Luke came and got me out. Which well … let's just say, it wasn't easy. But of course—" she smiled flatly "—that wasn't the story Jack told everyone."

Logan winced. It was the first real tell on his face that this was going in, that he had heard.

She knew it must contradict everything Jack had said. And she hated that she had to fight for her own truth to be heard. It made her angry and ashamed that she had to lay bare her own mistakes and vulnerabilities just so that he might not look at her the way he had since Jack had died.

"I made some mistakes, Logan. But I've paid. I've paid with humiliation, with fear, with the loss of my privacy, with everything that he's said about me. I've paid." She held up her hands, she was done. She was tired. Exhausted. She tried to push the tears back with her fingers. "And you know what's funny, is that sometimes, you know, I just wished you'd remembered me." She looked up at his clenched jaw and hooded, unreadable eyes, the tears spilling down her cheeks now, warm on her skin.

She closed her eyes, running her hand across her face. And she stayed like that, with her eyes shut and her hand in front of them because she couldn't bring herself to look up. And he stayed where he was and the gap between them seemed huge, but really small at the same time. Part of her ached for him to walk around to her. But the other part, the part that had gone through it all, didn't want him near her.

Shaking her head she forced herself to look up at him. At the hard blue gaze. "Do you still not think much of me?"

Logan laughed sadly, as if surprised by the question. "No, Bella. I think it's safe to say, it's myself I don't think much of."

They looked at each other but neither spoke.

She heard the breeze rustle the apple trees through the open window, the chime of the clock in the living room. As they stood, she felt her feelings change from anger to sadness. Regret, almost. She found herself wishing for just a glimpse of who he used to be. But then she'd have to find a glimpse of who she had been, too, and she felt the impossibility of that.

"I'll go," Logan said, voice tight.

She nodded.

He walked out of the room toward the front door while she stood in the kitchen doorway watching his back retreat. Halfway down the hallway, he paused for a moment and turned, like he was about to say something more. Her body braced for whatever it was going to be, and she wondered if he noticed the tension and decided against, walking away instead. At the front door, he looked back at her over his shoulder to say, "Goodnight, Bella."

She nodded. "Goodnight, Logan."

Chapter Fourteen

Logan couldn't drive away fast enough. His head reeled with what he'd done and what she'd said. At one point he had to stop, just so he could get out and breathe fresh air, because he thought he might be sick. He closed his eyes, hung his head low, but still the claustrophobic nausea pressed in on him. He felt the shame of his own feelings, actions, wanted to pack the truth away but the box was open now.

Images of whatever Jack had done to her in that house, behind those walls, crowded his head. He wanted to turn back time, be the one who smashed through the compound's defenses and forcibly yank his brother off her. He wanted to fight him, man to man, stare into his eyes, no games, no disguises.

But Jack was dead.

Logan gripped the car doorframe for a second, not certain what to do. He knew he had to rid himself of that fury. He couldn't go home feeling like this. Taking a breath, he got back in the car, U-turned on the spot and headed back to Main Street.

When he pulled up down a side street, Logan got out of the Porsche and stood for a second looking at the dirty, scuffed doorway. It looked exactly as it had when he'd last been there over a decade ago, give or take a few cracks in the wood. Even the air around it smelled the same: of the vent from Gino's pizza and the trash cans. Charlie's Gym. It was the only anonymous place he and his brothers could go when they needed to let off steam or get some training in. These weren't the kind of guys who tipped off the press.

Logan yanked open the door and jogged down the stairs. It was like stepping back in time.

Once inside the gym, he stood for a moment, hands in his pockets surveying the area. There were the same scuffed, utilitarian weights machines, the fraying medicine balls, the brown leather punchbags hanging from the ceiling, the spiders' webs and the bare lightbulbs, but most of all, there in the center of the room was the boxing ring, exactly as he'd left it. Sagging side ropes, the chipped paint, supports, electric striplights flickering overhead.

"Well, look who it is!"

Logan felt his mouth tip up in a grin before he'd even seen the guy. "All right, Charlie."

Nothing changed. Charlie was as old as the building and always had been. Lines on his face like grooves in rock, black hair now white, same red Adidas tracksuit.

"Do you know," Charlie swaggered toward him, arms crossed, "I saw you in the paper the other day and I wondered if you'd be back here."

Logan tipped his head. "You know me too well, Charlie." His smile however felt forced as he waited for the inevitable condolences about Jack.

Maybe there was something in Logan's eyes that he hadn't meant to show or maybe Charlie had a knack for reading emotions in men who didn't ever reveal any, because he just gestured to the dimly lit gym floor and said, "It's all yours, Logan."

Logan felt his shoulders drop a bit as he looked around, at the sweating boxers smashing at the punchbags, the teenagers banging out reps, the fighters in the ring dousing themselves with water, and nodded his head. This was where he needed to be. Then he looked down at himself and realized he was still in his work clothes. "I haven't got the right clothes."

Charlie smiled. "You're in luck, my friend. We sell merch now." He winked. "Gotta stay one step ahead, Logan."

Logan laughed, shrugging his jacket off. "Hit me up."

Half an hour later, warmed up and wearing a gray marl T-shirt with "Charlie's Gym—Home of Champions" scrawled on the front in red, and similarly logo'd tracksuit bottoms, Logan was beating the life out of one of the hanging punchbags. It felt good for his fist to connect with something. His muscles shuddering satisfyingly from the impact. Sweat beading on his forehead.

With each punch, he found his rationality. Was able to break down the things she'd said. Dispute accusations she had made of him. Build an argument. Yeah, he hadn't had loads of time in the past, but he'd had responsibilities, the band to look after, the fledgling Carter Media business. She knew that. Of course things had slipped his mind—

"Logan! You want in?" Charlie was leaning on the ropes of the boxing ring, there was a young, sinewy guy throwing warm-up punches into the air. Charlie beckoned with two fingers for Logan to join.

It had been a while since Logan had faced a real opponent. He strode over. "Why not?" he said with a raise of his brow that looked more cocky than he felt.

The young guy in the ring didn't smile.

There was nothing, Logan realized a few minutes later, like being smashed across the face to get one's thoughts in order.

"You okay, Logan?" Charlie checked.

He nodded. Ignoring the wooziness in his head that caused him to stagger, he got back into position, his opponent's blank, steely stare was like being forced to look in his own soul.

His body sparred on autopilot, shaking off blows, delivering his own, while his mind spiraled off to previously unseen places, moments he'd glossed past on his own single-minded journey.

He remembered Bella calling on his phone "Logan, where are you? We're waiting for you all."

He'd been so distracted by the list of people wanting to talk to him, the contract negotiations, the endless list of appearances. "I don't know what you're—" he started, glancing around the interior of the jet he was on with his brothers, and realizing as he spoke where he was meant to be, had promised they would be. Bella's *Vogue* shoot. He closed his eyes for a second. "We're on a flight to Tokyo, I'm really sorry." He tipped his head up to the ceiling. "There must have been a mistake in the scheduling."

"You can't be on a flight. Everyone's here—we've got it all booked." He knew even then that the clipped tone of her voice was covering up the fact he'd hurt her, but he didn't have the time.

The guy in the ring jabbed him hard in shoulder, pain ricocheting up his neck.

If he forced himself to remember the truth, he'd just wanted to end the call so he could close his eyes like the rest of the band and get some precious sleep. He sent her flowers as an apology.

An uppercut to the jaw sent him staggering back. Looking down he saw the sweat drip from his body. He felt blood trickle down his chin, across his collarbone and over the scar that cut him from breastbone to shoulder, which was now throbbing unreservedly.

He saw the missed calls on his phone. The conversations he'd only half listened to while typing emails or heading to a meeting. Or her name flashing on his screen and actively silencing the call because he had—he cringed —something better to do, somewhere more glamorous to be.

He wanted the memories to stop crawling back in. Why had he been such an idiot? Why had he let her slip out of his life?

Because he was pulled too many different ways. And then when the band split, time vanished. Logan's life was spent dealing with the fallout; Noah breaking down, Ethan going off the rails and disappearing, Brodie, lost and rudderless when it all fell apart.

Only Jack managed to get out unscathed. Climbing high on his solo Hollywood success. Logan understood that the band had to end, what he resented was being left to pick up the pieces—like it was expected of him, unquestioned.

Why hadn't he called her when her dad died? Why hadn't he made the time?

Because by then, he was head down, building his empire. Keep moving forward—only forward, that was his mantra. All that resentment, fear, failure, he could block it all out by working harder and smarter. Wasn't that always his advice? Stay ahead, never stop, never look back. Not even for a second. Calling Bella about her dad—that would have been too much, a catapult back to someone who knew him too well, who could see into him—right through to the chaos inside.

And then Jack had arrived at the polo with his arm around her, and he'd just felt so much envy, been unprepared for the ferocity of it.

A fist slammed into his face causing blinding white lights in his vision.

That was the emotion he'd never allowed himself to name. Envy. He had been jealous. Bone-crushingly, all-consumingly jealous.

Holding up his hand to signal a time-out to his opponent, Logan fell back against the rope, arms outstretched, chest heaving for breath.

I just wished you'd remembered me.

The memory felt worse than any punch. Guilt seeped

through him, dripping from head to toe. It had been so easy to make her the enemy.

Someone threw him a towel and he nodded in thanks, his eyes lacked focus, blood swirling heavy in his brain. He wiped his face and chucked the towel to the side. His jaw throbbed. His heart raced, and he felt finally like he was getting some of the punishment he deserved.

"Not like the old days, eh?" Charlie leaned up against the ringside and handed Logan a bottle of water.

"You can say that again." Logan exhaled, exhausted. "These guys are tough."

"Nah," Charlie shook his head, waving his hand as if dismissing the lot of them. "They just want to show the big, powerful Logan Carter they're stronger."

Logan laughed, pointing to his ravaged face and body. "I think they've got the wrong guy."

"There's a lot of ways of being the bigger man, Logan." Charlie picked up the discarded towel and walked away, the echo of a smile playing on his lips.

Logan took a swig of water and saw his opponent head back into the ring.

"Yeah?" the guy drawled.

Logan paused for a moment. Wondering whether this was such a good idea after all. But when he shut his eyes, he saw her, standing opposite him in that kitchen, the tear down her cheek, the hurt and confusion.

Logan nodded. "Yeah."

A group of teenagers had stopped warming up and were lounging around the side of the ring to watch with feigned disinterest. Logan clicked his neck and stood up. Felt suddenly very exposed.

That was why the first punch caught him off-guard, caught him with no defense, caught him wanting to lose. The impact vibrated through him, and he staggered for a second, absorbing the shock. The pain almost did what he had hoped it would.

I made some mistakes, Logan. But I've paid.

But was it really sufficient punishment, unless he put up the fight that it deserved?

As he pulled himself upright, Logan glanced around him, at the teenagers loafing around jeering at the side of the ring, at the cracked brick walls and the striplights and bare bulbs that lit the gym like a prison, at the man in front of him who seemed to be nothing but narrow, burning eyes, at the creaking ceiling above. And he made himself force up all the fury and the pain and guilt that had been plaguing him since going to Jack's house, since seeing Bella, since his picture was printed in the paper, since before that, since he'd lost her to his brother, since he'd let her down. Since—he winced in horror—he'd been so dismissive of her at the funeral, forced her to go to the wake. He felt his own stubbornness and frustration rise inside him, scorching hot.

And that was when the fight began.

When the laughing boys stopped laughing.

When Charlie looked up from packing away equipment and nodded in approval.

When the air became so charged, so raw, so electrifyingly intense, that slowly the crowd around the ring got thicker with people who had given up their own training to be a part of this.

Logan was muscle and dirt and sweat. He was eyebrows darker with moisture, and lips tight and body screaming. He was physically hurt and lungs burning. He was smashed and punched and bruised and bleeding. He was fighting for himself, against himself, for his brother, and against him. He was crying out for the pain of what Bella had said to him to be made physical, yet he was here to atone for leaving her alone.

He was deep in a world of his own. People and faces swam before his eyes. Conversations played out in his head. His father's constant disappointment, his brother smirking on the pitch, his mother at the sink with her back to him, *"What has happened to us?"* Bella standing with her head pressed against the glass.

For a second, he did the unthinkable and allowed himself to imagine what it would have been like if he'd been the one. If he hadn't let her slip away. If they'd got closer not more distant. If he had put her first. Perhaps she would walk in now and run her fingers through his hair, and cradle his head to her chest, and lean down and kiss him, and he would pull her into his lap and she might laugh. And then she would stand up and take hold of his hand and lead him home. And if that happened now, if he could just be given that small sliver of a chance, he would follow her with such reverence that it would hurt.

The roar of a crowd cut in startling him back to the present and he realized that he was coming to a point where he might win.

And he didn't want to win.

He wasn't there to win.

As swiftly as it had risen up the fight left him, drained out of him like pulling a plug. His armor was gone. His body throbbed. The pain was crippling. The shouts from the sidelines crowded in on him, distracting him, the focus he needed ebbed away. So, when it hit him, he realized he hadn't seen the final punch coming.

As he fell backward, he knew at some point he would hit the ground, but it took an eternity. When he did, he wished he hadn't. His back smacked hard against the floor, the shock reverberating through his outstretched arms, and when his head smashed down throwing his chin up and back, a pain like fire ripped through his collarbone.

Lying alone in the center of the ring, all sound seemed to retreat. He could see only the electric light as it flickered above him, the grooves of the corrugated roof, the spiders' webs that drooped with dust. He could feel the smooth chalky floor, cool against his skin. And a strange peace washed over him.

He would have lain there for the rest of his life if he could.

"Still alive?" Charlie's hand reached down to help him up.

"Just about." Logan shook his head to the proffered hand and pushed himself up on his elbow, wincing as every muscle in his body cried out for attention.

Charlie draped a towel over his shoulders. "That was a pretty good fight, Logan. I gotta admit, I didn't know if you still had it in you."

Logan looked up from where he was sitting, elbows resting on his knees, eyes sardonically narrowed. "I lost, Charlie."

Charlie raised bushy white brows. "There's a difference, Logan, between losing and throwing a fight."

Logan shook his head as he yanked his gloves off. "I didn't throw anything."

Charlie laughed. "If you say so."

Logan ignored him, downing the remains of his water and letting it splash over his face. When his opponent came over, hand out to shake his, Logan lifted up his arm but felt the throb of damage shoot through his muscles. He did his best to disguise a grimace of pain.

Charlie held the ropes open for Logan to step through. A couple of people patted him on the back. The teenagers skulked away. Weights were lifted again, the sound of the metal cracking to the ground echoing around the gym. He didn't know how much time had passed, there were no windows in the room so you wouldn't know the time of day. Logan rubbed the sweat off his body with the towel and slung it over his shoulders.

"I'm out of here. Thanks for the time, Charlie."

"Anytime, Logan." Charlie raised a hand to wave. "Hey, next time you have your picture taken try and smile."

Logan laughed and then winced from the pain in his split lip. "No chance."

Chapter Fifteen

Logan hadn't told any of his family that he was back in Autumn Falls and was staying the night at the house he owned on the outskirts of town. He'd never lived in it before, it had been decorated by New York's best interior-design company and most of the couches still had the plastic coverings on that they'd been delivered with. On the few occasions he stayed there, he just crashed on the bed, never even going into the other rooms. It certainly wasn't home, but the idea of heading to the ranch in the state he was in after the gym was laughable, his mom would be apoplectic.

When Logan pulled up at the desolate house, he was still wearing his Charlie's Gym gear. He stood for a minute by the car, not quite ready to go inside, not quite ready to assess how much damage and how much good he'd done himself in the ring. Or just not quite ready for the day to end.

Closing his eyes for a second, he tentatively touched his

collarbone, stifling a shout as he pressed the bruised skin with his fingers. Then he ran a hand over his face to check that it was all in one piece. His fingers came away with blood on them from the cuts.

Someone stepped off the front porch, whistling at the sight of him. Logan squinted in the darkness. For a moment he thought it was Bella. Hoped, perhaps. But, then he heard Brodie's voice saying, "Dang, Logan, what have you done to yourself?"

He realized he was seeing Bella everywhere. Like looking straight at the sun, her image imprinted on his retinas.

"Brodie! You scared me half to death." Then when he'd caught his breath, he added, "How did you know I was here?"

"Well, you weren't at the ranch and your office said you were in Autumn Falls, so I figured this was where you'd be." Brodie shrugged.

His brother sauntered over from where he'd been sitting, casually chewing Wrigley's and looking more and more pained the closer he got to Logan's injuries. "Do we need to call the cops or was this—" he glanced down and smirked when he saw the gym logo emblazoned on Logan's chest "—self-inflicted, I see." Brodie raised a brow like he could see the last few hours in a reel above Logan's head. "I was gonna ask if you wanted to go for a drink, but the ER might be more appropriate."

Logan shook his head but even that made him wince. "I'm not going to the hospital."

"Drink, then?" Brodie said, seemingly unperturbed by the state of his brother now he knew he'd done it willingly.

"Can I go and get changed first?" Logan replied, hobbling to the front door.

Brodie laughed as he followed him. "D'you know, that might be the first time you've asked my permission for anything?"

Logan glanced back at his brother. "I'm really getting some home truths today."

Brodie grinned, the gum he was chewing held between his teeth. "Brilliant."

Half an hour later, they were in The Firestone, a block from the gym where Logan had just had his lights punched out. Logan had cleaned up his face as best as he could, but kept pressing his bottle of Bud against the cut on his swollen cheek.

Brodie swigged his beer and said helpfully, "You're going to look bad tomorrow."

Clay Murphy, the bartender, who they'd known since school, said, "Logan, you want some ice?"

"I'd appreciate it, yeah." Logan nodded.

The bartender wrapped a couple of squares in some paper towel and handed it over. "Doesn't look good."

Logan said, "You should see the other guy."

Brodie's brows raised. "Seriously?"

"No." Logan laughed.

The barman chuckled.

Brodie grinned, taking another swig of his drink.

They never did this, just sat in a bar together. Logan

wondered what was going on. "Why are you here, anyway?"

Brodie put the bottle down on the scratched aluminum counter. "Came to check you were all right."

"Seriously?" Logan frowned.

"Yeah," Brodie laughed, eyes tilted up, glinting. "I saw the picture in the papers, wasn't like you to get caught. Figured something must have happened. So, I called your office, they said you were here." He shrugged. "I was in the vague area so thought I should come and check."

Logan didn't know what to say. For a second, he thought there was an embarrassing possibility he might cry. But he never cried. He'd certainly never felt like he couldn't speak before.

Brodie watched him, seemed to sense his crumbling façade and looked away at the rows of optics behind the bar, giving Logan a chance to swallow away the lump in his throat. When he turned back, fingers toying with a beer mat, turning it over and over on its corners, he narrowed his eyes and said, "So look, you can do what you always do and say everything's cool, under control, or you can tell me what happened? Because from here, I gotta be honest, it really doesn't look good."

Logan tried to laugh, then flinched from the pain.

Brodie didn't look away this time, didn't laugh. Just waited.

Logan turned so he was facing the bar, his forearms resting on the cool aluminum, so he didn't have to look his brother in the eye. Fingers tapping the sides of the Bud bottle, he said, "I think I may have made a few mistakes."

Brodie snorted. Then, elbow on the bar, he rested his chin in his palm, settling in as he said, "I think I'm going to like this."

But his smile slipped as Logan told him everything he'd seen at Jack's—the drugs, the signet ring, the folded photo—and everything Bella had said.

When he was finished, Brodie sighed. "Oh, wow. That's much worse than I was expecting."

"I know," Logan said flatly. "We've got to tell Mom and Dad."

"Good luck with that." It was an off-the-cuff remark, but it hit the nail on the head, it was always Logan who did the hard stuff.

Then Logan frowned as he took in his brother's reaction and said, "You don't seem massively surprised?"

Brodie sat back in his seat, seemed to think through it all, then he glanced over at the bartender and ordered another round. Turning back to Logan, he said, "Look, growing up it was always you and Jack and then the rest of us."

"That's not true."

"It is true. It's not a bad thing, it's just the way it was." The bartender put the new drinks down, Brodie thanked him and reached to pull his bottle toward him. He thought for a second then said, "In the band, you were like our dad, Logan." He swigged the beer, said out the corner of his mouth, "Darn sight easier to talk to than Dad." Logan snorted but Brodie carried on. "But still, you were like the authority figure. And for us, 'cause we were young, we needed that, we appreciated that. But Jack—" Brodie bit down on his lip, shook his head as he thought about it "—you could see him rallying against it."

Logan lifted the half-melted ice back to his cheek, wishing he'd just said that all was cool as he usually did. "That was just brotherly competition as far as I was concerned." Then when Brodie raised a brow, Logan shook his head. "Maybe I did see it, but I don't think I took it as seriously as I should have done."

Brodie laughed. "That's because you were at the top. That's what happens. You had stuff to do, you were moving us forward. Charting the course. You only see the other stuff when you're underneath." Brodie peeled the corner off his beer label. "Jack wasn't awful, he just wanted power and he got it how he could. I'll be honest, there was always an edge with him, like you didn't want to get on his bad side because he could be really mean. Yeah, it was funny sometimes, but as time went on with the band and he was less and less satisfied, really, he could be kind of a bully. Not to you, he wouldn't have dared, but the rest of us, we felt it."

Logan winced. He thought of Noah at the funeral saying he didn't buy the heartbroken stuff. Why hadn't Logan pushed for more at that point? Because Noah was the kind of guy you could trust with your life, but he'd never for one second tell you how he was feeling. He scrubbed a hand over his face, his skin still cold from the ice. "What about Jack and Ethan?" he asked, not sure he wanted to know the answer. "They were out all the time together when the band split."

Brodie made a face, picked some more at his beer label, seemed reluctant to reply.

"Come on, Brodie, just tell me everything."

Brodie sighed. "Thing is, Logan, when the band split it affected everyone differently. Jack had his movie offers, we all knew he wanted to go off, do bigger things. To *be* bigger, more famous. He was unstoppable. I think you were already more fulfilled by the business side of things."

Logan tipped his head in reluctant agreement even though he sensed Brodie didn't need it to know it was true.

"Noah, well, he'd been desperate to get back to the ranch from practically the word go, and then there was everything that happened with him and Livvy." Logan winced at the reference. Brodie paused for a moment as he thought back, then he half laughed. "But me and Ethan. It was our life. It was kind of all we knew. I was fifteen when we left home. Yeah, we knew how to farm but that was Dad, that was just following orders. We grew up in that band. It was who we were. It was our identity." He shrugged, like it didn't mean so much when clearly it meant everything. "And then it ended and we're suddenly like, what happens now!?" He held his hands out. "I knew I'd be okay, I'm happy anywhere." He grinned. "And whatever, I'd always have songwriting revenue. But Ethan." He screwed up his face. "I think Ethan *was* the band. It was his identity. What was he if it ended? He was back to being the kid who got kicked out of high school, got into fights and got hollered at by Dad for having no prospects. We all know he wasn't in a good place when we called it quits."

Logan nodded. Anyone could see that Ethan completely spiraled when Silver Sky ended, and if they couldn't, they just had to read the newspaper to get an idea. He was the only one of the brothers to launch a solo career and it was more successful than anyone would have thought—alone on stage, Ethan had a roguish, mischievous star quality that shone when given the spotlight. All the energy and disregard for authority that got him expelled from school, and constantly threatened by their dad, made him explosive on stage, but it also led to utter chaos in his personal life. Without Logan there to pick up the pieces, Ethan almost giftwrapped himself to the journalists, who gleefully photographed him drunk at festivals, new girlfriend on his arm every week, shouting about how much he loathed Silver Sky on one of his tours, trashing his brothers. It was when, soon after that, he was pictured staggering out of the hospital after wrapping his motorbike around a tree, that Logan had tried to force a meet-up with him, but Ethan had told him where to go. Walked away when Logan confronted him. Didn't want to hear anything he had to say.

Now sitting with Brodie, wanting and not wanting to know his take on the situation, he forced himself to ask, "And?"

Brodie made a face, uncomfortable with what he was about to say. "I think he found it difficult to be happy, couldn't get his head around everything that had happened —was happening—and he didn't really know who to blame for that. And I don't really wanna say it, Logan, but it's always pretty easy to blame the parent and, to Ethan, well you were the parent."

Logan's eyes widened with surprise. "He blamed me?"

Brodie shrugged in reluctant agreement.

Logan turned to stare down at his beer bottle, more than a little taken aback. But if he made himself think about it properly, his relationship with Ethan *had* been more father and son—almost in retrospect too much like their own father and his sons, impatient, misunderstood. Logan got frustrated with Ethan and tended to go in heavy where he was concerned, but only because he was so worried about him, because he was the one who seemed on the cusp of making the most dangerous mistakes.

"And you know what Ethan and Jack were like when they went out together," Brodie went on. "Jack would wind Ethan up like a spring and let him go. They'd go wild but Jack always knew what he was doing—pulled back at the last minute. Ethan's never been good at knowing when to stop. And at that time, Jack was hardly gonna paint himself as the bad guy who wanted out of the band more than anyone else, so he definitely didn't do anything to stop him believing that you'd pulled the trigger." Brodie raked a hand through his hair, he wasn't used to being the bearer of bad news, he was the happy-go-lucky one.

Logan put his head in his hands on the bar. "It was such a mess."

"It was," Brodie agreed. "But—" he shrugged "—I think it's better that it's out in the open. For me, anyway." He laughed. "I feel better being able to say it. Kinda relieved. And, you know Ethan, he's got himself together. Wherever he is."

Logan sat up, said dryly, "I don't know if you can use

the phrases 'got himself together' and 'wherever he is' in the same sentence."

Brodie's eyes crinkled—a more familiar sight.

Logan picked up the slivers of remaining ice and ran them over his cheek. "I can't believe I didn't do more to stop it happening." He felt a little like he was standing on the edge of a void. The whole world open below him.

"Don't beat yourself up too much, Logan." Brodie flipped his beer mat like a coin. "It wasn't your fault. I have a feeling this is what being a dad is like. Just a ton of blame, worry and responsibility."

Logan tipped his head. "Remind me never to have children."

"Tell me about it." Brodie grinned. "But on the other hand, we loved you, we needed you." He reached forward and patted him on the shoulder. "None of us could've done it without you there. And I think, with Jack, maybe that was why there was so much envy. He knew how much we depended on you."

Logan lifted his beer bottle with his right hand without thinking, the pain shot up his arm to his collarbone. He had to suck in a shout. Then breathe slowly through the aftermath of the pain.

It made him consider his competitiveness with Jack. While all the brothers used to pile onto the polo field on a Friday night, the whole town in the grandstand, polo was always the thing that Logan was the best at. He loved it. But so did Jack. And even though he played rough and aggressive, he showed real promise, always trying some clever new tactic to win. But on the flipside, he'd get really frustrated if he lost, blame everyone, have tantrums, blame Logan. And if Logan ever retaliated, his dad would say, "*Let it go, Logan, you're his older brother, be the better man.*"

Logan remembered when Jack turned up at that charity game with Bella by his side. Now he could bring himself to name the feeling, he could picture the savage jealousy, like fire burning through him. But he'd looked at Jack smiling and happy and he *tried* to be the better man. He *wanted* to be the better man.

Up until the very moment he'd mounted his horse, Logan was still persuading himself that he didn't care if Jack had Bella, didn't care if he beat him in the match, but then as he played, against his will the force arose and engulfed him. Everything seemed a little clearer, a little faster, there was a sickness in his throat and a burn in the fabric of his muscles. He could feel a relentless need to triumph. He wanted to show that whatever Jack thought he had, Logan, when it came down to it, wasn't secretly— morally—the better man, he was simply the better man all around—whether it was out there on the field or off the pitch, rising above Jack's attempts to make him jealous— and not just better, the *best*.

Exactly, he realized, what Jack had been determinedly trying to prove about himself over a lifetime spent snapping at Logan's heels.

That was the beast of competition. The whisper-thin line between love and hate.

"I should have done better," Logan said, staring down at his bruised, scratched reflection in the aluminum bar top.

Brodie flipped the beer mat again. "We all did what we

had to do." Then catching the coaster and resting it on the bar, he added, "We've all grown up, you know, Logan?"

Logan's eyes narrowed. "What are you saying?"

"I'm saying, you don't have to do everything," Brodie replied with a raise of a brow.

Logan snorted like that definitely wasn't the case. "Oh, yeah? You just said it would be me telling Mom and Dad about Jack."

Brodie winced. "Yeah, that was a joke."

"No, it wasn't."

"I will come with you."

Logan shook his head to say it wasn't necessary. "And where's Ethan, then, when you need him? What would Noah have done with the funeral—held it in the barn?" He stretched and yawned, which made his face hurt. "And where are you when Dad's chucking out the guilt trips like this whole mess is our fault. I don't see you squaring up to him."

Brodie tipped his head, looked at him with a rare hint of challenge before saying, "I didn't see you do it, either."

Logan paused, blew out a breath. His shoulders dropped. "No," he admitted.

Brodie's mouth tipped up in his usual half-smile. "Like it or not, we're all in this together, Logan. You can't solve everyone's problems. And you're never going to be everyone's hero," he said. "That's just the way it is."

Logan looked up, brows arched in surprise at the wisdom. Everyone knew Brodie's notion of wise was managing to do the least possible for the most gain—or maybe they didn't, maybe that was another assumption Logan had made.

Brodie threw him a knowing wink.

Logan smiled, it hurt his face but he didn't mind. He had never talked with Brodie like this before. He could chalk it up to another mistake or realize that perhaps he needed to hit this rock-bottom moment in order to hear what his brother had to say. That perhaps being the leader, the one out in front, had blinded him to so many other things going on behind him, other people.

Maybe Brodie was right, maybe they could all look after themselves. Maybe they all had to deal with their own mistakes. And he had to face up to his.

Logan looked at his brother who, spinning his beer mat on one corner, just sitting, nowhere else to be, had come all the way from wherever he had been to check on him. He could have gotten choked up again. Instead, he said, "Another drink?"

Brodie looked up with a grin. "Thought you'd never ask."

Chapter Sixteen

Bella was out in the orchard when John-Luke poked his head out the screen door and said, "People here to see you, Bella."

Bella presumed it was Logan and immediately braced herself to see him again after their altercation. She swept a hand over her hair just to check it didn't have apple blossom in it and walked toward the back steps.

But to her surprise it was Martha Carter who walked out first, Logan a few feet behind.

"Hello, Bella," she said. Martha had always been a strong presence in the boys' lives, tall and statuesque, brown hair so dark it was almost black, heavy eyes that looked naturally lined with kohl, long, straight nose. She was striking, not pretty. Today she looked tired, her skin pale and her shoulders low.

Bella stopped abruptly at the sight of her. Stunned to see her standing there in the orchard. "Oh, hello, Mrs. Carter."

"Call me Martha, Bella, please."

Bella nodded. It was late afternoon, but with brilliant sunshine, and the noise of the bees in the blossom hummed like crackling fire. The beauty of it felt surreal compared to the current reality of Logan and Jack's mom walking toward her. It was only when she'd recovered from that surprise that she looked up to see Logan's face and flinched back in horror at the angry black bruise down one side of it, the split lip and the cut that slashed through his brow. She opened her mouth to say something but then didn't, because this wasn't the time, Martha was walking closer. Instead, she held his dark, impervious gaze for a second, knew him well enough to know that the injuries were self-inflicted, she imagined the beating he'd taken at Charlie's, wondered if he'd won or lost.

Then she turned her attention fully to Martha who had stopped in front of her, her eyes red-rimmed and bloodshot, the fan of lines at her temples deeper from grief. "Bella, I hope you don't mind me coming over out the blue, but I knew that if I didn't come straight away then I might…" She was clearly nervous, and Bella's own heart was racing, "Oh, goodness, sorry, I…" Martha paused, put her hand to her chest.

Logan took a step protectively toward her.

Martha held up a hand to indicate that she was fine. "Let me start again." She cleared her throat. Bella remembered her in the kitchen of the ranch house, all wooden cupboards and old patchwork throws, laughing loudly, flipping pancakes, winning ruthlessly against the boys when they played board games, practicing their polo swings with them when they were out in the pasture, always so confident, so warm and enthusiastic. It was heartbreaking to see her so vulnerable. "Bella, Emmett and I spoke to Logan in depth this morning—Emmett would be here, but I thought it might be a little overwhelming, so many of us on your doorstep. But we would like to offer you an apology. For Jack. For what you went through."

Bella's eyes darted up to Logan. He had told them. All the tiny hairs on her body stood on end, a shiver prickling through her, even in the gentle warmth of the day. She wanted to press pause on the conversation, take a moment to adjust and hear properly every word that was being said. Wanted a second to understand all the million emotions that she knew were hidden in Logan's impassive, narrowed gaze, if only she had more time to look.

"I know it's not enough," Martha went on, shielding her eyes from the sunlight and moving into the shade of the trees, "and I know it can't put things right, but it's the only thing I have to offer right now. I'm sorry, Bella, for everything that happened with Jack."

Immediately, Bella stopped trying to work out what Logan was thinking, and let the words sink in. They felt like a release. Like Bella was at one with the ground beneath her, the delicate white flowers on the trees, the tributary of the Redemption River that trickled alongside the orchard. She hadn't realized, until that moment, how highly she regarded these people: the Carters. How ashamed she was of their judgment. Of her own behavior in their eyes.

"Can you please find it in your heart at some point, not now, to forgive us, Bella? For letting it happen."

"Yes." *Don't cry.* "Yes, of course." She swallowed over the lump in her throat.

Logan dipped his head, looked down at the ground, like he was separating himself from the moment to make it between Bella and his mother.

"No." Martha held up a hand. "Don't be hasty. Don't say it lightly. Just please, take the apology and in your own time, know that you are always welcome at our house. We're sorry."

Logan glanced up then, face shadowed darkly by the bruising but eyes softening slightly, as if adding his own agreement in a look.

Bella couldn't stop the tear that rolled down her cheek. She swiped it away with her hand. "Thank you, Mrs. Carter. Martha. I really appreciate you saying that."

"It's the least I can do, Bella—" her voice compassionate and homespun "—I'd like to know how I can do more."

"It's fine really. I…" Bella didn't know what to say, couldn't find the words to confess the enormity. "It's fine," she said again, looking fleetingly at Logan and seeing what looked perhaps like regret in the tightening of his jaw.

But then Martha's hand went up to her mouth to cover a sob and in front of Bella, this strong matriarch crumpled into tears. "I'm so sorry," she gasped, trying to catch her breath.

Bella reached out to support her, but Logan was there in an instant, wrapping his arm around Martha's shoulders, wincing instinctively at the pain in his rib caused by the movement but holding her firm and walking her back to the front door as she kept apologizing and Bella kept reassuring her that it wasn't necessary.

When they got to the car, Logan opened the door for his mom who had managed to compose herself, was wiping her eyes with a Kleenex, and said again, "I'm so sorry, Bella," as she reached to give her a hug—not the polite, impersonal gesture of the funeral but gentle and apologetic. "Please come and see us whenever you're in town. I know your mom and John-Luke have missed you very much."

Bella nodded, breathing in the warmth of the hug. "Yes," she said, still distracted and overwhelmed by it all. "I will."

Tearing up again, Martha got in the car and closed the door. Logan walked formal and businesslike around to the driver's side, as if he had no place there, like his presence was an intrusion because he and Bella had said everything they ever would.

So when Bella said, "Thank you, Logan." He paused, taken aback, and said, "What for?"

She wasn't quite sure how to articulate it. "For saying to them what I never would."

His expression softened, eyes creasing as he nodded, then after a moment he said, "I am truly sorry for what happened."

She nodded back, the tight knot that had lived inside her for years loosening its threads.

As Logan was about to open the car door, she added, "What happened to your face?"

"Charlie's Gym," he replied, confirming her suspicions.

"Did you win?" she asked.

He paused for a second then shook his head. "No."

"No," Bella replied softly, as if none of them had. Just various degrees of loss.

Their eyes met for a second and it seemed like everything that neither of them would say flickered in the air like a match. And for a fleeting moment, the raw intensity of his gaze made her breath catch. Then just as quickly it was over, he yanked open the car door and the spark between them went out.

When they had driven away, Bella went back out to the orchard, had to breathe the fresh air and lower herself to the ground, plunge her hands into the long thick grass just for something to grasp on to, to tether herself to the moment.

She felt the tears cascade down her cheeks and fall at will onto the grass. She lay back, arms outstretched, gazing up through the leaves at the azure sky and realized that *now* she was free.

Martha's visit had opened a door inside her and let out all the shame she carried in herself about how those people thought about her. All the judgment that she didn't realize kept her away. Kept her out. Kept her from life.

She knew then that it was time to go home. Back to New York. Her time at this safe, beautiful sanctuary was over. Because while it had given her the calm and protection she had craved, it suddenly felt like hiding.

Now she was free. It was over, she thought, staring up at the vast swathe of blue sky.

But then an image of Logan's dark ravaged face flashed into her mind, all the pain and regret in his eyes, and that hard-won freedom felt suddenly bittersweet.

Chapter Seventeen

It was just over a year later that the prestigious Cornelia Street Ballet Academy staged a show at the theater in Soho where Bella worked.

As the dancers were all piling out after their first rehearsal, Bella suddenly heard her name called from down the corridor. She looked up to see none other than Willow Carter running toward her, wild red curls piled haphazardly on the top of her head, dressed like such a dancing cliché in leggings, leg-warmers and a crop top, that Bella couldn't help but smile when she saw her.

"Willow? What are you doing here?"

"I'm the principal dancer! I didn't know you worked here!" Willow enveloped Bella in a giant hug that smelled of strawberry shampoo.

"You coming, Willow?" One of her friends called, holding the door open, the rest of the dancers having already left.

"One sec," Willow shouted back. Then returning her

attention to Bella, said hurriedly, "Listen, I have to go. But it's my birthday tonight and I'm having a little party—you should come!"

Bella shook her head. "I wouldn't want to intrude."

"Don't be silly. Brodie'll be there, he'd love to see you. No Logan unfortunately—he's away. But it'll be fun! Please?" She looked at her, wide upturned eyes beseeching. It reminded Bella of times in the Carters' hay barn when Bella would come and watch the boys rehearsing, when their band was just a hobby. Willow was a little kid then, ten or eleven at the time, and would sit on the highest bale of hay, her cloud of curls haloing her face, her legs swinging as she munched on peanut butter and jelly sandwiches. Bella would climb up to join and without fail be persuaded to let Willow do her make-up and plait her hair into all kinds of weird and wonderful shapes. Just as then, Bella found it impossible to say no to Willow's big-eyed pleading. And if Logan wasn't going to be there, it wouldn't be awkward. Brodie was always easy company.

"Okay," Bella agreed.

"Yes!" Willow clapped with delight. "I'll text you the address," she added as she flew out to catch up with her friends.

The party was on the rooftop of an old Brooklyn brownstone with a view out across the East River and the twinkling lights of Manhattan. By the time Bella arrived, it was already packed with people. It certainly wasn't the "little" party that Willow had called it. Bella was met with a sea of faces she didn't recognize, they all looked like dancers, glowing with radiant health, toned and poised like fashion models, it reminded her of the old *Vogue* parties, a far cry from where her life was nowadays. She had been in two minds about going, aware she wouldn't know anyone, and would definitely be out of place among the crowd of Willow's friends, but went in the end because the invitation felt too important, a bridge between the past and present.

She weaved her way through the crowd, twinkling festoon lights criss-crossing the sky above her, and headed to where a makeshift bar had been put together out of old boxes and a slab of wood. She poured herself a drink and looked out at the view. It was a cool, early fall evening, and from the rooftop they were level with the plane trees, the yellowing leaves sparking like gold in the setting sun.

"Hey! You made it!" Willow shouted excitedly when she spotted her. Wearing a little floral dress and her cowboy boots, her red curls knotted high on her head, she rushed over and hugged Bella tight.

It made Bella feel instantly at ease. Made the smile on the face feel more natural. "Happy Birthday," she said, handing her the flowers she'd brought her as a gift. "Sorry, I don't know what you're going to do with these, I didn't realize it was quite such a big party!"

"Don't be silly! They're gorgeous!" Willow grinned, smelling them before reaching over to grab one of the water jugs on the table and plopping the bouquet in. "Look, they're, perfect!"

Bella smiled at the flowers in among the bottles of wine

and jugs of cocktails. Then Willow said, "Come on, let me introduce you to some people," and ushered her toward a group of her friends.

Everyone Bella spoke to was lovely and really welcoming, but when Brodie came sauntering through the crowd toward her, it was a relief to see a face she recognized. "Brodie," she said fondly as he approached.

"Hello, darling," he murmured. Putting one hand on her waist, he leaned in and kissed her smoothly on both cheeks. He had the same expensive cologne, cute dimples, shaggy hair—was by far the best-looking guy in the place, and the twinkle in his eye said that he knew it. He surveyed the area and said, "Know anyone here?"

Bella shook her head.

He nodded in agreement. "Me, neither." He sipped his drink, eyes transfixed on the beautiful, tousled-haired dancers threading their way through the crowd, and said, "But you've gotta love Willow's parties."

Bella laughed. "Brodie, behave."

He chuckled, then turned and gave her the full radiant force of his attention. "So, what have you been up to?"

Chatting with Brodie was always easy, and he was his open, charming self, but while he was more than happy to devote his attention to Bella, every now and then she saw his eyes wander to the bare golden limbs and flirtatious glances of the women around them and felt she was unfairly monopolizing his attention, like a dog straining at the leash. When one girl knocked his arm as she passed, spilling his drink, she apologized profusely then taking a step back said, "Are you one of Willow's brothers?"

"Yeah, I'm the good-looking one," Brodie grinned. Which made the girl giggle and Bella roll her eyes and say, "I'm going to get a drink."

It was on the way to the bar however that the door to the rooftop opened and suddenly she saw Logan.

Bella stopped where she was, heart suddenly thundering, her eyes glancing left and right for an exit, but she couldn't move. He wasn't meant to be there.

Clearly fresh from the office, he wore a dark gray suit and white shirt, top button undone, hair rumpled and falling forward over his brow, there were dark circles under his eyes, a shadow across his jaw. He looked handsome in an exhaustedly disheveled way, like he had come to the end of a really hard week, but still there was that lazily crooked smile on his face as he searched the crowd for his sister.

But when the first person he saw was Bella, the smile vanished instantly, replaced with a frown of confusion, almost resignation, like he was expecting to whip in, say happy birthday to Willow and get out of there. Now he had Bella to contend with—something he wasn't prepared for and didn't look like he particularly wanted.

The look on his face made her stomach clench. She wanted to disappear. Wished she had never come.

But she had to just stand and wait as he took the couple of strides it needed to reach her.

"What are you doing here?" he asked.

His surprise may have made the words come out harsher than he intended, but even so it was a far cry from the infectious enthusiasm of Willow's and Brodie's greetings.

What was Bella doing there? She felt suddenly foolish for agreeing to come, she should have predicted this. "Willow invited me," she replied stiffly, "I didn't know you'd be here." She regretted it the moment she said it, annoyed that she'd implied that where Logan would or wouldn't be affected her choices.

But just then Willow came bounding over. "Logan! I didn't think you could make it."

"I just landed," he replied, all attention suddenly fixed on his sister, the smile back in place. "Happy birthday," he said dotingly, handing her a beautifully wrapped box.

"Oh, Logan, you didn't have to get me anything." She bashed him on the arm but ripped off the paper like an excited kid and gasped with delight at the tiny gold charm of a ballet shoe inside.

"I saw it in a little shop in Milan last week, made me think of you." Logan shrugged as if embarrassed by the effort.

"Oh, I love it!" Willow picked it up delicately and then showed it to Bella. "Isn't it so cute!"

Bella nodded, thinking how different, how caring, Logan was with Willow compared to how he was with her. She couldn't work out if what she felt was regret or envy, not of their relationship, but of the ability to take for granted the feeling of being loved so unwaveringly.

Willow hugged Logan thanks then slipped the little box into the pocket of her dress and said, "Right, we need to get you a drink! Bella, do you want one?"

Bella didn't want to drink. She didn't want to be there,

she wanted to be as far from Logan as she could get. "Do you know, I was actually just leaving."

"What?" Willow looked confused. "You can't leave, you've only just got here."

"Yeah, I'm really tired," Bella said regretfully. "I was only popping in to say happy birthday, that was all."

"No." Willow looked crestfallen. "Stay. Logan, tell her to stay."

But even with Willow's pleading eyes on him, Logan seemed as reluctant as Bella for her to be there and, without meeting her eyes, said simply, "If she wants to go, let her go, Willow."

"No, no, no!" Willow insisted. "Bella, have another drink, stay, dance!"

Bella tried to keep things light, despite the brooding presence of Logan next to her. "That's my cue to leave," she joked. "I definitely don't dance!"

She saw Logan's brows draw together in a frown at her comment and he said, almost despite himself, "Why don't you dance?" Because in the past, Bella was always the first on the dancefloor, she'd loved to dance at parties.

Bella swallowed under the wary scrutiny of Logan's darkening blue gaze, felt her heart beat too fast and her palms start to sweat. She hadn't thought it through, it was an automatic answer she'd got used to saying because Jack didn't like her dancing, didn't like other people looking at her, touching her. And as a result, she had stopped altogether. It was another thing that she had made smaller about herself. Another thing that she had to keep in check, remember who she was now and what she liked doing.

An awkward silence had descended on them all while Bella struggled to reply. Without having to verbalize it, the shadow of Jack suddenly seemed thick in the air.

Her obvious discomfort made Logan's jaw clench and his eyes narrow before he looked away at the concrete floor. Willow shuffled back a step and said, "Of course, you should go if you're tired, Bella. Sorry to be pushy, I know I get overexcited!"

Kicking herself for having said anything about dancing, Bella said, "Not at all!" And, refusing to look in Logan's direction, she reached forward and gave Willow's arm a friendly squeeze. "I really appreciate you inviting me. I'll see you at the theater."

Willow nodded, eyes wide with a sympathetic sadness. "Bye, Bella."

"Bye," she replied, slipping away past Logan without a second glance.

Chapter Eighteen

Logan watched Bella walking down the street toward the theater—he'd recognize that walk anywhere, hair bunched on top of her head, glasses on, sweater falling off her shoulder as she struggled with a heap of costumes on hangers.

In the past year his finger had hovered over her phone number more times than he could count, but he'd never dialed. He felt like he'd let her down and he hated that.

When she saw him, she paused for a second in shock, then schooling her features, rolled her lips together and walked more calmly toward him.

He didn't blame her wariness, he'd behaved appallingly the evening before at Willow's party.

When she got close enough, she said, "I'm assuming this isn't a coincidence."

Her hair fell into her eyes as she spoke, and she had to blow it away because her hands were full.

Logan shrugged, hands in his pocket. "Would you believe me if I said it was?"

"In a city of one and a half million people, it would seem strange," she replied, face still coolly impassive. Then she carried on walking toward the back entrance of the theater, the costumes over her arm clearly weighing her down.

"Do you need a hand with that," he asked, falling into step beside her.

"No, thank you."

A van was double-parked on the sidewalk, which made them have to fall into single file. Bella squeezed through the space, the costumes grazing against the brick wall, Logan followed.

"What do you want, Logan?" she asked, without turning.

Logan raked a hand through his hair, knowing this was going to be difficult. "I thought we could go for coffee."

She paused when they got back out in the open, the fire-escape doors of the theater propped open with a chair beside them. She turned to look at him, exasperatedly resigned. "I'm really busy."

"*I'm* really sorry," he cut in, making her inhale sharply.

He let the words hang in the air for a moment, then added, "I behaved really badly last night. I was caught off-guard, I'm sorry."

He watched her sigh up at the gray, brutalist theater building, clearly trying to decide what to do next.

Logan had gone back to New York after his drink with Brodie, feeling exhausted but strangely purged. Admittedly, he was disgusted with himself for how he'd treated Bella, and uneasy about what he'd learned about his brothers, particularly Ethan. His whole body had throbbed from the boxing, he could barely walk and had trouble breathing and felt like he'd broken a rib, but he'd felt, for the first time in a long time, a little easier. Which was odd considering he had learned all sorts of horrors about the lurking ghost of Jack, about himself, about his other brothers. But as Brodie said, it was kind of a relief to have it out in the open.

As gradually the cuts on his face healed, he'd tried to get back to normal, getting through the days as he always had, settling into the routine of life, mourning his brother, trying to piece back together his memory of him—swum through the sadness and come up on the bank on the other side—he still found he couldn't get Bella out of his mind.

Couldn't rid himself of the image of her in the kitchen in the orchard telling him what had happened, her beautiful face, her eyes, the trails of moisture down her cheeks. The naked vulnerability as she stood in front of him telling her story. He had done that to her. Or watching her face soften with relief when his mom came to offer an apology. She haunted him, surfaced in his mind when he was doing something as simple as ordering his macchiato or running in Central Park. He found his eyes scouring the crowds for her. He hated to admit it, but this wasn't the first time he'd taken a circuitous route to his office to pass by the theater. The idea of bumping into her causing a tingling of excitement to shiver over his skin. Something that he didn't like to admit because it was both wrong and impossible.

He was torn between the secret pleasure that he didn't have to compete with his brother for Bella's affections and a shameful self-loathing for even considering such a thought. When he'd seen her at Willow's party, he'd been so rocked at the sight of her, at all those feelings closing in on him, afraid that she could see it all in his eyes when he looked at her, that he'd ended up being standoffishly aloof, something his sister had given him an earful about after Bella had left.

Now, standing at the entrance of the theater, he said, "Let me buy you a coffee?"

Bella shook her head, hesitating a second before replying. "I really don't think that's a good idea."

"Please."

The word seemed to make her pause. She looked down at the sidewalk, there was an overturned Coke crate by the propped-open doors with a mug on it that had obviously been used as a table for coffee breaks. She kept her eyes on the empty mug. "Why?"

"Because I owe you a proper apology."

She raised a brow and said flatly, "I don't really want an apology, I just want to get on with my life."

Logan paused for a moment, wasn't sure what more to say to convince her. He glanced down at the Coke crate, taking a breath before looking back up into her steely brown eyes and saying, "I keep thinking about you."

The air changed. He watched her brain whirring in the expression on her face, as she seemed to weigh up the options, whether this was a can of worms she wanted to open or keep firmly closed. He heard cars driving past behind them, the bustle of the theater through the open doors, pigeons fluttering on the fire-escape ladders, his senses suddenly alert to everything and anything until finally she said simply, "Okay."

Logan felt his heart clench.

Then she raised the armful of costumes she was holding and said, "Let me just dump this stuff."

Logan nodded and, slipping his hands back in his pockets, waited for her next to the propped-open doors, feeling unfamiliarly bashful and more than a little out of his depth.

They strolled in awkward silence down the sidewalk to a little kiosk in the park. There was an awkwardness between them, neither knowing where to look. To make conversation he said, "So you're not at *Vogue* anymore?"

"Fashion wasn't for me in the end. Can't you tell?" she added, joking as he always remembered her doing, to cover the unease, gesturing down at her tatty jeans and the loose scoop-neck sweater she wore that had pins stuck for safekeeping in the fabric by the neck.

He smiled along, but to him she looked the most relaxed he'd seen her in years. Made him war with himself for having turned up out of the blue, for forcing the wariness back into her gaze.

They sat at a table and chairs laid out by the kiosk, under the dappled shade of a plane tree.

Silence again.

The air between them seemed to crackle. He looked away for a moment, down at the coppery carpet of fallen leaves. Then he leaned forward, arms crossed on the table, and said, "Let me just say this—I'm sorry for the way I treated you, Bella. Not just last night but all of it. At the funeral, at your house, last year, last whenever. Forever." He sat up straighter, hands braced on his thighs, and looked away for a moment. When he turned back, he looked at her, almost willing her to hear the sincerity.

The sound of the coffee machine and the conversations of other people in the park around them softened into the background.

She looked down at the tabletop, cradling her cup in her hands, and then back up at him. Her eyes were the size of dinner plates. When he saw her hesitation, he wanted to say it again and again until she would hear it, be able to forgive him.

"Okay," she said, more formally than he could handle. "I appreciate that."

Birds pecked around them at crumbs on the ground, pigeons fighting off sparrows who fluttered down, jumping in the dust and leaves.

Logan sat back, running a hand through his hair feeling the least composed he'd ever been. "I find it really hard … I look back and don't like who I was. I can't believe I didn't call you when your dad died. And you and Jack, I admit, I was jealous, I was. I just couldn't admit it. You were my friend and I let you go." He ran his hand over his mouth trying to pin down what he wanted to say. When it came down to it, it was simply, "I was wrong, Bella, and I'm sorry for it all."

She traced her finger down the side of her cup then glanced up, brow raised as she said dryly, "It's quite a monumental moment—Logan Carter apologizing and admitting he's wrong in the same sentence."

He chanced a laugh. Her lips twitched and he felt himself relax, blew out a breath of relief. "I'm sorry I didn't see what was happening."

"It wasn't your fault."

"I knew Jack could be tricky. I chose not to see it, I suppose."

She looked down at the leaves and he saw her swallow, perhaps nervously, before she said, "I know I could have told you how bad everything had gotten for him, but I hated him, Logan..."

He flinched at the word *hate*.

She looked away at one of the little sparrows.

He didn't want her to look away. "It wasn't your responsibility. It was mine."

"No!" She seemed to surprise herself with her sharpness. "It was Jack's responsibility. You can't just absolve him." She shook her head, tucking the strands of hair that came loose behind her ear. "We all played a part and we all paid."

Logan didn't say anything, just watched her across the table in the cool sunlight. Thought about what she'd been through at his brother's hand and said plainly, "Yes, you're right. I'm sorry for my part in it." Then he sat back in his chair, and shaking his head said, "I wish you'd been able to come to me."

"Yeah," she said, almost resigned and he couldn't get over how it felt to have let her down, it made his heart actually hurt.

Neither of them said anything and he felt the silence stretch on between them, it felt like a spotlight on how distant they'd become. He knew, from his conversation with Brodie, that he had to dig a little deeper, had to say what he didn't want to say.

He focused on her fingers toying with her coffee cup and said, "I'm so angry with him." Her fingers stilled. "He was my brother, and I don't want to feel like that about him, but I'm furious with him, and I'm envious of him. And I love him. And I don't know how to align all those things." He glanced up, saw her watching him with wary sympathy.

She shook her head, her hair slipping in front of her eyes. "I don't know either, Logan." Then she stood up and chucked her cup in the recycling. "I should get back."

He didn't want her to go. He tried to summon the cool rationality that he would have used to deal with this a year ago. But he couldn't make it go away. All he wanted was to keep talking to her.

"Can I walk back with you?" he asked, standing up.

She paused for a second, seemed to consider it and then nodded. "Yeah."

It felt like the tiniest of wins.

But then as they started to walk back through the park she said, "Why *didn't* you call me when my dad died?" and he felt the shame of his own actions like a punch of regret once again.

"Because I'm an idiot," he replied flatly.

She looked up at him, brows raised in vague surprise at the answer.

He raked a hand through his hair, unused to hauling so much of his own wrongdoing out into the open for scrutiny. "I didn't even know for ages, for exactly the reason you said

—I was just too busy—and then I suppose I blocked it out." They reached a fountain, the water swishing with iridescent carp, Logan stopped walking to say, "Everything to do with home—with Autumn Falls—it was just easier to turn away from it." He put his hands in his pockets and shrugged. "I'm not trying to make excuses. It was selfish, there's no doubt about it. I kept thinking I'd call you, but time went by and then I think I felt too much time had passed. But also, I kept getting distracted." He sighed looking down at the water, the fish twisting like ribbons in the pond. "I seem to have gotten distracted from a lot of things."

She stood next to him, their reflections looking back up at them as she nodded, as though possibly appeased by the answer, or for finally getting one. She said, "What's weird is the people I ended up needing were John-Luke and my mom. The man who I'd blamed for moving to Autumn Falls and ruining my life! It turns out he was worth a hundred times what my dad was." She looked sidelong at Logan. "I wasted a lot of energy trying to impress Dad."

"Yeah, well," he said resigned, looking sidelong at her, "we all make mistakes."

There was a pause, the words hung between them. The white noise of the fountain in the background. When she turned her head to look at him and their eyes met, he felt his breath catch, because as he looked, her mouth tilted ever so slightly into a smile, and it felt like in that moment she might be forgiving him, and the feeling spread slowly through him. Filling chasms that he didn't realize had been cracking for so long.

They walked on in silence to the entrance of the park.

When they got to the crosswalk opposite the theater, Bella said, "I really have to go." But before she walked away, she paused and said, "It was nice to see you, Logan." Then added, wryly, "I'm glad you happened to walk past."

He tipped his head in acknowledgment. "So am I."

Then he watched her cross the street, push open the doors of the theater and disappear. When she was out of sight, he turned and walked away, looking up at the clouds and exhaling long and slow, like a huge weight had lifted from his shoulders. While also painfully aware that he had to see her again. Even if it meant the purgatory of being so close to something he could never have.

Chapter Nineteen

Logan sat at his desk unable to concentrate. Figures jumped across the screen, his cell phone vibrated with contacts that he wasn't interested in. He leaned back in his chair, leg bouncing impatiently and looked around the room. The tall, slatted blinds over the window carved up the view of Manhattan on his left. On his right were shelves of all his own trophies and certificates, platinum disks of top performers on his label hung on the walls, awards glittered in the dusty rays of sun. He had everything he could ever want and still not what he really wanted.

Marianne poked her head around the door, her gray hair swept neatly back. If she caught him daydreaming, she didn't let on. "Ah, sorry Logan, I was just checking you've remembered the board meeting."

He glanced across, stirred from his trace. "Yep, I'll be there."

She raised a brow, somewhat quizzically. "Feel free to answer the phone, by the way, any time you like."

He snorted a laugh. "Will do." But when the door closed, he found himself staring blankly at his desk again, willing the only person he wanted to hear from to call.

It was a couple of months since he'd had coffee with Bella in the park, the holiday season had come and gone, snow had dusted the skyline, but he couldn't stop thinking about her. Against his better judgment, his mind would drift back to the past. To the early days in Autumn Falls when it had just been the two of them.

He remembered the first time he'd invited her to one of his polo matches. They were only sixteen, but she seemed to know exactly what she wanted to do with her life, whereas he was stuck staring down the endless barrel of the ranch. She was the first person he'd met who just did exactly what she wanted. He remembered during the game, when he looked over in the half-time break to see if Bella was enjoying it, he saw her in the stands, glasses on, halfway through reading a book, and snorted a laugh.

"I came, didn't I?" she said when he galloped over to accuse her of not paying attention, "I didn't necessarily mean I was going watch it all." She pointed to her book. "I'm really enjoying myself."

"Good," he said, a little bemused by her lack of interest. "Glad I could be of service."

She'd shooed him back to the pitch.

As he'd taken up position again and seen her out the corner of his eye, still nose in her book, he'd realized that it was quite nice to have someone be there for him but not be there at the same time. Just someone to live side by side with.

It occurred to him that he'd never had that before or since. Someone either not wanting a piece of him or not simply doing something because he'd said to do it. He'd got too used to being at the top.

There was another knock on his office door. Marianne said, "Everyone's waiting in the boardroom."

"Okay, thanks." Logan was about to get up when his phone rang.

Bella.

His whole day immediately brightened. "Hey."

"Is this a bad time?" she asked.

Marianne tapped her watch at the door.

"Not at all," Logan said and gestured five minutes to Marianne.

"I'm calling because a UPS guy has just dropped off a huge box at my apartment and in it is all my stuff from Jack's house."

Logan swallowed, aware suddenly that she might be angry, that he should have warned her rather than assuming it would be a surprise. His heart paused for a second.

"I just wanted to say to thank you, Logan. I really appreciate you doing that for me."

He could breathe again. What was happening to him? Second-guessing his every move. He felt like a teenager. "You're welcome," he said.

"There were some very precious things in there that I'm really glad to have back. Things I never thought I'd see again. So, thanks."

Logan had flown to LA over the weekend to finally

supervise the packing up of Jack's house. He'd thought it might be cathartic, but it was mainly just painful. Sending Bella her things felt like at least something good could come of it.

But he also knew, the moment he'd received the notification, that the package had been delivered, that the gesture hadn't been completely altruistic. He'd wanted exactly this, to make her happy, to have the opportunity to talk to her again. "I'm glad it arrived safely."

"Yeah, it did," she replied.

There was a pause. Words seemed to be failing him. He'd been waiting for this call and now couldn't for the life of him think of anything to say. He just knew he didn't want her to hang up.

She said, "Well, thanks again. It was really thoughtful of you."

"It really was no problem," he replied.

He could see Marianne waiting impatiently in the corridor.

"Well," said Bella, "I'll let you go. I'm sure you have a meeting or something."

"Yeah."

"Okay, well thanks."

"That's okay."

"Bye, Logan."

"Bye."

Marianne made a gesture with her hands to hurry him up.

He was about to hang up when he swore he heard her say, "Logan?"

"Yes!" The phone went straight back to his ear. Marianne looked heavenward.

"I wondered if you wanted to have dinner or something, nothing special, you know, just as a thank you—"

"I'd love to," he cut her off, his words quicker than his conscience. Aware he was walking a fine line, one he knew he should turn back from, but the smile tugging at the corner of his mouth making it impossible.

Chapter Twenty

Bella stood in her bedroom staring down at the selection of clothes lying sprawled on the bed.

Since leaving everything behind when she'd fled Jack's, she hadn't lived with many possessions. Living from a suitcase had become her safety net. So now, after suddenly having all her stuff back, even with some of it in bags packed and ready for Goodwill, she felt overwhelmed by choice.

She FaceTimed Claudette. "I don't know what to wear."

"Don't be ridiculous."

Bella could see herself in the camera, her hair had gone fluffy and she'd put on too much make-up to cover her flushed cheeks, so she'd washed it off and now her skin looked blotched. "I can't believe it, look at me. My face is all red. I can't make a decision about what to wear. I can't think straight. It's like I'm sixteen again!" Her heart was beating too fast at the thought of seeing Logan again.

When she'd suggested dinner, it had been spur of the

moment, overwhelmed by gratitude for him having thought of her and saving her belongings. Small items like the necklace her dad had given her on her thirteenth birthday, a wool sweater knitted by her grandma, the handbag she'd bought with her first *Vogue* paycheck. Things she didn't need but that had unquantifiable sentimental value and that she had resigned herself to never seeing again.

But now they were having dinner together.

"Just breathe, Bella," Claudette ordered in her usual no-nonsense fashion. "And just wear what you feel comfortable in. Call me back when you've decided." She hung up.

Bella sat on the edge of the bed, her hands either side of her, palms flat on the quilt and took a couple of calming breaths. There was a flutter in her stomach every time she thought about seeing Logan again, but it was difficult to tell if it was good or bad. She didn't know if she wanted to step down that path again. The minutes clicked past. Panic short-circuited her brain. She kept seeing all her lovely, cherished memories of the past; when they'd first become friends and they'd drive out to nowhere in Autumn Falls, the road stretching out like they could keep going to the edge of the world together, or just lying on their backs in the orchard, hidden from everyone lying under the trees and eating sweet ripe apples with the sun shimmering on their skin. Or her sitting on the fence by the horse barn on the ranch as Logan broke in the new horses, or freefalling together from the lip of the waterfall, crashing into the ice-cold water below. She saw just wide smiles on their faces, the warmth of his body as they lay side by side, the trust and the friendship and the shared hopes and dreams.

They were a clutch of precious memories kept safe in her mind, wrapped up like treasure.

Turning to look over her shoulder at all the clothes spread out on the bed, she felt like she was deliberately sabotaging what was to come, because deep down she feared inviting Logan back into her life. Because there hadn't been much happiness in it since those recollected moments, and she didn't want being with Logan now to change who she remembered him being then. Who she remembered herself being.

She wanted to keep her precious memories safe.

"It's just dinner," she reminded herself. And returning to the pile of clothes, picked out a pale gray cashmere sweater with a low V-neck that Claudette had given her for Christmas, and a pleated satin skirt in emerald green. Then she pulled on her dark leather boots with a little block heel, favorites that Logan had rescued from the LA house. Looking in the mirror, she felt nicely herself, not too dressy, not too shabby. She sent Claudette a selfie and the reply came back, *"Perfect."*

But while she at least looked good on the outside, inside Bella's heart thrummed like hummingbird wings.

Her intercom buzzed.

Uncertain who would be at her door at this time, she went to answer it. "Hello?"

"Car for Bella Jameson."

She paused with her finger on the button. "I didn't order a car."

"Logan Carter sent me. I'm here to take you to dinner."

She peered out the window and saw a black Cadillac waiting at the curb. A small smile played on her lips.

When she got downstairs, she said to the driver, "I can't believe Logan sent a car. I could have gotten the subway."

"Logan didn't want you getting caught in the rain," he told her.

She laughed, a little bewildered. "It's not raining." Then, as she said it she saw that the sky had darkened and it was just starting to drizzle. "Trust Logan to know it was going to rain," she said. "Let me get my umbrella."

Before she could head back, the driver held up an enormous black umbrella and flicked it open. "Will this do?"

"Right, yes, of course." She hesitated between the doorway and the vast umbrella. Then pulled the door closed, locked it and let herself be escorted to a cavernous sedan that filled the sidewalk. "I can't believe he sent you."

"Can't you?" the guy chuckled.

Bella shook her head as if it were all unnecessary.

He opened the car door for her. "Sit back. Enjoy yourself."

As they purred their way through the traffic, Bella gave into the luxury, snuggling back into the seat and chatting with the driver. Out the window, she saw people rushing along the sidewalks to get out of the rain, sheltering under awnings, the sky a dark blanket of cloud.

"Indigo House," the driver said ten minutes later, as they pulled up outside the plain double doors of the private members club.

Bella bent her head and peered out through the rivulets of rain on the window. And there he was. Collar up on his dark gray jacket, eyes hooded by shadow, hands thrust deep into his pockets as he leaned with his back against the wall under the awning, waiting. She couldn't help the shudder of trepidation that went through her. She knew it would probably be a safer idea to stay in the car.

Then the door was opened for her and of course she stepped out, an umbrella held above her head. Logan pushed off the wall and started strolling toward her. She purposely avoided his eyes, turning instead to thank the driver. "You saved me from the rain."

He laughed. "It was my pleasure. Have fun."

"I'll try." She smiled.

Then she turned to Logan and she felt her heart skip a traitorous beat. She looked up at him, wondering at how he still managed to make her breath catch after all this time. "You shouldn't have sent a car."

His mouth tilted up in a half-smile. "You look beautiful."

She batted the compliment away. "Be quiet." But a blush crept up her cheeks. She tried to think of something to say but nothing clever came to mind. Then the moment passed, and it was too late to say anything. Even thank you.

She saw him schooling his features, but the smile still flickered in his eyes. Drizzle tapped on the awning above them. She felt like he could read all her nervous thoughts as if they were drawn like pictures on her body.

He gestured ahead at the entrance to the club. "Shall we go inside?"

She nodded. "Yes." Glad to be able to walk side by side, not have to look at him as she tried to make her heart slow down.

Inside was a blast from the past. The place was a low-level hum of busy, nothing too ostentatious but dimly lit, faded glory. The furnishings were dark velvet, candles on every table. Above them, old crystal chandeliers glistened and the open windows let in the cool smell of winter rain. It had always been one of Logan's favorite places and in the very early days of arriving in the city they would meet there for dinner.

They went to the bar, ordered their drinks, made small talk about the weather and how arctic it was, like everything was completely normal, like there wasn't a slight tremble in her fingers just from being there with him.

She had tried to keep her distance. She had tried to block out any thoughts of him but her mind kept circling back to him standing in the shadows of the orchard as she spoke with his mother, his face battered and bruised, the shame and regret in his eyes, the sympathy. And then in the park the other day when he had finally talked to her with unaccustomed honesty. She knew Logan—all the Carter boys—they tended to do rather than say.

While she was a bundle of nerves, Logan on the other hand seemed unfazed. He directed her to a table alone in the far corner. When the tiny touch of his hand to her back ricocheted through her, it confirmed how on edge she was. Age-blackened mirrors surrounded them, and she saw the slightly wild nervousness in her eyes. She was conscious of other diners glancing their way. It wasn't the kind of place where people asked for autographs but she couldn't help but notice the covert looks and subtle nods and felt herself shrink from the attention.

The waiter came over with a carafe of water, then placed down a bottle of red wine and two glasses, complimenting the vintage as he poured, then slipped away, all very discreet. Bella couldn't think of what to say. Everything seemed either too trite or too serious.

She couldn't look at Logan too long, found herself too self-aware in his company, so she looked about her, at the people on other tables who'd gone back to their own conversations, at the waiters weaving their way around the room.

"Are you okay?" Logan asked.

"Fine," she replied too quickly.

His eyes narrowed a little to suggest he wasn't convinced but he didn't push it.

She watched his hand as it swirled the drink in his glass.

"So," he said with a slight tip of his head.

"So," she replied, mirroring his pose.

"You got all your things from the house."

She nodded. "Yeah. I hadn't realized how much I wanted some of it back. Like I said, I really appreciate you thinking of me."

He thought for a second, eyes looking everywhere but at her, then said, "I'll be honest, I think it was as much for me as it was for you."

She frowned. "Why?"

"This," he replied, holding his hand out to gesture to the fact she was sitting there opposite him.

She went to say something, but surprise made her unable to.

Their eyes locked in the candlelight.

His mouth tilted up at one corner, eyes sparkling with a mischievous glint.

Which, against her better judgment, made a smile twitch on her lips, too, and suddenly the atmosphere between them changed.

She looked away with a disbelieving shake of her head and he laughed. She took a sip of her drink, felt herself relax. He did the same.

She crossed her legs, leaned forward, elbows on the table, the shoulder of her sweater slipped and she left it, noticing Logan's eyes flick dangerously to her bare skin. "This place hasn't changed," she said.

He gave the surroundings a cursory look then shook his head. "Do you remember we'd come here whenever we were in town?"

"Yeah," she laughed. "It was a nightmare, you having to sneak out of your hotel, loads of security guards escorting you, me having to wait by my phone for exact timings! Like some sort of military operation, just so we could have dinner."

His eyes creased at the memory, making him look instantly like his old self, younger than when she'd seen him in the park. "It was a crazy time."

"Sure was." She shook her head thinking about it. The times they'd dashed out the back doors, sped through town away from chasing paparazzi, swapping cars down side streets to get away, fans swarming around Logan if they caught even a glimpse, clawing at his clothes, arms thrown tight around his neck as they snapped photos on their phones, hammering on the tinted car windows. "It's almost surreal to think back on it."

He leaned back in his seat, fingers still resting on the stem of the glass. "Sometimes when I think about it, it's like it wasn't happening to me but that I'm watching someone else's life. It was all so fast, it's a blur in my memory." He swallowed, then looked up at her, blue eyes suddenly serious, "Moments like coming here with you, they're the bits that are clear. The rest is a haze."

As she looked at him, it felt like the restaurant around them retreated. She wanted to tell him that she felt the same. About the precious pockets of memories with him that she kept so well protected because they were the solid, reliably true moments of her past. Instead, she cocked her head and said conversationally, "When you look back, are you glad you did it?"

"I don't know." He rubbed his hand behind his neck for a second as he thought. She watched the movement, the tensing of his forearms, his shirt rolled up just below the elbow, the expensive watch on his wrist. "I mean it got me away from the ranch—it got me freedom. I'd be with living with Noah in his trailer if not."

She snorted into her drink. "No, you wouldn't."

He smiled, probably enjoying having seen her splutter. "Some of it was good," he said. "I'm making it all sound bad, I know, and I do have some great memories but those are mainly just from being with my brothers—not the band. I feel like I haven't stopped."

"Probably because you haven't!" she suggested, twirling the stem of her glass.

He sat up straighter, his eyes darkening as he said, "I regret how it ended. It felt like we went in brothers and came out strangers. Crawled out," he added. "Yeah, we made a lot of money, but I honestly feel like we lost pieces of ourselves along the way that we never got back."

She nodded. "I know." Her time with Jack felt painfully similar.

"People warn you that it's going to happen but—" he did a resigned shake of his head "—you don't believe it until it does."

"No," she replied, every word resonating. "We all fell for it."

His mouth tipped up in a sad smile of acknowledgment. "A while ago, I talked to Brodie about it all. It was hard hearing it from someone else—about how it affected the others." His eyes narrowed. "Made me realize I've got to try harder to find Ethan."

"When was the last time you heard from him?"

Logan thought for a second, trying to remember. "Two years ago? Maybe even three? And then it was just a call to Mom. I haven't seen him since he got through his selection for the SEALS."

"And presumably you take responsibility for his disappearance," she said wryly.

His glass stilled at his lips. "How well you know me."

She laughed.

The waiter came over and Logan apologized because

they hadn't looked at the menu. Then he said to Bella, "Although it's the same as it always was."

"Oh, well, I'll have the Ceasar Salad. And fries on the side." They had always made the best Ceasar Salad. It had been her favorite dinner in the city.

Logan had the steak. He only ordered it when he knew it was going to be good and he knew it was because it came from the Silver Sky ranch, he'd made sure of that years ago.

When the waiter left, Logan said, "So you like the theater where you're working now?"

She flicked her hair out her eyes. "Yeah, I like it. I don't love it."

He frowned. "No?"

"I like the people," she said. "But I think probably my time in New York is coming to an end." It was an opinion she hadn't voiced out loud to anyone and it surprised her that she was telling Logan.

His dark brows drew together. It clearly wasn't news he wanted to hear. "Why?"

"It's too much. It's too busy. I feel like I've lived a thousand lives, Logan. I need a break." She laughed but it came out more desperate than she'd expected. When she looked at him, she felt his watchful concern and realized how much she'd missed that about him.

"What will you do?"

"I don't know. I've enjoyed being back in Autumn Falls, which I never thought I'd say." She'd gone back for a couple of days at Christmas and been surprised by how much she loved it there in the winter, when the snow settled on the branches of the apple trees and the river crackled with ice. She'd gone for long walks in the orchard and sat around the table with her mom and John-Luke playing Scrabble, drinking tea and curling up under the crocheted quilt in front of the fire. But it wasn't just the coziness of the season, it was because, for the first time in years, when she returned now, she didn't fear bumping into anyone who she might have to avoid. When people saw her being enveloped into a hug by Martha Carter after church on Sundays, that was enough for them. "You won't believe it but I'm going back next weekend to help John-Luke with the pruning."

Logan choked on his wine. "Now that is something I never thought I'd hear you say."

"I know, right?" she laughed. "All that time I was desperate to leave, now I'm old and world-weary I want to go back."

Logan hooked her with his gaze, dark lashes lowered. "You're not old and world-weary."

"Yeah, okay, that is probably a bit of an exaggeration."

He said, "Honestly, you don't look any different to when you were sixteen."

"Now you're lying," she laughed.

He shook his head, completely serious as he locked her with a look that she felt shiver over her skin. "I'm not."

She felt herself blush, had to look away at the bustling restaurant and the low flickering light. When she looked back at him, Logan had a cocky grin almost imperceptible on his lips, like he knew he'd unsettled her.

She tried to play it cool. Glossed over it by saying, "Maybe I'll go traveling, something like that. Be a tourist.

Explore." She picked up her glass and took a sip. "I'd like to go where no one knows who I am."

He raised a brow, like wouldn't that be the dream?

She smiled. It was nice to be with someone who understood who she was, who had lived how she had lived.

"How about you?" she said, "What are you doing now?"

"Same as always, working harder, getting better." He shrugged a shoulder. "Making people's dreams come true," he added with a slow smile.

This time it was her turn to raise a brow. They both knew that the music industry definitely didn't make every person it swallowed up's dreams come true.

He held his hands wide. "I don't know why you're looking at me like that."

She just shrugged but her mouth twitched in a smile. "I didn't look at you like anything."

"Yes, you did," he said, half laughing, half confused. "What?"

"Nothing."

"There was definitely something." He wasn't going to let it go.

She leaned back against her velvet seat. "I guess I find it interesting that you spend your life signing people up for something that you've just said you didn't know you liked while you were doing it."

He looked affronted. "I said I liked some of it. And I make certain that all my artists are looked after way better than we were ever looked after. That was the problem, there was no one looking out for us."

She sipped her drink, narrowing her eyes. "You liked

being around your brothers. You liked being able to step in and manage it when things were going wrong. I think setting up the record label was exciting to you, but I know you, Logan, I don't think you *care* about the industry." She bit her lip, took in the slight defensiveness of his posture and considered stopping, self-preservation kicking in, but reminded herself it was Logan she was talking to. And she was done not saying what she should say to Logan. "I don't think it's your passion."

He scoffed, "Of course it is. Of course I care. Why would I do it otherwise?"

She shrugged again, tried to keep it light but knew it was something she'd wanted to say to him for years. "The fear of getting off the wheel, maybe."

Logan shook his head, then laughed, incredulous. "You don't know what you're talking about."

She smiled. "No, maybe not."

He took a gulp of his drink. Still smiling as he rolled his eyes at her crazy opinions.

A warmth spread through her chest, just at being there with him, being able to say stuff to him, tell him things. It was like being back in the apple orchard, lying on the ground with their heads together gazing up at the sky.

Chapter Twenty-One

Logan couldn't take his eyes off her. All through the food, all through the coffee. When her hair fell from behind her ear he wanted to reach over and catch a strand of it between his fingertips. When she laughed, when *he* made her laugh, his chest actually tightened.

He had been wrong about many things, but never more so than when he had told himself that he could sit opposite her over dinner and it would be enough.

When the waiter came over to clear their coffee cups, he said, "Can I get you another drink?"

Logan wanted to say yes just to keep her there, sitting in front of him. But Bella shook her head, "I think I've had enough, thank you, though."

The waiter nodded and disappeared.

Bella bit her lip, half smiling, half wide-eyed apprehensive.

There was a band playing in another room of the club,

the music drifted around them and seemed to grow louder as they didn't speak.

Logan wanted to say a hundred different things. He wanted to tell her how much he'd missed her. How there was no one else he could talk to the way he talked to her, how he could look at her forever. He wanted to say, come back to mine and never leave. He wanted to lean forward and say that losing her from his life was the biggest mistake he'd ever made. But he didn't, he picked up his napkin from his lap and laid it on the table beside his water glass and said, "Well, thank you for a lovely evening."

Unexpectedly her mouth stretched wide into a smile. "No, Logan, thank *you*."

It was all perfectly polite, but the look in her eyes suddenly took him back years to the moment at The Music Box where she'd looked at him with those mocking, narrowed eyes and seen straight through to his boyish, infatuated soul, or when she'd climbed onto the back of his bike in a pencil skirt and sky-high heels, to the snatched moments of just them when she smelled of vanilla and apple blossom and her laugh made everything else disappear. And he suddenly dared wonder if in that look was possibility. Maybe he was imagining it, but maybe she was thinking what he was thinking. Maybe it was a date. Maybe it was there on the table, exciting and thrilling, like a note passed in school. Maybe, his hand edged forward, it just took one of them to take the risk.

Chapter Twenty-Two

She was so caught by the look in his eye that when the camera flashed she didn't notice at first.

"Smile Bella, darling!" The voice echoed around the table. She couldn't breathe as the words hit her.

"What the—!" Logan's glass smashed down onto the floor as he swung around. Bella pushed herself as far as possible into the corner of the little table booth. Her hand reached up to cover her face. The lights kept flashing. Over and over.

She heard Logan shout. His chair crashed to the floor as he lunged for the photographer. People on other tables gasped. And still the flashes went. The man thrust the camera in Logan's face, clicking on repeat, the light blinding him so that he had to steady himself on the table.

"Got a quote for us, Mrs. Carter?" The man shouted. "Wouldn't even have to change your name!"

Bile rose in Bella's throat. The comments rang in her

ears. A ream of flashes blanked out her sight. Suddenly waiters were there, someone called for the bouncers.

Her lungs tightened. She couldn't catch her breath. Stars glinted in the corner of her vision as she panicked, hand clutched to her chest.

There was suddenly a crowd, people getting in the way, pulling at the photographer, pushing at her as she tried to stand up, as his camera snapped erratically.

Then Logan had his arm around her, keeping her head down with his hand, urging her through the crowd. And still the camera clicked.

"Get out my way!" he snarled at the photographer who took no notice, shaking off the grip of the waiters trying to eject him from the room. Bella could feel the tension in Logan's arm around her, the muscles clenched, the urgency as he marched them past concerned diners. The rogue photographer's camera still firing, shattering the privacy of the little bar that had been their safe place.

As they neared the exit, suddenly the bouncers appeared, charging toward the pap. But clearly going for one last attempt, the photographer lurched forward, and Bella felt his hand on her shoulder, the force of strength as he pulled against Logan's hold wrenching her back, her heels slid on the shiny wood and she stumbled, slipping through Logan's hold and tumbling to the floor, the back of her head thwacking on the corner of a table as she fell.

There was a blazing crack of pain through her skull. A hazy daze clouded her eyes as she saw Logan reach forward, almost slow-motioned and soundless, dark rage in his eyes, taking the man by the throat, pushing him back against the wall. He ripped the camera off him with his free hand and hurled it to the floor. Jaw tight, the muscles bunched across his back. But the photographer kept goading. She saw his mouth moving, his hands flailing as he punched uselessly at Logan. She tried to get up, but her feet kept slipping, she couldn't get her balance, her head throbbed.

And then suddenly Logan's eyes met hers. As if coming to his senses, he'd turned and seen her hurt.

"Come on, Logan, hit me." The photographer goaded.

But Logan had already let him go and was striding back, blazing blue eyes fixed on Bella's. Silence suspended thick in the air. The noise from the bar receded. She saw his hand reach down to grab hers, hauling her effortlessly to her feet and catching her with his arm tight around her waist.

The manager was there, apologizing profusely, couldn't understand how the man had gotten past security.

Logan's hand reached up and touched Bella's face, his thumb brushing away the trickle of blood down her neck, his eyes looked so pained, so sorry that he had left her even for that moment.

Around them was the clatter of glasses, the photographer being dragged away, hurling baiting insults behind him.

Bella put her hand gently on Logan's forearm, her eyes not leaving his. "I'm fine," she whispered.

A waitress appeared holding a clean, cotton napkin, folding it and telling Bella to press it against the cut. There were suddenly lots of people, everywhere. A waiter brought ice. Someone else knew first aid. Bella didn't really hear the words, just stayed looking at Logan. If she focused on him all the rest would go away.

"Can we get you anything, Mrs. Carter?" asked someone else in management.

"It's Jameson," was all she found herself saying. "Ms. Jameson."

"My apologies, of course." They wanted her to sit down, to call an ambulance.

"What do you want to do, Bella?" Logan's voice cut through the fussing. His arm holding her close.

Her breath caught at the concern in his eyes for her. Her whole body started to shake from the adrenaline. "I want to get out of here."

"Let's go." He steered her away, the crowd of concerned staff unzipping to let them pass, his fingers tightening protectively on her waist. "Are you sure you don't need to go the hospital?"

She gave him a look like now he was being overprotective. "No, I don't need to go to the hospital, I need to get *away* from people, Logan."

His mouth tipped up. "Understood."

Then she added, "If that photographer knew we were here, then others will, too. There'll be more outside." But she realized she needn't have said it because Logan was already on the phone to his driver and leading them away to the side where the manager was holding open the door to the kitchens and pointing toward the back entrance. It was like old times.

By the time they got outside, the car was pulled up as

close to the doors as it could get, an umbrella shielding anyone getting in from sight.

"I didn't see any more of them out the front, Logan," the driver said when he got in the car.

Logan nodded, he was already scrolling for another number on his phone. "Okay, well I'll get in touch with Greg, see what he can do."

Bella sat back against the leather seat bereft from the sudden lack of his hold. She knew Greg was Logan's communications director from briefings around the funeral arrangements. It was all immediately too real, too businesslike. "Why are you getting in touch with anyone?" she asked, her head throbbing, she touched it tentatively and found the bleeding had stopped. "They'll print what they like, they always do."

Logan had his eyes on the phone. "Well, we can try to mitigate—"

"Mitigate what?" she said, exasperation in her voice. He was gone, locked in his phone. "They have the photograph!"

He threw her a sidelong glance. "You're my dead brother's wife, Bella."

"*Ex*-wife, Logan." The curt authority in her voice was enough to make his fingers momentarily pause on the screen. She wanted to shake him, to make him stay in the present. She could feel the familiarity of him slipping away into managing, firefighting, controlling, ignoring, like muscle memory. It was so familiar that she could kick herself for forgetting. She could taste the memory of regret. The physical ache of it.

Logan lifted the phone to his ear. "I don't want you to have to go through this scandal."

Bella felt tiredness creep over her, she wanted to go home, to get away from this. "I'm used to scandal," she said, turning away from him and staring out the tinted window, at life streaming past in the evening light. "If you call anyone, you're doing it for yourself, not me."

She heard the moment Greg picked up in the background.

But then she also heard the hesitation after the guy said, "Logan? Everything all right?"

She glanced back, saw the muscle taut in Logan's cheek. Saw him look down as he said, "Yeah, sorry, all fine. I'll talk to you tomorrow."

When he looked up, their eyes locked in the rear-view mirror.

Logan slipped his phone into his pocket.

Chapter Twenty-Three

They drove on through towering buildings glinting in the streetlight, neon signs for shows reflected in sidewalk puddles, snaking lines outside clubs.

"Do you want to stay at mine?" Logan asked.

Said into the silence it sounded like a cheesy chat-up line. Bella laughed.

Logan rolled his eyes. "I didn't mean it like that. Just so that you're safe tonight, I don't really want you to go back to your apartment on your own."

"I'll be fine," she said.

He shook his head. "I don't want us to drop you off there and you suddenly get hounded. You don't need any more trouble tonight. At mine, we can drive in underground, no one will know you're there."

She shook her head to say no, but felt the dull throb of a headache when she did and couldn't help reaching to touch the cut on the back of her head.

That was enough for Logan. "Okay, seriously, you're not

going home on your own. You've had a bump to the head and people hounding you. Just let me keep an eye on you tonight. And then—" he held his hands wide to say that would be it.

She glanced out the window, saw people piling out of restaurants, chatting arm in arm, living happily, anonymously, in the busy streets. She thought about her flat, cold and alone. The panic of the photographer's lens in her face. "Okay," she said. "It's probably a good idea." She looked back to where he was watching her, face serious, and wondered if he, too, was thinking of how moments before, they had been the ones laughing and chatting, dreaming stupid dreams, before real life intervened. "Thanks."

The driver dropped them in the basement garage. They could take the elevator up to Logan's apartment. Not see a soul.

Logan put his arm around her as she stepped out the car and kept it there as they walked through the cool concrete belly of the building. She told him she was fine as they stepped inside the polished gold elevator, but she didn't want him to take his arm away, felt cocooned in the warm strength of it.

It was all very gentle and protecting. Until suddenly, it wasn't.

Until suddenly, they were side by side, their reflections staring back at them in the gold doors; her, pale-faced, pressed tight against him, his eyes still holding the dark remnants of fury. She could smell his skin, feel his heartbeat, the pressure of his palm against her upper arm. The numbers counted slowly up to Logan's apartment.

Where he lived. Where he ate. Where he slept. The tension rising with the numbers as the elevator rose.

Bella looked into her own wide eyes in the gold mirrors, saw her own desire clash with apprehension. For a moment, Logan bent his head, looking down at nothing, but then when the elevator pinged at their destination, he looked up, and their eyes met in the reflection, dark, doleful, wanting, and she felt her heart shudder. The heat, the longing. A single look shooting through her like an electric current. Then the doors slid open.

Logan dropped his arm to gesture for her to step out first and she felt the sudden loss of his hold. A coolness where his hand had been as she stepped out into a private hallway, waited as he unlocked the door, flicked on the lights.

It was a vast, loft apartment, concrete-poured floors, walls covered in art and photographs, shelves stacked with books, enormous sofas that took in the spectacular view. She gazed around open-mouthed. "Logan, this place is amazing." She glanced back and saw him watching, waiting boyishly for her reaction.

"Thanks," he said then, playing it cool.

She walked around taking in the mix of modern and vintage furniture, the elegant sculptures and music awards that shared space with sprawling plants, their leaves obscuring probably priceless works of art. But it was the view that she could stare out at for hours. One wall of towering windows high above the city, where they were level with the birds. "It's so…" She didn't know what to say as she gazed out at a horizon that it was impossible to see on the street.

"Freeing?" he offered, coming to stand beside her.

She nodded, entranced. "There's so much sky."

He nodded, "Yeah."

She could feel him next to her. Almost sense the heat of him. The familiar smell of him in the apartment. She suddenly didn't dare look away from the view.

He said, "Do you want anything? A drink?"

She shook her head.

In asking, he'd moved closer as he gestured to the drinks cabinet but then stopped. She made the mistake of glancing from the skyline to him. Her eyes saw now the buttons on his shirt. The cuffs of his sleeves rolled up. The light tan on the hollow of his neck. *Don't look up*, her senses warned.

But she didn't have to look up because he looked down. She saw him swallow from the closeness of them. He took a breath. He let the hand that had pointed to ask if she wanted a drink reach fractionally forward as if it were going to touch her hair but then didn't. She followed his hand, watched as he pulled back, slipped it in his pocket. She wondered if he could hear her heart as loudly as she could. Her eyes flicked from his wrist up to his face, to the roughness of his jaw. The dip of his lips, the shadows under his eyes. *Don't look in his eyes.* The simmering longing in his hooded gaze.

She knew he was waiting. Would do nothing unless she did it first. She felt her hand raise and her fingers reach to gently brush against his face. Run her thumb along the sharpness of his cheekbone. She felt him tense slightly as she traced the line of his jaw, the rigid set of his face hinting at a barely restrained control, then she let her palm rest softly against his cheek. She felt like she could hear his thoughts through her fingertips. They stood, gaze fused, connected only through her hand against the sharpness of his jaw, the silence like a thousand words between them. She heard her own breath. Felt the urge in her to pull away yet step closer.

But then, before she could move, he reached across and ran his fingers from her shoulders down the soft fabric of her sweater to her wrists, interlacing her fingers with his and resting his other hand lightly on her waist. The touch burning through the fabric of her top.

She felt the warmth of him as he took a step closer. Felt the whisper-light touch of his shirt, saw the familiar outlines of his face, and his eyes that she knew so well. She never thought she'd stand this close to him. She thought the possibility had gone forever. She saw the darkening in his eyes as she lifted her chin. His hand threaded around the back of her waist, drawing her toward him. Her skin prickled at the closeness. She wrapped her fingers around the muscles of his upper arm. He let go of her other hand and reached up to gently cradle the back of her neck, his fingers toying softly with her hair.

Around them, the night seemed to get darker. As her eyes drifted closed, the image of the photographer flashed into her head. *You wouldn't even have to change your name.* Her lungs had constricted in panic. The grim look on Logan's face as he held the man by the throat. The determined line of his lips. The photographer's goading, antagonizing grin.

And she suddenly stepped back, eyes wide.

Logan immediately dropped his hold.

"I can't do this again," she said. Everywhere he'd touched on her body felt cold from an absence of him.

She saw his lips move as if to speak, but he said nothing, just nodded.

"It's madness," she said.

"Yes."

She couldn't look at him directly. Looked instead at the view, at the amazing apartment, at the rug on the floor. "Maybe we *should* have a drink."

"Absolutely." Logan moved on autopilot, seemed, like her, to be catching up with himself, with the sudden about-turn of events. He gestured for her to take a seat on the couch. "Make yourself comfortable."

"Thanks."

The polite distance was back. She perched self-consciously, knees pressed together, hands clasped on her thighs, her heart regretting what she'd done but knowing she had to do it.

She braced herself for stiff formality and awkward small talk when Logan came back with a bottle of wine and glasses, but when their eyes caught he grinned, crooked and conspiratorial, and she realized it wasn't the same as before. They were different, closer. The surface had been smashed.

They sat up for ages, Bella with her shoes off, feet tucked up underneath her on the giant couch, Logan relaxed back opposite, chatting about old times, funny memories, moments she'd forgotten but he'd remembered, which made her flutter inside that he had pockets inside his brain reserved for them, too. At one point he leaned forward, forearms braced on his thighs and said, "I can't believe we missed your *Vogue* shoot."

He looked up at her through raven's-wing lashes. "I was an arrogant idiot."

She laughed out loud. "Yes, you were."

He shook his head, biting down on his lip. "What happened when we didn't show?"

She shrugged and her sweater slipped off her shoulder again. When she slid it back, she felt his eyes trace the movement on her bare skin. "I was the laughing stock of the office," she said, trying her best to ignore the undeniable tension back between them.

He hung his head. "I'm ashamed."

"So you should be." She reached forward and bashed him on the wrist. He caught her hand in his. She watched him, heart thumping as he turned her palm over, let his thumb stroke gently over her skin.

She gently tugged her hand back, tucked it underneath her against the cushions. "Don't worry, I got over it, found someone to fill the slot." She paused. "Can't actually remember who. You know when you were saying earlier about Silver Sky being a blur, a lot of that time at *Vogue* was a blur, I was working so hard! I thought that job was the most important thing in the world. I had no life at all outside of it." She shook her head at the memory. "In retrospect, if feels like a bit of a waste, I was young and single in New York!" She laughed. "I definitely spent too much time trying to prove that I was good enough—that I didn't need anyone—and that can be quite a lonely way to live."

He watched her unreadably as she spoke, she couldn't tell if he was pitying her or empathizing.

"I mean, come on, who was I kidding, the whole fashion world ... it wasn't for me."

"No? I thought you were great."

"I think you were biased," she laughed. "No, I think I'm happier working at the theater, I feel like I understand it better, it's a bit more down-to-earth."

Logan frowned. "I don't know, I've seen a couple of Willow's shows, and they can be pretty avant-garde—I wouldn't call it down-to-earth."

She snorted a laugh. "True. But I'm backstage. I can hide out there."

"Unless you happen to bump into me," he said, holding his hands wide as if their meet-up really had been a coincidence.

She sat forward, elbows on her knees, wrists crossed, and replied wryly, "Unless I happen to bump into you."

She held his gaze for a moment, saw the soft amusement dancing in his eyes, and the hint of something else, a glint of a challenge maybe. She wondered if hers said the same.

"Anyway," she glossed over it. "Weird ballet aside, backstage it's small and intimate and it suits me." Then she paused and said, "Stop smiling at me."

He held his arms wide. "How can smiling at you be bad?"

"It's distracting," she said.

"Sorry."

"Be serious."

"Okay." He schooled his features, but couldn't hide the hint of what she knew was smug amusement that she had let slip a desire to simply see him again when she'd invited him to dinner. "So, you're happy?" he asked.

"Yeah, I'm happy."

"Good."

She widened her eyes to make him stop with the subtext of the look he was giving her, then said, "Are *you* happy?"

The question seemed to cause him to pause, to make the sly, cocky smile slip slightly. For a moment, it seemed like a shadow skated over his features and the ease left his face. Then he shrugged and said, "Sometimes."

She narrowed her eyes, trying to read him, but too quickly the smile came back, the confident certainty. Then he stood up and said, "It's pretty late, we should probably go to bed."

Chapter Twenty-Four

Later, Bella lay in the darkness of the guest bedroom, the sheets cool and crisp, the pillows exquisitely comfortable. She had everything she needed but was completely unable to sleep. Logan had loaned her a T-shirt to sleep in and it smelled of him, of his washing powder. It conjured too many thoughts and pictures in her head. Too many times her heart rate rose as she thought about standing with him by the window, his lips a fraction from hers, wondering what might have been. She rolled over, flumped the pillow in frustration. *Go to sleep.*

But then she heard a really faint tap on her bedroom door. She sat up, ran her hand through her hair. "Yeah?"

The door eased open, Logan stood on the threshold, the moonlit hallway silhouetting him as he said, "What is it you think I'm afraid of?"

Bella frowned, drawing her legs up under the sheet and resting her arms on her knees. "What do you mean?"

He took a couple of steps forward. He wore gray marl

tracksuit bottoms and a T-shirt with Charlie's Gym written on it.

"You said earlier that I stayed in music for fear of getting off the wheel. But I don't know what it is you think I'm afraid of?" He didn't say it accusingly, he said it like he was interested. Like he'd never paused to consider but had been lying in the dark, too, and found when he repeated the question he wasn't sure of the answer.

A shaft of light came in through the open door, illuminating half his face and the whiteness of his eyes in the dusky light.

"I don't want to tell you," she said.

He laughed and came and sat down on the side of her bed. "Why not?"

She was dangerously aware of him in her room, on her bed. Of the actuality of him rather than just the washing-powder scent of his T-shirt. Suddenly nervous, she swept her hair out her eyes and tucked it behind her ear. "Because I think you'll be annoyed."

He blinked in surprise. "I promise, I won't be annoyed."

She flicked her hair again, adjusted her T-shirt, anything to swerve the issue.

He said, "Come on, tell me." Moving closer to her, wanting to hear. "You can say anything," he added, using against her the words she'd once said to him.

If she put her hand down on the bed their fingers would touch. She swallowed. "I think you're afraid of having nothing to stop you from having to go back to the ranch. Having to be a rancher again."

He scoffed a laugh, almost in relief, like that was just the stupidest thing he'd ever heard.

She didn't say anything, she just watched him.

He raked a hand through his hair, leaving it messy and disheveled. "Why on earth would you think that?"

"Because I saw you with your dad at the funeral. When you look at him, you still look guilty. The same as you always have. You still look like you think you've got something to make up for, like you let him down."

Logan leaned back on his hands, looked up at the ceiling, the light flickered on the planes of his face making it difficult to distinguish between emotion and shadow. "We did let him down. He wanted us to stay there, work the ranch, that was how he saw the future. But that doesn't mean it's how I see it." He chuckled at the idea. "That is ridiculous, you know that, don't you?"

She looked into his eyes. "See, I knew you'd be annoyed."

"I'm not annoyed, I'm laughing." He held his arms up incredulous.

Her mouth tipped in a half-smile. She nodded. "Okay. You're laughing."

"I am seriously laughing. I would *never* ever go back to ranching," he said, leaning forward, his weight on his hand, inches from her toes on the bed.

"What if your dad called and said he needed you," she countered, "said you were the only option?"

"Well, then, yeah. Of course." He rolled his eyes like that was a given. "Who wouldn't?" His voice was more serious now.

She leaned a fraction closer. "Well, how about if you weren't working at the label?"

"What do you mean?"

"What if you gave it up?" she asked, watching his confusion at the idea. "What if you decided to just do *nothing*?"

He frowned, like the idea was preposterous. "I couldn't do nothing."

"Why not?" she shot back, not missing a beat.

"Because then I'd have to—" He stopped talking. Paused for a second as his mind caught up and then he swallowed. She watched him, her eyes on his face, on his eyes, as the idea dawned, she saw the flicker of panic that he'd been about to say he'd have to go back to the ranch.

She could almost see his brain working as he looked up to the ceiling, as he sighed, this time definitely in annoyance, as he clenched his fists and raised his hands in a movement that made her suddenly flinch back, before she realized he was going to clasp them behind his neck.

She couldn't hide her reaction. The whole area around her had moved when she'd tensed. The sheet had pulled taut, the pillows parted as her back pressed into them, her hair fell from behind her ear over her face.

Logan immediately dropped his hands. It was his turn to scrutinize her. His expression apologetically confused as he said, "Bella, I'm frustrated with myself, I'm not angry with you. Even if I was, I wouldn't…"

He looked at her with such concern, such tender care that it was her turn to be caught off-guard. Tears unexpectedly pressed against her eyes.

Logan paused for a second then shifted his position so he was next to her on the bed, his arm along the pillows behind her. "You have to trust me. You can say whatever you like to me. Anything. I might not like it, but I'm not going to get mad. Not with you. Not like that."

She nodded, blinking away the feelings, the sudden spike in fight-or-flight adrenaline, the memory of Jack's hand raised, of the narrow-eyed anger, of the fear of having nowhere to run to. She pushed her hair back. When she tried to smile, though, it felt a bit too vulnerable.

She felt Logan's hand tentatively stroke her hair. "Did you ever think about going to the police?" he asked, in a tone that implied he wanted more to have been done to help her, rather than suggesting she hadn't done enough.

"Sometimes," she replied, looking down at the sheet, pleating it in lines with her fingers. "But for the same reason I didn't tell you. The same reason I didn't make a statement to the press. I didn't think anyone would believe me." She shrugged, like it was that simple when it was clear it was no such thing. "Jack would have sworn up and down that I was lying. And then what?" She let the pleats she'd made in the fabric go and turned to look up at Logan. "The press have always loved to hate me, Logan, even in the early days I was always referred to as the hanger-on, the desperate groupie, so I've got used to everything I say being twisted." She shrugged. "And Jack was their golden boy. One wink at the camera and everyone went weak at the knees. Anything I said against him, well..." She focused on the sharp contours of his face in the darkness. "You know what they'd say. 'Must be her fault. No smoke without fire. She must have had something to do with it.'" She drew her knees up again, wrapping her arms around them. "Logan, I couldn't even get him to sign the divorce papers, yet there were all these stories branding me a gold-digger. People sneered at me in the street. I've been spat at..." She held her hands out in exasperation.

She watched a guilty shadow skate across his features, as if he was remembering everything he and Jack had said about her.

"I didn't want people taking something that was devastating to me and using it to sell newspapers, as clickbait. For it to become gossip." Logan seemed to notice that her hand was shaking the same time she did and he reached over and took it in his. "There's only so much humiliation and failure a person can take. It's exhausting." She leaned back again, felt the imprint of his arm behind her neck, turned to look at him with a tired smile.

He said, "I don't know how to say it without sounding patronizing, but I think you're really brave."

She scoffed. "No, I'm not."

He shrugged. "I think you are."

She looked into his eyes, looked at the dark lashes and the flecks of gray in the blue, and the kindness. She found that she didn't want him to leave, didn't want him to look away and stand up politely and go back to his room, so she stayed looking as she said, "Don't go."

She saw his moment of hesitation, where he knew he should walk away. But instead, when she moved so she was lying down, he did, too, keeping his arm outstretched so she could slide across and lay her head in the crook of his shoulder, feel the slow, soothing beat of his heart.

She placed her hand on his chest, her fingers tracing the outline of the Charlie's Gym logo. "Nice T-shirt, by the way."

She felt his chest rumble as he laughed. "Yeah. I took quite a beating there last year."

Her finger kept drawing the line of the lettering. "The fight you didn't win?"

"Yeah." He laughed again. Then paused and said, "Except, I'm starting to wonder if I did."

She didn't move, just nodded as she studied the fabric, the muscles beneath it, she imagined him taking the hits as some kind of punishment. She wanted to reach up and touch his face, run her hand over his jaw, his cheekbone, where he'd been hit. But she stayed where she was, just raised her chin so she could see his eyes.

The sounds of the city below them filtered up through the window, the curtains billowing in the breeze. She could hear the rain tapping on the glass and felt herself relax into the warmth and safety of lying there beside him.

Then, into the darkness, Logan said, "Why do you think we never got together?"

Her eyes widened at the question, at the weight of such simple words. "Because we were friends."

She felt him nod, but then say, "There's got to be more to it than that."

She ran it over in her own head, tried to remember them together in Autumn Falls laying out all their hopes and dreams for the future, confident in their paths to success, the whole world out there waiting for them, but what she found she remembered most was the feeling of utter certainty that they would go and do all that they dreamed of but when it was done, one day they would come full circle together again. She allowed herself a small smile at the blind confidence of youth. "Because it was the wrong time in our lives. We were young, we wanted different things." She sat up, pressing her hand to his chest to support herself. "I was going to conquer the world."

His eyes creased when she looked at him. "Do you still want to conquer the world?" he asked.

"No," she laughed, lying back down, trying to find the exact same spot she was in before, his hand moving to rest lightly on her waist.

"Why not?"

"Because I think I was doing it to replace something within me. A feeling of self-worth." She paused to think about what she was trying to say. "I think I understand myself better now—I don't need to conquer the world to prove my own value."

As the words hung in the air, Bella found herself believing them. Felt the thought spread through her veins into the very fabric of her being.

The rain tapped gently against the glass.

Logan said, "Why do I feel like there's some veiled message in there for me?"

She laughed and sat up again. "Only you would think you'd conquered the world, Logan."

He looked uncharacteristically abashed. "That wasn't actually what I was implying."

"Course not." She lay back down with a wry look on her face. "Go to sleep, Logan."

She felt like she could see his smile without having to look. But she looked anyway and saw it there, even his closed eyes with their thick dark lashes had the fan of laughter lines.

Bella stayed watching him for a second then put her head back on his chest, moving to get comfortable, she felt his arm tighten around her and closed her eyes, her whole body aware of where his hand touched, lulled by the naturalness of it. Like in this room, she was home. And she drifted off to sleep to the slow steady rhythm of the rain and the quiet, steady beat of his heart.

Chapter Twenty-Five

When Bella woke up, Logan was asleep next to her. It took her a moment to think of doing anything else than look at him. It was a snatch of time, like someone had paused the world for her just to look, and to imagine. She stopped herself, reaching over and tracing the calmness of his face, or moving closer and resting her head on his chest.

She looked around her in the misty light of the early morning, at the colorful prism of the glass on the table as it caught the rising sun. The coolness of the room ran over her body as she lay still, thinking of the evening, the good bits before it was ruined, and then falling asleep with him there in the room beside her. And she let a small smile creep through her, gave free rein to her imagination, pictured him waking up and telling the world that he wanted her, no matter who was damned along the way. She could savor that little burst of happiness for just a minute, and then she would put it in its box and go on with real life.

Then suddenly a phone rang in a different room, shrill and intrusive.

Logan sat bolt upright, hair all rumpled, eyes alert but still with the heaviness of sleep. "What time is it?" With just a cursory glance at the bedside clock, he got out of bed and jogged out the room to answer his phone.

It all happened so quickly, Bella was left slightly stunned. One minute he was lying there, beautiful in repose, now she could hear him in the other room. "Yeah, I know, just busy this morning. No, I haven't actually seen it. Yeah. Yeah." His business voice echoed around the apartment. "Absolutely. Nip it in the bud."

She sat for a moment, listening. Outside of this room, of this apartment, she knew there was no hope for them. Once she stepped outside there would be someone else wanting a picture, someone else shaming them, someone judging her and judging him. And Logan had a reputation to protect and an empire to safeguard.

She pushed her hair away from her face and turned to let the sunlight hit her skin. No. She couldn't take this path again. Her future had to be different from her past—if only for her sanity's sake.

Standing up, she pulled her skirt on, tucking in the T-shirt he'd lent her and tying up her hair. She was slipping on her boots, when she realized that she couldn't hear his voice any longer and glanced over to see him standing in the doorway, still wearing the clothes he'd slept in, hair mussed from sleep, eyes watching her warily. It felt as if a little of the air left the room. Like she had to breathe a little deeper to fill her lungs. She knew it wouldn't be as easy as she thought to walk away now.

He came into the room. "You're going?"

"Yeah." She went around and stood in front of him, had to stop her hand from reaching out and resting her palm on the warmth of his skin.

"Sorry, I can't believe I slept so long." He shook his head. "I haven't slept like that for years."

Outside, the rain had stopped and the morning sun sparkled through a crisp, icy-blue sky. She felt a shiver on her skin, a sad awareness of an ending.

She smiled, then nodded toward the phone in his hand and said, "I take it they've printed the pictures."

"Yeah." He ran a hand through his hair. "It's not great."

"No," she replied.

He looked her up and down, taking in her clothes, her hair. "Are you just going to go? Do you want a coffee? Breakfast?"

She scrunched up her face and shook her head. "I have to go, Logan."

"You don't have to leave right away."

"I do."

"Why?"

"Because nothing's changed. You're going to go back to work." She gestured to the phone in his hand. "I'm going to go back to my life." She smiled.

He didn't.

She reached up and tentatively touched his face, he closed his eyes for a second. She stroked his skin with her thumb. He held her hand, turned his face so his lips were against her palm. They stood like that for a second, the sun dancing on the dust in the air.

"So, that's it," he said, in almost a whisper, as if said only to himself.

She moved her hand away, trying her hardest to ignore her feelings as she looked into his eyes. "Logan, you know as well as I do that there will always be someone there waiting to take a picture. And it will always end like it did last night."

His face hardened.

"I've lived that life—being constantly on guard, or hiding away in case someone catches me out. I've had enough of hiding."

His eyes narrowed. "So, what are you saying? What do you want?"

"To be ordinary." She laughed, then when he sighed like she wasn't playing ball said, "I don't know." As if the thought had trailed off to nowhere. But she did know, of course she knew. She wanted to grab him by the shoulders and say, for you to be ordinary, too! Let's be ordinary together! She wanted to look into his shuttered blue eyes and say, you'll only be happy when you're honest with yourself and realize what you're running from! But she'd told him as much last night, and Logan never listened to what he didn't want to hear.

Right now, he seemed to be looking everywhere but at her, as if by looking at her he'd be forced to push for a better answer. Instead, he said sardonically, "That's very helpful."

"Isn't it?" She laughed, then gently put her hand on his arm. "It's okay, Logan. We're okay now." She immediately wanted to move away because the warmth of his skin made her nervous, hampering the courage of her conviction. Made her add, jokingly, "You're free to go."

As if on cue, his phone rang. He didn't seem to know what to do, just looked at her, the phone cutting through like a siren. Then he said, "I have to sort it, Bella, I can't leave it like this. For the business, for the family..."

She nodded, perhaps a little too vigorously. "I know. I know, it's fine, Logan."

He answered the phone. "I'll call you back in a second. Yeah, I know, yes..." She could hear the stress in his voice. He looked at her and laughed as he repeated back the words she'd said, "It's fine." He shook his head, utterly disbelieving. His hand reached out as if to take hers, but then his phone rang again almost immediately pulling his attention away as he checked who it was. "It's my mom."

Her lips pressed together in a smile, she crossed her arms over her chest, the sun warm on her skin now, waiting as he said, "Two minutes" and stepped outside again into the hallway.

Bella pulled on her sweater and looked around for her bag. When she couldn't find it in the bedroom, she went to look in the living room, pausing for a moment to take in the majestic view of the skyline in the morning sun.

"Yes, I know it's a small town and people talk." She heard Logan's voice coming from over by the kitchen.

She turned, saw him standing by the countertop, his back to her.

"Just tell them it's nothing," he said. There was a pause

while Martha obviously said something, and Logan, more emphatic this time, added, "Because it *is* nothing."

The words shot through her as she stood there in front of the big picture window.

Logan seemed to sense suddenly that someone was watching and turned. When he saw her, she watched his jaw tighten. He said, "I have to go," and hung up the phone. Then he crossed the cavernous space to stand in front of her. "I didn't mean that the way it came out."

She shrugged a shoulder, wasn't quite able to get her words together quick enough.

His phone rang again, he held his hands wide in a gesture of frustrated apology. "I'm really sorry!"

She pulled herself together and smiled and said, "Don't worry. It's okay, I'll go."

"You don't have to." He silenced the phone but still it vibrated away in his hand. He cut the person off, chucked the phone on the sofa.

She could see his frustration, torn between it all. She took a step forward, put her hand on his shoulder, went up on tiptoe and kissed him on the cheek, inhaling the soft morning scent of his skin. "Goodbye, Logan."

The phone started vibrating again. He closed his eyes for a second. Sighed. "Goodbye, Bella."

Chapter Twenty-Six

Logan sat in a meeting, staring absently at a droplet of condensation on the fancy water bottle in the middle of the boardroom table. The path it took, collecting other little bubbles along the way.

He'd spent the previous day in various discussions with his comms team, trying to quash the fallout from the debacle with the photographer. The focus was as much on Logan losing his cool as it was on him having dinner with Bella, which wasn't great for business. His comms director, Greg, had sat forward, tapping his pad with his pen, recounting the list in front of him. "Okay, just for clarity, we're going with apology for threats made, difficult time personally, emotions high, just friends, looking out for brother's wife, et cetera."

"Fine, just get it sorted."

It didn't make much difference, the stories ran with salacious headline puns and opinionated copy that cast every type of aspersion about Logan's stability, his relationship with Bella, him muscling in on his brother's widow. Just looking at it made him want to punch the computer screen.

In the meeting room, someone said, "Logan?"

He looked up. "Sorry, what was that?"

From the surprised faces all around him he sensed he might have missed something quite important. They'd poached a big star, this was an exciting time in the business, he should have been all over it. But he couldn't concentrate. "Sorry," he said again, then glanced at the slide deck on the screen and added with a self-deprecating raise of his brow, "could you just remind me which section we're on?"

There was polite silence as one of the VPs said, "It's fine, we were just talking about…"

In the office, everyone had politely glossed over the paparazzi shots, but he could sense the pulse of gossip in the air. It wasn't good for the business. Or for him. He didn't want to be the star attraction.

Logan forced himself to concentrate, but as well as the distraction of the news story, he couldn't shake the fact of Bella saying he was only in the industry for fear of leaving it. Was this him? he wondered as he looked around, feeling like he was floating above them all as they sat in their buttoned-up suits with their brains engaged on the topic.

The meeting ended. When he returned to his office, Marianne shot up from her desk by his door and said, "Coffee?" at the same time as surreptitiously trying to close the browser on her computer that showed the paparazzi picture of him and Bella.

When she looked up, Logan raised a brow and he saw

her cheeks flame red. Old enough to be his mother, he was not used to seeing Marianne as anything but one hundred percent composed. "I don't think I've ever seen you blush, Marianne."

"Sorry, Logan."

He shook his head. "It's none of my business what you read."

"I wasn't reading it, I was just—" Embarrassed, she rested a hand over her beaded necklace, her skin speckled red.

He walked over to his office door and pushed it open with his shoulder. "It's fine, Marianne."

Alone in his office, he leaned back against the door, gripping the handle behind him, head against the wood, feeling like an imposter in his body, untethered to everything he could see around him. His desk was exactly as he'd left it, his laptop with its million emails waiting, his jacket slung over the back of his chair, a glass of water half-drunk, but it was like it all belonged to a stranger. When he tried to concentrate, he kept seeing the spark of surprise on Bella's face when she'd overheard him telling his mom on the phone that it was nothing. He feared that if he started to open more emails, he wouldn't know what to do, how to reply. His phone was piling up with missed calls. There had been some from Brodie, a couple from his sister, and his mom had rung. But he couldn't talk to any of them. Nothing felt normal anymore.

Suddenly the door to his office flew open and Bella stormed in, a newspaper in her hand, folded to the page with their photograph.

He barely had a chance to register Marianne in the background standing up from her desk still telling her she couldn't go in before Bella slammed the door shut.

"Just friends? Looking out for your brother's wife?" she spat, chucking the newspaper down on the table in his office with such force it slid along the polished surface and fell to the floor.

Logan came around his desk.

"How dare you?" She moved closer, eyes blazing, cheeks pink from annoyance, her hair falling loose from its ponytail. "Fine if there's nothing between us. But don't pretend that you were there looking out for me. Don't align me with Jack in your statements to the press. Do you understand?"

He stood where he was, felt his heart racing in his chest, wanted to dial back the clock, anything to not have her standing there looking at him with such dislike, such mistrust, everything he'd worked for gone in a couple of ill-considered throwaway lines in a press release. He went to speak but she cut him off.

"I'm free," she said, jabbing her finger at him. "*I've moved on. This is *your* issue.*" She flung her arm out gesturing to the newspaper sprawled on the floor. "This is you who can't face the truth, can't be honest." She swept her hair back from her face, kept her steely gaze fixed on him as she took a step closer. He could smell her perfume, it brought back memories of falling asleep next to her, he wanted to reach out but slipped his hands in his pockets, bracing for her onslaught. "Say it's nothing," she said with tightly controlled annoyance, "say we're just friends, but don't you *dare* use my marriage to trap me again. Understood?"

They were a whisper away from each other. He could see the anger and hurt in her eyes, see her chest rise and fall.

He nodded.

She swept out with the same fury she'd come in with.

Logan stayed where he was for a second, took a moment to absorb what had happened. Straight ahead of him, Marianne sat awkwardly with her head down at her computer trying to carry on as normal.

He walked over and closed the door, then stood with his head against it.

All his adult life he'd battled the press. Smoothing over scandals to protect his brothers. Ethan stumbling out of a club underage, too drunk to answer a question, Logan put in motion the "suffering from exhaustion" line; Brodie gets caught in a kiss and tell, Logan sorts it. Noah tries to punch a photographer when their questions get too intrusive, Logan sorts it. Jack tries to steal the limelight on stage and upsets the others, Logan sorts it. Cameras chasing them down the street, crowding outside their hotel windows, sneaking in with recording devices in housekeeping trolleys, bugging their phones, stalking ex-girlfriends. Hands grabbing at their clothes, ripping the chains around their necks, tugging clumps of hair from their heads. Ethan, wide-eyed and shaking in the back of the limo. Honesty. Logan couldn't—wouldn't—tell the press anything true if his life depended on it.

But when he walked back to his desk, he saw the

newspaper on the floor, the image of him and Bella cozying up in the restaurant staring back at him. He went and picked it up, stared at the picture till it blurred into a swirl of colors. And for the first time in a long time, he had no idea what to do. Suddenly, he couldn't breathe. He sat down on one of the chairs around the table, ripped off his tie and had to undo his top button, brace his hands against his knees. What was happening to him?

He pushed a hand through his hair and exhaled slowly. Then he looked again at the photograph, saw the smile in Bella's eyes, so different to when he'd seen her at the funeral or when she'd revealed what had happened with Jack. He thought for a second how free she looked compared to him, who had the haunted expression of having seen the photographer approach. That split-second caught on camera seemed to tell it all.

Suddenly Logan found himself grabbing his keys, phone and laptop from his desk and stalking purposely out of his office.

"Hold my calls, Marianne. I'm going to be away for a couple of days," he said as he strode past her desk.

"Very good, Logan."

Chapter Twenty-Seven

There was a light dusting of snow on the ground when Logan touched down in Autumn Falls, of course there was no one there to greet him, no Brodie on the tarmac. He hadn't told anyone he was coming back. He waited in line for a cab and had them drive him to the house he owned.

Logan's property was just outside the main town, surrounded by its own ten acres. The house itself was nothing too flashy, but he'd bought it because of the views. He'd liked the idea of being able to gaze out at the mountains when he was lying in bed, figured it would make him remember there was more to life than his small part in it; but he had never been back enough to be reminded of that.

The cab dropped him at the front door. He rang his housekeeper to let her know he was staying a couple of days, and she got in a tizzy about not having prior warning to air the place. He told her it didn't matter at all but when he walked in, the musty, unlived-in smell made it feel more like a mausoleum than a home. But in a way, that was what it was. He barely went there. He kept the place almost out of politeness, to give his mom the impression that he would sometimes come back for longer periods, but he never did. It was a gesture rather than an actuality, and they all went along with the pretense.

Logan dumped his bag in the hallway. Looking around, it felt suddenly as stark and impersonal as Jack's place. Uninhabited, decorated with possessions that weren't his but were chosen off a shelf by a decorator. He flicked on a side light and walked through the semi-darkness to sit down in one of the chairs that flanked the staircase. Chairs that, as far as he could remember, had never been sat on. Props used to fill a space.

It was always strange to be back. He didn't know what to do with himself with no one to see or nothing requiring his immediate attention—except work, but he was ignoring that for the moment. The best thing he probably could have done was go to bed, but he was restless, his mind felt mid-morning awake. He needed a drink.

No, the last thing he needed was a drink.

He stood up and walked from room to room. It felt like a hotel. The cushions plumped, the art chosen by someone else. He went into the kitchen, flicked on the lights, saw all the fancy appliances, the unused oven and fridge. It felt like he'd arrived at a show home, an alternate bland reality. He couldn't stay here. He looked around for something to do, there was nothing, no books, not even a pack of cards. Why hadn't he furnished the place properly? Because he assumed he'd never live there.

He'd needed to escape, not feel more trapped.

He needed something now to take his mind off everything.

Next thing he knew, he was striding back through the hallway, past the staircase and the doors to the living room and into the back corridor. His eyes adjusting to the shadowy darkness as he reached the garage.

Logan pulled back the bolt and pushed open the door. The smell of the room smacked him in the face—of cold concrete, grease and engine oil. As he flicked on the bare bulb, he closed his eyes and breathed deeply—this was the smell of freedom. When he opened his eyes, he looked around and saw the ledges of paint cans, tools and stacked boxes. Then there, underneath a sheet so thick with dust he could have written his name, was his motorcycle.

Yanking off the cover, the dust engulfed the air making him squint away for a second. But there it was. Shimmering as if newly polished. He ran his hand along the body and over the soft leather of the seat. Images of Bella flashed furiously through his mind, her arms tight around his waist, her legs straddled against him, her soft cheek pressed to his back.

Where he'd left it, slung on the back of the door, was his jacket. The smell of the dark leather was so evocative it almost knocked him backward. The helmet was resting on the back of the bike, his old, battered gloves inside. His boots sat waiting for him on the floor by the back wheel, the weight of them making him clomp heavily as he walked to open the garage door. Then he got on the bike, turned the key and kicked the stand away. The engine roared to life. Logan felt his heart jump with adrenaline. He pulled his helmet on and, getting used to the feel of the bike beneath him again, cruised his way out of the garage. It was like getting back on a horse, his body knew what to do. He felt suddenly young again, out on the road, visor up, cold night air whipping against his face, the full moon lighting the night like a ghostly morning.

He drove for miles out to nowhere. The mountains in the distance like a mirage. The land on either side unchanged from his memory, the grassy plains undulating as far as the eye could see, glinting like waves in the moonlight. He absorbed the solitude of being alone on the road, he remembered driving this same route with Bella on the back of the bike, the wideness of her smile, the smell of her skin against the leather, her chin resting on his shoulder. It was like seeing snippets of freedom, his life being stripped off his back the further he rode. He was no one out here. The landscape could suck him up and never let go. Pine trees loomed above him, darkening the road, throwing shadows like phantoms across his path as he kept on riding. Kept on heading for those mountains, a blanket of stars above him, the streetlights of Manhattan felt like another world, another life.

When he finally stopped, he pulled over, got off his bike, and sat at the foothills of the dusky mountains he'd climbed as a boy, his body shivering from the frigid cold, above him the quiet, looming presence of Starlight Mountain that had been the backdrop of his childhood. The craggy black shadow that he'd always seen as a barrier keeping him trapped but that now seemed more like a guide; a watchful, protective eye. He lay on his back against the crisp, crunch of frost, staring up at the moon, breathing in what felt like courage spreading through his lungs.

Chapter Twenty-Eight

In the morning, Logan pulled up at the Silver Sky ranch on his bike. The tires leaving tread marks in the red earth, his heart thumping, his palms sweating, his whole body psyched and ready for the confrontation ahead.

But when he cut the ignition and yanked his helmet off, he heard all the familiar noises of the farm, the hum of the tractor and the braying of the horses and it suddenly all seemed too mundane, too normal for his intrusion.

His immediate thought was to back away, kick the bike back to life and head for the hills. But then Noah came into view, strolling from the paddock toward the main house, his hat pulled low, his big jacket zipped up almost over his nose from the cold. Rocky bounded ahead of him and when the dog saw Logan, it barked excitedly.

When Noah looked up to see what had caught Rocky's attention, he allowed himself a wry grin at the sight of Logan getting off the bike. He blew on his hands as he sauntered over, "Well, look who it is," he drawled, while his gaze admired the shiny black frame. "I always loved that bike."

"Me too," Logan replied.

Noah didn't ask why he was there. He took after their father, wasn't one for questions.

"Dad home?" Logan asked, removing his gloves and tucking his hands into his jacket pocket.

Noah tipped his head in the direction of the sunlit horse barn, remnants of frost still on the roof, next to the paddock with a couple of grazing horses in their colorful winter coats, and the big hay barn behind.

Logan nodded, then he ran his hand over his mouth, steeling himself. It wasn't too late to leave. Only Noah had seen him, and Noah wouldn't say anything to anyone if he suddenly took off.

But Logan had had enough of running away. He set off in the direction of the horse barn.

Noah walked part of the way with him across the yard. Their feet scuffing in the sandy dirt. The sun was blindingly low in the sky making them squint. Logan glanced across at his brother, he was always familiarly unchanged; same battered flight jacket same layers of shirts and T-shirts underneath, same battered sun-bleached hat, same stubble in need of a shave. All he cared about was getting the job done.

Thing with Noah was, if you showed him something he couldn't do, he put all his focus into working out not only how to do it, but how to be the best at it. When they were in the band, ask him to play anything—saxophone, piano, drums, keyboard—he could either do it or taught himself how, no hassle. But all Noah had really wanted when they were in the band was to be back out there on the land with no one to bother him, except maybe his girlfriend.

It was that brooding disconnect that had girls practically fainting at Noah's feet, but he barely gave anyone the time of day. Hated the attention. And that, Logan was now realizing, was what put him at odds with Jack who wanted all the attention he could get, every last scrap. Jack could never understand why all the fans went wild for Noah. Always winding him up. Logan had brushed it off as brotherly banter at the time but of course, he now understood all too well the insidious nature of envy. And as someone who refused to fight back, Noah was an easy target.

"Everything okay with you?" Logan asked, knowing the response he'd get.

Noah shrugged a shoulder.

They walked some more. Logan shielded his eyes from the sun, looking past the barn at the pine-covered hill behind and the high slate peaks beyond.

Noah said, "Saw the picture of you and Bella in the news."

Logan blew out a breath. "Yeah."

"She okay?"

Logan winced. "She's not okay with me, but otherwise, I think so."

"You think or you know?" Noah checked, more serious now.

"I think I know," Logan replied, because that was the best he could offer.

"Well, make sure she is," was all Noah said.

"I'll try."

Although Noah's warning had an edge of accusation, what Logan hadn't been expecting was the touch of sympathy directed his way in Noah's glance, like he was sorry for the fact he was still getting hounded.

Logan looked away, out across the pasture to the pine trees and the mountains. He took a breath. Then he felt a touch on his shoulder and saw Noah's hand rest briefly there before he took it away and shoved it back in his pocket.

Logan kept looking at the spot on his shoulder for a moment longer. Thought of Brodie telling him they'd all grown up.

Noah said, "You come all this way to speak to Dad?"

He nodded but felt his courage dip momentarily.

Noah narrowed his eyes. "You sure that's a good idea?"

"No," he replied and watched the corner of Noah's mouth tilt up.

They reached the wide-open door of the barn, Noah said, "He's in there." Then after a pause added, "Good luck," before walking away.

Logan entered the building. The warm, familiar scent of the horses bringing with it memories of early mornings when his eyes were still half-shut, endless sweat-soaking jobs to do and one-word orders to get them done. But alongside it came a satisfaction, an almost addictive ache in the muscles, and—one of the new horses he hadn't met before, Jo-Jo it said on the name plate, poked her head over the stall door and looked at him with her wide, silken eye—the delight of these perfect, gorgeous beasts. Logan walked over and ran his hand down her soft chestnut coat just as his dad appeared at the other end of the barn. Logan let the horse nuzzle his hand as he turned toward his dad and said, "Hi."

Emmett Carter put his hands on his hips and, eyes narrowed, said almost accusingly, "Were we expecting you?"

Logan shook his head. "No." He gave the horse a pat and then walked over toward his dad. "I need to talk to you."

Emmett huffed. "I'm working." And made to move toward the back exit.

Logan said, "I need to talk to you now."

"Well, I'm working." Emmett didn't look around.

"Well, you'll have to get someone else to do it for you." Logan put his hands in his pockets, held his ground. "This is important."

Emmett kept walking. "I can't talk right now."

"Yes, you can!" Logan's raised voice echoed around the giant structure.

His dad paused. Logan felt his heart rate increase a notch. Emmett turned. They squared off against one another along the length of the barn.

This time, unlike after the funeral, when his dad locked eyes with him, Logan refused to flinch, just stared right back.

After a beat, and barely moving his head, his dad called

to one of the ranch hands to take over. Then he walked out the back of the barn in the direction of the house, presuming Logan would follow.

Chapter Twenty-Nine

Logan and his dad sat opposite each other in the kitchen. Across the big slabs of wood that made up the table, where Logan and his brothers had done their homework, eaten their meals and been given stern lectures by their mother when they'd been told off at school for not listening or getting into fights. All standard boy stuff, but sitting back there across from his father, Logan felt like that boy again, like the years of work, of social standing, of success, peeled away from him at the sight of his old man, gnarled-faced and heavy-set.

Hold your nerve, Logan.

He remembered the boxing ring. Imagined suddenly going a couple of rounds against his dad. It would be quite some fight. Emmett had determined strength ingrained in his work-honed muscles. Neither would back down, that was for certain. The idea of it made Logan smile inside, which actually helped him relax, his shoulders drop. He'd made coffee while his dad cleaned up and he took a sip of it, scalding-hot and familiar; same cups, same beans. It tasted like mornings at home.

"So, you'd better get talking, 'cause I haven't got all day." Emmett was drying his hands on a towel.

Logan put his mug down, said, "Do you want to say hello? Ask me how I'm doing first?"

His dad glanced at him from underneath stern black brows. "I don't have time for that."

Logan reached into his pocket and took out the signet ring. He placed it on the table between them. The gold sparked like flint in the sunlight streaming through the kitchen window.

Emmett had taken a gulp of coffee and paused with it in his mouth when he saw the ring. Logan watched him swallow, watched him put the cup down slowly on the table and before reaching for it, throw Logan an is-this-what-I-think-it-is glance. His dad could convey an expression in the infinitesimal hitch of a lip or vague narrowing of an eye. That was his language and they'd all learned to read it since infancy.

Logan kept his face impassive.

His dad's cracked-skinned fingers picked the ring off the table, holding it like a jewel, bringing it close to his face to inspect the insignia.

He looked at Logan over the top of it. "Where d'you find it?"

"Jack's house."

Emmett's mouth tightened. He focused back on the ring. Logan wondered for a ridiculous moment if he might apologize for the crushing silent treatment he'd subjected him to for losing it.

But Emmett was a "never apologize, never explain" kind of guy. He just placed the ring back in the center of the table. "So, what is it you want to say?" he asked, one hand now on the handle of his mug, the other flat on the table.

Logan cleared his throat. "I want to talk to you about us, about the past."

"Really, Logan?" his dad winced. "I don't have time for that." He started to push himself up from his chair. "There's nothing to say."

"Sit down!" Logan surprised himself with the hard flatness of his voice.

His dad paused.

Logan looked up. "You're going to hear what I have to say if I have to pin you to that damn chair. I'm not doing this anymore. I'm not going to let you disappear off, still judging us all for what we did. I'm not going to do your job because you refuse to do it."

"I don't know what you're talking about."

"If you don't, then you're blind as well as stubborn."

"You watch your mouth, son."

"Or what, Dad? You going to fight me because you're too scared to listen."

"I'm not afraid of anything you have to say."

"Oh, no?" Logan narrowed his eyes. "This family is broken. *We* are broken."

Emmett scoffed. "Don't give me that. Don't come into my house and start telling me what we are and aren't." His eyes blazed with the harsh ferocity that always made Logan shrink back as a child. "You gave up that right a long time ago."

But he wasn't a child anymore. He held that terrifying gaze and sneered back, "Oh, what, so no one's allowed to say anything anymore? Have an opinion? Should we just keep on going exactly as we always have?" Logan's lip curled in distaste as he glared at his father across the table. "Where's that got us? Jack's dead. Ethan's who-knows-where. Who's next, Dad?"

The clock ticked in the background. The only giveaway that his father had heard was the tightening to his mouth.

Logan felt his blood pounding in his temple. There was a tremor in his hand. He sat back, could still hear his own words like an echo in the room.

Emmett took a slug of coffee, seemingly for something to do, for a moment to think. When he put the mug down, there was a long pause before he spoke. Logan was glad he'd left his phone in his jacket in the hall because he'd be checking his emails by now if not, something to distract him from the fear that still resided in the pit of his stomach when faced with his father.

Emmett focused on the mug as he spoke. "Jack was never satisfied. Never happy with what he had." He turned the cup around in his hands. "None of you were. Apart from Noah, maybe."

Logan's brows drew down in disbelief. "I don't think that's true," he said. "I don't think any of us had any idea what we were." His pulse was still pounding, his body on high alert. He wondered if he'd have the courage to say what he was saying if he wasn't brimming with adrenaline. "We all knew what *you* wanted us to be."

Emmett's head jerked a fraction.

Logan flinched, couldn't help himself, it was a preprogrammed reaction, the terrifying apprehension of crossing a line. But he carried on, there had been no point coming if he didn't. "We certainly never knew ourselves, or what we could be."

"Oh, right," his dad replied with a barely-there mirthless laugh. "And singing and playing the guitar was the answer, was it? Taught you all how to be the men you wanted to be?" Both hands on the table, he stretched back, tanned forearm muscles flexing. "Because as far as I can see, all that's happened is you all lost your way." He said it slow and demeaning. "None of you are here. None of you know a darn thing about *who you are*." He sneered the last three words, drawing them out slow. His eyes drew to the ring, sparkling again in the low sun. "I never should have let you go."

"*Let us go*?" It was Logan's turn to scoff. "We were teenage boys, how could you have stopped us?" He glared at the man across the table in his red checked shirt faded to pink, the neatly clipped beard, the deep furrows between his brows that never softened. "What you *could* have done," Logan said, forcing himself to counter with restraint, "*should* have done—is tell us that it was okay. Tell us to go and see the world and bring it back here if we wanted to." Logan's hands mirrored his father's, flat on the table, but his were almost pushing him out of the seat to get closer in his urgency to speak. "*You* could have supported *us* so that I didn't have to. *You* could have understood that if you give people the freedom to leave, they're more likely to come back!"

"But you *didn't*, did you!" Emmett bashed the table.

"Because no one wanted to!" Logan almost shouted. "No one dared. Because you were so furious with us all, but you wouldn't say anything!"

Silence. Just the metronome of the clock pendulum. And the remnants of Logan's words in the air.

His father glared. Hooded eyes impenetrable.

Logan sighed. He looked away, out the window, saw the shadows of the clouds on the mountains. "I think part of why I'm here is to tell you that I never will come back." He felt all his muscles clench like bracing for a punch. "I've never dared bring it up before. But I'm not coming back here, Dad, not to the ranch." To his horror, his voice wavered as he said it, not like he was going to cry, but like he was admitting a wrongdoing; terrified, like a small boy, of the consequences. He was a grown man, for goodness' sake, he'd closed billion-dollar deals, he'd stood on stage in front of millions of people, and yet he could barely tell his father the truth. Logan thought suddenly of Bella having to stand in her kitchen and admit to him what had happened to her, the naked vulnerability of it.

Emmett scoffed like Logan had wasted his time. "You done?"

Logan sat back in his chair, feeling the shame of foolishness for having tried. "Yeah. Fine."

His dad stood up, chair scraping on the floorboards, then turning his back on Logan, he walked across the kitchen and out the back door, the screen thwacking with finality.

Chapter Thirty

Logan closed his eyes. Listened to the familiar tick of the clock and the hum of the fridge from where he sat at the table. He breathed in and out, feeling like an idiot and wondering why he'd even bothered.

"He may not be very good at showing them, Logan, but he does have feelings."

Logan's eyes snapped open to see his mom leaning in the doorway between the kitchen and the living room. She wore jeans and a black sweater, arms crossed, hair tied up in a scruffy bun. She had her apron on, and he wondered if she'd watched them approach from the barn and gone to sit in the living room.

"Did you hear all that?" he asked.

She nodded. "I did." Her eyes sparkled with their usual knowing as she came over to where he was sitting and bent to hug him tight around the shoulders. "It wasn't your job to save Jack. If anything, it was mine, or your dad's, but not yours, Logan. We let him down."

The last person Logan wanted to take any of the blame for what had happened was his mom, and he said as such.

"Honey," she said, pulling out the chair next to his; the shape of her hands, the carved back of the chair, the sweetness of her perfume all so familiar to him and yet had become so distant. "When you're a parent you take on a responsibility to take care of your kids. I spoke to Jack on the phone, he never hinted at any problems beyond those with his marriage. His career was going brilliantly, he had that beautiful house, he went on amazing vacations. Yes, he was angry about the divorce but he didn't give any hint that there was more going on." She shrugged in disbelief. "But we were wrong. All of us." She turned so she could rest her clasped hands on the table. "He was a very good actor. Very good at hiding things." Her eye caught on the ring, and she reached over and picked it up. "I wondered what it was you'd found." She turned it over in her hand, then put it back. "I'm sorry that happened."

"I don't want *you* to be sorry," Logan said.

"But you want your dad to be?" she asked, dark brows raised in question. They had the same eyes, he and his mom; Logan understood her expressions as he understood his own and knew she was the same with him.

He remembered when she'd told them that she was ill. That they had found a lump but it would be okay. Always quick with the reassurance, but Logan could read the fear in her eyes. Six kids, Willow only twelve at the time. All in desperate need of their mom and she knew it, because the alternative was Dad: outstanding with the practical, gruff and distant with anything else. Ten times worse when her health was in jeopardy. If he didn't say much day to day, he said nothing while his wife was ill.

Logan clenched his fists, unable to quash his own frustration.

Martha smiled, wide cherry-red lips, kind eyes. "I'm as much to blame, Logan. I'm sure deep down your dad would say that you all took off because I encouraged you too much with the music and the singing. That was my passion." She put her hand on her chest, over the gold cross she always wore. "I brought that to the house. The Carters were not musical people before I came along." She smiled wryly as if it were the biggest understatement of the year. Logan thought of Granddad Carter, if he thought his dad was a man of few words, then Granddad Carter said even fewer.

"It wasn't your fault." Logan wouldn't stand for that. "You were ill." He could still remember so vividly Ethan pausing the TV when a commercial came up for a big talent show, and saying, *"We should do that for Mom."* They'd all been sitting in the living room, none of them with a clue what to do because Aunt Eleanor—who'd come to stay because Emmett had the ranch to run, or hide in—kept telling them that the doctors thought they had it under control, but she refused to say for certain that Martha would survive. At that point, no one was making any guarantees. Putting the band together became something, anything, to get them all through. To give them something to talk about when they went home and their mom looked so terrifyingly, helplessly fragile. He could still picture Willow dancing around as they practiced in one of the disused barns, cheeks wet with tears.

They had entered the competition when Mom started chemotherapy. And by the time she watched them win, the treatments were finished, and the guarantees were more forthcoming. To the boys it felt like a miracle. To their dad, less so.

"I loved what you did, Logan." His mom reached over and squeezed his hand, hers cool over his. "I was so proud. *Am* so proud of all of you. But your dad, he loves this ranch, and his dream was all of you here." She smiled softly, her eyes tipping up like a cat's. "Some things we win and some we lose. No one likes to lose, Logan. No one likes to feel that the part they play isn't good enough. Is second best." She moved her chair closer to his so she could sit with her arm over the back of his chair and turned to look out the window, at the sun bright on the pasture. She sighed. "There's a lot of egos in this house, always has been." She glanced back at him, one brow shrewdly arched. "Stubborn, competitive egos."

Logan had to look away to hide his complicit smile.

His mom nudged his knee with hers. "It's tough to take when you're not the one who's winning. I'm not excusing it," she added more seriously. "I'm just explaining it." Then she stood up and kissed the top of his head as if he were ten years old. "You've always been a great kid, Logan."

"Mom, I'm not a kid, look at me." He gestured to his fully grown self.

She wrapped her arms around him, smelled him,

squeezed him tight. "My lovely boy," she said ruffling his hair.

"Get off," he laughed, pushing her away.

She stood back, hip leaning against the table. "Listen to me," she said, the smile fading to seriousness in her eyes. "We've never talked properly about any of it—it's always been easier to sweep things under the carpet—but I'll tell you one thing, it's your life, Logan, and you live it any way you like, understand? Don't listen to me, don't listen to your dad. Don't worry about what we think. Do it your way, yeah?"

He paused for a moment, then nodded. Now he feared there might be tears in his eyes.

She went over to the coffee pot on the stove to pour herself a cup. "But don't be a stranger, Logan. That's all I ask."

Chapter Thirty-One

Logan left the ranch on his bike without looking back toward the horse barn, didn't want to even catch a glimpse of his dad.

By the time he pulled up outside the orchard, his palms were sweating inside his gloves from nerves. When he rang the bell, he just hoped that Bella had stuck to her decision to help her stepdad with the apple-tree pruning.

It was John-Luke who answered the front door, dressed in cargo pants, old cable-knit cream sweater and heavy boots, he'd clearly come in from working in the orchard. He was shorter than Logan by quite a bit, but the stony look he gave him on seeing him made Logan feel suddenly very small. He swallowed. "Is Bella home?"

John-Luke glanced behind him, which Logan took as a yes, then taking a step forward, he said coolly, "I think it's best if you stay away, Logan. I've picked her up once already after the damage one of you boys did, I don't want to have to do it again."

Logan was about to protest, try and reason with him, but he saw the stark warning in the man's eyes and found himself having to look away in shame. "I understand," he said, taking a step back and turning to leave the porch, his heart catching in his throat at what John-Luke had had to do, to face, when it came to protecting his stepdaughter.

But then he heard Bella's voice say, "It's fine, I can talk to him. Honestly, don't worry."

Logan turned back to see her standing there, wrapped up in a long blue coat and chunky black turtleneck, passing her stepdad and giving him a reassuring squeeze on the arm that she could handle herself. "Thank you, though," she added with a soft smile, and after a moment's hesitation John-Luke reluctantly conceded, stepping back but keeping his hard gaze locked on Logan.

When he was gone, Bella glanced at the street behind Logan, and the possibility of prying eyes, and said, "You'd better come through to the orchard."

He followed her through the house, glancing at the familiarity of the furnishings, out through the ramshackle sunroom and through to the rows of trees with the shadow of the mountains behind.

Bella pulled her coat tight around herself as they went out into the cold. She led them between the trees, the grass crunching beneath their feet in patches where the snow hadn't thawed.

As they walked, Logan said, "I went to see my dad." Bella glanced briefly his way. "I told him I wasn't coming back."

She paused for a moment. "What did he do?"

"Walked out."

She raised her eyebrows as if she wasn't surprised but was still waiting for what that had to do with her.

"I came here because I wanted to say that I was wrong about what I said about Jack." He reached up and ran his finger along the prickles of frost on one of the branches. "I'm sorry," he said, looking back at her. "I know I keep having to apologize but this is all pretty new to me."

Her eyes narrowed. "What's new?"

He shrugged ruefully. "Having to account for my actions."

She rolled her eyes and looked away, maybe to hold in a smile of disbelief—he hoped.

A couple of rows ahead of them, John-Luke was up a step ladder, pruning shears in hand, keeping a wary eye on them.

Bella headed over to a rickety bench woven together with apple branches. She swiped the frost off with the sleeve of her coat before sitting down, Logan didn't bother. He leaned forward, the bench creaking beneath him, elbows on his knees, chin resting on his steepled fingers, eyes straight ahead taking in the endless rows of trees, then the pines, then the mountain like a layer cake.

"I'm not good at having my life—my choices—in the public eye any longer. I'm not sure I ever was. I'm not good at not being in control."

She sat a foot or so away from him, leaning against the apple-wood armrest. "You can't stop every story, Logan. People will always have opinions."

"I know and I hate it." He sat back, raking a hand through his hair in frustration.

She gave him a resigned look. "At some point, you have to let go." Then she paused, taking a steadying breath before adding, "Unless you still see me as your brother's wife."

"No, I don't," he said quickly, "but…"

The *but* hung in the air.

Bella tilted her head waiting.

Logan couldn't formulate an answer. He stared back at the view. His breath a cloud in front of him, the wind bitter against his cheeks, his brain warring between saying nothing and what it was he actually felt. He remembered the picture in the newspaper, the goading headlines. "I feel like you're off-limits," he replied finally, looking regretfully back at her.

Bella closed her eyes for a second.

Logan sighed.

When she looked at him again, he could see only annoyance in her eyes. "Don't you think that should be up to me?"

He paused again. "Probably, yes."

She ran her fingers through her hair. "Logan, you're so frustrating."

He laughed in surprise. But she shook her head, exasperated. "I should get back to work," she said, standing up and gesturing to the trees around them.

Logan took the hint. "Absolutely."

When he stood up to go, he waved to John-Luke in the

distance, who gave a wary, almost suspicious, wave in response. Logan didn't like how it made him feel.

As he walked with Bella back through the house, he didn't feel any better than he had when he'd arrived, perhaps worse. Hollow, like pieces of him were suddenly missing when he'd only just felt what it was like to have them back.

But then just as he was leaving, he heard Bella say, "Well done for saying what you did." He glanced back. "To your dad," she clarified.

He paused. Not wanting to show quite how much it meant to him, he raised a brow and replied flippantly, "Can I remind you that he walked out of the room?"

"It was just the first step," she countered, eyes serious. "You still have to try again."

He winced. "I don't think so."

She shrugged like it didn't matter to her either way, but to him, seeing his refusal through her eyes made him feel suddenly as blinkered and set in his ways as his dad.

Chapter Thirty-Two

The next afternoon, the back door opened and Noah walked into the ranch-house kitchen, Rocky trotting obediently behind him. When he saw Logan sitting at the table and his mom standing by the cooker, he started to back out, but Martha said, "Noah, come in and sit down."

"You said this was a planning meeting!"

Martha shrugged. "Yes, I lied. Sit down."

Noah hesitated. Logan could see he was desperate to leave. But he'd never say no to their mom, so he schlepped across the kitchen, head hung like he was a kid.

Rocky seemed to sense the mood and flopped down under the table. Noah pulled out the chair opposite Logan. Sitting across from one another at that kitchen table, it felt very much like when they'd been growing up.

Martha strode over to the back door and opening it up, shouted, "Emmett!"

After a second, "What?" came the reply.

"You're meant to be in here! We have a meeting remember?"

"I'm busy, Martha. It's going to have wait."

Logan glanced at Noah who raised his brows like, here we go.

"He's so stubborn," Martha complained. "You're all so stubborn! How did I manage to have six children and a husband all as stubborn as the other?" She pushed her feet irritatedly into her boots that she kept under a small bench by the back door and stalked out across the yard.

Across from him, Noah gazed longingly out the window, leg jiggling under the table. When he realized Logan was watching him, he said dryly, "And we were all doing so well as we were."

Logan held back a smirk.

The back door flew open and Martha came back in, kicking off her boots and stalking back to where her coffee cup waited on the kitchen counter. She stood, arms crossed, blue eyes blazing.

They sat in silence. Just the clock again. Logan couldn't look at Noah, feared he might get the giggles like they did when they'd been told off, five wild boys hauled in around the table for a stern talking-to by their mother.

They waited.

Logan didn't believe for one moment his dad would come. But then suddenly the screen door banged and Emmett appeared in the kitchen doorway, taking off his hat and running his hand through his hair in weary annoyance.

Logan straightened up in surprise. He glanced to where his mom was standing, hands now cradled around her coffee cup, eyes fixed on her husband as if tethering him to the spot, and he suddenly realized who it really was that he wouldn't want to face in the ring.

Martha walked around to the chair next to Logan and sat down, placing her cup in front of her. "It's been too long since we've really spoken, any of us." She glanced sidelong at Emmett who stood by the fridge, eyes downcast, giving nothing away.

"We see each other at Christmas and birthdays, if we're lucky, and no one dares broach anything for fear of upsetting someone and ruining the day." She clasped her hands, like she was chairing a meeting. "So, is it my fault you all left and the family has become so fractured? Because I encouraged you all to play an instrument, to sing, to enjoy music in a house where no one had played a record unless it was carols at Christmas and even then—" She shook her head in despair at the memory.

Logan opened his mouth to refute what she said about it being her fault, but she went on. "But no, you can't blame me because then we take away from the fact you kids did it *for* me, to make me smile, to make me happy at what was a very ... difficult time." Her voice caught.

Logan chanced a glance at his dad, but Emmett stayed, head bent. Same as Noah. No one looking.

To Logan, the band and their leaving the ranch had forever existed like Starlight Mountain dominating the horizon out the window, a dark looming monolith casting its shadow over all of them, a beast that no one dared prod for fear of revealing their part in it. Now his mom was practically detonating it and the risk of what might happen as a result made Logan press his back against the chair.

Martha, however, seemed unfazed, as if she'd been waiting a lifetime for this moment. "Or should you boys go through life feeling varying degrees of guilt for having left? Of leaving your dad hurt and let down by the change in what he thought was your future together."

Emmett did look up then, but away at the wall. Jaw tense. He would be hating this. Any mention of emotion was like a big arrow pointing weakness at him. The discomfort radiating from his dad was so acute it made Logan want to just raise a hand, accept the blame and be done with it.

But his mom wasn't finished. "Or maybe," she went on, sitting back, legs crossed, arms crossed, "we finally say, it is what it is. What happened happened. And get on with our lives. Start a new chapter. Something we will forever have to know that Jack didn't get the opportunity to do. But that's on us. Me and your father. And I refuse to let it happen again."

There was a pause. She let the words hang there between them.

Logan looked at Noah, Noah at Logan. Logan could hear his heart thumping in his ears, wondering what his dad might say now, might do with that option.

But, predictably, instead of saying anything, Emmett took the end of the speech as a chance for dismissal and turned to leave.

Martha sprang up from her chair so fast it almost

toppled over. "Don't you dare walk out that door," she hissed.

Logan's eyes widened. Noah shrunk in on himself.

"Emmett Carter, for once in your life, you are going to admit that you are a terrible loser and always have been. Too proud to look at anything you don't agree with a different way. Because if you carry on pretending that you'd rather have nothing than make the best of what we have, then we will continue to have *nothing*." She stood tall, cold fury in her eyes. "*We've* let this distance happen in this family, all of us. Through stubbornness and pushing away what we don't understand—or *want* to understand."

Logan had never seen his mom get angry like that, unless it was scolding them as kids when they'd been really bad. He glanced between her and his dad, fearing for a second that his dad might storm out regardless, and if he did, what then? He wondered how certain his mom was of the odds of him staying or leaving but she was as poker-faced as Emmett.

The clock ticked. They waited.

The moment when it came could never be called monumental, a half-turn of the shoulders back toward the people in the room, mouth set in a thin, terse line, but it was monumental to them.

Logan's breathing returned to normal.

More composed now, Martha carried on as if there had been nothing amiss, "It's up to us now to put things right." She smoothed her hair back that had come loose when she got angry and returned to her chair. "If we can do anything now, we remind you boys that this is your home. I want you all back, Logan," she said, frank and unapologetic. "I want you to *want* to come here. Not circle around us. I want you to live at least a couple of days a year in that house you bought."

Logan felt his cheeks color with shame at the mention of the long-ignored house.

"I want you to feel you are welcome here," she said more gently, reaching across the table and squeezing both his and Noah's hands.

Noah rolled his eyes, couldn't seem to help himself.

Martha smacked his fingers to behave. "We've let you down by letting this fester. We let Jack down, *us*, not you." She looked pointedly at Emmett, daring him to question.

Logan looked, too. As did Noah. And watched in disbelief as very slowly and imperceptibly to the untrained eye, his dad nodded.

Martha closed her eyes for a second, her relief palpable. Then when she opened them again, there were tears dampening her lashes. His mom never cried, not in front of them anyway. Logan felt his heart constrict.

She pressed her fingers to the corners of her eyes to stop herself from crying. Emmett made to move across the kitchen toward her.

She held out a hand to stop him. "I want something good to come out of this. Anything we can get. For a start, I want you two to try and understand each other," she pointed between Logan and his dad. "To stop being so darn stubborn, for once, and forgive each other."

Logan felt defenseless against his mom's tears. His face

got warm as he stared down at the table, felt fourteen, then up at where his dad stood, waited for him to look heavenward with a sigh of irritation. But maybe he was defenseless, too, because instead of sighing, Emmett looked at Logan for a good long while, long enough for Logan to look back and for what he saw to become a face that was human rather than just his father, long enough, he wondered, for his dad to see his son rather than a businessman.

Then when it felt like no one would ever move again, Emmett crossed to the table and held out his hand, calloused and dirt-stained, and without question, Logan stood up and clasped it, as firm as he could considering how astounded he was. When he looked up, it was possible that he saw the lines at the sides of his dad's eyes crease with some semblance of affection.

For once, Noah looked equally as mind-blown by the whole exchange as Logan, which must have meant it was as momentous as Logan felt it was.

Martha blew out a breath in relief. Then she got a Kleenex out the pocket of her jeans and wiped her face.

Logan reluctantly let his dad's hand go and sat back down, Emmett pulling out the chair opposite.

Martha said, "That's a good start."

His dad seemed surprised by the word start but seemed to know better than to say anything.

Resting her arms on the table, his mom leaned forward and said urgently, "I want to make sure that what happened to Jack doesn't happen to any of the rest of you. I don't want anyone to slip through the net, hide who they are.

I want us to be a family again who know one another. *Really* know one another."

Logan nodded even though he was pretty sure it was a pipe dream. Noah focused on the grains of wood in the table.

"This includes you too, Noah—" Martha tapped the table where he was staring to get his attention "—don't think just because you're here, you're exempt."

Noah looked up with a frown. "I haven't done anything. I'm fine."

Martha sat back again, gaze fixed now on Noah. "Right, yes of course, living in a trailer over there—" she pointed out the back door "—and working every hour of the day is *just fine*. It's not sustainable, Noah. It's hiding not living. It's not reaching your potential."

Noah tipped his head up to the ceiling. "Can we not bring me into this, please? I'm pretty happy as I am." He threw Logan a glare like it was his fault all this was happening.

Martha glossed over Noah for the time being. "You have not lived normal lives. None of you. You need to decide who you are. Settle down." Her hands gesticulated impatiently as she talked, as if all these thoughts had been building inside her, bursting for the opportunity to be voiced. "You need to get some *normality* and some *balance* in your lives. Logan, you're chained to your desk or your phone all the time. It's either work or nothing. Or—what was it?—punching photographers?" She shook her head in disappointment.

While obviously ashamed of his actions with the

photographer—and knowing this wasn't the right time to say that he didn't actually punch the guy—what struck Logan was that was what his life boiled down to in their eyes. Not, Logan you're out there killing it, high up the Forbes list, building careers, basking in the glory of success, but that essentially, like Noah, they saw him as hiding, but behind a computer not in a trailer. No balance, no normality.

He thought about Bella telling him he didn't love the music industry he was just afraid to get off the wheel for fear of what? Of having to go back to the ranch. He looked across the table at his dad, sitting with his arms out in front of him, fiddling with the pads of his fingers with his thumb, nodding a little more definitively at everything Martha was saying. Logan had told him now that he wasn't coming back. He'd jumped the hurdle and hadn't come crashing down. Made things better, if anything.

"Brodie's drifting around with no responsibility," his mom went on.

At that Emmett nodded. "Yes, he is."

As Logan sat listening to the idea of pulling his brothers back together again, he felt a warmth spread through him that he hadn't felt in this house since he was a kid. He could feel his shoulders dropping, like the weight of the world had been eased from him without him even realizing he was carrying it. He found his mouth involuntarily smiling. A calm spreading through him. It was over. One chapter was closed.

"And then there's Ethan." Martha put her hand on her heart.

Logan glanced up, drawn from his reverie. "No one knows where Ethan is. I had people trying to find him for the funeral. Nothing. Zilch."

His mom wouldn't have it. "We have to get Ethan back."

Noah shook his head like it was an impossibility.

Martha banged the table with her fist. Emmett flinched. "I want us to find him, and bring him back. He needs us! We *all* need each other," she implored, pinning each of them with a stare of calm determination, the same one that as children was the most terrifying because it brokered no arguments. "We're a family. It's the only way."

Chapter Thirty-Three

When they left the kitchen, Logan wasn't quite sure what to do with himself. Noah was walking off in the direction of the horse barn and as if sensing his brother's lack of purpose, he turned and said, "If you don't have anything better to do, Logan, I could use a hand to check the fencing."

Logan thought about all the work he had to catch up on, about how he wanted to tell Bella what had happened, but there was something about Noah's offer that felt too precious to turn down. A shared moment that he knew instinctively would cement everything that had been said.

They saddled up and rode out to the perimeter, but the further they went it felt more like an excuse to get away out into the open and let everything sink in. Noah barely glanced at the fencing.

They didn't talk about much, just felt the afternoon sun on their backs and the chill air in their lungs. For Logan it was good just to be out riding again. He couldn't remember the last time. Didn't realize how much he'd missed it until all the easy familiarity of it came back. Although he felt annoyingly out of practice next to Noah who wouldn't ever get down from his horse if he didn't have to.

At one point, Noah made a show of hanging back so that Logan—who had actually slowed to take in the scenery—could catch up, and said, "If it's too much for you, bro…"

Which led to them galloping side by side fast as they could go on the scrubby stretch of grass, Noah edging ahead, Logan, muscles burning, T-shirt sweat-soaked, urging the little chestnut mare, Jo-Jo, forward. And she almost caught them up, but Logan had to admit defeat as the river up ahead cut off their path.

"That felt good," he said, breathlessly, leading Jo-Jo over to the water for a drink and jumping down to splash some on his face.

Noah stayed in the saddle. The exertion was nothing to him. "What did you think about all that, back there in the house?" he asked, gesturing away into the distance back the way they'd come.

"Good, I thought." Logan put his hat back on and hoisted himself back up. "You?"

Noah shrugged. "Yeah, good."

Logan smiled to himself. He said, "What's this about you holed up in the trailer?"

Noah said, "What's this about you having dinner with Bella?"

"Touché." Logan laughed.

"You stay out of my business, I'll stay out of yours."

"Wasn't that what we just said we'd change?"

Noah pulled his hat lower and turned his horse away. "I think we said Dad was a bad loser, Brodie was a drifter and we had to find Ethan."

Logan rolled his eyes as he tugged Jo-Jo's reins and went after him.

Noah glanced over his shoulder. "I'm totally fine, Logan."

"I'm sure you are, Noah," he replied, as his horse drew up level.

They trotted back in the direction of the house.

About halfway home, Noah said, "That dinner with Bella as cozy as it looked in the paper?"

It was Logan's turn to shrug, noncommittal.

"You ever gonna admit you like her?"

His head whipped around, caught off-guard by the casualness of the comment. "I don't know what you're talking about."

The first real easy smile spread across Noah's face. "I think you're blushing, Logan."

"I'm just hot, Noah."

"Sure you are," he laughed.

Chapter Thirty-Four

This time, when Logan drew up at the orchard, he said to John-Luke, "I'm not staying long, I promise. I just wanted a quick word with Bella."

John-Luke sighed and said, "It's okay, Logan. I was probably a little overprotective last time."

Logan shrugged. "It's understandable."

"I just don't want to see her hurt again."

"No," Logan replied, meeting the older man's steady gaze, "Neither do I."

Appeased enough, John-Luke nodded and led Logan through to the orchard where he gestured over to the left and said, "She's up a ladder somewhere in that direction."

Logan wove his way through the trees, the low winter sun flickering through the bare branches.

When he saw Bella, he paused for a moment before saying hello just to take in the image of her, her long hair tied up with tendrils around her face, the collar of her jacket turned up against the icy cold, the pinkness of her cheeks and the tip of her nose, the cloud her breath made when she breathed.

But clearly sensing someone was there, she swung around and nearly fell off her ladder when she saw him. He rushed forward to hold it steady. "Sorry," he said, "I didn't mean to startle you."

She regained her balance and climbed down. "Just for future reference, Logan," she said, "sneaking up on people when they're up a ladder tends to startle them."

"Noted," he replied with a wry half-smile. Then gesturing to her clothes said, "This apple farm look suits you."

She swept her hair away from her face. "I'm not sure if that's a compliment or not."

"It's a compliment," he replied, tipping his head, lazy smile playing on his lips.

She threw him a sidelong look and walked over to where there was a bottle of water on the floor by a stack of branches. "I'm presuming you didn't come here to talk about my fashion choices, Logan."

"No," he replied. "I came to say that I tried again. With Mom's help."

She paused, water bottle paused at her lips. "And?"

"And he shook my hand."

Bella choked on her water, had to cough a couple of times before saying, astounded, "He didn't?"

Logan laughed at her reaction. "He did. And I think he might have even smiled."

Bella screwed the cap on the water and put it back on

the ground, then she slipped her hands in her back pockets and said, "That's brilliant, Logan," her gaze soft and genuine as it met his. "I'm really pleased for you."

"Thanks," he said. "I couldn't have made any move without you, so thanks for pushing me to do it, I appreciate it."

"I think you'd have gotten there in the end."

"I wouldn't be so sure," he replied.

When she looked at him, he could feel the scrutiny of her big brown, all-seeing eyes, like she could see inside him, knew how out of his comfort zone he was, awkward—vulnerable even—having to confront all these feelings.

He had to glance away, focused on the surroundings instead. "How's the pruning?"

"Tiring," she replied. "Have you seen how many trees there are?"

He laughed, taking in the endless branches, rising like broomsticks all around them.

Then as they stood facing each other under apple boughs, he said, "You know there aren't many people that I really trust enough to listen to and act on what they say."

She tipped her head, assessing him, checking his sincerity, then nodded like she understood, appreciated the magnitude of what it meant to him. "I know."

He said, "I've missed having you in my life, being your friend."

There was a pause. He added, "And I appreciate we might not be friends after everything, but I've still missed—"

She cut him off, "We're friends, Logan."

"Yeah?" He found himself smiling unexpectedly, warmth flooding through him.

"Yeah," she replied, her lips twisting, eyes glinting in amusement.

Chapter Thirty-Five

It was after dinner that things felt really different at the ranch.

When they'd cleared the dishes away, instead of going back outside as was his usual routine, to the brothers' surprise, Emmett stayed at the table. He even went and got the good bourbon off the shelf.

Logan gave his mom a surreptitious look of amazement, but she just smiled, like she wasn't too surprised, she knew the possibility was there deep down. Then she stood up and said, "Well, I'm off to the new yoga class at the church hall."

Noah made a face like that was the weirdest thing he'd ever heard.

Emmett frowned. "Really?"

"Yes," she replied innocently, going over to get her car keys from the bowl on the kitchen counter and picking up a gym bag that she'd obviously packed ready to go. "You boys have fun!" she called as she headed for the front door.

The three of them watched her go from where they sat

around the table. Logan felt a small lump of panic creep up his throat. They needed her. She was their safety net. The buffer between them and their dad, the linchpin they could all focus on.

Logan cleared his throat but suddenly didn't know what to say.

Emmett concentrated on pouring the whiskey into three lowball glasses.

It was Noah who said, "Logan got Jo-Jo moving."

His dad glanced up. "You did?"

Logan frowned. "Yeah. She's quick. Responsive. I didn't know she was a problem."

"She's been stubborn and temperamental since she arrived," Emmett said, passing out the glasses. "Doesn't let half the people here within three feet of her."

Logan looked incredulously at Noah. "Why didn't you tell me?"

Noah grinned over the rim of his whiskey glass.

Emmett swirled the deep amber liquid in his and said, "Maybe you should take her down to the Silver H, see what she's like on the pitch?"

From anyone else it would be a throwaway suggestion, but to Logan it felt like a peace offering. A return to the type of conversations they used to have around this table. "Maybe I will."

His dad nodded, taking a sip of the bourbon.

And from that point, it was like they'd been handed the freedom to reminisce. To remember the worst and the best of the horses they'd ever bought; Bumblebee always the flat-out winner because they'd hand-reared her when she'd been orphaned at birth, she'd sat with the boys as a tiny foal and watched TV with them.

"Do you remember that bull, Winslow?" Logan said and his dad groaned. "He escaped and that woman from the diner—"

"Loriana?"

"Yeah, Loriana, she still around?"

Emmett nodded and Logan carried on. "She rang because Winslow was charging up and down Main Street chasing cyclists."

They all laughed.

They were memories that Logan didn't even know he had, which came from a time before the band that he barely thought about.

As the evening went on, they even slipped into talk about the band itself. Accidental at first, when Noah compared something to how embarrassing their audition had been.

Logan cringed, waiting for the reproachful well-you-shouldn't-have-done-it-then glare across the table, but it didn't come. Emmett just refilled their glasses. Logan could see his dad was trying, even asked how things were going at the label and Logan replied honestly—that it was good, better than good, even—without fearing Emmett's silent, guilt-inducing departure from the room.

If he was honest, Logan still wouldn't dare mention the money they'd made or the loan he'd paid off on the ranch without his dad's knowledge, but he did notice that the hay barn had a new roof so maybe some of the money he'd put in the account was finally being spent, even if begrudgingly.

And maybe one day things would change and they would talk about it, because clearly things could change; he certainly didn't think there would ever be a time he'd be sitting around the table as his dad said things like, "And you had to name the darn band Silver Sky. Had them here all the time." Emmett sat back in his chair, long legs stretched out under the table. "Selfies at the gate."

Noah frowned. "Since when did you know the word selfie, Dad?"

Emmett ignored him. "Do you know how often they stole that star on the front? They still come, you know that?" His eyes widened accusingly across the table at Logan. "Your mom gives them coffee."

Logan's mouth twitched at the idea of his dad being forced to socialize with the die-hard fans. He laughed, couldn't help himself. "Sorry."

"It's not funny." Emmett raised his brows disapprovingly.

"It is kind of funny," Noah offered.

Emmett rolled his eyes. "Pain in the backside, that's what it was."

Noah's eyes met Logan's across the table sparking with amusement, while at the same time an almost boyish grin appeared on his dad's lips, something Logan hadn't seen in years.

It made him feel suddenly hopeful. The fact that things he thought were set in stone weren't necessarily.

It made him think of Bella. The eternal gratitude he owed her for forcing it all into motion. For having the courage to challenge him when no one else would.

Chapter Thirty-Six

Logan lay on his bed staring out at the view of the mountain, a black shadow on a gray sky. The full moon casting an eerie glow over the horizon. He couldn't sleep, his mind was too busy with everything that had happened, everything that had been said. He'd be back in the city tomorrow, no more mountain, no more bike, no more Autumn Falls.

He got out of bed and pulled on his clothes, then strode through the unlit house, down the stairs, shrugged on his jacket and went out to the garage. The bike was waiting like a bird of prey, patient yet eager to spread its wings.

Frost glittered on the road as Logan cruised down Main Street. The shops all shuttered, the sidewalks empty.

He told himself he didn't know where he was headed, and again the bike took him where he wanted to go.

He drew up at the side of the house, underneath her bedroom window, where he used to throw stones at the glass to get her to come out as a teenager.

Searching the ground for a decent-sized pebble, he picked one up from the curbside and threw it so it tapped and bounced from the glass.

Nothing.

He had to do it three times before the window opened, Bella squinting down at him, hair ruffled and bleary-eyed from sleep. "What are you doing here? What time is it?"

"Do you want to go for a drive?" he said, looking up, feeling suddenly foolish, wondering if this was a really bad idea as she looked at him with sleepy confusion—that he'd relied too heavily on the nostalgic memory of their teenage selves.

She rubbed her eyes and, running a hand through her hair, glanced back to the warmth of her bedroom.

His heart paused, breath stilled.

She looked back, eyes narrowing down at where he stood, at the bike poised beside him.

And he watched as slowly a smile started to spread across her face and she said, "Give me five minutes to get dressed."

Logan felt like punching the air.

Less than five minutes later, Bella came dashing out the front door, wearing leggings and sneakers, and the navy-blue coat she'd worn the other day when they'd sat in the orchard.

"This is not the way to get into John-Luke's good books," she said breathlessly.

Logan handed her a helmet. "We just have to not get caught."

She laughed as she climbed on the back of the bike. The

cuffs of her big black sweater hung down from the sleeves of her coat making just the tips of her fingers visible when she gripped his shoulders. "This is fun!" she said, wiggling closer to him to get comfortable.

Logan narrowed his eyes. "It's not fun, Bella, it's fast and furious."

She scoffed. "Please!"

He hit the throttle with more pressure than necessary and the bike sped away from the curb. Caught off-guard, Bella screeched at the speed and had to grab hold tight around his waist. When he slowed down to normal, she bashed him on the back. "Don't do that!"

"Sorry." He grinned but pressed the accelerator harder again, hurtling them down the wide, empty road toward the mountain, but this time she was ready and he could hear her laughing, feel it in her body behind him, her hands locked snugly around him, her chin pressed into his shoulder so she could see what was happening up ahead.

They drove out for miles, the moon lighting the way, flecks of snow swirling in the air around them encased by the pine trees, fronds dusted with frost, that darkened the roadside.

When they reached the base of the mountain he pulled over. Bella tugged off her helmet. "That was amazing."

Logan could have driven on forever.

It was too cold to sit so they walked along the side of the Redemption, the tang of fresh cold river water and pine in the air. Snow started falling gently, speckling their clothes, melting into their hair.

When they heard the roar of the waterfall in the

distance, Bella sped up, glancing excitedly at him and saying, "Do you hear that, Logan?"

They climbed up the rocky path, ice glistening on the needles of the pines, and came out at a ledge just underneath the top of Autumn Falls, the endless cascade of water almost white in the moonlight.

"Wow!" Bella gasped with delight, icy spray kicking back, stinging their faces.

Logan couldn't work out whether to look at her or the waterfall.

"When was the last time you swam here?" she asked, staring up at the falling rapids.

"Couldn't tell you," he replied. "Ten years ago? More, probably."

They moved closer to the edge and both looked down at the pool beneath them, the falling snow merging with the frothy spray. Bella threw a stone, they watched it plummet, the rings on the surface as it plunged to the bottom. The moon was high above them, casting shadows and blackening the water like tar.

When she let her hand drop back, her fingers unexpectedly grazed the back of his.

The contact caught his attention, he stared at where their hands met, then up to where she had looked to. The sudden sparking current between them made his breath catch, the feel of the cold skin against his stirred a sudden longing to gather her closer.

He found himself saying, "Maybe we could try again? Would you have dinner with me when we're back in New York?"

There was a pause.

"I'm not going back, Logan," she said, moving her hand away to brush a flake from her cheek.

He felt his whole body tighten. "What?"

She shoved her hands into her pockets and looked up at him. "I'm not going back."

"Where are you going?" This didn't make sense. He frowned down at her, this was meant to be all good, this was change, friendship, this was putting the past behind them and moving on.

"I don't know. Away—I'm going to travel. I don't want to be in New York anymore. I don't feel like that person anymore." She tucked her hair behind her ears like it was something to do rather than look at him.

Logan couldn't understand. The waterfall roared in his ears. "Why didn't you tell me?"

The snow fell heavier, dusting the shoulders of her coat, resting on her hair, on her eyelashes. The blanket of white dusting away their footprints. "Because I knew it would be really hard."

He looked down at the sheer drop to the pool. He wanted to tell her that she couldn't go. That he wouldn't let her. That she had to come back to New York, while at the same time knowing the impossibility of it. Knowing he wasn't and never would be that person. But he did find himself saying, almost in a whisper, "What about—" He was going to say *us*, but there wasn't an us, he knew that too well.

She took a step closer and smiled sadly up at him. He didn't want to hear what she was about to say. Didn't want it confirmed what he knew deep down by having it said out loud.

"There will always be a photographer, Logan, always someone waiting with a comment or a judgment."

He felt his jaw clench, wanted to dispute it but couldn't find the words. He watched her throat as she swallowed, the sweetness of her eyes as she tried to keep it light. "Being with me will ruin your reputation with some people. You won't always be the good guy. You won't always be in control." Her eyes glistened, snow settled on her lashes, and she reached up and her cool hand touched his cheek. "I know you, Logan, it will eat you up and then it will just be another life spent running away."

Chapter Thirty-Seven

Logan sat at his desk eyes narrowed at his computer screen. On it, side by side, was the picture of him with Bella in the restaurant, him looking furiously at the camera. Next to it, he'd placed a picture published that morning of Bella and Brodie. She'd met up with his brother in Sydney and they were walking side by side on Bondi Beach, looking happy and relaxed as they smiled at the camera, Bella's skin glowing with the touch of golden summer.

He was so lost in the comparison between the two images that he didn't hear Marianne come in.

As she put some papers down on his desk, he saw her eye glance to the photographs on his computer screen. He couldn't have closed the browser quick enough to stop her seeing it. He huffed a laugh at the fact he'd been caught, exactly as he had caught her when the first picture came out.

Marianne nodded toward the more recent photograph and said, "Bella looks happy."

Logan ran his hand over his face. "The story's pairing her up with Brodie now."

Marianne tutted in annoyance. "Of course it is."

Logan of course had bristled when he'd read it, but he'd already had a message from Brodie telling him what a great time they'd had together, and that he'd finally learned to surf. He'd mentioned the picture as an afterthought, said the same thing as Marianne just had, how lovely Bella looked in it. Logan found it hard to look at it objectively, every part of him tingling to have a retraction printed by the press, to have the record set straight. He was reacting, he realized irritatingly, exactly as Bella had predicted.

Marianne tapped the contracts she'd put on his desk and said, "These both need your signature." Then she walked away, back across the office.

Logan picked up the papers, then out the corner of his eye he saw her pause, hesitate for a second and turn back to say, "Logan, do you mind if I sit down for a moment?"

He tipped his head in surprise. Marianne had worked for him his whole business life and she had never once asked permission for anything. "Be my guest," he said, and gestured to the seat opposite him.

Marianne came back across and sat down, pushing up the sleeves of her navy suit jacket then removing her thick-framed glasses.

Logan sat back, watching her consider how best to say what she was intending to say.

"Logan, it's none of my business what you do." She folded her glasses in her hand.

He raised a brow. "But presumably you're going to tell me anyway?"

She ignored the retort, crossing her legs and smoothing her suit skirt. "I should have retired years ago, Logan, I'm only still here because I didn't want to play endless golf with my husband." She made a face and Logan laughed.

"But he's wearing me down," Marianne went on. "I'll give it up soon and join him out there on the course. Life's too short not to spend it with those that you love. That's what he tells me, anyway." She gave a wry little smile.

Logan folded his arms, waiting for what wisdom was surely about to come.

"Logan, I've also stayed so long because I like you."

His eyes widened. That wasn't what he was expecting her to say.

"And because of that," she said, "I don't really like seeing you unhappy."

"I'm not unhappy, Marianne," Logan waved the concern away on instinct. "Don't worry."

"Logan, please," she said in a tone a schoolteacher might use when gently reprimanding a student.

He smirked at it.

Marianne kept up the teacherly stare.

"Go on, then," Logan said, settling back in his chair. "What do you think I should do?"

She lifted her hands. "I didn't come in here to tell you what to do."

"No, you came in to bring me these contracts to sign, but look at us now."

She ignored him. "What I want to say is, whatever you do, don't let it be because of that—" She pointed to the pictures on the screen. "Don't let the press dictate the way you live your life, Logan."

There was silence for a moment.

He looked at her over the desk, mouth rested against steepled fingertips. Then he sat back and said, "So what do you propose I do?"

Marianne frowned. "I don't want to overstep the mark by giving you too much advice."

"You're well over the mark, Marianne. Go ahead."

She thought for a moment, then said, "For as long as I've known you, Logan, you've always done everything for everyone else—which is no bad thing. You're a good boss, everyone enjoys working here, your artists are happy, you keep your siblings in vague degrees of order."

He snorted a laugh.

She suppressed a smile, eyes watching him with fond amusement. "I wonder, though, whether it might be time to do not what you're supposed to do—not what's right or fair or just—but what *you* want to do. Maybe it's time to do something for yourself."

He sat still, letting the words sink in.

Marianne slipped her glasses back on. "You're a good man, Logan."

He glanced up, not quite certain that was the truth.

She smiled fondly, said again a little more softly, "You *are* a good man and there is no point punishing yourself any longer for things that have already happened. After everything, I think most of all, you deserve to be happy."

Then she stood up, smoothing down her skirt, and said dryly, "I've definitely overstepped the mark now."

Logan laughed.

When she got to the door, she added, "By the way, I always liked Bella the best out of everyone."

"Subtle, Marianne, very subtle."

Chapter Thirty-Eight

Bella ended her travels back in Autumn Falls. And she loved every minute of being back. She spent a couple of days hanging out with her mom and John-Luke, having dinner in The Firestone or coffee in the orchard sunroom with Heather before her shift at the hospital, and lazy strolls through the apple trees, the air heavy with the hum of bees and the blossom soft like cotton candy.

One day she went for a walk on her own with no true purpose, and found herself on Main Street, feeling less like a tourist and more like a resident.

She paused outside Joe's Diner and looked in at the owner, Loriana, waiting tables. She thought how last year she had walked on, believing she'd been deliberately ignored and maybe she had been, but this time she didn't put her head down and walk past, she didn't hide away ashamed and afraid of other people's gossip. She went in, head high and sat down at one of the vacant tables. When Loriana came past carrying vast stacks of pancakes, she paused when she saw her and said, "Oh, Bella, just the person! Could you do me a favor and tell your mom that I'll be about an hour late tonight? I keep meaning to message her, but I'm rushed off my feet."

"Yeah, sure," Bella replied, a little taken aback by the casualness as Loriana carried on to deliver the precariously balanced plates to another table. It seemed to put so clearly into perspective how everyone was just getting on with their own lives, just rolling forward. Maybe a year ago Loriana *had* deliberately ignored her but now she needed a messenger. They were peripheral characters in each other's lives and Bella could choose to take things as they were, there and then, or get hung up on the past. It was a no-brainer. So when Loriana came back to take her order, Bella said, "How are things?"

Loriana had one eye on a bunch of people who'd just walked in through the door. "Oh, busy, always busy! How are you getting on, honey? What can I get you?"

"Just a coffee, thanks."

"Lovely, be right back."

The encounter at the diner inspired her to pop in and see Dusty in The Music Box afterwards. She took him a coffee and his eyes lit up when he saw her, clearing a stack of papers off a chair for her to sit down. She should have been in months ago, she realized. She told him all about her travels while he fixed a guitar wearing three different pairs of repair magnifying glasses on his head. Then later, in the early afternoon, she borrowed her mom's car and drove out to the pine forests. She walked along the river, spring flowers bathing the banks, and climbed up to the waterfall where she remembered standing with Logan in the falling snow. She realized she didn't have to go all the way to the other side of the world to find the normality—the peace—she was looking for.

And yes, on the way back, she might have driven past Logan's house, just for a casual glance, and of course found it shuttered up as always. But she carried on till she got back into town where she pulled up in front of the theater. Stepping out the car, she took a deep, reassuring breath and then pushed open the ornate doors of the old Art Deco building, the exact opposite of the bare concrete brutalist theater she'd worked at in New York. Passing the ticket booth, she went through the *staff only* door to the wardrobe room.

Claudette was leaning over the huge wooden table, spreading out pattern paper and holding it in place with whatever she could find. When she heard the door she said, "Alice, what have you forgotten this time?"

"I'm not Alice."

Claudette gasped. "Bella! You're back! And you're so tanned! Oh, that's so unfair!" she sighed at the sight of her then enveloped her in a giant hug. "Did you have a wonderful time?" she asked into her hair. "I'm so jealous."

Bella nodded, "I did."

Claudette let her go and stood back. "You look *really* well," she said, sounding more surprised than Bella would have hoped for. Then she went off to the little kitchen and made them both coffee. Coming back, she dragged over another high stool so they could sit by the cutting table. "So, tell me all about it!" Then, before Bella could answer, said, "How long are you staying?"

Bella bit her lip. "I'm thinking maybe forever."

"No!" Claudette's face lit up. "That's so exciting! That could literally be the best news I've ever heard!" She paused, eyes narrowing with suspicion before adding, "Are you serious?"

Bella nodded.

Claudette looked around the cluttered workshop and, holding her arms wide, said, "You could come and work here!"

Bella felt her stomach flip. "That was actually one of the reasons I came by."

"The first being to see me, your friend, yes?"

"Yes," Bella agreed.

Claudette widened her eyes like she wasn't quite convinced. But then her face broke into a smile again as she said, "We could have so much fun if you worked here!"

Bella nodded, eyes alight, the plan that hadn't even been definite when she walked in, coming together too easily.

Claudette screwed up her nose. "I won't be able to pay you very much."

Bella shook her head. "I don't need very much."

Claudette clapped with delight.

Chapter Thirty-Nine

Logan stood in front of his office window, looking out at the skyscrapers like building blocks. The Empire State Building piercing the clouds. A metropolis of stepping stones he could leap across to freedom.

He glanced at the clock.

Five minutes.

He went back to his desk, straightened up the laptop and water glass, aligning them with the notebook. Then he sat back in his leather chair and put his hands in his pockets.

His fingers touched on the cool metal of the signet ring. He'd taken to carrying it with him everywhere. He took it out and placed it in the center of the yellow notepad.

He thought back to where he'd found it in the pool house of Jack's place, along with the photograph of the day at the polo, the one where Jack had folded Logan's image back.

He thought about the photo: him, Bella and Jack, all their grinning, youthful faces.

Keeping his gaze on the signet ring, Logan reclined back in his chair. He tried to picture his brother riffling through his stuff to take it, slipping it into his own pocket and having it all those years.

He saw all the envy and the competitiveness, the jostling for hierarchy, the secrets and the hurt. But he also saw the little kid with the dirty-blond hair and the scrunched forehead desperately determined to keep up. He saw the brother he'd played baseball and polo with out in the fields, hidden within the barn, their bodies shaking with suppressed nervous laughter as their dad shouted for them to get back to work. He saw the friend who, despite what else had happened, had been a polo teammate, had made them laugh on the tour bus with his quick comebacks and his limit-pushing and his cocky swagger. Yet he had also been cruel and bullish and overly thirsty for his own gain. Everything that was once bright was now tinged forever with a veil of gray.

Logan stared at the ring, his jaw tight with all the conflicting emotions. He breathed out through his nose and said, "I'm sorry."

Of course, he didn't expect the ring to reply but Logan nodded all the same. After a moment he felt a sad smile pull on the edge of his lips. "And yes, I accept your apology, as well."

Then he reached forward and, picking the ring up, slipped it onto his little finger, absently rubbing the dented band at the back with his thumb.

There was a short rap at the door and Marianne poked her head around. "Ready, Logan?"

Logan stood up, buttoned his suit jacket and said, "Ready."

Chapter Forty

In the spring, Main Street lit up like a film set. Sunshine reflected off the big chrome theater sign, illuminated the old cola advert painted on the side of the diner, and twinkled in the mist soaking the bouquets outside the florist. Bella drank it all in as she walked to the theater, carrying three coffees in a cardboard tray.

A battered green pickup drove past and she recognized Noah Carter at the wheel.

He didn't wave or anything so she presumed he hadn't seen her and she kept on walking in the direction of the theater. Seeing any of the Carters made her think of Logan and that made the healing wound in her heart open just a little bit.

Then she watched as the truck cruised to a stop just ahead of her.

When she got closer, Noah took off his aviators, tanned arm resting along the window. "I heard you were in town."

Seeing Noah always made her smile. He took everything

in, saw what was going on in the world, let it play out. "Yeah, I'm back," she replied.

Noah nodded. He glanced up ahead at the mountains. When he looked back at Bella there was a hint of a smile on his face. "Logan'll be happy to hear that."

She felt a sudden hot rush of anticipation that Logan was in town or about to be in town. But she put a stop to it immediately. She couldn't wait around on the off chance of a fleeting visit from the great Logan Carter. No. She was definitely done with that. "Oh, I don't think Logan will be too bothered." She could feel she was blushing and tucked her hair behind her ear self-consciously.

Noah didn't contradict her, just tapped the steering wheel with his fingers.

To Bella, it felt like he had something else to say but she certainly wasn't going to press him for it. She had some pride. So she nodded toward the coffees in her hand and said, "I'd better go. It was nice to see you, Noah."

"You, too, Bella," he replied, slipping his aviators back on.

She started walking, really wanting to know what it was he was going to say. The truck cruised along next to her, picking up speed ready to drive off.

Then she heard Noah say, "You see him on the news?"

She stopped. The truck stopped. "See who?"

Noah grinned. "Logan." Then he drove off.

Chapter Forty-One

Bella practically ran the rest of the way back to the theater, sloshing the coffee as she put the tray down on the counter in her hurry to get her phone out of her pocket.

Claudette jumped up from her seat, waving the scissors in her hand, looking around as if there was an emergency. "What's going on?"

"There's your coffee," Bella said absently, searching on her phone for Logan's name.

She clicked on the first news video that had Logan in it.

Claudette peered over her shoulder. "What's happened?"

"Shush!" Bella waved her hand at her to be quiet.

Intern Alice hovered behind them.

Bella turned the sound up on Logan as he was saying, "Over the years there have been a number of offers made for Carter Media. They've always been great offers from some great companies—so the possibility's always been there—but it's never been the right time." He was wearing his suit and tie, slick and confident, looking straight at the camera. "Now feels like the right time."

Bella's heart paused.

The interviewer nodded. "And I'm told there were a number of rival bids."

Logan tipped his head diplomatically. "There were a few."

She could barely believe what she was hearing.

The interviewer chuckled. "Am I also right in thinking you didn't actually sell to the highest bidder?"

"What you're right in thinking is that I would only hand over the reins of the company I've built, in an industry I've grown up in, to people renowned for taking great care of their artists and employees, who have long and trusted relationships in the business. For me to sell the company it had to be with the core values and long-term vision front and center."

Bella's hand was on her chest, a smile she didn't realize she was smiling on her face. "Did he just say he'd sold the company?"

Claudette took the lid off her coffee and blew on it. "That's exactly what he said."

Bella stared wide-eyed at Logan on camera. How could he look so impassive?

The interviewer said, "Not so long ago you were reported as saying on a podcast that you'd never think about stopping because, and I quote, 'life's great.'"

"And it was. It is. But life has that annoying habit of changing." Logan's eyes twinkled.

Bella covered her mouth, watching on tenterhooks as if the ending still might not turn out how she hoped.

Intern Alice slurped her coffee. Claudette shushed her.

"When you talk about change, Logan, I'm sorry to ask but are you referring to the death of your brother, Jack."

Bella tensed and Claudette put her hand gently on her shoulder.

Logan didn't flinch. "I think it's made all of us pause and take stock. Shown us what's most important in life."

"I'm sorry to bring this up, Logan, but there's been a bit of gossip about you lately—"

Logan cut him off. "There will always be gossip, people like to talk, I just don't need to hear it. It's taken me a long time to learn not to listen."

For a second, Bella could hear only her heartbeat.

"So, what now for you, Logan?"

"Well, I've been in this business since I was eighteen years old, I figure it's time for a bit of a change."

"And what does a bit of a change look like?"

"The exact opposite of this." He sat back, his arms wide, gesturing to the office around him.

Lots of laughter.

"Seriously," the interviewer pushed.

"I don't know yet. Maybe I'll just do nothing for a bit." For the first time ever, Logan smiled wide at the camera.

The video clip ended.

Bella's hand clutched around the phone. A grin to mirror Logan's on her face.

"Well, that's exciting," said Claudette, fixing Bella with a knowing look, then putting the lid back on her coffee and taking it with her to the workbench. "Good for him."

Bella stood for a moment, feeling the warmth of his decision spread through her. The lightness of his face when he smiled. If it was ever only that one small thing that she did for him, it could be enough. "Yes," she said. "Good for him."

Chapter Forty-Two

Bella was running along the bank of the Redemption when her phone rang. She went there for the space at the end of her workday, to drink in the light. When she heard the call cut in over her headphones, she let it ring out. She'd only been running for twenty minutes.

Her voicemail kicked in.

She carried on running. This was the new her, lots of running and yoga and cycling. She realized that what she had loved about both her time away and being back in Autumn Falls, was the space, the majesty of the landscape that made her remember her own insignificance while at the same time somehow making her value herself more than she ever had. It reminded her to be the person who smiled at the camera.

Her phone, which she wore in an armband with a clear plastic cover when she ran, rang again. She made an awkward attempt to see who it was by lifting her elbow and craning her neck around. When she saw Logan's name flashing on the screen, she stopped still.

It kept ringing.

She went over to a fallen tree and sat down, slipping the phone out of the plastic case.

It stopped.

Just over a month had passed since she'd watched him talking on the video about selling Carter Media. A month of glancing hopefully at the screen on her phone every time there was a message or a call—but telling herself she wasn't doing just that—until this moment, when she hadn't been expecting it at all.

She took a swig from her water bottle. Could she talk to him? What would she say? Part of her said ignore it, the other part traitorously pricked up its ears with excitement. She pushed the water-bottle cap back down with the palm of her hand.

Her work at the theater was so busy, so much to do and such a small team, that she didn't have much time to think about him during the day. But at night. At night her mind drifted off with endless possibilities.

Closing her eyes she ran the cool water bottle across her forehead.

The phone rang again.

Opening her eyes she looked across at the trees and the light dancing between the pines. Then suddenly she reached forward and pressed the answer key. As if her fingers had a life of their own.

"Hello."

Nothing.

Then a deep, drawling laugh. "I wondered how long it would take you to pick up."

She felt an involuntary smile tug at the corners of her mouth and tried to hide it in her voice. "Oh, no, I just had it on silent."

There was that laugh again. "If you say so, Bella."

She felt herself start to blush and fanned her face to cool down.

"So, you're a free man," she said.

"I am indeed."

She smiled again at his voice, drawing her legs up on the fallen log, she wrapped her hands around her shins. "How are you finding having nothing to do?"

"Yeah, I'm not coping that well with that," he said ruefully.

Bella looked across at the river, the water rippling over the rocks. Life moving on while hers felt stilled in that moment with that voice.

"So, what can I do for you, Logan?"

He didn't answer immediately. She could hear from the background noise that he was outside. "When I set up Carter Media, all five of us were investors."

"Right." She frowned, this was not what she'd been expecting him to be calling her about. She sat forward, engaging her brain.

"Jack had money in the business, Bella, which presumably he didn't mention because he didn't want me or any of us to know that he was having money trouble."

She bit her lip. Tried to think about what this meant, having to get her lawyers back on the case.

"By selling the business, each of the investors gets their share—as of course you know. I've spoken to Jack's lawyers, Bella, and we've used his share to pay off the outstanding debts that he'd accrued."

"Okay." She sat back, looked up at the sky. "That's a relief." She hated that there were people left owing after he died.

"The rest Bella, what's left after those debts are paid, is your money."

She made a face. "No, it's Jack's money. I don't want it."

"No, Bella." Logan's voice was firm. "It's your money. It's money owed to you as part of your divorce settlement."

She felt tears press against the back of her eyes. "Logan, I don't want his money."

"Then give it to a good cause. But the money is rightfully yours. *By law*, it is yours."

She pressed her hand against her forehead. "Okay. Thank you." She knew that she would give it away. She would find a charity that helped women who didn't have the support that she'd had from her family and friends when in desperate need of help.

There was a pause before he said, "It's the least I could do."

She said, "It's good that it's done."

Neither of them spoke.

She tucked her hair behind her ear, stared down at the scrubby forest ground beneath her feet. She couldn't help a vague sadness that it felt like she was one of the loose ends Logan was tying up. "Okay, well…"

"I also called to invite you to a party."

"A party?" Another thing she wasn't expecting. She had started to stand up from the fallen tree and immediately sat back down again.

"Yes." Amusement laced his voice.

"Where?" She cocked her head in confusion. "I'm not in New York, Logan."

"Neither will I be soon. I bought the polo club. The Silver H."

"In Autumn Falls?"

She heard his name being called, and for a second he was clearly distracted. "Listen, I'm going to send you an invite to the grand reopening, whether you decide to come or not is up to you."

Her brain was still catching up. "You bought the club?"

"Yeah, I told you I'm terrible at doing nothing."

Bella sat back, wide-eyed. "Oh, my goodness, Logan."

"The invite's in the post." He hung up on a deep laugh.

She bit her lip and smiled. The conversation couldn't have lasted more than five minutes, but it had been enough to spin her world on its axis again. He'd bought the Silver H Polo Club. Did that mean he would be back living in Autumn Falls? Why would he invite her to the party and not just meet up with her? Was it a way of getting their first meeting over with, out in the open? She went back to her phone and googled "Logan" and "polo." Sure enough, his acquisition of the club was there in black and white. There was a letter on the club's website written by Logan, talking about preserving the history of the place while also investing in facilities, looking to broaden the scope of the club, his new coaching role and many new initiatives, including free youth classes and scholarships to encourage young kids of different financial backgrounds to enjoy the sport.

Wow. She stared up at the towering pines, dumbfounded. Logan had finally recaptured his dream.

Chapter Forty-Three

The invitation arrived at the theater. There was one for Claudette, too. The envelopes were thick and cream and inside the card was embossed black lettering. Bella turned hers over but there was nothing else written on it aside from the standard print. No sign that Logan had had anything to do with it, no scrawled, personalized note or signature. She felt silly for building herself up to be a bit special when it was just an invite to a corporate event.

Claudette plucked Bella's invite out of her hands and inspected it. "You'd think he would write a note."

Bella shrugged like she hadn't just been thinking that at all. "That would make it too personal. He's using it for what it is—a good neutral place for us to be in the same room together."

Intern Alice nodded, pins in her mouth as she spoke. "Especially if the press are there."

"Yes, exactly!" Bella agreed, wishing it didn't make quite

so much sense. Then she paused and said, "But I don't think Logan would invite the press."

Claudette scoffed, chucking the invitation down on the table. "Either it's nothing or it's something. Either way—" she glanced up with mischief in her eyes "—you're going to need a *very* good dress."

There was a pause before Bella cottoned on and then they all started walking, slow at first and then speeding up to almost a dash out the wardrobe workshop and up a flight of stairs to the costume store.

It was nothing like the one in New York, where delicate costumes hung in sealed bags, beautifully arranged on endless racks and all carefully labeled.

Their room was barely-organized chaos. Outfits squeezed into minimal space, boxes teetering lethally up to the ceiling, old papier mâché puppet heads hanging and laughing eerily down at them from the rafters.

The three of them rushed in like giddy children, nudging one another out the way to get to the bursting rails.

Bella skimmed through hangers, immediately realizing what a bad idea it was when all she could find were bright, flouncy dresses that had been made for *Oklahoma!* or ruffled Shakespearean shirts.

"How about this?" Intern Alice held up a 1950s polka dot skirt that looked just like the dresses she wore herself.

Bella shook her head as politely as she could.

"Over here," called Claudette from over in the far corner of the room. She pulled one of the polyethylene dress bags from the hanger. "I hoped this was still here."

They wound their way through the rails over to where Claudette hooked the bag so it lay flat against the other clothes on the rail and unzipped it with a flourish.

Bella gasped.

Intern Alice giggled with delight.

Inside the bag lay an eye-wateringly gorgeous dress. Claudette lifted it reverently out and held it up for them all to admire.

It wasn't a structured designer number with an inbuilt corset like Bella used to wear on the red carpet, but soft, gunmetal silk, whisper-thin straps and a low V neckline edged with a delicate strip of net. Nipped in at the waist, the skirt was gathered in tiny pleats at the front, then drifted lazily down to skim just below the knee.

When Bella reached forward to touch it, the material rippled through her fingers. It was the exact right dress—feminine but not overly showy, sensuous while at the same time coyly demure—waiting and ready for this very occasion. This moment.

Claudette's lips pouted, her eyes glinting with pride. "I made this," she purred. "It won't let you down."

Taking the dress from her, Bella held it up against her body and looked down at herself. The watery gray silk catching in the low light. "It's exquisite," she said.

"Yes," Claudette agreed. "It's the perfect dress."

Chapter Forty-Four

Logan wasn't a hundred per cent sure Bella was going to come. He was pretty sure, but not certain.

"Everything's ready, Mr. Carter."

Standing out by the stables, Logan nodded to the organizer, who stood with her clipboard smiling with polite efficiency.

"Thank you," he said, "I appreciate all your effort today."

"It's no problem at all, just doing my job." She gave a self-deprecating shrug and then ventured in a lighter tone, "You'll ruin your suit out here, Mr. Carter."

Logan had intended to go straight to the main clubhouse but got sidetracked by the horses. He was currently leaning over a stall chatting quietly to Jo-Jo, the feisty little beauty from Silver Sky who his dad had given Logan as a present when he announced the purchase of the club. Never had a single horse meant more. Logan looked back at the woman with her clipboard then down at himself, his jacket on one of the stable hooks, his sleeves rolled up, he'd be happy never to wear a suit again. "Yes, you're probably right."

She smiled endearingly, like she could sense the apprehension in him, then she turned to walk over to her car. "I hope it's a fabulous evening, Mr. Carter."

"Thank you." He paused for a second and looked over to the clubhouse, all decked out and ready. "So do I."

Chapter Forty-Five

There was a slight shake to Bella's hand as she put on her make-up. As she slipped on the dress and the fabric slithered like cool water over her skin. She thought about the polite hello that she and Logan would share amidst the crowds of people waiting to congratulate him.

When she was ready, John-Luke gave her a lift to the Silver H. He was coming to the party later when he'd picked up her mom from the hospital. In the car on the way he said, "Calm down, Bella. Take a deep breath."

She glanced down and saw her foot was tapping like crazy. Her hands were clammy, her heart thrumming. "I'm fine," she said, and he laughed like after all these years he knew her better than that.

He dropped her off by the path that led to the first field and the club house. It was a thirty-second walk that felt like eternity. Her emotions oscillating between fear and excitement. This could be everything or nothing. Because while it was most likely a polite reintroduction, a friendly kiss on the cheek in front of the Autumn Falls crowds, there was a chance it could be what she lay in bed at night dreaming it might be. She took long deep breaths, reminded herself that either way, it was okay, her heart had broken before and she had survived. She stroked the soft silk of her beautiful dress. Up ahead she could see where the path ended and the grass began, and she counted down the seconds.

Chapter Forty-Six

Music playing softly, Logan took the opportunity to sit down with his drink. His tie felt too tight, so he pulled it loose and undid his top button. The lighting across the whole club was low, string lights twinkled around the ceiling beams and threaded through the vines out the front.

He had an urge to get out of there and go back to see the horses. But he didn't want to leave in case she arrived. He closed his eyes for a second to block out the room, and wondered how he'd be feeling tomorrow.

Chapter Forty-Seven

The path carried on along the sideline of the field, lined with tealights in little paper bags flickering in the breeze, past the stables, toward the clubhouse. Perhaps she could just sneak in and see the horses, ignore the party? No. She was too caught up with the pulsing, nervous thrill of being in the same room with Logan again to do that.

Just outside the door she stopped, straightened the straps on her dress, ran her fingers through her hair and puffed it out a bit, trying to give herself an air of casual indifference. Then she put her shoulders back, breathed in, told herself she'd been through much tougher things than this, and pushed open the doors.

She walked into an empty room.

Logan stood up as she entered. Dressed like it was the end of the evening rather than the start, hair a little disheveled, shirt sleeves rolled up, top button undone. A drink untouched on the table next to him.

"Where is everyone?" Bella looked from side to side and

saw no one, just a beautifully decorated room with colorful hanging lanterns and strings of lights.

He didn't take his eyes off her. "Who?"

"The other guests."

A smile tilted the corner of his mouth. "They're coming later."

She frowned in bemused confusion. "So, it's just me?"

He nodded.

She didn't know what to say. Too perplexed to question it, just aware of all the apprehension vanishing and in its place, Logan walking toward her, unhurried but purposeful. Her brain tried to catch up, but her attention was caught only by the image of him as he got closer, filling her vision, kind eyes dancing with mischief and intent till he was there in front of her, close enough for her to breathe in and smell him, close enough for her to take a step forward and be closer.

"I um…" Her brain fought for some words. "I thought there'd be more. More people."

He shook his head, dark hair messily tousled over his forehead like he'd run his fingers through it nervously waiting for her to arrive.

She bit down on a growing smile.

He reached up and touched her hair, twirling a lock of it around his fingers. "I know what I want now," he said, without taking his eyes off hers.

"You do?" she replied.

There was a sliver of a gap between them. She could hear the sound of her heart, feel the prickle of anticipation on her skin, see the bright brilliant blue of his smiling eyes.

"It's not a lot," he said.

Cautiously, she lifted her hand, let her fingers stroke along the buttons of his shirt. "No?"

"No." He put his hand over hers. She felt the solid strength of his chest, his heartbeat against her palm.

"So, what is it you want?" she asked, breath hitching in her throat.

He ran his finger down her cheek. "Well, I want a place to work," he said, nodding slightly toward the luscious green fields outside.

"Uh-huh," she said, still feeling his touch on her face.

"And my family around me," he went on.

She nodded, her heart almost bursting against her ribs. "Yeah."

He tilted her chin a fraction so she was looking straight up at him, into the smiling blue gaze and the thick ebony lashes.

"And that's it, really," he said.

She stepped back sharply and bashed him on the arm. "Oh, Logan! You've just totally ruined the moment!"

He laughed, deep and rumbling, then reaching out, he gathered her up close against him as he said, "You! *You're* all I want."

She bit down on her smile but knew it shone out of her eyes all the same.

Then the next instant his hand was cupping her cheek and she was on her toes, her arm thrown around his neck, and his mouth pressed hard against hers in a kiss that was everything she had been waiting for, everything that she had wanted, and never wanted to end.

As their lips met, his arm snaked tight around her waist, hauling her closer, crushing the delicate silk of the dress, their hands roamed with an urgency and desperateness of years of waiting and wanting. And still she wanted to be held tighter, she wanted not to be able to breathe. She wanted his mouth never to leave hers, she wanted forever that feeling, that taste, that pressure, that shivering thrill. She felt herself mold to him, an almost desperate desire in the kiss, in the touch, their lips crushed. Her fingers pushed into his hair. His hand splayed firm and cool against her bare back.

When he pulled back, she didn't want to let go. He looked down at her with such twinkling triumph in his eyes that she drew his mouth back down to hers and kissed him again, soft and smiling this time in the radiant confidence that she could, they could. And then he held the back of her neck and kissed her forehead and said, "I'm so pleased you're here."

She tried to rein in her smile that seemed embarrassingly wide. "So am I."

He tucked her hair behind her ear and, almost like he didn't want to lose contact, let his hand trail down over her shoulder and back around her waist. "I didn't stop thinking about you."

She felt a burst of silent joy inside. She shook her head. "Me, neither."

She kissed him again, just because she could. There was a warm familiarity to it, a rightness, that she thought she'd lost. It felt too precious, she wanted to lock it up tight, like something might come along and take him away. But then in the way he looked at her, with such tender fondness, she knew in that second that she could let it breathe, let what they had be free and know it would always be there.

He led her over to the giant wall of windows that overlooked the training track and she held his hand in both of hers just because she could, because she didn't want to let go. He pushed open the door with his shoulder and led her outside.

Above them moths danced around the globe lights strung along the terrace. Uplights on the trees at the back of the track gave the forest an eerie majesty. Above them a blanket of stars popped in the black night sky. She glanced back over her shoulder and took in the decorations, the music, the champagne for the party to come, but in that moment of emptiness it was just them.

When she turned back, she realized he was looking her up and down. "That's one heck of a dress," he said.

She blushed. "Thanks. Claudette made it." Then she paused, looked back again at the party ready and waiting. "Did she know about this?"

He grinned boyishly, "Might have done."

Bella gasped. "I'm going to kill her."

He raised a brow, let his finger run under the thin strap of her dress, rubbing the silken ribbon with his thumb. "I'll be thanking her."

It was hard to concentrate when he touched her like that. She gazed up at him, unable to keep the smile from spreading on her face, just wanted to keep looking, wanting to reach up and touch his face to make sure it was all real. "Do you think this can work, Logan?"

"Yes," he said absently, fingers tracing the V at the front of her dress.

She moved her head to make him look her in the eye and concentrate. "I'm serious."

"So am I," he replied dryly. Then he stopped his wandering fingers and focused on her, locked his hands behind her lower back and said, "I can't be certain, Bella. But I think I've—we've—been through enough to face pretty much anything that comes our way." He smiled, the kind of smile that told her that he could see straight into her head at her deepest fears and desires and wants. "Listen," he said seriously, "I would be proud to go anywhere with you by my side."

She rested her forehead on his chest so he couldn't see her bubbling smile. He put his hand under her chin, lifting her face up to his, making her look at him. "I don't want to be in the public eye anymore, Bella, and I'll do my best not to be. I'm going to hide away here. Not from people but from everything that doesn't matter. From the noise. I want a normal life. A smaller life but a better life. And the only person I really want to be in it with me is you."

She beamed. "I would really like to be in it with you, Logan."

She threaded her arms around his waist and buried her face into his shirt. She felt his mouth press into her hair, and she inhaled as deeply as she could to smell him, to know that maybe, actually, now this would be where she could be for years to come. She felt his hold tighten around her and knew that it could never be tight enough.

"I've missed you."

"I've missed you, too, Logan."

He said, "Really, really missed you. For years." When he kissed her, it felt like the sealing of a new future.

Then she heard the muffled words through his lips. "Do you want to see the horses?"

She raised a brow as she pulled away. "You know how to kill a moment, Logan."

He laughed, and she saw an excitement in his eyes that had been there all those years ago when he'd been out on the field. The buzzing excitement of freedom.

"These are some of the finest beasts in the country, Bella." He held out his hand, an easy grin on his face. "Some of them perhaps in the world. The offer is not to be sniffed at."

She slipped her hand into his. "Lead the way."

They left the clubhouse terrace and walked around to the barn. Where Logan led her inside the light, open building that smelled of warm wood and the earthiness of the horses. He quietly introduced her to the inquisitive ones with their heads over their stalls.

"This is my new mare, American thoroughbred, trained in Mexico. Bella, meet Bella." He glanced over to her as he scratched the horse's neck.

Bella walked over and let her namesake sniff her hand, then stroked her fine coat. "I'm not sure whether to be flattered or not."

Logan shrugged. "She's exceptional, clever, stunning. And cost a fortune but worth every penny. I'd be flattered, if I were you."

Bella gave a wry smile. "He knows how to say the right

thing, doesn't he?" she said to the thoroughbred mare, as it nuzzled for more attention.

She felt Logan watching her. Really looking at her.

They walked further up the barn. Logan introduced her to Jo-Jo and some of the others. All of them eliciting the same relaxed happiness in him.

When they got to the end of the walkway, they stepped outside where the paddocks stretched on as far as she could see, the light from the moon giving everything a supernatural glow. She said, "I'm glad you gave it up—Carter Media."

Logan looked out toward the moonlit grass, the planes of his profile lit by the stark light. "So am I."

Then he turned to face her. "And I want you to know that I didn't give it up for you."

She frowned, taken aback for a moment, not totally sure what he meant.

He winced, took her hand in his. "I don't mean it in a bad way. I mean that I gave it up because I had to. I gave it up for me." He pointed to himself. "Whatever happens between us—" he gestured to her "—has no impact on that decision."

Before she could reply, he ran a hand frustratedly through his hair, like he was struggling with what he was trying to say. "Basically, Bella, I don't want you to ever have to feel responsible for it. It was something that I couldn't have done without you, but not because of you. I had to free myself, I suppose. So, I did it for you, but also not." His brows drew together. "Do you understand what I'm saying?"

A smile tugged at the corners of her mouth and she rolled her lips together to stop it from looking like she was laughing at his rambling speech. "I think I can grasp the gist of it."

He shook his head at his own inarticulateness and then laughed. "Sorry. That was a dreadful explanation." He sucked air in through his teeth. "I'm better in the boardroom or on the pitch."

"I think you're doing all right." She felt her teeth dig into her lip as her smile started to spread.

His eyes glinted.

They walked over to the wooden fencing around the paddock. Bella leaned against it, Logan stood in front of her, hands resting either side of her on the fence.

She tilted her head to the side, looked up into his eyes, narrowed and assessing. "So, what now?"

He looked at his watch. "Well, the other guests arrive soon."

"I meant in life," she laughed, "not the party!"

"Oh!" He grinned, then shrugged. "Well, I've got everything I need right here." He moved his hands from the fence and placed them on the cool silk of her dress, drawing her in toward him. "Bella, I don't ever want to let you go. I want everything. With you."

She felt her heart explode like a firework.

"And I promise you that, if you want that, too, I will give all of it my absolute best." He paused and a wicked glint appeared in his eyes. "And so far in life, my best has been better than average."

She was flooded with a feeling of such uncontainable

happiness she wondered if her whole face was alight. She wrapped her arms around his neck and said, "Then I'll have your best, Logan Carter."

"It's all yours," he replied, and kissed her with a smile on his lips.

Chapter Forty-Eight

If there was one thing the people of Autumn Falls did spectacularly well it was a party. At the Silver H Polo Club there were waiters serving delicate miniature appetizers, a cocktail bar, the champagne flowed while the sound of chatter and laughter filled the room. The music came from the community band—John-Luke on guitar, Dusty on sax, Hank Murphy, who owned the Supply Store, on the banjo, and Claudette on vocals.

Bella put her champagne glass down on the table and said to Logan, "Do you want to dance?"

Logan cocked his head with a frown. "I didn't think you danced anymore?"

"I dance," she replied and, determined brown eyes locked on his, she held out her hand to lead him to the dance floor.

A smile spread across his face as he slipped his hand in hers and, feeling the slight nervous tremble, squeezed reassuringly. Then raising their entwined hands to his chest, he held hers there as they walked together into the crowd.

The music went on late into the night. All of them dancing together in the dusky light, laughing, grinning, Logan twirling Bella around like they were teenagers, all except Noah who didn't dance no matter how hard Willow, who had flown in especially for the party, tried to drag him onto the dancefloor.

When the sky darkened to black, it felt like a lifetime had passed and no time at all.

The band took a well-deserved break and Logan went to get some water at the bar. As he was topping up his glass, his mom came to stand beside him, looking elegant in a long red dress cinched in with a leather belt. In front of them, Willow was still lighting up the dancefloor, his dad was by the open window, as far from the crowds and the music as possible, talking to Hank as the band took a break. Noah, who'd been up most of the night because one of his horses was sick, and didn't want to risk being cajoled onto the dancefloor again by his sister, had his feet up on a chair, his hat over his face and, while wanting to support his brother's venture, was also trying to catch up on sleep.

Logan glanced at his mom. "We're getting there," he said.

He watched her survey the members of the Carter family in the crowd, then lift her glass to her lips and take a thoughtful sip. "One day, Logan," she said, "I'd like us all to sit down for Sunday brunch again. You remember, after church, we used to have eggs and you'd all want different ones?"

"I remember."

She smiled softly at the memory. "That's what I'd like, that would be the dream for me—all of us together." She paused. "Except Jack." Her lip trembled as she said his name.

Logan put his arm around her and hugged her tight. "We'll get there," he promised.

But looking around at his dad, clearly itching to leave, Noah detached and snoozing, Willow checking her watch because she was catching a plane at midnight. No Brodie—and no Ethan, either.

"Maybe," said Martha and she walked away, going over to say hello to someone she knew.

Logan looked around for Bella and saw her standing by one of the tables. She turned, and when she saw him she smiled. That was *his* dream, he realized, and he was living it.

When she came over to join him she said, "What are you smiling about?"

"Can't a guy just be happy?" he asked.

"You're not saying you're actually happy are you, Logan Carter?" she said jokingly, eyes narrowed and sparkling, as if it were an unimaginable feat.

He wrapped his arms around her, drawing her close, let his forehead rest against hers, eyes adoring, and said, "I am now."

Bonus Chapter
ETHAN CARTER

Even if someone had been there, they wouldn't have seen him. He'd blended into shadows half as dark as these.

The leaves didn't crunch under his feet as he walked slowly, looking around for something. Pausing every now and then, the whites of his eyes glowing in the moonlight.

Then suddenly, he stopped, dropped into a crouch, arms resting over his thighs as he found what he was searching for, lips moving ever so slightly as he read:

In loving memory of Jack Oliver Carter.

He swallowed. Face set, steely and unmoving.

He could picture the end of the mission without having to close his eyes. The relief, the euphoria, the slumping back in the Jeep, hair long, beard tangled, mouth stretched into an unaccustomed smile, when suddenly they pulled up back at the base and he caught the look on his commanding officer's face as he strode over to meet him.

After everything he'd endured over the last months,

only when he heard the news about Jack did his body start to shake and his mind fracture. Back in his room he poured over the headlines the pictures of his brother's all-too-familiar cocksure, laughing eyes staring back from the screen. Like the joke was on him.

He stared now at the grave, jaw tight, eyes unwavering at the carved, headstone lettering, the flowers, the handwritten cards faded from the weather.

He looked up at the church, the familiar white spire framed by the pine forest, then behind him at the ornate streetlights, the church hall, the glow of the shops at the end of the road, finally up at the mountain, which cast it's ever-watchful shadow over them all.

Ethan Carter had fought and survived in more hostile territory than he cared to remember, but in that moment, none of it compared to how being back in Autumn Falls made him feel.

Palms sweating, pulse racing, he stood up straight, and with a final eyes-glistening nod, he was gone. Not a single trace of his presence left, just the throaty roar of his bike out on the highway.

FALLEN IN LOVE WITH THE CARTER BROTHERS?
DON'T MISS OUT ON WHAT HAPPENS NEXT...

The Carter brothers were once inseparable – five boys, a band, and a bond that seemed unbreakable. But it's been ten years since the band broke up and even longer since they left the family ranch and the wide-open skies of Autumn Falls. Fame, secrets and time have left cracks that no one wants to face...

Meet Noah in Silver Sky!

Acknowledgments

I've loved every minute of writing *Autumn Falls* and I'd like to take the opportunity to thank all the One More Chapter team for making the experience so brilliant. Extra special thanks go to Charlotte Ledger for being so creative, enthusiastic, dedicated and incredible at her job. Also huge thanks to Sofia and Kara for all their hard work and for going above and beyond. And thanks to Rebecca Ritchie, my hugely talented agent.

I'd also like to thank my friend Lucy for happily sitting through endless cappuccinos to talk about the Carter brothers. And for having a granny who brought music to the house.

Thanks to my husband for watching *a lot* of boyband documentaries with me. Thanks to my mom for offering the kind of advice that Martha does in these books and my dad for not being like Emmett (and *loving* a TV talent show!)

And for readers everywhere who find so much joy in the rush of falling in love. (Me too!)

The author and One More Chapter would like to thank everyone who contributed to the publication of this story...

Analytics
Imogen Wolstencroft

Audio
Fionnuala Barrett
Ciara Briggs

Contracts
Laura Amos
Inigo Vyvyan

Design
Lucy Bennett
Fiona Greenway
Liane Payne
Dean Russell

Digital Sales
Laura Daley
Lydia Grainge
Hannah Lismore

eCommerce
Laura Carpenter
Madeline ODonovan
Charlotte Stevens
Christina Storey
Jo Surman
Rachel Ward

Editorial
Janet Marie Adkins
Rosie Best
Kara Daniel
Charlotte Ledger
Jennie Rothwell
Sofia Salazar Studer
Emily Thomas
Helen Williams

Harper360
Emily Gerbner
Ariana Juarez
Jean Marie Kelly
emma sullivan
Sophia Wilhelm

International Sales
Peter Borcsok
Ruth Burrow
Bethan Moore
Colleen Simpson

Inventory
Sarah Callaghan
Kirsty Norman

Marketing & Publicity
Chloe Cummings
Grace Edwards
Katie Sadler

Operations
Melissa Okusanya
Hannah Stamp

Production
Denis Manson
Simon Moore
Francesca Tuzzeo

Rights
Ashton Mucha
Alisah Saghir
Zoe Shine
Aisling Smyth
Lucy Vanderbilt

Trade Marketing
Ben Hurd
Eleanor Slater

The HarperCollins Distribution Team

The HarperCollins Finance & Royalties Team

The HarperCollins Legal Team

The HarperCollins Technology Team

UK Sales
Isabel Coburn
Jay Cochrane
Sabina Lewis
Holly Martin
Harriet Williams
Leah Woods

And every other essential link in the chain from delivery drivers to booksellers to librarians and beyond!

One More Chapter is an award-winning global division of HarperCollins.

Subscribe to our newsletter to get our latest eBook deals and stay up to date with all our new releases!

signup.harpercollins.co.uk/join/signup-omc

Meet the team at
www.onemorechapter.com

Follow us!

@onemorechapterhc

Do you write unputdownable fiction?
We love to hear from new voices.
Find out how to submit your novel at
www.onemorechapter.com/submissions

The Heart Stone

by Raynor Woods

© Copyright 2009. Raynor Woods. All Rights Reserved.

All characters and events in this publication are fictitious and any resemblance to real persons, living or dead is purely coincidental.

No part of this book may be reproduced, stored in a retrieval system, or transmitted, in any form or by any means, without the prior permission in writing of the publisher, nor be otherwise circulated in any form of binding or cover other than that which it is published and without a similar condition including this condition being imposed on the subsequent purchaser.

Printed in the United States of America

ISBN 978-1-60693-552-1

Published by Strategic Book Publishing
An imprint of AEG Publishing Group
845 Third Avenue, 6th Floor - 6016
New York, NY 10022
www.StrategicBookPublishing.com

The Heart Stone

by Raynor Woods

Strategic Book Publishing
New York, New York

"For Nana who knew about faeries."

I would like to thank my family for their solid support and belief in this book.

This book was inspired by the books and artwork of Jane Roberts and Rob Butts.

ILLUSTRATIONS BY STEPHANIE McINNES

The Heart Stone Verse

There is a stone, a gem, so pure,
so brilliant that it can melt even the coldest heart.
It is as old as time yet as fresh as tomorrow,
for it is a living thing.
Within it is contained every foolishness
and all the wisdom of humankind.
And from this knowledge comes its power,
the power to grant all that the heart desires.
Many have sought to find this stone
and harness its might.
That is but more foolishness,
for the stone cannot be found,
It will find you, when you are ready.

Table of Contents

Chapter 1: The Neg Invasion..........................1
Chapter 2: Meet Susan Grey,
              Her Friends And Enemies!...................5
Chapter 3: A Game Of L.A.R.P.
              And A Budding Romance...................12
Chapter 4: A Good Game Spoiled By Bullies.............19
Chapter 5: Puppy Tails And Granny Wails!..............27
Chapter 6: Susan And Seb Serve It Up Italian Style!.......37
Chapter 7: A Faerie Emissary Is Sent To Susan..........47
Chapter 8: Susan Visits The Faerie Realm..............53
Chapter 9: Susan And Hawthorne
              Return To Bring Help......................79
Chapter 10: Susan Takes Seb To The Faerie Realm.......89
Chapter 11: A Food Reward!
              For A Strategic Victory!...................101
Chapter 12: Peace With Gran And Ten
              Go To The Realm Of Faeries 111
Chapter 13: Victory! And George's
              Incredible Story!.........................134
Chapter 14: Susan, Aliya And
              The Voice Of Nature 140
Chapter 15: The Return Of The Negs 148
Chapter 16: Susan Returns To Earth To Ask
              A Neg Child For Help....................157
Chapter 17: Susan And Hawthorne Take The Neg
              Child To The Realm Of Faeries 167
Chapter 18: The Heart Stone And The Neg Child........173
Chapter 19: The Arrival Of The Slegna................181
Chapter 20: The Children Carry The Heart Stone
              To Earth 196
Definition Of A Neg.................................203
Definition Of A Faerie 204

Chapter 1
The Neg Invasion

"They're approaching from the north this time," cried Laurelei, the oldest and most experienced of the warrior faeries. "Prepare for battle!"

The blood-curdling battle cry of the warrior faeries rang, shrilly, out into the ether. Their voices echoed from every tree, through every valley, and across every meadow of their beloved realm. Clad in battle armour, their tall, elegant frames vibrated with the collective power that was needed to meet their formidable enemy. Together, they would stand and fight to the death to defeat the negs.

In unison, the battalion of faeries rose into the air to meet their foe, their breastplates glinting in the last vestiges of sunlight. The approaching negs were obliterating the brilliance of the sun with their huge, grotesque forms. As they drew closer, the clear blue skies grew as dark as night and a bone-chilling cold fell upon the land.

"On my command, begin your projection!" cried Laurelei, who was circling the battalion. The battalion of faeries stood ready, their bodies vibrating stronger as the enemy drew nearer. They hovered in the air fifty feet above the ground in a triangular formation with the strongest and most powerful faeries positioned in the wide-fronted battle line.

"Begin projection now!" shouted Laurelei, taking his place in the front line. The projected vibration that began in the faeries' minds blazed out through their eyes in a brilliant stream, emitting a shining mist that seemed to hover over the land. It acted as a strong force field that protected their territory for many miles. The faeries didn't use weapons to defend their land, as it was forbidden for them to take a life, no matter the circumstance. They were only permitted to use their powers of projection to protect themselves and their beautiful land. Despite their amazing abilities, the negs were already gaining faerie ground.

In one swift and terrifying motion, the gigantic negs advanced to within three miles of the faeries' battlefront and launched another devastating attack upon them. The neg attack was directed at the minds of the faeries; they began flooding their minds with dark, negative energy, which was disastrous, as it disunited them and caused chaos. When they were separated and weakened, the negs began to plant disorienting, sinister images into their minds, robbing them of their strength and ability to think clearly. Some of the younger faeries struggled desperately to neutralize the dark images, but to no avail. They didn't have the mind strength of the older ones and, sadly, began to fall and die upon the field of battle. Even the older, stronger faeries were falling in this terrifying onslaught through trying to protect their younger brothers and sisters.

All loathed the fact that the younger faeries had to stand in battle, but the situation was critical. Every faerie in the realm was needed, either on the battlefront or behind the lines to keep the warriors fed and to help nurse them back to health. There was no other choice—the faeries had to defeat the negs or they would be destroyed along with their magical realm.

For more than three months, the faeries had bravely stood their ground. As one warrior fell, another would move up to the front to take his or her place. Some of the fallen could be restored to health, but now many were beyond help. As the faerie ranks became depleted, so did their land. The lush, verdant, meadows and hills were left as drab, ashen expanses with once exquisite trees standing like gaunt, skeletons in the eerie light. The negs had evolved rapidly and were now able to consume light, beauty and goodness and turn it into the dark, negative energy that fed them.

The negs were like no other invading force; they

originated from negative energy produced by idle humans who had ceased to use their imaginations and creative abilities. Now they had evolved into a dark, fearsome enemy that overwhelmed the minds of their unsuspecting victims with negative thoughts. They preyed upon their victims when their minds were idle and unfocussed, eventually leaving them drained, desolate and isolated from their true sense of self. They were particularly drawn to Earth children, whom they robbed of dreams, hopes and expectations.

Earth was a rich feeding ground for them, as her children had grown lazy over the years and had allowed their minds to be influenced by others. They rarely used their own imaginations. The negs were quickly growing stronger from the negative energy that the children were emitting. As a result, there were very few children left whose inner strength and imaginative ability was strong enough to withstand the onslaught of this monstrous foe.

The faeries were under attack because they were trying to shield the Earth children from the dark influence of the negs. The negs believed that by attacking and destroying the faeries, they would be allowed to infiltrate and control the minds of Earth children. Their master plan was to enslave the people of Earth and use the planet as a base for invading and draining other worlds of their positive energy. Now the Realm of Faeries, and potentially the Earth, stood in great peril from this devastating force of evil.

The entire faerie battalion heard Iridaan's telepathic command simultaneously. "Retreat! Retreat!" came her urgent summons.

"No, my queen, we cannot let them take more of our land," protested Laurelei who was close to exhaustion.

"We cannot afford any more losses," Queen Iridaan said resolutely. "Let them take the land, we can still hold out for a while. The negs will have to rest in order to digest all the positive energy they have consumed. This will give us time to regroup." She couldn't bear to have any more of her faeries destroyed in this way. With each wound they suffered, the pain struck her like a knife, with each death, a piece of her soul departed with them. She too needed respite in order to rethink her strategy. The weight of her burden was so great that, for a moment, she almost lost hope of ever defeating the negs.

In her despair she became aware of Hawthorne's steady, reassuring voice speaking into her troubled mind, whispering words of hope and encouragement. She brightened at the sound of his voice. Drawing up to her full six feet in height, Iridaan shook her auburn mane of silken hair down her slender, winged back and regained her former positivity. She strode purposefully over to Hawthorne, her closest advisor, and looked at him with warm affection, thinking how gallant and chivalrous he was. He was always at her side in times of need.

Hawthorne stood a few inches taller than Iridaan, his lean, yet powerful frame standing in readiness for his queen's command. Kindness seemed etched into his handsome face, his eyes reflecting the deep warmth that came from his gentle and generous soul.

"You are right, Hawthorne, the time has come. We can hold out no longer. If she will come, bring her to us with all haste!"

Chapter 2
Meet Susan Grey, Her Friends and Her Enemies

Susan Grey was eleven years old and was, in many ways, a very ordinary girl. She didn't excel at anything. She was quite good at reading and writing, but her spelling let her down because of her mild dyslexia. She was also good at sports. Running was her best one, but she usually came in second to Alison Wilcox. She really would've liked to excel at just one thing to make her mum and dad proud of her (even though they already were).

Susan was not pretty in the conventional manner, but she had an inner glow reflecting in her eyes, making them sparkle like fabulous gemstones. When people looked into her eyes, they often felt happy. Indeed, Susan was a happy girl despite the fact that she was often bullied at school.

Susan didn't spend a lot of time worrying about the bullies, as she would rather daydream about something that made her happy. Indeed, it was her fertile imagination and her ability to daydream that made her "extraordinary." That is to say, extraordinary in the good sense of the word, not the weird sense.

For Susan, life was full of intensities. For her, rain was never just a shower, but a tropical monsoon that might engulf the whole of England. Complicated strategies would need to be thought up in order to escape the deluge.

A walk on a hot, sunny day might become a gruelling trek through the Sahara Desert with only a half full canteen of water to survive with. Snow showers would become a blizzard in the Antarctic. Skill and accuracy would be needed to navigate back to base camp. Even while doing boring things like "swiffing" the floor for her mum, Susan would imagine that the Swiffer was a metal detector used to discover treasure buried in the sand at the seaside.

Susan's life was never dull. Her main interests lay outside of school where she and her best friend Aliya would invent games and adventures to be played out or go for long, rambling walks in the nearby countryside. If it rained, they would often listen to the latest pop music and dance energetically, play board games, or even just talk.

As the last week of school before the summer holidays began, Susan stumbled into the bathroom, still groggy from sleep. Her thoughts turned to the upcoming summer holidays as she splashed water on her face. *Yes,* she thought. *Wonderful adventures will begin again!* She almost shouted the words out loud in her excitement. The anticipation of having no more school for weeks was sending thrills of excitement through her. No more bullies to contend with! No more homework to do! Just weeks and weeks of freedom!

She calmed herself realizing that there were still a few more days of school to get through. Susan was not the most popular girl in school. She didn't have many friends at all. It didn't worry her too much because the few friends that she did have were loyal and kind.

Looking in the mirror to brush her teeth, she stared menacingly at her unruly brown hair that needed taming with lots of leave-in conditioner and wished with all her heart to have sleek, shiny hair like the "hair spray" models on TV. Her thick, wavy hair was such a problem to manage that she usually had to plait it. Plaiting was considered a heinous fashion crime by the "Beauty Parlour Brigade" at school (they were given that name by Susan's mum). They were the "perfects" that had unsubtle, highlighted, blonde hair and the latest fashion clothes. They paraded around the school as if they were on a catwalk and belittled anyone that stood in their way or didn't slavishly follow their way of dress.

There's no chance of me ever becoming one of the "perfects," Susan thought to herself with a sigh. *But then again, I don't really want to be part of all that. It's one thing to look like a Barbie doll, but quite another to behave like a hooligan.* The Beauty Parlour Brigade thought nothing of bullying and tormenting the less pretty girls in school and intimidating vulnerable boys.

Susan accepted that she was in the less pretty category. She was small for her age, but fortunately, was quite slim despite the large appetite she had. Her face was somewhat babyish; people often said that she looked younger than her eleven years. Even the glasses perched on her little, turned up nose didn't make her look any older.

Returning her thoughts to the present moment, she opened her rather wide mouth to examine the results of her vigorous tooth brushing. *Oh, rats!* she thought. *I haven't brushed my teeth properly. They still look the colour of the chocolate milk I drank last night before bed. I'm going to be late for school,* she wailed internally. *I am just a higgledy-piggledy mess!*

Susan didn't manage her appearance very well. She wasn't sufficiently interested in clothes to bother herself with how they actually looked on her when she put them on. She could look nice if her hair stayed tidy, her face stayed clean and her clothes stayed un-crumpled. This didn't happen very often, especially since Susan rarely looked into a mirror to check her appearance. There was always something more interesting going on in her head than giving attention to her appearance.

"Susan!" cried her mother from downstairs. "Aren't you ready yet"?

"Nearly!" she replied.

"Well, you had better get a move on! Aliya is here waiting for you," her mother said.

Good, thought Susan. *I like it when I can walk to school with Aliya because I don't have to listen to the nasty comments of the Beauty Parlour Brigade all by myself.*

Susan always found it easier to manage when Aliya was with her. She was better able to withstand the taunts and jibes of the "perfects." Aliya Khan lived just down the road. Her parents ran the local newsagents. Susan and Aliya often walked to school together. Aliya had been off school for two days last week feeling a bit poorly, Susan was delighted that she was now back.

Susan ran downstairs to the kitchen in a dishevelled mess. "Come here luv, what do you look like?" said her mother, adjusting the tie of her school uniform. "You look like Joe Smith's donkey." Susan's mother was what the local people called "bonnie." She was neither fat nor thin just "cuddly." Her face was softly round with large, clear, deep blue eyes. She had a small, upturned nose and a smiley mouth with lips like plump red cherries and a determined little chin that Susan had inherited.

Susan always wondered why her mother compared her to Joe Smith's donkey. She wondered who Joe Smith actually was and in what way she looked like his donkey, but that was what her mother always said to her when she looked a mess.

Aliya was sitting at the kitchen table and was smiling at Susan in her quiet, shy way. She was happy to be walking to school with her best friend and was also happy to have an ally to fend off the daily dose of bullying that she had come to expect from the Beauty Parlour Brigade.

"Come on now, you two," said Susan's mum, whose name was Sylvia. "You had better get a move on. Here, Susan, don't forget your lunch!" She pushed Susan's lunch bag into her hands.

"Thanks, mum," Susan said, kissing her on the cheek. "See you at four o'clock.

"Goodbye, Mrs Grey," Aliya said politely.

"Goodbye, luv. See you on your way home."

Susan's mum had a strong, broad Yorkshire accent, but

she never allowed Susan to speak with one. When they moved to Hardingate, a rather posh North Yorkshire town, she decided that Susan would need to be well spoken, more like her dad. Susan was never allowed to drop her H's or miss letters at the beginning and end of words.

The two girls set off for their fifteen-minute walk to school, chatting amiably and enjoying the warm July sunshine.

"Isn't it great?" Susan remarked gleefully. "Only four more days to go and then we're on summer holidays!"

"Yes, it's really brilliant, no more school for six whole weeks!" Aliya responded.

"What's even better," exclaimed Susan, "is that we're never coming back to this school again. We're off to senior school!"

"I'm really glad that we're going to be at the same school," Aliya said, turning to smile at Susan.

"Me too," said Susan. "Let's hope that the Beauty Parlour Brigade won't be coming to our school."

The "Beauty Parlour Brigade" was how the two girls always referred to the "perfects." Susan's mother had first used the expression when she saw the stylish group coming home from school one day. The brigade were doing their "catwalk" strut and flicking their blonde tresses about as they spoke. Susan and Aliya had roared with laughter when her mother had coined the phrase in her broad Yorkshire accent, and from then on that was what they called them.

"I really, really, hope they won't be coming to our Secondary School, as I've had enough of them to last a lifetime," said Aliya emphatically, stopping to tie her shoelace. "Uh, oh, don't turn around, Susan," she continued with alarm rising in her voice.

"They're behind us on the other side of the road!"

Susan and Aliya walked on, chatting together and trying to ignore the fact that the Beauty Parlour Brigade would soon catch up with them. However, the sound of clattering high heels soon announced their unwelcome arrival.

"Aw, don't they look sweet," taunted Kerry Boswell, referring to the colour of the girls' skin. "Just like vanilla and chocolate ice cream!"

The rest of the Beauty Parlour Brigade laughed loudly. Kerry was the undisputed leader of the gang and no one dared to cross her. To look at her you would not imagine the cruelty of which she was capable. She had naturally dark blonde hair made lighter with artificial highlights. Her blue eyes were large and soulful and she had a pert, straight nose and a perfect Cupid's bow mouth. She was tall for her age and had a slender frame that was just hinting at adolescence. Most grown-ups and teachers thought she was "a little angel."

"Hey, curry breath, you should pluck those eyebrows, or should I say, eyebrow!" Kerry said insultingly to Aliya.

Susan was immediately incensed with rage. How dare she say that to Aliya! Aliya was beautiful. She had glossy, straight black hair and skin the colour of milky chocolate. Her features were delicate and refined. Her lovely, dark, arched eyebrows framed her almond shaped, amber coloured eyes. She was tall and willowy and Susan thought that Aliya could even be a model when she grew up if she wanted to.

Susan saw tears spring to Aliya's eyes. "Never mind them," she said gently. "They have no manners and are ignorant."

Aliya swallowed hard and said, "I'm okay, let's walk a little faster."

"I don't think we should. They'll think we're scared of them, and we've managed to hold our own so far," Susan said in a decided manner.

"Alright then," Aliya said resignedly.

"Hey, Suzy squint eyes, if you wore some wedge heels you might look as if you were nearly eight years old!" shouted one of the other girls.

"And if you wore your skirt at a decent length, you wouldn't show everyone your knickers!" retorted Susan defiantly. The Beauty Parlour Brigade always hiked their skirts up on the way to and from school to make their legs look longer. They weren't allowed to wear skirts shorter than four inches above their knees for school.

"At least she wears knickers," interjected Kerry. "I bet you still wear nappies!"

The group roared with laughter and began speaking among themselves again, content that they had upset Susan and Aliya enough for the morning at least.

"Oh, I really, really hope that they don't come to our senior school," Aliya said.

"Me too," said Susan wistfully. "What have you got for your lunch?" she asked, changing the subject abruptly.

"Veggie Samosas and Tandouri chicken and fruit yogurt."

"Can I swap you half of my cheese and onion quiche for one of your Samosas?" Susan asked sweetly.

"Of course you can," said Aliya, smiling once again.

Chapter 3
A Game of L.A.R.P. and a Budding Romance

The summer holidays began for Susan and Aliya in a balmy haze of fun and freedom from the tyranny of the Beauty Parlour Brigade. The two girls were passing the days in a delightful mix of play, sports, and helping Aliya's dad in his shop on busy days. If the weather was really bad, they spent a bit of the day watching telly. Fortunately, the English summer weather was being kind and the two girls were able to get out most of the time.

It was nearly ten o'clock and Susan and Aliya had just finished watching their favourite TV show about a girl with magical powers. They were at Aliya's house and were wondering what to do next.

"I'm enjoying these summer hol's so much that I wish we never had to go back to school," Susan sighed longingly.

"Yes, me too," responded Aliya with an equally wistful sigh. "Do you realize that we only have two and a half weeks left now?"

"No, I can't believe that!" cried Susan indignantly, "It only seems as if we started the holidays last week!"

"Never mind that," Aliya said consolingly. "Let's go to The Stray and walk for a while."

The Stray was a lovely, preserved green belt that encircled Hardingate. A Royal Proclamation many years ago had ensured that it could never be used as building land and was kept as a beauty and recreation area for residents. There was plenty of space for adults, children, horses and dogs to have fun. There was always something of interest going on.

The two of them marched off to see what was currently happening on The Stray after informing their parents where they would be. They walked for a good thirty minutes before deciding to sit down on one of the green benches and watch a young boy losing the battle to launch a large, colourful kite. The weather was very calm with only a slight breeze. Every time the determined child managed to launch his kite aloft, it would come tumbling down again. The girls were absorbed watching this sight when they heard a voice ring out behind them.

"Hiya, you two! Got nothing better to do than kite watching?" the voice said in a pleasant, teasing manner.

Susan turned around sharply to see who had spoken. "Oh, it's you," she said without much ceremony. She was, despite her dismissive tone, quite pleased to see Sebastian Alameda standing there. He was in their class at school and was a nice kid. She was not unaware of his Mediterranean good looks either!

He had eyelashes that most girls would die for and dark, mysterious, brown eyes that seemed to hold magical secrets in them. He was tall-ish and a bit skinny, but altogether quite an attractive package. However, she didn't wish to give him any hint that she found him attractive, lest it put him off her. He seemed to be responding well to her feigned indifference.

"What are you doing that is so much more interesting?" challenged Susan.

"Well, nothing really," he said, dawdling the toe of his tennis shoe in the grass.

"Can I come and sit with you two?" he enquired boldly.

Susan looked at Aliya for agreement and then answered with a shy nod.

"Okay then, got any ideas about what we can do?" she asked.

"Actually, yes. Have you heard of larping?" he asked eagerly.

"What on earth are you talking about?" Susan asked, somewhat scornfully.

"Well, it's really L.A.R.P.," he said spelling out the letters. "It stands for Live Action Role Play."

"And what does that mean?" demanded Susan.

"You know the Sword and Sorcery games that you can play on the PC?"

"Yes," both girls said in unison.

"It's like that, but all the players dress up in Medieval or alien gear and act out roles. We set up scenes to act out and make rules that we follow. Our characters have special powers to help us defeat our enemies. The one with the most points wins," he concluded with an inviting smile.

"Where did you hear about this game?" enquired Aliya with obvious interest.

"Oh, my older brother, Steve, is in University studying Archaeology and he has joined a L.A.R.P. (larp) group. He goes to all the big conventions and has a brilliant time," Sebastian responded enthusiastically.

"Well, it all sounds a bit complicated," Susan interjected hastily.

Susan loved Aliya, but felt that she was much too pretty to be carrying on such animated conversation with Sebastian.

"No, no, it's not," he insisted, not wishing to displease Susan. "You can make it as easy or as complicated as you like."

Sebastian really liked Susan; he admired the way that she stood up to the bullies at school. She was just a little thing, he thought, but she was tough. He often hung behind Susan and Aliya in the distance when they walked home from school in case they got into difficulties. He knew that Susan sometimes went overboard with her comments and feared that she might come in for more than just a verbal assault if she wasn't careful.

Sebastian wasn't sure what he'd be able to do against all seven of the Beauty Parlour Brigade, but at least he'd be there to help. He wasn't sure why he felt so protective of Susan, but he did and somehow it felt right to him. His friends were a bit sceptical about his attraction to Susan, telling him that she wasn't exactly "babe," material. He told them she wasn't an "airhead," and was fun to talk to and be with. Usually, they let him get on with his infatuation with only the minimum of teasing.

"Seb, if we're going to play this larp thing," said Susan, "will it take a long time?"

"Uh, um, yes it does," he replied, scratching his head trying to remember what his brother had told him.

"And what about the characters?" interjected Aliya. "When we play these games on computer there are usually lots of characters and we're only three."

"Mmmm, that's true," Sebastian replied, beginning to feel a bit daft for suggesting the game.

"Well, I'll tell you what," said Aliya brightly, "I have to go home for my lunch now, but I'll phone some of my cousins and see if they want to join us."

"Alright, we can meet back here on The Stray at two o'clock," Susan said, taking control of things again.

Aliya took her leave of Susan and Seb and went quickly home to phone her cousins.

"Aren't you going for your lunch too?" queried Seb hoping that Susan would stay a while.

"Not just yet. My mum won't be home yet, and I don't want to spend two hours talking to my gran. She's half deaf and always in a bad mood!" she said emphatically.

"Does your gran live with you?" enquired Seb.

"No, she just comes over once a week while mum goes over to my dad's work to do the books and the filing," Susan responded.

"What does your dad do?" asked Seb interestedly.

"He has a joinery business and makes all kinds of things. What does your dad do?" asked Susan.

"He's a cook in Federico's Italian Restaurant," he replied, shifting his gaze down to the floor wishing that he could

The Heart Stone

impress Susan by saying that he was a big business tycoon or something.

"He's a cook at Federico's?" she reiterated questioningly.

"Uh, um, yep," he said, thinking that she was about to say something uncomplimentary.

"Wow, that's awesome! Federico's is my favourite restaurant of all time! The food is fantastic! You are soooo lucky, getting all that lovely food to eat every day!" Susan said with great enthusiasm.

Seb was most surprised and relieved at Susan's response. "Well, it's not all that good. My dad works so many hours that he's not usually in for meals, and when he is, the last thing he wants to do is cook," he replied feeling much encouraged. "My mum, unfortunately, is not such a good cook!" he added gesturing toward his skinny frame.

They both enjoyed a good laugh and continued talking for another twenty minutes or so enjoying a pleasant time. However, Susan began feeling the pangs of hunger that soon became the main focus of her attention.

"I think I had better go for my lunch now, Seb," she said.

"Okay. I'll walk you home, it's on my way!" he offered brightly. Susan and Seb set off towards her house chatting amiably on the way. All too soon, they arrived at Susan's house where Seb, reluctantly, took his leave of her.

Susan ran into the large kitchen where her mum and gran were having a cup of tea and chatting.

"Mum, we're going to play this great game after lunch," she said, gasping for air after trying to talk twenty to the dozen.

"Now then, Susan say hello to your gran," said her mum, reminding Susan of her manners.

Susan's gran was a tallish woman with a back as straight as a ram-rod. She never slouched in chairs and never, ever, lay on the sofa to watch television. She was stick-thin and her clothes hung off her loosely. She always wore dark clothing and very sensible shoes. She looked much older than her fifty-five years. Her face always looked pinched as if she was cold or hungry. She was not ugly; she had lovely blue eyes, a nice straight nose and beautiful skin. The problem was that her gran never smiled, her lips were always pressed firmly together as if she was afraid of what might happen if she ever moved them to smile.

"Oh, hello, Gran. How are you?" Susan enquired perfunctorily.

"Fair to middling, not that you'd likely be bothered," Gran replied acerbically.

"That's a bit unfair, Mum," Sylvia (Susan's mum) said. "Remember, when you came home from hospital after your little operation? It was Susan that did all your shopping and chores around the house until you were back on your feet." Susan's gran just snorted and pretended that something interesting was going on outside the window.

Sylvia turned her attention to Susan again. "So what's this new game that's got you so excited, love?"

"Well, Sebastian Alameda met Aliya and me on The Stray and he told us about it and asked if we wanted to play it with him."

A knowing look came into her mum's eyes when she mentioned Seb. His name had been mentioned to her more than once and in glowing terms.

Susan continued, trying to explain all the intricacies of the game in ten seconds. "It's called larp and we have to choose a plot to act out and choose our characters and we can have magical powers and we dress up in costume and Aliya is going to ask her cousins to join in and..."

"Steady love," interjected her mum. "You're going at eighty miles an hour, calm down and let's get your lunch."

Gran snorted again. "I don't know about this larp business. Kids these days have to have fancy names for things. It was just called playing when I was a kid,"

"Now Mum, don't be harsh, it's a different time and kids do things differently. Anyway, I'm just glad that she's happy to play outside and isn't stuck in front of a computer screen all day,"

Susan bolted down her lunch of baked beans and sausages and ran to her room. *What can I take with me that will be useful to dress up in?* she thought frantically.

Rummaging around in her wardrobe she found some stuff that she had worn when she was in the Christmas play at school. There was a dark blue cloak and a silver foil crown and a shiny belt. Deciding that they would be just the job she began to relax a little. Susan glanced at her watch and found that she still had about forty minutes before she was to meet the others. She got her note pad out and started composing a larp plot that she hoped the others would like. It revolved around a young peasant boy who was left alone in the world when his only parent, his beautiful mother, vanished one night while he was sleeping.

The only clue that she left him was her sole treasure, a pendant with a large red stone that had a broken clasp on its chain. The quest would be to find out where his mother was and to discover the significance of the pendant. This would lead him into many encounters with magicians, confidence tricksters, genies, and eventually, some good guys. As her inspiration was running out, she decided to leave the ending of the plot for the others to work out.

She looked at her watch again and rejoiced to see that it was time to meet the others. She hurtled down the stairs carrying her costumes and script. "I'm going now, Mum!" she yelled from the hall.

"Wait!" shouted her mum. "Where are you going to be and what time are you going to be back? Have you got your mobile phone with you?"

Susan reassured her mum that she wouldn't be far away and wouldn't be late and that she did, indeed, have her mobile phone. She left the house in high spirits, clutching an old rucksack containing her make-shift costume, ready to enjoy the afternoon's adventures.

Chapter 4
A Good Game Spoiled by Bullies

Seb was already waiting on the bench when Susan arrived; he had also brought some dress up clothes. They were both looking eagerly at what the other had brought when the sound of laughing, noisy children enveloped them. It was Aliya and five of her cousins, some of whom were brandishing plastic swords in their hands and wearing metal colanders on their heads as helmets, pretending to vanquish some unseen foe. They made a happy, if somewhat comical, sight!

"Brilliant!" shouted Susan at the top of her voice. "We can have a great game because there are so many of us!" Aliya looked quite pleased with herself. It had taken a few phone calls, but very little persuasion to get them all there. The cousins were all pretty much at a loose end having exhausted all of their PC games during the early part of the holiday, and the cartoons on telly had also started to be bit repetitious and boring.

Some of the younger ones had grasped the concept of larp very easily and had come prepared with swords and makeshift helmets. Rather imaginatively, some were also wearing coats that were fastened at the neck with the sleeves hanging back into the folds of the coat to resemble a cloak.

The motley crew of girls and boys gathered together, and after much discussion, managed to work out the intricacies of Susan's plot. With the appointment of villains, heroes and sorcerers, the game got underway.

"Let's go to the middle of The Stray, guys," volunteered Seb. "We can make as much noise as we like and we won't disturb anyone."

He was mindful of his parents' warnings every time he went out to play. They never failed to remind him to be quiet and considerate of other people. It had taken them a long time to be able to get enough money to come and live in England and they were very wary of doing anything that would make people think badly of them. His mother was very proud and wanted everyone to think of them as Italians of the highest order.

"Yes," agreed Susan, noting the unrestrained yells of some of the younger ones. She too had been told repeatedly to consider other people when she went out to play. Whilst she couldn't guarantee that it would happen every time, she did her best.

As they were walking over The Stray, they encountered George Slater. George was a lanky, blonde haired boy from their school who seldom mixed with anyone. He had delicate features and was sometimes accused of being "pretty" or "gay" by some of the bullies in school. He was always a bit of loner, but to their surprise, he called out a greeting to them all.

"Hiya Seb. What are you all up to?" he enquired in an interested sort of a way nodding at the others in greeting.

Seb explained the complicated plot of the game they were about to begin.

"Would you mind if I joined in?" he asked with obvious interest.

Seb looked at Susan and Aliya for guidance. Susan quickly took charge.

"Well, we've got everyone sorted out into their roles and it would be difficult to sort out another one for you. But, you can be a Marshall and make sure that no one cheats and keep score," she said in a decisive tone.

"Oh, right. Thank you," he said, grateful to be allowed into their game. The game got underway with few problems and they soon found that they were able to improvise and ad-lib the script without having to stop the game. It was, however, noisy and robust but extremely good natured!

About an hour into the game they were hailed by an all too familiar voice.

"Ah, look at the little children having so much fun," Kerry's sarcastic voice rang out above the noise of the game, joined by the chorus of laughter from the rest of the Beauty Parlour Brigade.

"Just shut up and mind your own business!" Susan said, furious that their game had been interrupted.

"You shut up, you little pip squeak!" retorted Kerry vehemently. She turned her gaze to Seb and her attitude changed and a soft inviting look came into her eyes. "Sebastian," she drawled out his full name softly. "Why don't you leave these losers and come with us?"

"Why would I want to do that?" asked Seb, astounded by her offer.

"Well, Sebastian," the sexy intonation was in her voice again. "We're going to the mall first and then back to my house to play," she sniggered when she said the words "to play."

"No thanks, Kerry," he replied politely. He'd got the none-too-subtle message from Kerry as to what might go on at her house and he wasn't interested. He was having lots of fun playing with his friends here.

Kerry was taken aback; she wasn't used to being refused. Her stunning, good looks guaranteed that she could pull any of the boys at school. Most would have given anything to get the offer that Seb had just refused.

"What? You mean you'd rather stay with this ragamuffin lot than come with us?" she exclaimed in an incredulous voice.

"Yes, but thank you for the offer," he replied politely. Kerry became enraged at Seb's answer.

Susan too was livid with anger at Kerry's intrusion into their game and her brazen attempts to lure Seb away from them. She struggled to keep her mouth shut. She wanted to tell Kerry what she thought of her and exactly where to get off.

Aliya came up beside Susan and put her hand on Susan's arm in a gesture that said she understood how she felt.

Kerry turned her wrath onto Susan. "You little shit! Don't think that you have won any victory here today? You and your Paki friend had better watch your backs!" she shrieked, her voice contorted with anger.

Susan couldn't hold back any longer. "I'm not scared of you! You're pathetic, you have nothing but your obsession with fashion and make-up to show for yourself, and you torment others just to make yourself look important!" she said with equal anger.

Kerry crossed the twenty feet to where Susan was standing in an instant and grabbed the front of her tee shirt. The force of her grasp almost knocked Susan off her feet.

"You little cow!" she exclaimed, her face red with anger. "How dare you speak to me like that!"

The Beauty Parlour Brigade had begun to close in around Kerry, but Aliya, her cousins, Seb, and George also started to gather around Susan. Seeing that they were well outnumbered, the girls began to back off, leaving Kerry facing a very angry Susan who had all of her group standing behind her. Kerry looked at her followers in dismay as she saw them backing off. For a split second Susan thought that she detected fear in Kerry's eyes. Kerry toughed it out and stood her ground long enough to hurl a little more abuse at Susan.

"You're in for it the next time you're on your own, you fricking little bitch!" she hissed at Susan.

There was a tense silence as the whole of the Beauty Parlour Brigade took their leave and Kerry's followers gathered around her sympathetically.

Kerry turned around and screamed back at Susan, "You've had it bitch, just wait!"

The larpers all stood around not quite knowing what to do next. The unpleasant encounter had taken the spontaneity out of their game and they looked to Susan, Aliya, and Seb for direction. Susan looked at Seb, feeling very unglamorous. Kerry's comment about them being a "ragamuffin lot" had hit home. Seb was a very good-looking boy and she knew that she was not in the same league as him.

"You know, you can go with them if you want to, Seb," Susan said meekly.

"What for?" he asked, surprised at her comment.

"Because they're the "in crowd" and we, well, I mean me, I can't compete with them," she responded candidly. Susan looked down at her baggy jeans, last year's tee shirt extolling the virtues of Tenerife, and her scruffy tennis shoes. She was sure that her hair would've escaped from the neat ponytail that she had started the day off with and wondered why on Earth Seb would want to stay in her company.

"If they represent what the "in crowd" are I would rather be in the "out crowd," he responded with a big smile. "Besides, I think that we're the "happening crowd." We're having fun aren't we?" he chirped, trying to cheer her up.

"Are you sure?" she asked looking directly into his eyes.

"Of course I'm sure," he responded.

"Well, let's get on with the game!" she shouted loudly, her spirits returning.

As she ran off to her former position in the game she was startled by a loud rustling in the trees. For a second she thought that she saw a figure concealed amongst the leaves. Stopping, she took a closer look, but on further scrutiny she could detect nothing and so returned happily to the game of larp. Seb looked at Susan, pleased that he had restored her wavering spirit with his words.

He looked at her small, slightly dishevelled form and

thought how good she looked. Her face was still slightly flushed from anger and the vigorous intensity of their game. Her eyes were captivating, they shone with adventure and daring. When she looked into his eyes he felt himself drawn into a magical place that held untold treasures. He knew without a doubt that she was the girl for him.

The game of larp continued until late in the afternoon when Aliya's mother called her on her mobile phone to say that it was time for her and the cousins to return home. The group reluctantly broke up but not before agreeing to continue with the game the next day. Aliya left with her cousins but Seb and George hung back and chatted for a while.

"Better be off now," Susan said, looking at her watch.

"I'll walk you home, it's on my way," said Seb.

"Okay," she agreed.

"I'll come too," said George.

"Okay," she agreed again.

Sebastian shot George a look that suggested that he wasn't too pleased about him accompanying them. However, George was oblivious to this and the three of them made their way back home discussing further potential plots for larp

Susan ran into the house glowing with exhilaration and joy. "Mum, when's dinner? I'm starving!" she yelled, shouting in the direction of the kitchen.

"No need to shout, luv", replied her mother appearing behind her in the hall. "Just look at you, you're all higgledy-piggledy", she said with a broad smile whilst surveying Susan's unruly hair and dishevelled appearance. "It looks as if you've been having fun. I hope that you didn't get into mischief?"

"No, Mum. Of course I didn't. We were just playing larp in the middle of The Stray," she replied in a slightly wounded voice.

"Well, you've just got time for a nice, warm bath before

dinner."

"Oh, Mum, do I have to? I'm absolutely starving," Susan whined.

"Yes luv, you do. You know that we never sit down at the table for dinner until we're all clean and tidy," she said emphatically and walked off to the kitchen with no further ado.

Susan ran her bath and decided to make it more interesting by adding some of her mum's bubble bath. Unfortunately, her hand slipped as she poured it out and about half the bottle went into the bath. As the bath water plummeted into the bath, the foam began to increase at an alarming rate. None the less, she decided the best thing to do would be to get into the bath and hope that the bubbles would dissipate. She stepped into the bath and promptly went flying onto her bottom as she stepped onto some undissolved bubble bath liquid.

Oh my God! she thought. *If Seb knew what a klutz I am, what on Earth would he think of me?* Then she laughed at herself despite the pain that had accompanied her unceremonious fall into the bathtub. *Why do I care what Seb thinks of me?*

A little soul-searching provided the answer that she was looking for. She was forced to admit to herself that she was totally smitten by him. With this realization, she snuggled down into the warm, soapy, bubbles.

Seb had made it quite clear that he was interested in her, although she felt quite undeserving of this. To convince herself of Seb's interest, she re-played the scene in her mind where he had refused Kerry's invitation to go off with her and the Beauty Parlour Brigade. She recalled how her heart had been thudding in sick, anticipation as she waited for Seb to respond to Kerry and how her spirits soared to the moon as he politely declined the offer. She played this scene over and over in her mind until she eventually wore it out. She emerged out of the bathtub thinking how pleasant an interlude it had been and also how her hunger had diminished during her reverie in the bathtub.

She spent the next ten minutes trying to get rid of the masses of foam that still towered in mountainous peaks in the bathtub. Dinner and the ensuing evening went by in a blur for Susan, only when she went to her room and lay down on the bed was she finally able to release her innermost thoughts again. She sat on her bed and hugged her knees and thought about Seb and all the fun the larping group had experienced that afternoon.

Susan's mum popped her head round the door to say goodnight. "Something tells me you will be having sweet dreams tonight, my dear," she said with a knowing smile. Susan had told her parents about her afternoon's exploits and her mother had been quick to note that Seb had been a major player in the tale. She had also noticed the flush of anger in Susan's cheeks as she recounted the story of Kerry and her gang of fashion slaves. It concerned her that Susan was having her happiness eclipsed by Kerry and her gang. So far, they had only been verbally abusive, so she didn't feel that she needed to intervene. She knew, full well, that Susan was never short of a quick, smart answer to their taunts and hoped that things would settle down once they all went to Secondary School.

Regarding Seb, she was not worried. She could see that Susan was experiencing her first taste of puppy love. Even though she thought Susan a little young to start courting, she trusted Seb. He was a well-mannered lad and she knew his parents to be decent, hard working people. If Susan had to have a boyfriend she couldn't choose a better one than Seb.

Susan fell into a sound sleep minutes after her mum left her room and did not stir until seven o'clock the next morning.

Chapter 5
Puppy Tails and Granny Wails

The next morning Susan woke to the pleasant thought that there was no school and there would be more fun to be had playing with the others later that day. She sauntered slowly down to breakfast, unlike her usual procedure of dashing down the stairs and stuffing her mouth with food as if there was going to be a famine.

"Not hungry this morning, luv?" enquired her mum smiling.

"You know, I don't think I am," Susan said in a puzzled voice. "That's not like me!" she said with a broad grin.

"No, it's certainly not!" rejoined her mum chuckling with her. Susan did eventually manage a small breakfast of Muesli and yogurt. Her mum sat down next to her and asked what she would be doing all day.

"I'm meeting the others at two o'clock and we're larping again," she said with great enthusiasm.

"Well, that will be nice for you. I'm going to your dad's office today to do the books, so your gran will be coming to the house. Make sure that you don't upset her," she said in a cautionary tone.

"Oh, Mum, why does she have to come? You know that I can look after myself," Susan moaned.

"Because, my dear girl, it's against the law to leave you on your own in the house at your age," she said firmly.

"Don't you think it's a bit daft that I can go out into the streets by myself at my age, but I can't stay in my own house?" Susan countered, her voice rising to a crescendo of indignation.

"Well, it might seem daft, but laws were made for a

The Heart Stone

reason and I'm not going to break them. Besides, it's good for your gran to get out into the community and feel useful," she concluded emphatically.

Susan knew from her mother's tone that there would be no arguing with her, so she resigned herself to washing her breakfast dishes up and helping her mum with the morning chores. Between them they were finished in no time.

"I'm off to the garden to read now, Mum."

"Alright, luv," answered her mum.

Susan collected an old rug and a couple of cushions from the den and laid them on the lawn in the back garden and then returned to get a pile of old comics. She set herself up next to the flowered border of the garden and lay on her stomach with her legs bent up behind her and began gazing intently at the flowers.

Ever since she was tiny, she loved to look at flowers. They seemed to possess a magical quality that never failed to entrance her. She particularly marvelled at pansies that seemed to have mischievous faces painted onto their velvety heads. She wondered how a stalk so thin could support the big flowered head. Moreover, Susan wondered how the little pansies could flower through the winter. She would watch them being buffeted in gale force winds and still the tiny, thin stalks would holdfast even though large branches were being ripped from trees by the force of the wind. She thought it a miracle of nature. It also made her think of what her mother used to tell her when she complained about being rather small and weedy for her age. She said, "Strength has got nothing to do with size. It's got to do with the way you conduct yourself."

Today the marigolds and lobelias were the focus of Susan's attention. She was fascinated by the bright orange of the marigolds and the deep blue of the lobelias. She had helped her mum plant them before they had come into flower and now she had the pleasure of seeing them in full bloom. She smelled the marigolds, enjoying their rather medicinal odour and gazed deeply into the lobelias, entranced by the depth of their blue colour.

Lost in the moment, she was suddenly startled by a rustling sound behind her. She twisted herself round quickly to see what had caused the sound, but there was nothing to be seen. She shrugged and turned her attention to her comics.

Before long another sound assaulted her ears, but this time she could see clearly the cause of it. It was Rocky the neighbours' new Golden Labrador puppy that was pawing at the loose plank in the fence.

"Come on boy, you can do it!" she coaxed the playful, young, puppy. The pup needed little encouragement and negotiated the loose plank that swung back and forth with little problem. He crouched down on his front paws and slithered under the fence with tail wagging twenty to the dozen. He bounded over to her and jumped up to her, stretching up onto his hind legs to plant multiple, sloppy, licks onto Susan's willing face.

"Good boy," she purred at him in great pleasure. She grabbed him under his front paws and rolled him over on his back, playfully, much to Rocky's delight. The two of them romped happily in the garden for a good half hour before she heard the neighbour calling the puppy.

"Rocky! Rocky, come! Where are you hiding, Rocky?" the slightly worried voice rang out.

"Mrs Robinson, Rocky is here!" cried Susan, concerned that she might be causing undue concern to Rocky's owner.

"Oh, thank goodness for that," responded Mrs Robinson in her broad Yorkshire accent. "I was busy making lunch and forgot about him completely. He looks as if he has been having a grand time," she chuckled.

Mrs Robinson was a rotund, middle-aged lady who was a bit forgetful, but who had a heart of gold. Everything about her seemed jolly, her eyes were always lit up with an inner glow, her mouth was always ready with a warm, comforting, smile even at the worst of times. Her hair was always nicely done because she had been a hairdresser when she was younger. Now she and her husband were retired. They had no children and were always very kind to Susan, remembering her birthday and bringing her presents at Christmas. They would often baby-sit her when her parents went out. Susan particularly enjoyed those evenings as they would play board games with her and were quite amenable to having several chocolate laden snacks during the course of the evening.

"We've been having fun together. He's a great puppy," Susan said, wishing she could have a puppy too.

"Well, you know you can play with him anytime that you want to, Susan," said Mrs Robinson kindly.

"Thank you very much," Susan said, happy to have been given unlimited access to Rocky.

Mrs Robinson called Rocky again and he responded eagerly especially when she told him that his "din-din" was ready.

Susan spent the rest of the morning reading her comics, stopping intermittently to watch the various birds that visited their bird table. She checked her watch at regular intervals wishing away the hours until she could meet the others. Time was dragging by excruciatingly slowly despite her doing all the time-wasting things that she could think up. Finally, she decided that she would ask Mrs. Robinson if she could take Rocky for a walk.

Mrs. Robinson happily agreed, clicking Rocky's lead to his collar and handing over the excitable pup to Susan. "He's a bit awkward still with his lead, Susan luv, so be patient with him."

"Don't worry, I'll look after him and teach him to walk nicely," responded Susan brightly. She felt much cheered at the prospect of a walk with Rocky. The happy twosome set off down the road with regular 'sitting downs' from Rocky. He was not sure what a lead was required for. It only seemed to impede his freedom. Susan was in full flood of coaxing Rocky to walk nicely when she was accosted by a distant voice that hailed her.

"What are you doing, Miss?" Susan spun around to see her Aunt Jill with her small border terrier walking up behind them.

"Oh, Aunt Jill, I'm trying to get Rocky to walk nicely," she lamented.

As Aunt Jill drew close, the two dogs started wagging their tails in a delighted manner and greeted one another effusively. Jill's dog, Trixie, was little more than a puppy herself, but had mastered the art of walking on a lead.

"Where are you going?" Aunt Jill asked.

"Just down to the edge of The Stray," replied Susan.

"Well, shall I come with you and see if we can get Rocky sorted out between us?" offered Aunt Jill kindly.

"Yes, that would be lovely," responded Susan happy to have some help with Rocky. He was proving to be more of a problem than she had anticipated. The pavement was rather narrow for them both to be walking side by side, so Aunt Jill went ahead with Trixie. Rocky adopted the "sit down" mode again and Susan had to drag him to his feet once more. However, this time, Rocky stood up and looked at Trixie walking in front of him. He looked at Aunt Jill, he looked at the lead and then he looked at Susan and his own lead and then began walking perfectly! Susan had watched this little scene with disbelief realizing that Rocky had just used his intelligence to see what was required of him when on a lead. From that moment, Rocky walked perfectly with Susan. His demeanour seemed to say that, if it was alright for such a distinguished lady as Trixie to walk on a lead, then it was alright for him too.

Aunt Jill looked over her shoulder to see how Susan was getting on and was amazed to see Rocky walking so nicely, "Well, I never!" exclaimed Aunt Jill. "I've never seen a dog learn something so quickly!"

They continued on to the middle of The Stray to where Aunt Jill decided it would be safe for the dogs to go off lead and have a run. The two dogs ran off wildly, taking it in turns to chase each other, sometimes barking in sheer delight of the run and the feeling of the fresh breeze whooshing past them. Rocky walked home just as beautifully as he had earlier. Susan was eager to tell Mrs. Robinson about his progress.

"Look," said Susan, wheeling Rocky around the garden expertly. "He really knows what he's supposed to do now. He just watched my Aunt Jill's dog walking on the lead and he seemed to figure it all out for himself."

"Well, I'm truly amazed!" exclaimed Mrs. Robinson. "I've been trying for weeks to get him to walk properly and he goes out with you once and you've got him trained."

"Well, I think he trained himself really. You know, the last time Aunt Jill was here with Trixie, Rocky came through the fence and they played in the garden together. I think that they made friends then and that helped Rocky," announced Susan in a decisive manner.

"Well, whatever it was, I'm very grateful. Here, luv, have a chocolate bar for that," Mrs. Robinson said, rummaging in her apron pocket for a chocolate bar to reward Susan for her efforts.

"No thank you," she replied, surprising herself with her lack of appetite for chocolate.

"Are you sure?" enquired Mrs. Robinson equally surprised by Susan's refusal of the chocolate bar.

"Yes, honestly, and besides I am a bit late for my lunch and I am meeting my friends soon," said Susan, surprised at how quickly the time had passed while she had been out with Rocky. She took her leave of Mrs. Robinson and ran into the house in search of her mother. However, her mother had already left and her gran was sitting with her usual stony face waiting for Susan to arrive.

"About time, Miss. I've had your lunch ready for half an hour now and I shouldn't wonder that it's spoiled," she grumbled. Susan wondered how her gran's food could get any worse than it was. It was the most tasteless, bland food she had ever eaten. Gran believed that basic was best and didn't agree with any embellishments to food nor, indeed, did she believe in any embellishments to life. Sylvia and her sister Jill had been brought up in Spartan conditions. No frills, no extras, no special treats despite their father earning a decent wage. Susan wondered how her own mother and her Aunt Jill could be so different from their mother. They loved to indulge their husbands and children and every weekend was made to be a special occasion for both of their families.

However, Susan knew that there was nothing to do other than sit down and force the bland food down. The alternative was to hear a ceaseless ranting of how she should be grateful for what she was given and how kids didn't know how good they had it these days and that children in Africa would be eternally grateful for a mere

The Heart Stone

morsel off her plate. Susan thought, unkindly, that *even the starving children in Africa would probably spit out her gran's food*. None the less, she forced the unpleasant food down in record time, encouraged by the fact that it was almost time to meet the others for larp.

"You'll get wind if you bolt your food down like that," observed her gran dryly.

Her gran wasn't entirely displeased at seeing Susan eating so quickly. She was under the misguided notion that it was due to the delicious nature of the food. Usually, Susan would dawdle over the food her gran cooked, looking uncomfortable until she finally finished her plate.

"I'm not getting wind," she assured her gran. Finishing her plate, she ran to wash her hands, informing her gran that she would be on The Stray for several hours with her friends.

"Well, don't you be disturbing other people and mind your manners if anyone speaks to you," she grunted.

"Yes, Gran," she sang out as she ran through the door, free at last.

She covered the distance to The Stray in record time. As Susan approached the seat where they had all arranged to meet, she saw Seb approaching with his mobile phone in his hand. He waived at her with his other hand and loped over to the seat, talking in rapid Italian into his mobile. Joyful noises in the distance heralded the arrival of Aliya and her boisterous cousins. Susan waived cheerily at them whilst Seb mouthed to her that he would be only a minute. Well, actual he mouthed "uno momento" as he had not made the mental transition from Italian to English, but Susan knew what he was saying.

Aliya and her merry throng arrived before Seb had finished on the phone and they began, enthusiastically, discussing the plan of campaign for the afternoon's larp session. Seb seemed to be in a heated discussion as much arm waving and body posturing was taking place. Finally, with a resigned "Si Papa," he clicked his mobile phone shut.

"Everything alright?" Susan enquired gently, hoping that whatever had transpired would not affect him joining in this afternoon.

"Sort of," he said uneasily. "My dad wants me to come and help in the kitchen at his work at 5:30 p.m. tonight. There's a panic on because the staff have had a family crisis and can't get into work until later tonight. My mum is going in to help too," he concluded. All the staff were members of Federico's extended family and were all affected by the crisis.

"If you like, I could ask mum if I can come and help too," Susan offered.

Seb immediately brightened and phoned his father who thought this was an excellent idea.

"That would be brilliant, Susan. When the other staff get in, Dad will make us some food and we can eat it in the restaurant," Seb responded brightly.

Susan phoned her mum and after some complex arrangements had been made about who would be collecting her from Federico's, her mother agreed to let her help out at the restaurant.

Underneath a nearby Chestnut Tree, Susan had noted that Aliya was holding an animated conversation with another cousin, Omar, who had joined them today and was just their age. He was extremely handsome, tall, with broad shoulders and a slender waist, large, animated brown eyes that could melt a heart of stone, a straight, medium sized nose and a well proportioned mouth that seemed always to be ready to break into a wide, toothy grin.

"What are you two talking so passionately about?" demanded Susan cheekily. "I wish my cousins were as lively as yours."

"Oh! Omar's not my cousin," Aliya replied, blushing readily. "He's the son of my father's best friend."

"Aha!" said Susan none too discretely as she eyed them

The Heart Stone

both up and down. She wasn't displeased with the fact that the two of them were obviously interested in each other. That meant that she didn't have to worry about Aliya being attracted to Seb.

Susan's spirits soared; her day was getting better and better! All the larpers congregated together and finalized their plot for the afternoon, allowing enough time for Seb and Susan to leave for the restaurant. The afternoon's session passed uneventfully with no unwarranted disturbances from the Beauty Parlour Brigade. The time sped by and it seemed as if no time at all had passed before it was time for Seb and Susan to leave.

"Have fun and enjoy your dinner," shouted Aliya as they left.

"Okay, see you tomorrow," Susan replied.

"See ya!" shouted Seb in Omar's general direction, not wanting to be left out of the little exchange.

"Yeah, see ya!" echoed Omar.

"Have a good time!" exclaimed George cheerily.

Chapter 6
Susan and Seb Serve It Up Italian Style

Susan and Seb arrived at the restaurant in good time. As they walked towards the kitchen they heard Seb's parents talking happily from within.

"Allo children," said Seb's father, Gino, in a heavy Italian accent. "You're Susan, yes?" He directed his gaze at her.

"Yes, Mr. Alameda, pleased to meet you," she said, sticking out her hand importantly.

"I am very pleased to know you too and please call me Gino. This is my wife, Rosa," he said, shaking Susan's hand vigorously.

"Allo Susan," Rosa said in an equally heavy Italian accent. "I lika to say thank you very much for you coming to help us this evening. Your'a mama talk to me and say it is okay that you work."

"You're welcome, Rosa," responded Susan feeling very grown up in calling Seb's parents by their first names.

Susan's parents always insisted that she address adults formally unless they specified otherwise. However, Seb's parents were very young looking for their age, which Susan estimated to be around forty, given that Seb had an older brother of nearly twenty. They had such a happy, carefree, demeanour that it seemed quite appropriate to call them by their first names.

Gino was a tall, broad shouldered man with handsome regular features and an olive complexion. He had long, wavy hair of a dark auburn colour that was tied up neatly in a ponytail.

Rosa was petite with a girlish figure and was very

pretty. She had large hazel eyes that sometimes shone green depending on the light, a pert little nose and a gently curving mouth that seemed ever eager to break into a smile. Her shoulder length hair was also neatly tied into a ponytail of golden brown that shone with subtle threads of pale blonde.

Smiling at the two youngsters, Rosa invited them to follow her into the back of the kitchen; she led them to a very large sink and asked them to wash their hands thoroughly with hot water and antibacterial soap. Then she led them to the side of the kitchen that was full of fitted cupboards and drawers.

"All'a the knives and a forks are here," she indicated a large set of drawers that was full of clean cutlery. "We need'a to set up all'a the tables in'a the restaurant. Do you know'a how to do that Susan?" she enquired.

"Yes, I do," she answered confidently. Her mother had taught her all about etiquette and the proper way to lay a table.

"Well then, you and Sebastian can'a start wi' that please," she said with a big smile.

Susan and Seb gathered up the cutlery and serviettes into a large wicker basket and set off into the restaurant. No sooner had they begun the task of setting the tables than the front door of the restaurant opened and a small, rotund man with a loud, jolly voice greeted them.

"What a blessing, we have two sweet cherubs to rescue us tonight," his voice boomed warmly with only a hint of an Italian accent.

Susan immediately recognized the man as Federico, the restaurant owner. He was often seen strutting round the restaurant, enquiring if all was well with the diners and generally letting everyone know that he was the Federico, owner (not waiter!) of Hardingate's magnificent Italian restaurant. He was short in stature with a large belly. His small, rather beady eyes were always darting around looking to see if the customers were looking satisfied with their meals. His large nose sat over a small, well-trimmed moustache and his thin lips would willingly break out into a beaming smile. Federico was known to be rather pompous but was still well liked because of his good nature and sense of humour. He wanted everyone who ate in his restaurant to enjoy their food and have a smile on their face. As the food was good and the atmosphere pleasant, this was usually achieved.

"Hello, Mr. Cellini. This is Susan, my friend," said Seb politely.

"Ciao, Sebastian," Mr. Cellini's Italian accent became more and more prominent as he spoke. "I have seen this lovely little lady in my restaurant before, have I not?" He raised an eyebrow questioningly at Susan.

"Yes sir," she replied. She wasn't quite sure what Federico's surname was, as she hadn't heard what Seb had called him. "I come in with my parents about once a month," she replied politely.

"Yes, your father has a joinery business. I know him," he said loudly, mentally congratulating himself on his memory. "Anyway, you may call me Mr. Federico," he left the two of them to get on with their work.

They managed to set up the tables quickly and report back to Rosa who directed them to the next job, which was to empty the industrial sized dishwasher and put everything away. Before they had completed the job, the first customers had arrived in the restaurant. Rosa quickly took off the overall that she had been wearing in the kitchen to reveal a straight black skirt and a pristinely white shirt. She picked up an order pad and walked quickly into the restaurant to greet the diners. From that time onward, the restaurant began to get busier.

Gino had fired up the ovens and was dealing with several orders at once. Susan and Seb were kept busy setting plates of cooked food onto a hot plate ready for Rosa to take to the

The Heart Stone

customers in the restaurant. Even Federico had his jacket off and was serving the customers too—a rare sight! Susan couldn't believe the speed with which Gino and Rosa were working. It was as if their feet were flying!

The next time Rosa came to the kitchen, she looked rather flustered and spoke in rapid Italian to Gino who then turned to Susan and Seb and translated what Rosa had said to them.

She wanted them to help her serve the food to the customers. He explained that there were quite a few children in the restaurant and it would be better if Seb and Susan served them and Rosa served the adults.

Susan felt a pang of excitement shoot through her at the thought of actually serving food to the customers. She felt extremely grown up. She was also pleased that she had worn a tidier outfit than the day before. She was wearing black cargo pants and a fitted, sky blue v-neck t-shirt. The colour of her shirt was particularly becoming to her lightly tanned complexion, and its style showed off her tiny waist.

Under Rosa's watchful eye, Susan and Seb began to serve the children in the restaurant. Susan was a bit apprehensive and nervous when first serving the food, but she soon relaxed and began having some friendly exchanges with the children. The customers kept coming in thick and fast. It was as if Federico's was the only restaurant open in town!

Susan and Seb managed to take mini breaks in between serving and helping Gino. Sitting down for a couple of minutes, Seb brought Susan an ice-cold cola to drink. "Here, I should think that you're ready for this," he said, smiling at her. "You're a great girl. Thank you for helping out like this," he said appreciatively.

Susan was unaccustomedly embarrassed and blushed to a beetroot red at Seb's words. "Oh, you're very welcome. I'm actually enjoying myself," she said honestly. "Thanks for the cola." She held the can up in salute.

"I wonder when the rest of the staff is going to get here?"

Seb asked to no one in particular.

"I hope they won't get here for a while. This is such fun!" Susan said, enjoying her first work experience.

Gino noticed that the food on the hotplate was beginning to back up again and asked the two of them to help Rosa.

Rosa came in at that moment and instructed them where they should deliver the food. Susan had to serve at the table in the far corner of the restaurant. Rosa told her that there were two children at that table for her to serve and Rosa would serve the two adults. While carrying the two plates of food across the restaurant, Susan became aware of a woman's loud, raucous voice piercing through the usual bevy of restaurant noises. As she approached the table where she was to deliver the food, she realized that the woman's voice was coming from that table. As she looked at the other people sitting at the table, she saw, with horror, that Kerry Boswell was sitting there with her little brother and that she would be serving them both.

Susan noticed that Kerry was not her usual brash self and that she was staring studiously down at the tablecloth. As Susan approached the table with her food, Kerry looked up and, for a moment, Susan saw a look of pain and embarrassment in her eyes. Susan's kind heart went out to her; Kerry seemed to be embarrassed by her mother's loud behaviour. Kerry's mother was not only loud, but very provocatively dressed, showing far more cleavage than was necessary for an early-evening family meal. Her make-up was excessive and her hair was bleached to an almost white colour. Despite this, she was not an unattractive woman, just inappropriately dressed.

Kerry's eyes met Susan's and, in an instant, the old malice was back in Kerry's eyes. She looked over and saw Seb serving food. "Boyfriend got you working for him then?" she asked sarcastically. Susan was mortified to have Kerry speak to her like this in front of Rosa. She had no need to worry. Rosa quickly spoke up for her.

"Susan is' a so kind to give her free time to us, to help us out tonight. Our staff is'a late and she has'a been working very hard, she is a very nice'a girl."

"Yes, luv. You tell her," boomed Mrs. Boswell's raucous, alcohol laden voice. "If you want to keep a feller you got to do summat to keep 'is attention." At this, she leaned in the general direction of the man who was accompanying the family and gave him a knowing wink.

"Is 'a this spaghetti for you or your husband?" inquired Rosa sweetly.

"Oh, ee's not me 'usband, at least not yet!" replied Kerry's mother giving her escort another knowing wink.

Kerry was staring down at the tablecloth again, her face bright red. Her little brother was tugging at her sleeve trying to tell her something, but she would not answer. Susan guessed correctly that Kerry was on the verge of tears and was fighting for control.

Susan asked Kerry's little brother if the margherita pizza was for him and placed it in front of him. They exchanged a pleasant smile of recognition. She put the other plate in front of Kerry and said with sincerity, "I hope that you'll enjoy your food."

Kerry didn't look up or thank Susan; she was so ashamed of her mother's behaviour that she wished that a hole in the ground would spring open and swallow her up. Every time they went out in public it was the same. Her mother would have a couple of drinks and think that she was supposed to entertain all of the people around her. No amount of pleading from Kerry could persuade her differently.

Tonight was even more embarrassing, as Susan Grey was there to witness it. She hated Susan, she hated the way that she was never intimidated by anything, even the comments that the Beauty Parlour Brigade levelled at her. Kerry hated the fact that Susan never worried about dressing in the latest fashions or adopting the "in" hairstyles, and yet could find a boyfriend like Seb with little effort.

Kerry's little brother, Mark, managed to gain Kerry's attention. "Kerry, that's Susan. She helped me on the playground when I fell down and cut my arm!" he said with great enthusiasm.

"Oh, God, not you too! Is there anyone in the world that doesn't think Miss Prissy, Susan Grey is a blooming saint?" she said, her voice laden with venom.

"She was nice to me," said Mark in a sad little voice.

Kerry didn't enjoy her food, she didn't enjoy the evening, and she was glad when it was time to leave. She vowed to take revenge on Susan Grey at the next possible opportunity.

When Susan returned to the kitchen, Seb asked her in a concerned voice if Kerry had upset her.

"Not really, Seb. In fact, I really felt sorry for her. She was so obviously embarrassed by her mother's loudness that she wasn't able to be too obnoxious herself," she replied openly.

"I would've gone and served her if I had seen she was in the restaurant," Seb said reassuringly.

"It really wasn't a big deal. Let's just forget it," Susan said with a bright smile. She was still enjoying the thrill of working in the restaurant and didn't want thoughts of Kerry Boswell spoiling it.

Shortly after this little encounter, the four tardy staff members arrived. They congregated into the kitchen discarding their coats hurriedly and thanked Rosa, Susan, and Seb for their help. Federico walked into the kitchen and a heated conversation was exchanged in rapid Italian. The four staff members looked suitably penitent for their lateness and resumed their jobs. Although they were all relatives of Federico's, he didn't cut them any slack.

After the staff had all been delegated their jobs and the restaurant was running smoothly, Rosa invited Susan and Seb into the dining room.

"Come on you two. I have a table just'a for you," she said

motioning to a small table by the window. "You deserve a very good dinner. Gino will fix, you choos'a whatever you like," Rosa said smiling.

Susan was very hungry. It was eight o'clock and she had not eaten since lunchtime. However, it seemed a little strange to be eating with Seb, but quite nice too.

They ordered their food and discussed possible locations for future larp games; they thought that the Pine Woods would be a great place.

"Yeah, if we stay at the top end of the woods there aren't too many trees, but there are enough bushes to provide hiding places if we get into any battles," Seb said with enthusiasm.

"And there's that big Willow Tree where we could make our headquarters," responded Susan with equal enthusiasm.

Their conversation was interrupted by a rather noisy rendition of the William Tell Overture playing on Susan's mobile phone.

"Oh, bother. I hope I haven't disturbed the customers," she cried in embarrassment. "I forgot to turn it to silent mode when we came to work. I never hear it if I'm outside, so I have it turned to loud."

"No harm done," Seb said, looking around at the other diners in the vicinity who looked to be rather amused by the unexpected musical outburst.

"It's Mum," she whispered to Seb. "I'll go into the loo and answer it."

"Okay," Seb replied.

Susan's mum informed her that she would be coming to pick her up as soon as she had finished her meal, as it was getting late. Susan rushed back into the restaurant to finish her meal with Seb.

"Mum is coming in half an hour to pick me up," she said with a twinge of sadness in her voice. She had so enjoyed herself that she really didn't want the evening to end.

"This has been a great day," Seb said, smiling at her. "I know my mum and dad really appreciated your help."

"Oh, it was a pleasure. I'd do it again in an instant," she replied honestly.

The next half hour just flew by and before she knew it, her mum walked through the restaurant door and over to their table. For a second, Susan didn't recognize her. She had been so engrossed in talking to Seb that she had forgotten that her mum was coming for her. Seeing her from this different perspective, she was struck by how nice looking her mother was. Her mid-brown, wavy, hair swung around her shoulders and her blue eyes sparkled with fun. Dressed in jeans and a light camisole top she looked half her age.

"Now what have you two been getting up to?" Sylvia asked, smiling broadly at them.

"Mum," said Susan obviously startled. "You're here!"

"Well. It would appear that way," she answered in an amused voice.

Seb jumped in. "Susan has been great tonight, Mrs. Grey. She's worked really hard."

Susan's mum seemed pleased at this and a moment later Federico and Rosa came over to extend their thanks too. Susan spent the short journey home and the rest of the evening telling her mum and dad about her experiences in the restaurant. When she told them about Kerry and her mother, Susan's mum chipped in.

"Yes, her mother has had a rough ride in the last few years, I've heard. It seems that her husband was a bit of a so and so and used to knock her and the kids around. In the end, she took the kids and left him. Then she had to find a job to support them. She didn't have any qualifications or any real job experience because she left school early and stayed at home to look after the children after marrying very young. Eventually, she got a job as a barmaid. I think the man she was with is her current boyfriend," she concluded.

Susan began to revise her opinion of Kerry. Now, instead of disliking her, Susan was beginning to pity her. Susan looked at her mum and dad and thought of how much she loved them. She could never imagine her dad raising his hand to her mum. Her father was a big man, but he was like a big, cuddly, teddy bear. He stood about six foot two and was well built without being fat. Lifting heavy materials and wood in his joinery business kept him in good physical shape. His hair was a sandy colour and his eyes were a piercing blue. He had a straight aquiline nose and a generous mouth that had the most amazingly white teeth. She felt a sudden rush of emotion come over her as she thought how lucky she was to have such loving parents.

"I think that the boyfriend might be going to marry Kerry's mum," Susan said, returning to the topic of conversation.

"Well, that would be nice. Perhaps then Kerry will stop being such a little horror and behave a bit better," concluded Susan's mum.

Chapter 7
A Faerie Emissary is Sent to Susan

Susan was glad to go to bed that night, the demands of working at the restaurant had taken its toll and she was feeling exhausted. She took a moment to pause at the window and admire the bright moonlight and the starry skies above her. It was a warm August night with barely a rustle of wind to disturb the calm. Susan fell asleep almost the minute her head touched the pillow. She slept soundly in her cosy bedroom which was adorned with the things that she felt were important in her life. There was a small collection of sea shells from various seaside holiday locations that ranged as wide as from Scarborough to South America. Susan's parents believed that it was important to take holidays in as many different parts of the world as they could afford. The whole family always enjoyed sitting down together before their holiday and opening the encyclopaedia to find out all the information about their chosen destination.

Her dressing table had a glass top to protect the wood underneath. Between the wood and the glass she had an assortment of photos of people she and her parents had met on holiday. Next to the dressing table there was a large wooden bookcase which, along with all the other furniture in the room, had been made, lovingly, by her father. The bookshelves were crammed full of books that Susan refused to part with. She had books there from when she first learned to read.

The walls of her bedroom were painted in a delicate pale blue and adorned with posters, hastily stuck up on the walls, of her current musical idol. She loved music and had a CD

The Heart Stone

player on the top shelf of her bookcase that she listened to when she was tired of watching the telly with her parents.

Susan's deep slumber was disturbed in the early hours of the morning. She woke up with a start and quickly looked at her bedside clock to see the time. The illuminated numbers told her that it was precisely 2:22 a.m. She was startled again by the rustling sound of pages of a book being turned over.

"This is not a bad likeness," a gentle voice rang out in the still night.

Susan gasped and was about to shriek in terror when the voice gently informed her that there was nothing to get into a tizzy about and that she should calm down. As her eyes became accustomed to the darkness she made out the silhouette of a small puck-like figure about two feet in height, perched on the end of her dressing table flipping, rudely, through the pages of one of her treasured faerie books. As she peered closer, she noted that this creature was small but perfectly proportioned. She had decided that the entity was a male and could see that he had up-slanting eyes, something of a button nose, and ears that were rather pointy at the top.

He had a mischievous grin playing on his lips and was dressed in a tunic of pale green that set atop a cream-colored cambric shirt.

He wore dark brown, knee length boots over leggings of the same colour. Upon his head he wore a pointed, green cap with a large scarlet plume that partially covered his, shoulder-length, brown hair. A wide cloak of deep forest green fell from his shoulders to his heels.

Susan's fear began to subside and curiosity and annoyance took its place.

"What are you doing in my bedroom and what are you doing with my book? Who are you?" Susan demanded, her courage growing as she began to speak.

"Oh, my name is Hawthorne. That's Hawthorne with an 'e' at the end. Well, it's actually Hector Hawthorne, but everyone calls me Hawthorne. It's an honour, you know, because I'm the eldest of the House of Hawthorne," replied the diminutive figure, looking perfectly at ease in Susan's room.

"You don't look very old to me," Susan interjected.

"Ah, I'm lot older than you perceive me to be," he said with a secret smile. "But to continue, I have come here purposefully to find you, and while you were asleep, I was having a look at this book of Faerie Stories. The illustrations are very good you know. Here, look at this," he proffered a page with a picture of a Buttercup Faerie on it. "This could be my cousin Belinda. It is really astonishing," he shook his head as if in disbelief.

"Well, as I don't know your cousin Belinda, I couldn't say whether that's a good likeness or not," Susan replied matter-of-factly while gesturing towards the book. "And why are you looking for me, anyway?"

"Oh," said Hawthorne remembering his primary mission. "The queen has asked me to bring you to her," he informed her in a more serious voice.

"What are you babbling about? And what's more, I think that I should ask what you are, not who you are. You don't look anything like anyone I've ever seen."

"Do you always ask two questions at once?" replied Hawthorne.

Susan's impatient look told Hawthorne that he had better start explaining himself a little better or he might well be brought to the attention of her parents and that was not the object of his mission. He hopped off the dressing table and onto the end of her bed and took his cap off and began to speak in a serious manner to Susan.

"I am what you call a faerie and I have been entrusted by Iridaan to come here and—"

Susan interrupted. "Who, or what, on earth is an Iridaan?"

"Iridaan, my dear Susan, is our queen. She is Queen of

the Realm of Faeries, and by the way, the correct spelling is f-a-e-r-i-e-s." Susan gave him another withering look for going off the point again. He continued, this time, with a look of seriousness that could not be disputed. "Dear Susan, our realm is in grave danger and we need you to help us," his voice had lost its amusing, if rather impertinent, tone and now resonated with a deep sorrow.

Responding to the note of sadness in his voice, Susan began to pay attention to what he was saying. She could hardly believe that she was having a conversation with a faerie, but the urgent pleading in his voice was tugging at her kind heart.

"Now, let me get this right. You're telling me that you come from a Realm of Faeries, and that you've been sent by your Faerie Queen to bring me to help you?" her voice ended on an incredulous questioning note.

"Yes, that is correct," he assured her.

Susan swallowed hard and also pinched herself rather painfully on the arm to make sure that she was awake and not dreaming. Ascertaining that she was definitely awake, she tried to make sense of things.

"Okay, Hawthorne. If I'm to believe what you're saying about your realm being in grave danger, what on earth do you think that I can do about it?" Susan enquired.

"Susan, believe it or not, the very fact that you have this book of Faerie Stories still on your bookshelf is enough to let us know that you are exactly the kind of human who will be able to help us," he said with great sincerity. "I beg of you, will you come with me to our realm and let Queen Iridaan speak with you?" he pleaded.

Susan thought hard and fast, she thought about all the things her parents had taught her about going off with strange people. *And heaven knows, he's strange*, she thought to herself. However, there was something about him that encouraged belief. She didn't feel in any danger, so she decided to ask where their realm was located.

"The Realm of Faeries is not located on what you call your Earth; it is not even located on one of your planets or stars in the solar system. It is a universe, but not one that you are consciously familiar with. It is a realm that resides in the inner world. My dear old friend, Don Rooibos, once called it an Innerverse and I think that is the best explanation that I can offer you now," Hawthorne concluded.

"How am I to get to this Innerverse?" Susan asked in confusion.

"It is not very hard for individuals like you. Indeed, you have visited us before in daydreams and in your sleep."

Susan looked at him in disbelief, again wondering whether she was imagining this encounter with Hawthorne. Perhaps she was overtired; her dad always said that you could get a bit "spacey" if you were over tired. *That must be it*, she thought. *If I just go back to bed all this will go away.*

Hawthorne looked at her and could sense her confusion. "Susan, this is all very strange to you and I know you have to take a lot in. Perhaps I should return another time when you have had time to think all this over?"

Susan's curiosity overcame her state of confusion and her impetuous nature got the better of her. She made a bold decision. "Hawthorne, I'm ready to go now," she stated bravely, "I only have one question. How long will I be gone for?"

"You will be back in no time at all, you will certainly be here for your breakfast," he assured her with a twinkle in his eye. Hawthorne jumped down from the bed and asked her to come and stand next to him. He would assist her on the journey.

Susan looked down at herself and realized that she was still in her nightclothes, "Wait! I can't go like this. I'm in my pyjamas!" she wailed.

"It does not really matter, but if it makes you feel better please change," Hawthorne told her.

The Heart Stone

Susan hastily put on her jeans and a t-shirt and tried to convince herself that she was doing a sensible thing. She didn't quite manage the "sensible" part, but she presented herself next to Hawthorne in a reasonably tidy manner.

"What do I have to do now?" she asked, hoping that she wouldn't regret what she was about to do.

"Hold my hand and think of the happiest thing that you can," he told her in a kind, reassuring manner.

It wasn't hard for Susan to think of a happy thing, the hard thing was deciding what the happiest thing was. She settled upon the last holiday that she went on with her parents to the Austrian Alps. She recalled the wonderful scenery, the scrummy food and the great fun they all had trying to learn to ski. As a smile formed on her lips she felt a strong force propelling her forward.

"Don't worry, it's all okay," said Hawthorne. "It's just a bit different doing this when you are in a waking state. Just keep holding my hand. I have got you," he said squeezing her hand in encouragement.

Chapter 8
Susan Visits the Faerie Realm

Susan felt a powerful whoosh and opened her eyes to see vibrant colours flying past her and then as suddenly as it had begun, it ended and she found herself standing still in a fantastically beautiful garden. At least, she thought it was a garden, but she could see no hedges or walls around it and it seemed to go on forever. She had never seen grass so green or flowers so vibrantly coloured. There was nothing organized about the garden. The grass wasn't particularly short or particularly long. It didn't appear to have been cut lately. The landscape rolled away into small hillocks that were strewn with assorted clumps of flowers that seemed to compete with one another in their beauty. Bushes blazed in glorious hues of every colour imaginable, some colours Susan had never even seen before, she could almost feel the colour it was so intense. Trees stood in majestic splendour, raising their branches to the skies as if to proffer their fruits to the heavens. Multicoloured birds and butterflies fluttered from tree to tree adding to the orchestra of colour.

As far as the eye could see, there was the sheer beauty of nature. A narrow river meandered round the hillocks some two hundred yards away adding to the picturesque scene. Susan also spotted some small woodland creatures scurrying around collecting some kind of food. In a brief glance, she saw rabbits of different sizes and breeds. There were also red and grey squirrels and what appeared to be albino squirrels that had long, soft looking fur. There were foxes that seemed unusually friendly with the smaller creatures that were loping around a small copse of trees. She even spotted a beaver, busily constructing a dam down by the river.

"Are you alright Susan? You are very quiet," enquired

Hawthorne.

Susan was visibly startled at Hawthorne's words. Lost in awe of this beautiful place, Susan had forgotten all about Hawthorne even though she was still clutching his hand very tightly. She turned to answer him and once again jumped in surprise. Hawthorne looked totally different. Most obviously, his size had changed. He now stood a good six foot in height and towered above Susan. His puckish features had evened out to a reveal a remarkably handsome face and he now looked to be about thirty years old.

"Oh my goodness, what has happened to you?" cried Susan in great surprise.

"Well, nothing actually," Hawthorne replied. "This is how I really look. When faerie-kind comes to your realm we are subject to the diverse electro-magnetic fields that operate there and it distorts our shape," he said informatively.

"Oh," said Susan, once more nonplussed by the information that she was being given. After thinking for a moment she continued. "But I'm still the same size as I usually am," she observed.

"That is because you are not projecting," said Hawthorne, a broad smile lighting up his handsome face.

"What do you mean by projecting?" asked Susan.

"Well, think of how you would like to appear to others and see what happens," he told her.

Susan doubted that her thoughts could make the slightest bit of difference to how she appeared, but was game to try it anyway. Everything else he had said so far had been beyond belief and turned out to be true, so maybe she would succeed.

Suddenly faced with how she would actually like to look, Susan didn't really know where to begin. She wasn't overly enamoured with her appearance, but somehow, had become accustomed to it and found herself more attached to it than she had previously thought. Nonetheless, there were a few things that she wanted to change, so she immediately thought of being about six inches taller. As the thought formed in her head, she felt a gentle shift in her physical structure and became aware of being taller.

"Unbelievable!" she cried and immediately thought of her hair and wished for straight, silken locks that behaved beautifully.

She touched her long hair and ran her fingers through it and pulled it in front of her eyes to confirm what she was feeling. She had, indeed, got her wish for lovely locks!

"Don't get carried away with all that now," said Hawthorne, beaming. "The queen will be on her way and it would be nice if you were still recognizable!"

"This is amazing!" Susan cried. "Do you change the way you look every day? How do you recognize each other?"

"You're doing it again," said Hawthorne, "asking two questions at once. No, we do not change the way we look every day. We inherit some characteristics from our parents which forms our basic structure. From there we can tweak our appearance to project our own individuality. This is not usually done until our fiftieth year when we have gained a true sense of self. However, usually during our teenage years, there is a period of intense changes and experimentation as we leave childhood. Even then, our primary characteristics are identifiable to each other; it is very rarely that we choose to be so very different from our birth appearance. Besides, as I told you, we use our senses differently than you humans and we know each other by vibration rather than appearance," he concluded.

"Wow!" said Susan, lost for words, trying to digest all that Hawthorne had told her.

"I feel Iridaan's vibration approaching now," Hawthorne said, becoming more serious.

Susan could see a tall figure striding purposefully towards them in the distance. As she drew closer, Susan was struck by the energy emanating from the queen. She was astonished to see that Iridaan was wearing leggings and a tunic similar to that of Hawthorne's. However, her cloak was more impressive and appeared to be made out of some velvety type of fabric and edged with a gold border. It was of a russet colour and was very full and draped in soft folds down to her heels. Susan imagined that her wings would be beneath the cloak.

The queen was a little shorter than Hawthorne, Susan guessed around six feet in height. She was slender, but still looked muscular, and her hair was vibrant chestnut in colour with several distinct flashes of white running through it. Her face was lightly tanned and her brow was slightly furrowed with concentration. As she neared them a warm smile developed on her generous lips which spread to her piercing blue eyes.

"Why is she dressed like that when she is queen and where are her guards and attendants?" Susan asked Hawthorne conspiratorially.

"Oh, now it's three questions at one time!" he responded in mock irritation, "Iridaan dresses like that because she is going about her day to day business, she does not wear her royal regalia unless there is an official matter of state to preside over. And as to her guards and attendants, Iridaan does not have any, she does not need any—"

Hawthorne cut his explanation short because at this point Iridaan arrived. Turning to Susan with a welcoming smile on her lips she began to speak.

"Susan I cannot tell you how pleased I am that you have come here," and as an aside to Hawthorne, she added, "Well done, Hawthorne for bringing her."

Her voice was deep for a female and it had a strong resonance within it. It was a voice, thought Susan that invited trust.

"Your Majesty, I am truly amazed that I'm here, and am glad that I came because I've never seen anywhere so beautiful or amazing in my life!" Susan exclaimed.

"Do you like it?" Iridaan asked with a note of pride in her

voice. "We all created this in our collective consciousness and projected it into physical reality. Oh, and please call me Iridaan as everyone does!"

"Oh, I thought that Kings and Queens should be addressed as Majesty," Susan said, a little confused.

"You are correct in relation to your realm, but you will find that things are very different here," Iridaan confided.

"I do know about projecting though," offered Susan, fearing that she might have sounded less than intelligent about the Majesty thing. "Look, I've made myself taller!"

"Yes, I had noted that and you have done a very good job for a first timer!"

Susan swelled with pride at this; however, she was becoming rather distracted by a small event that had started taking place ever since Iridaan had joined them. Out of the corner of her eye she had noted that the beautiful Oak Tree that stood to the right of them had started changing shape and it was now showing very definite signs of becoming an even more beautiful Weeping Willow Tree. Susan felt very rude in turning her gaze away from Iridaan, but she had never seen anything like it in her life.

Noting the direction of her gaze, Iridaan offered, in an amused tone, an explanation to Susan. "This is the only tree that all we faeries have never been able to agree upon. Some have thought that it should be Larch others believed that it should be Horse Chestnut, still others thought that it would be more suited to being a Cherry Tree, there were many suggestions. In the end, we decided that we would allow each other the pleasure of projecting the tree into whatever type of tree that we felt appropriate when we passed by it."

"But, what if a group of you all walk by together and you all project something different?" enquired Susan a little confused.

"Clever girl! You are beginning to understand the mechanics of projecting! The answer, dear Susan, is simply that the faerie whose wishes are the strongest will prevail. When you arrived here with Hawthorne he, naturally, projected his wish upon the tree and it became an Oak Tree. When I arrived, it became a Weeping Willow because, at this moment, my wish or desire is stronger that Hawthorne's. On another occasion it might be that Hawthorne's desire for it to be an Oak Tree that will prevail. The tree then remains in the form that the last faerie wished upon it until the next one comes along."

"Isn't that very tiring for the tree?" Susan asked.

"No, it isn't. The tree has agreed to become a changing tree and it enjoys its uniqueness amongst trees," Iridaan said smiling.

"Do you have conversations with trees then?" asked Susan astonished.

"Susan, we are so close to them that we can hear their every whisper. We hear their songs; we feel the strength of their limbs. Yes, Susan, we speak to them and they answer," Iridaan said with emotion.

Susan felt very reverent at this point and did not venture to ask any of the many questions that were burning inside her. A gentle silence fell upon the three of them. Hawthorne was the first to speak.

"Iridaan, I have not spoken of the reason that we bring Susan to our realm. Only just to say that we need her," Hawthorne said with some seriousness.

"How can you possibly need me when you have all of this magic at your fingertips?" Susan asked.

"Dear Susan, what you see around you is our creation, we have brought into being this beautiful realm for us to exist in. However, the reason for our existence is to serve the realm of humans, especially the children," Iridaan replied.

"I can't imagine why you would want to serve us. We're not very good about looking after the things in nature," said Susan sadly, remembering the school lessons where she had learned about human wastage and pollution.

"That is true," said Iridaan. "But there was a time when you excelled at it; many eons ago you had a civilization known as Arbouria where you humans worked in harmony with nature and had an unrestrained imagination that brought forth wonders akin to what you see here."

"What happened to us that made us forget all these things?" asked Susan in awe.

"Many things happened, but the main event that changed your history was, sadly, a venture that was meant to be the ultimate gesture of peace amongst your kind. The scientists of that time were instructed to alter the genetic make-up of the race to eradicate aggression in the hope of preventing violent confrontation and wars. They succeeded only too well but this produced a race of people who became increasingly unmotivated, uninspired and lazy with each succeeding generation. They lost the impetus to use their imagination and, in time, all the great works of art and engineering and all the learning about human health disappeared. That civilization died out all but for a few rebels who broke away from the others. These rebels managed to keep their genetic make-up intact so did not succumb to the same fate as those that stayed in Arbouria. Initially, they prospered in the new colony that they founded. However, their success was short lived as a catastrophic ice age befell them. They endured much hardship as the cold and lack of food bore down upon them but in the end they prevailed and it is from those people that your current civilization evolved," she paused to allow Susan chance to digest this information.

"That's amazing!" was all that Susan could summon as a comment on Iridaan's words.

However, after a moment's pause Susan was full of questions. "So if humans are the descendants of these rebel people are we capable of doing the things that they did. I mean all the technology and working with nature and all

The Heart Stone

those things?" she asked in a doubtful manner.

"You most surely are, my dear, but therein is the problem. You have lost your way as a race of people; many have become selfish and do not care for others or the creatures and plants that live in your realm. With a new and positive attitude you could regain your capability of creating a truly wonderful realm. All it would take would be for your people to cooperate and respect each other, then you could all share equally the gifts and wonders of your realm and work closely with nature again," Iridaan said with hope in her voice.

"I wish we could do that," Susan said hopefully,

"Unfortunately, it is because you have lost your way as a race that we are at war now," said Iridaan gently.

"I don't understand," said Susan feeling concerned.

"Let me try and explain things better to you. The purpose of our lives is to help the human realm to fulfil their dreams."

"How do you do that?" asked Susan, still feeling a little confused.

"We are able to feel the vibration of your imagination and when your creativity is at its highest and most beneficial to humankind, we are able to help you to fulfill your potential. We begin working with children when they are very young and their imagination has no limits. During sleep and daydreams we, invisibly, help to direct their thoughts in a positive and beneficial way. We help them to learn that they only have to believe in themselves and they can create wonders. Then we interact with the elements to facilitate their good intentioned dreams to be fulfilled," Iridaan replied.

Susan's eyes were as round as saucers in total amazement at Iridaan's words. Her mind was whizzing trying to absorb all the information that she was receiving.

Iridaan continued. "But for some time now, we have not been able to do our work, as there is a malaise in you humans. There are few of you left who can interact with the faerie race. Your imaginations do not call to us in the way that they have done before, they are captivated by a dark force. This has caused a devastating war in our realm," she concluded looking sadly at the ground.

"But this place is beautiful," exclaimed Susan gesturing all around her. "How can there be any war here?"

"What you see here is but a remnant of our beautiful realm. Our borders are being driven back every day. Our warriors are fighting bravely against the most fearful of enemies and we are losing the war," Iridaan said tearfully.

"Who is this enemy?" asked Susan feeling alarm at the thought of these beautiful creatures being killed.

"They have many names, but we call them the negs because they emanate soul-destroying, negative, energy which is fatal to us. Their armies have become vast over the last few decades and they become stronger each day. With each attack we are weakened."

"But," interjected Susan insistently. "You have magical powers; surely you can overpower them with that?"

"Therein is the greatest sadness, my dear. The negs are able to withstand our magic. Our fight is a desperate one."

"Where do these negs come from?" inquired Susan.

"This will be sorrowful for you, dear Susan," said Iridaan not wanting to upset the kind-hearted young girl who stood before her. "They come from the human realm."

"Oh!" gasped Susan in horror. "What makes them come here?"

"They come here to stop us doing our work with Earth children," said Iridaan.

"What are they?" asked Susan wanting to know more about these dreadful creatures.

"They are the product of idle imaginations, especially those of children. Many children do not use their imaginations to play anymore, nor do the adults. They are happy to sit transfixed to a TV or computer screen and

The Heart Stone

let someone else create their play. A little TV and some time spent playing on computers can be very beneficial but things have got out of control. Children are becoming dull and unmotivated; they have no spontaneity of their own. This is caused by the influence of the negs, a dark, depressing blackness that, when fully developed, spawns the most hideous of creatures. They find their way to our realm in order to prevent us doing our work with humans. We are their absolute enemy. When they are weak they cannot infiltrate our realm but they come now in their hordes and we are overwhelmed," Iridaan said.

"I'm so, so sorry!" said Susan mortified at the thought of human children being the cause of something as horrific as the negs.

"You are not to blame, dear child, neither are the children who are now in the thrall of the negs. Somewhere in your evolution the path forked and you lost your natural instincts that lead you towards harmony with others and the Earth. Those instincts, if followed, would have protected you from the influence of the negs. Now your realm is vulnerable, and although the negs cannot kill you, they can control you to the point where you have no more free will. Moreover, the negs will not stop at our two realms, they will go on to eradicate all the imagination and spontaneity out of every realm within their reach."

"That is dreadful, why is this happening now?" exclaimed Susan, shocked by what Iridaan had told her.

Iridaan continued. "In the distant past, when there were very few negs in your realm, they saw the potential to gain a strong foothold in the land and began plotting their vile strategies to enslave your people. Invisibly, they infiltrated the minds of vulnerable Earth people and cultivated their greed for money. With this, your society started to focus away from that which is natural and look for fulfillment in material things. The negs hoped that soon all focus would be upon material things and away from nature and the development of the inner-self which is extremely beneficial to you. So they lay dormant, waiting for the moment of greatest opportunity before they struck. For some fifty years now, the negs have been, invisibly, preying upon children. They have been feeding upon their undirected energy leaving them lethargic and drained. Now, many Earth children just follow, slavishly, the dictates of the latest fashion or play PC Games, without using their mind or imagination. They have become, unknowingly, servants to the negs and we faeries are powerless to help them. Now is the strongest that the negs have ever been. That is why they strike at this time. Without the happy dreams and imaginings from the Earth children our realm is threatened and, without us your, future is bleak too."

"How are you able to hold on now?" asked Susan wondering how bad things had become.

"It is only the old guard of children and those like yourself who are keeping our realm in one piece," Iridaan sighed sadly and looked to Susan as if for salvation.

"Who are the old guard of children?" asked Susan thinking that they must be teenagers or the like.

"They are the children who are now, in your years, around eighty or ninety. They belong to a simpler time when believing in faeries and other nature spirits was easier. It is these children and their lasting beliefs that are keeping the foundations of our realm together," the queen replied.

"But they aren't children!" cried Susan in surprise. "They're old and usually pensioners,"

"My dear, remember that we live very long lives, often many hundreds of years, so to us they are still children. They have also retained their youthful beliefs in magical things. Because of this belief, you will find many of them embarking upon what might seem impossible feats for their age. They run marathons and go parachuting and go dancing until the small hours. They have learned that they can achieve almost anything that they set their minds and

The Heart Stone

beliefs to. They do not let age stand in their way; they use it as a tool. All the wisdom they have collected over the years gives them a firm foundation with which to embark on their adventures," Iridaan explained.

"Oh," said Susan a little dumbfounded. She had never really thought about older people being anything other than, well, rather boring. However, now that she thought about it she had met some oldish people that seemed to be very young at heart who had a twinkle in their eyes that seemed to light up their whole face. *Mmmm,* she thought. *Mr. and Mrs. Robinson next door are a bit like that.*

"Do you mean that children who have strong imaginations and hopes and dreams are safe from the negs?" asked Susan seeking clarity.

"Yes, although one can never be too complacent, one should regularly check ones own thought processes and ensure that a wide variety of subjects are being considered. It is when one begins to become fixated on one subject or event without variety that the negs can find their opportunity to strike," said Iridaan seriously.

"I understand, it is important to do a variety of things, like different games and hobbies that stimulate our minds and keep us entertained and focused," Susan said.

"Precisely, that is your best protection," said Iridaan, pleased that Susan had grasped her words so well.

Susan enquired again about the attacking negs in the Faerie Realm. "If the negs are attacking you why can't I see any sign of it? Where are they?"

"Two questions at once again!" interjected Hawthorne.

"They are here, Susan, do not doubt that. They are pounding at our borders as we speak," Iridaan said.

"Can we go there and see them?" asked Susan wishing to see things for herself.

"Most definitely not," replied Iridaan emphatically. "I would not dream of exposing you to such danger. That is why you are here in the safest place there is at this moment."

"But I'm not afraid to see what is happening," argued Susan.

"Susan," said Iridaan sharply, "there is no way that I will allow you to come to harm in this realm. However, there is a way that you can safely see what is taking place." Iridaan closed her eyes and concentrated for about one minute.

"She is summoning," explained Hawthorne.

"Who is she summoning and is she doing it in her mind?" asked Susan.

"In answer to *your two* questions, I believe she will be summoning the empaths, and, yes, she is doing it in her mind. Most of our communication to others is done telepathically. When we use our voices it is usually to speak pleasant thoughts or to sing or recite poetry. We use our voices to emphasize our pleasure; or in this case, with you, when we need to communicate information to another person," Hawthorne replied.

Two happy looking young girls came into view. Susan guessed them to be about sixteen years old. They were both about her height, now that she had made herself taller. As they drew closer, she could see that they bore a striking resemblance to each other. The word "twins" popped into her mind. She instinctively looked at Hawthorne who said, "See, I told you, you could use telepathy," he said with a big grin.

"So they're twins?" she asked him.

"Yes, dear Susan, they are the empaths from the family of Catkin," he responded

"They look very young to be empaths. Although I am not sure what an empath is," Susan said, a little confused.

"An empath, in our realm," explained Hawthorne, "is an individual who has extra strong telepathic powers and who can accurately portray events that are happening in another place. And yes, the twins are quite young about thirty of our years but together their powers are exceptional, you will see what I mean."

The Heart Stone

Iridaan began to speak as the two girls drew near. "Welcome dear ones come and meet Susan."

The two girls touched Susan gently on the shoulder in greeting and she felt a little tingle run through her at their touch, as if a breeze had blown through her hair.

"We are so happy to meet you," uttered the girls excitedly

in voices that sounded like tinkling chimes.

"They are not used to using their voices and have not tuned their pitch to normal conversation level," explained Hawthorne.

"Oh, I hope that they never do. They sound wonderful!" cried Susan in admiration.

Iridaan interjected at this point. "Susan this is Tina May and Laura June of the House of Catkin."

"I am so happy to meet you too!" cried Susan excitedly.

"Why are you called May and June?" asked Susan hoping to hear the wonderful tinkling voices again.

Hearing Susan's thoughts the two girls obliged and spoke to her again in tinkling tones. Tina May began the sentence and informed her that they she had been born on May 31 at a minute to midnight.

"And I," interjected Laura June, "was born on June 1 a minute after midnight. So although we are twins we were born on different days and thus we are called May and June."

Susan was fascinated with Tina May and Laura June; they were very pretty with large, luminous dark brown eyes that shone with deep intensity. Their eyes were framed by beautifully arched brows and long dark eyelashes that contrasted with their glowing pearl coloured complexion. They had pert little noses that sat atop generous lips that were upturned at the corners from frequent laughter and smiles. Their curly hair, which fell in beautiful soft ringlets down their slender backs, almost persuaded her that her own curly hair could be as beautiful as theirs. They wore the same outfit as Iridaan and Hawthorne but they wore no cloak so their wings were clearly visible. They were not gossamer wings, as she had always read in stories, but a more sturdy looking material that shimmered like Mother of Pearl. Their wings fell from shoulder to heel and were folded down like birds wings when not in flight. Susan couldn't keep herself from staring at the twins' magnificent appearance.

As if in accordance Iridaan said, "They are lovely, are they not?"

"Oh yes! They are so beautiful," agreed Susan.

"I have summoned them here for a purpose," turning to the two girls, Iridaan said, "Show us what is happening on the battle front my dears!" Tina and Laura lost their sparkle and became more serious and moved about sixteen feet away from each other. Turning to face one another the two girls unfurled their lovely wings and rose with a whoosh about six feet into the air and for some sixty seconds they closed their eyes and concentrated as their wings vibrated rapidly to keep them in a fixed position. Suddenly their eyes flew wide open simultaneously and projected a strong light in the space between them. Susan felt slightly afraid at the intensity of their actions and the seriousness that emanated from the two empaths.

Iridaan moved over and put her arm around Susan's shoulders for which she was grateful. As the beam of light between the twins grew stronger, forms began to take shape. Soon Susan could see what looked like a holographic image of a battle scene take shape. She began to see a long line of faeries, both male and female, facing a dark void.

Behind the faeries was the lush and beautiful land that was as unspoiled as that on which she stood. The land ahead of them, however, was a desolate wasteland. The warrior faeries were dressed in what she imagined to be battle armour; a shiny breastplate covered their chest, which was strapped over their shoulders, allowing their wings to be free. Underneath this, they wore a tunic that fell to their knees. On their heads they wore a shiny helmet of the same material as the breastplate. In their helmets they wore large plumes that matched their tunic, some were blue, some were red, in fact, noted Susan, most of the colours of the rainbow were in evidence. On their legs they wore thick boots of a leathery consistency that flared out just above the knee allowing them room to bend their knees comfortably.

Susan wondered if the coloured plumes had special significance.

Reading her thoughts Hawthorne interjected, "The colours that they wear represent their family house, my family's colour is maroon," he said with some pride.

"I can see your plumes," said Susan. "There must be many of your family there."

"Yes, we are one of the oldest and largest of all the Faerie Realm. My heart is with them," said Hawthorne with sadness. "I will not fight until the last battle; we older faeries will make the last stand as we are able to hold out longer."

"That's strange," said Susan. "On our Earth the old do not have to fight because they are weak."

"Here it is different. The old have greater wisdom and experience that strengthens their powers. They are able to project their energy to those who are weakening in battle," Hawthorne said in reply.

"What weapons do you fight with?" inquired Susan unable to see either gun or sword in the hands of the warriors.

As Susan spoke the scene that the empaths were displaying burst vividly into action. There was a deep, baleful sound that emanated from the black void and a horrifying shape loomed up from it. It was about twenty feet in width and forty feet in height and was rising swiftly. It had no recognizable form, just a mass of solid darkness that swirled in a monstrous formation that eradicated every ray of light in its path.

"That is a neg," said Hawthorne with loathing. It struck terror into Susan's heart. Iridaan pulled her cloak around Susan obscuring the menacing view from her. Susan was comforted by the warmth of Iridaan's body and steady, strong beat of her heart. Unable to restrain herself from looking at the horrible spectre, Susan peeked out from

The Heart Stone

under the cloak to see about twenty faeries fly into the air above the monstrous neg.

As they rose upwards, their battle cry filled the air. A vibrating chorus like she had never encountered in her life; both chilling and harmonious. With this sound a brilliant light shone forth from their eyes in the same manner that it had with the empaths. This time the combined, piercing light from the faeries eyes was directed at the neg. Captured in the light, the neg was immobilized for some seconds. However, the victory was short lived; the darkness was beginning to swallow up the projected light from the faeries eyes as, one by one, they began reeling backwards and falling to the ground.

"What's happening? What's happening!" cried Susan in confused terror.

"The neg has overpowered our forces. We use no other weapons than our power to project. We try to hold on to our land by projecting our wishes onto the neg but, again, they are swallowing our land into their filthy blackness and feeding off our positive energy. I must focus now, Susan, please excuse me!"

Susan felt Iridaan's body stiffen and felt a rush of wind sweep past her and out towards the horizon. Susan imagined (correctly) that this was energy being sent to the battle-front to help the weakening faeries. She saw Hawthorne stiffen in a similar manner and felt the rush of energy pass her too. Hawthorne became unsteady on his feet and began to sway a little.

"Steady, Hawthorne!" commanded Iridaan. "You cannot give all your reserves now! There are still battles ahead!"

"But its Laurelei, he is almost gone!" cried Hawthorne with great emotion.

"You cannot save him, Hawthorne, without damaging yourself beyond repair. Let him go. That is what he would want," replied the queen with gentleness.

Hawthorne let out a heart-rending sob and cried,

"Farewell, my good friend, you have stood in battle for forty days without rest. Fly swiftly now; go to your peace with the father in the sky. All who remain here will know of your courage, we will sing of your wonderful life and you will feel our love rise up to you. "

Susan had come out from the shelter of the queen's cloak feeling a little braver now that she understood what was happening. She felt the deepest of sorrow for the brave faeries that she had seen fall in this foray. She wanted to comfort Hawthorne, seeing him in such distress, but she could think of nothing that would help him so she stood in respectful silence for some moments.

Susan looked over to the queen who had moved a little distance away and watched in awe as Iridaan threw back her head and sent forth a wail that shook the ground beneath their feet.

"Don't fear, dear girl, she speaks to the spirit of Laurelei and bids him farewell and tells the father in the Upper Realm that he leaves Iridaan's protection," said Hawthorne.

"Is he dead?" she asked timorously.

"Alas, it is so. He goes from us this day. There were too many casualties who needed our energies in this foray to keep him alive. He has fought tirelessly on the front lines and taken the brunt of every attack. Now he leaves us," he concluded sadly.

"The father in the Upper Realm is he God?" asked Susan reverently.

"You would think of him as God, he is our creator and he is the husband of Iridaan. Together they are the loving force that first breathed life into us," replied Hawthorne with equal solemnity.

Susan wanted to ask more questions but the spectre that the empaths were projecting was becoming animated again. Susan looked once more at the scene of the battle and witnessed the advance of the neg. It drew closer devouring everything in its path and turning it into blackness to feed the void.

"With each advance, they take more of our land and our lives. Our situation is critical," said Hawthorne.

Susan watched as the faeries regrouped to face their enemy. This time there was some help for them. Susan's eyes were drawn towards the projected image of the sky and she saw an amazing sight. A fleet of six shimmering, silvery white dragons soared through the sky; they encircled the neg and began strafing it on all sides with their fiery breath.

At these scorching blasts the neg withdrew from sight. However, nothing of the land of the Faerie Realm was restored as it withdrew. A bleak, ashen wasteland was all that remained.

"How wonderful," cried Susan "the dragons can beat the neg! You will be able to win the war now!"

"I wish that it were that simple, my dear Susan. We only have six dragons and they cannot defeat the negs when they strike in greater numbers. Besides, we only have the dragons because of a careless projection by one of our young faeries. Toby, of the House of Allium, forgot that we are not allowed to create living creatures. Only the Father and the Mother may do that and even they must seek authority from a higher power to do that."

"How did Toby manage to create them then?" asked Susan full of curiosity.

"Well, Toby is a faerie who loves to read adventure stories and one day he thought he would try his hand at writing a story of his own. He became so absorbed in the mystical story of magic and sorcery that he was writing that his imagination intermingled with his projecting ability and whoosh! We had six dragons circling over the main street of our town! Normally, they would have been de-materialized straight away but everyone found them so beautiful and entertaining, they can be very funny you know, that we were allowed to keep them!" said Hawthorne with a nostalgic and approving smile.

"And," interjected Iridaan, "many a long hour was put into the training of them!"

"Ah, yes, there was that," acknowledged Hawthorne. "But it is a blessing that we have them now."

"I do entirely agree, dear Hawthorne," she responded.

After the dragons' defeat of the neg there was some respite for the faeries. At Iridaan's request, the Catkin twins ceased their projection and gently lowered themselves to the ground. Susan thought that they looked very tired.

"Yes," said Hawthorne responding to Susan's thoughts. "They are exhausted. They are still very young and we do not ask them to project unless it is really necessary."

Iridaan interjected, "It is indeed crucial that you see what damage we are suffering at the hands of the negs. We so desperately, need your help."

"You need my help?" responded Susan incredulously. "I'm just a nothing, a very ordinary person. I'm not very clever either. I couldn't be of any use to you, although, I wish with all my heart that I could be. I'd do anything to help all of you!" she concluded woefully.

"Susan, you under-estimate yourself," said Iridaan with a kind smile. "It is your heart and your courage that makes you so special and your fine imagination that inspires others. You are still an innocent; you have not become hardened and cynical to the world. You are still able to enjoy the magic that is all around you each and every day. Your friends hold you in very high esteem too and happily follow you. They are strong and full of heart like you and we need you to talk to them and ask them to help us too."

It took Susan a moment to digest all that Iridaan had said to her. She would do anything to help these dear creatures, so, taking a deep breath she said, "Whatever I can do, I will do for you."

"That is the spirit dear one; I should explain some things

The Heart Stone

to you. Because of the dark nature of the negs, we must fight them with light and positivity and a strong heart. It is for this reason that I ask that you and your friends might come here to help us," her voice sounding more hopeful now that Susan was agreeable to her request.

"I'm not sure that they could help much either," said Susan doubtfully. "We're just children. We don't have your powers," she concluded wishing with all her heart that she had more to offer these lovely faeries.

"You all have untold power in your minds. If all of you will only come here willingly and lay some stones around our final stronghold then we shall be helped beyond words," Iridaan said brightly.

Susan was confused again. "I don't understand, do you mean to say that if we children place stones somewhere in your realm it can actually help in this awful battle with the negs?"

Iridaan was quick to explain. "If the stones are placed by children who are uncorrupted by the negs it will afford us extra time to prepare ourselves for the last stand against them. We have no record of the stones ever being used before but it is believed that they have a great power. The negs will not be able to penetrate beyond the stones as the stones will be empowered by the light of children's imaginations and the purity and strength of their hearts. The stones are then thought to create a field about them that the negs cannot pass through."

Susan was encouraged by Iridaan's words, but she felt a concern about the other children.

Hearing Susan's thoughts she said compassionately, "Speak little one."

"I will do anything for you Iridaan, but I am concerned about the others. Will there be danger? Some of them are very young," Susan was a little hesitant.

"My brave one, you are a good leader. You think about others' safety above your own. We will make you as safe as we possibly can. I do not believe that they will be in any danger. However, you must tell them of everything that you have seen here and they must agree to come willingly," Iridaan said in reply.

"I'll tell them everything, but I'm really afraid that they won't believe me," said Susan with a note of sadness in her voice.

"Do not concern yourself about that, my dear, I will ensure that Hawthorne is available to you to help the process along," said Iridaan confidently. "Now young lady, it is time for you to return home and get some sleep."

"Sleep!" said Susan with some disbelief. "It must be morning by now, I've been here for hours, I just hope that Mum is not looking for me!"

"You will be very surprised at how little time has passed, dear one, in this realm we do not measure time the way that you do on your Earth," answered Iridaan with a twinkle in her eyes.

Susan looked at Iridaan with her twinkling eyes and bright smile and thought how beautiful she was. If she had to guess her age it would be impossible, she didn't appear to be young yet she did not appear to be old either. Just her amazing beauty shone through and lit up everything around.

Hearing her thoughts, Hawthorne whispered to Susan, "She is so old in your years that you could not count them. The beauty that you see comes from within her. She radiates the love that she has for all of us faeries and you mortals and that is what you see. There is no greater beauty than that of unconditional love."

"Thank you, Susan, for your compliment and Hawthorne, for your testimony, it is an honour to love and protect you all. Without that, my life here would have no meaning," she responded with feeling. "Now, Susan", she continued after a moments pause, "it is home to bed for you, take her hand Hawthorne and stay in the Earth realm until you have news

The Heart Stone

for me" she concluded firmly.

"Come Susan," said Hawthorne extending his hand.

Susan's gaze had returned to the changing tree and she could not resist trying to have a go at projecting her thoughts upon it. She concentrated very hard and, with a whoosh, the tree transformed into an Apple Tree laden with rosy red apples ready for the picking.

Hawthorne and Iridaan clapped their hands in pleasure at her remarkable feat.

"Oh! Well done, my dear!" exclaimed Iridaan, her face radiant with happiness. You are learning our ways fast! Now take Hawthorne's hand and begin your journey home." she instructed.

Susan looked longingly at Iridaan wishing that she did not have to leave this warm, loving person. Sensing her emotion, Iridaan walked to her side and gently stroked her hair and kissed her cheek. Susan could feel the strong power of her presence that contrasted with her gentle touch and she smelled the heady essence of flowers clinging to her warm body.

"Now, Susan, close your eyes and think of your parents and your home. Concentrate on your bedroom and you will be home in no time," said Hawthorne confidently.

Susan felt the same rushing sensation that she had when she arrived in the Realm of the Faeries. As she opened her eyes she found herself in her bedroom staring at the clock that was showing the time to be 2:28 in the morning. Just one minute later than it had been when she left. She looked up to speak to Hawthorne and was startled to see him in his diminutive form again instead of towering above her. Hearing her confused thoughts he spoke and gently reminded her that he was unable to project in the Earth realm and that he was subject to Earth's gravity and was small again.

"Oh! We're both small," she cried, dismayed that she no longer had the extra height that she had projected for herself in the Faerie Realm.

"Susan," said Hawthorne with great seriousness, "It is only our actions and deeds that make us small."

Susan nodded in understanding and immediately thought of Iridaan and her kindness and warmth. *She is a great person and if she came to Earth, and was only the height of Hawthorne, she would still be great.*

Hawthorne nodded in agreement as he heard her thoughts. "Iridaan would like to think that you are in bed by now and getting some sleep," Hawthorne added.

"Yes, yes, I suppose that I had better," Susan replied feeling an irresistible sleepiness come over her. "Can it really be that I have only been away from here for one minute?" she asked, her voice trailing off sleepily.

"Yes, remember what Iridaan told you about time. Now close your eyes and dream sweet dreams and I will be here whenever you need me. All you have to do is call out with your mind and I will hear you."

"One more question, Hawthorne," said Susan sleepily.

"Very well," agreed Hawthorne.

"How do the negs get to your realm?" asked Susan.

"Ah, a good question, my dear girl. The Negs are an amorphous mass so are able to shrink themselves down to a miniscule size and project themselves at amazing speed through time and space. When they arrive at their destination they reform themselves," said Hawthorne eloquently.

"Umm," said Susan unable to comprehend what he was saying.

"It is akin to Black Hole Theory, my—" Susan cut him short.

"Okay Hawthorne. I'll take your word for it," she said with an enormous yawn.

With that, Susan drifted into a gentle slumber. Hawthorne crept out of her bedroom and went into her garden and settled himself amongst the shrubs acknowledging a

The Heart Stone

scurrying field mouse and other assorted night creatures that were about their business in the garden. He took out a small flute from his cape and started playing a gentle tune that melded with the wind to become a soft lullaby.

Chapter 9
Susan and Hawthorne Return to Bring Help

"Susan, Susan!" cried her mother rapping on her bedroom door. "Are you ever going to wake up this morning?"

Looking around drowsily, Susan saw that it was past nine o'clock and realized that she had slept later than usual.

"Sorry, Mum. I'm getting up now," she shouted sleepily to her mother as she raised herself up onto her elbows.

"Well, your gran is here to keep an eye on you, as I have to go and help your dad at the office again today," Sylvia said apologetically, knowing that Susan was not the greatest fan of her grandmother.

"Okay, Mum. I'll see you when you get back."

"It might not be until about five this afternoon. I've got a lot of accounts to go over. The computer went down and I lost all the work I had done," Sylvia said unhappily.

"Sorry about that, Mum. Maybe you should've stuck to doing them by hand like you used to," she shouted unhelpfully through the door.

"Mmmm, yes. Well, be a good girl then and tell your gran where you're going if you go out and keep your mobile on!"

"Yes, Mum. Bye, love you!"

"Love you too!"

Susan flopped her head back on the pillow and thought how strange it was for her to have slept so late. She remembered the previous evening and all the fun that she had helping Seb in the restaurant. She glazed over, remembering the dinner that she and Seb had enjoyed together after all their hard work. *That's probably why I've*

The Heart Stone

slept so late, she reasoned with herself. As she hoisted herself up in bed again she felt something roll down her right side. Reaching down, she found a large red and delicious looking apple. Mystified, she picked it up and looked at it, wondering how on earth it got into her bed. She reached over to get her glasses from the night table, and in doing so, felt something prick her left arm. Startled, she felt for the offending item and found a Hawthorn twig with luscious green leaves on it. "What in heaven's name is going on?" she cried out loud.

As she spoke, her mind took her back to what she had thought to be a dream the night before. *Was it a dream?* she thought to herself, still confused. *Surely it must've been a dream. Is it possible that such a thing could happen to me in real life? And yet,* she thought, *this apple looks exactly like the one from the tree that I projected in the Realm of Faeries. And this Hawthorn twig, could it be a sign that the faerie person that I dreamed of named Hawthorne was real?*

She recalled her dream in vivid detail, from the moment she arrived in the Realm of Faeries and met Iridaan and the lovely twins and witnessed the battle with the horrible negs to her return home. Her head was spinning. Could it have been real?

A somewhat dishevelled Hawthorne, obscured from sight in the bushes, heard Susan's confused thoughts penetrate through the half doze that he had slipped into during the night.

He jumped to his feet and slipped stealthily through the garden and into the house, whizzing past Susan's gran who was pottering about the kitchen and mumbling to herself about the lack of proper organization in the house.

He reached Susan's bedroom and tapped gently on the door. Susan wondered who it could be, as her gran always banged loudly on her door and usually berated her about some misdemeanour that she had committed. She got out of bed, opened the door, and looked straight ahead, but saw nothing until she felt a tug at her leg. Jumping in surprise, she saw Hawthorne standing there.

With a look of disbelief on her face she gestured for him to come in and she shut the door behind him.

"It can't be real, can it?" she asked him incredulously.

"It is as sad as it is true, dear girl," he answered forlornly.

"But where will I start? Who shall I tell first?" she wailed in confusion.

"Ah! The two questions at once again! That's my girl!" said Hawthorne trying to lighten Susan's obvious distress and confusion. "I think we had better begin with enlisting the aid of one trusted friend who you believe will understand and support you. Can you suggest one?"

Susan thought hard about whom she should tell about what had transpired between her and the faeries. Aliya was her oldest and closest friend, but Susan didn't think that Aliya's gentle disposition would provide the strength that she needed right now. Her thoughts turned to Seb and how many things they had in common and their love of adventure. In an instant, she decided that Seb would be the one that she confided in.

"An excellent choice, my dear girl," Hawthorne said approvingly after hearing Susan's thoughts.

Susan was startled at Hawthorne's words. "You know, reading my thoughts can sometimes be very scary," she said.

"Would you like me to stop doing it?" asked Hawthorne openly.

Susan thought for a moment before replying. She decided that, on balance, it was probably better that he be able to hear her thoughts. It might be beneficial for her should she need his help in the future.

"No, I don't really mind you doing that, but I'm still not used to it and it seems especially strange here on Earth."

The Heart Stone

"Well in that case, I suggest that we get in touch with him as soon as possible."

"I'll phone him right now," Susan said enthusiastically.

Seb's phone seemed to ring for an eternity before he answered.

"Oh, hello Seb, this is Susan. I hope I didn't disturb you," she said coyly.

"No, no, not at all," he hastened to assure her. "I was in the garden helping mum move one of the big pots of flowers and I had my phone charging up inside."

"Seb," she began haltingly, "I have something to tell you and it may seem a bit strange, but can you please meet me on The Stray so that we can talk?"

"Of course," he said without hesitation, happy to have the chance to have her to himself again. "Just give me about half an hour to finish helping mum, and I'll meet you at the usual bench."

"That's great," she said, thankful that he was available to see her so soon.

Hawthorne smiled at her and asked where she and Seb would be meeting.

"Oh, yes!" he said picking up the mental image of the bench on The Stray from her mind. "An excellent place to meet. I will see you there."

"Wait!" cried Susan in alarm. "What if you get lost and aren't there to help me talk to Seb?"

"Don't worry. That is not going to happen," Hawthorne reassured her.

"But can't you just come with me?" she wailed feeling a little insecure.

Hawthorne took a deep breath and cleared his throat. "My dear girl, I understand very well how you are feeling right now, but consider this. How would it look if I walked down the street with you? Do you not think that people would be a little surprised at seeing me walking beside you? It could lead to a lot of explaining on your part. Besides, it is not our way to reveal ourselves to any but the most trustworthy of humans. Do not fear, I will be there with time to spare. I will take my leave of you now and allow you to wash and dress and get some breakfast."

"Okay," Susan said, feeling a little more reassured. "But how will you get there without being seen?" she asked inquisitively.

"We are still able to use some of our faerie powers here on Earth," he said with a twinkle. "Just watch."

Susan was startled as Hawthorne took a step towards the door. One minute he had been standing right next to her and the next he had vanished with only a slightly retained image of his plumed hat.

"Oh!" she gasped out loud as she watched Hawthorne's amazing exit. *What's next? I'm in a bit of a tizzy*, Susan thought to herself. She remembered her mother's words in her head. "Always stop and take a deep breath and think about what the next thing you need to do is. Don't try to rush at everything at once."

Yes, thought Susan. *That seems like a good idea*. She collected her thoughts and did one thing at a time, which helped to calm her down. After washing and dressing she went downstairs to face her grandmother. Susan took one look at her and could see she was in granny "gross" mode. Susan had heard that expression on a cartoon and adopted it as a reference to her grandmother when she was being difficult. It was quite evident by her gran's mutterings, as she flicked a duster about the house in a vicious manner, that she wasn't in a good mood.

"Morning, Gran," Susan offered sweetly.

"Morning? More like afternoon if you ask me! You had better have some breakfast," she hissed.

"Okay, Gran. I'll just have some cereal and get out of your way."

"Going out again are you?" she asked acidly.

"Yes, Gran. I'm going to The Stray to meet some of the

The Heart Stone

others."

"Up to no good I'll be bound. And what time do you propose to be home? I'm supposed to be making your lunch, you know," Gran said grumpily.

"Um, not quite sure, Gran," she said hoping to avoid her grandmother's flavourless food at all costs. "I'll phone and let you know in about half an hour. I've got some pocket money left and my friends and I were talking about buying some sandwiches and having a picnic in the Pine Woods."

"Humph," retorted her grandmother. "Children have it all their own way these days!"

Susan went to the kitchen and gobbled down her cereals as quickly as she could, washed up her dishes, and made for the door.

"Is that you sloping out of the house?" shouted Gran, her shrill tones echoing loudly around the house.

"Yes, Gran. I was just about to tell you I was going," she said meekly, not wishing to incur anymore wrath than was necessary.

"I suppose your bedroom will be a pigsty as usual," Gran said accusingly.

"No, Gran. I've made my bed and tidied up. I'm going now. Bye!"

"I've seen your tidying up before," she grunted. "Get on with you now and don't you forget about phoning me about lunch either!"

Susan left as swiftly as possible to the sound of her gran muttering about young people and their mobile phones and not knowing that they're born.

Susan walked purposefully to The Stray trying to get her thoughts in order so that she could communicate to Seb the amazing things that she had encountered the night before. She realized that she might be a bit early, but she was glad of that. She wanted to be calm and composed when Seb arrived.

When she got to the bench where they usually met, Susan

plonked herself down and stared around for a few seconds. She slowly became aware of a rather loud rustling sound in the large Chestnut Tree that shaded the bench she was sitting on. As Susan turned her head, she heard a whispered voice.

"It's only me!" said Hawthorne in a stage whisper.

"Oh! I'm so glad to see you. Did you have any problem finding this place?" Susan inquired.

"No, my dear child. You envision things so beautifully in your mind that I found my way here easily. Besides, we are greatly attuned to places of nature and that helps too. Um, I think that is your young man on his way over." Susan looked up in surprise. She hadn't expected Seb to arrive for another fifteen minutes or so, but was pleased to see his gentle, friendly face coming towards her.

"I am going to be up in the tree," Hawthorne informed her.

"No, no. I need you here to help me explain things," wailed Susan.

"Susan, until I have heard Seb's reaction to your story, I cannot reveal myself. I need to be sure about his willingness to help us."

"Oh, alright," said Susan, aware that Hawthorne was probably right. She smiled at Seb as he approached, returning his large friendly grin that lit up his rakish good looks.

"Hi Susan, you're up bright and early this morning, I thought you might be tired after all the work we did last night," Seb said, still grinning broadly.

"No, I didn't get tired last night at all. It was really fun and your mum and dad are great!" Susan responded.

"Well, my parents really liked you and they said to tell you thanks again for your help."

"They're very welcome," she said with a bright smile, finding herself joining in with Seb's obvious light-heartedness.

The Heart Stone

Susan had not formulated any plan of how she would tell Seb about the faeries, so she began in the best way that she could. "Seb, I've got something to tell you and it's going to sound very strange. I hope that you'll not think that I'm weird or something."

Seb's grin started to fade from his face at her words. He had wondered why she wanted to see him so early in the morning. Now he was beginning to worry that she might want to end their blossoming friendship.

"Please tell me what it is. I won't think you're weird, honestly," Seb said encouragingly. He just wanted to hear whatever it was and quickly.

"Seb," Susan looked at his face and seeing the alarm growing upon it she gave him a warm smile. "What I have to say is as strange to me as it will sound to you, but I want you to try and believe me," she said earnestly.

"I will, I promise," he said, feeling a sense of relief that what she had to say wasn't likely to be about their relationship.

Susan began the tale of what had happened to her in the middle of the previous night and her encounter with the Faerie Realm. Seb only interjected once to ask whether she had been dreaming, but after he heard about the apple and the Hawthorn twig which she had brought along with her, he was both persuaded and intrigued by her story.

"So you say that Hawthorne came back here with you?" asked Seb incredulously.

"Yes," said Susan glancing up towards the Chestnut Tree, hoping that Hawthorne had made some determination about Seb's belief by now. Hearing nothing from the tree she continued her tale about the negs and how the faeries needed their help.

Sebs' thoughts were racing, he believed that Susan was telling him the truth and he would certainly help her if all this was true, but his logical mind was struggling to believe that it wasn't just a dream. Even with the apple and the twig he still found it really hard to believe.

A loud rustling could be heard in the branches of the large Chestnut Tree above them and in a flash, Hawthorne stood before Susan and Seb. Seb jerked back in surprise. Susan put her hand on Seb's chest comfortingly and told him not to be alarmed.

"This is Hawthorne," she said indicating the diminutive form that stood before them. "It took you long enough to reveal yourself" she hissed at him with slight annoyance.

"Greetings, dear Sebastian. I am sorry to have delayed our introduction, but there was a matter of trust that I needed to be sure of before I could proceed. I am most delighted to make your acquaintance."

Seb was rather stunned but, nonetheless, was in command of himself enough to speak coherently. "You must be Hawthorne then?"

"Yes, I am," Hawthorne said, warmly extending his hand. "I believe it is customary on Earth to offer your hand to shake in greeting, so I extend it to you in greeting and friendship, dear boy."

Sebastian leaned forward to take Hawthorne's extended hand, feeling his normal senses returning to him again. "I am pleased to meet you Hawthorne."

"It is a pleasure to meet you too, Sebastian. Susan may have told you about the telepathic powers that we faeries have. I needed to observe your reactions and feelings to Susan's story to be sure of your imaginative capacity and your willingness to believe in us and help us in our battle with the negs," he said with sincerity.

"That's quite alright, Hawthorne. I would've done exactly the same as you if I was in your place," Seb said, feeling a bond developing between himself and Hawthorne. "But the question is, what are we to do next?"

"Well, now that I've ascertained your suitability for the work ahead, I want you and Susan to speak to—"

Hawthorne's words were cut short as his face contorted

The Heart Stone

in pain.

"Dear children, I hear Iridaan calling to me. There have been grave casualties from the last onslaught of the negs. We are losing ground by the minute, I must return at once!" he said in alarm.

"Wait!" cried Susan. "If you can make that time thing happen again, may I come with you?"

"Me too!" volunteered Seb without hesitation.

"Dear children, the Faerie Realm will be greatly helped by your presence and, yes, the time that you are away from Earth will not pass in its usual way. As it was with you, Susan, just seconds of your day will pass," he said, thankful of the children's offer of help.

"How does this work? Seb asked.

"Why don't you tell him, Susan?" suggested Hawthorne with a slight smile.

Susan remembered all that Hawthorne had told her last night and encouraged Seb to think of the nicest time he could remember and to hold hands with Hawthorne and herself.

"That won't be hard," Seb said, thinking that the evening he had spent with Susan last night, working and sharing a meal together was one of the nicest times he could think of.

The three of them held hands and together they whooshed speedily into the Faerie Realm.

Chapter 10
Susan Takes Seb to the Faerie Realm

"That felt quicker than last time," Susan said to Hawthorne.

"Yes, dear girl. You are very observant. It is because the more of us that are projecting our imaginative thoughts together, the more power is given to our journey."

Sebastian was looking around in awe, in much the same way as Susan had when she first arrived in the realm. They had arrived at the same spot as before and Susan couldn't resist a quick projection onto the changing tree. This time a Cherry Tree appeared.

"Well done, my dear. Your powers of projection are improving all the time," Hawthorne said.

With that, Susan remembered that she could be taller in the Faerie Realm and immediately made herself a few inches taller. Sebastian was amazed at what he was seeing. First it was the incomparable beauty of the place and then it was seeing Hawthorne's transformation into a tall and noble warrior. Not to mention seeing Susan grow a few inches!

Picking up on Seb's thoughts, she said, "You can project your appearance here to be the way that you want, you know. Do you like me a bit taller?"

"Yes, but I like you just the way you are too," Seb responded honestly. He thought that everything about Susan was lovely and needed no improvements.

Hawthorne looked over at Seb and gave him a knowing, man-to-man type of smile, indicating his agreement about Susan's appearance. Within seconds, Susan saw Iridaan striding over to where the three of them were standing. Her face looked drawn and pale, but there was obvious relief when she saw that Susan and Sebastian were standing there.

"Children, children, I am so glad to see you here. We are being attacked on many fronts and we need some respite to gather our wounded. First, let me welcome you, Sebastian," she encircled her arms around Seb and kissed him gently on the cheek. "All of this must be very strange to you, dear child. I wish that you were here under happier circumstances and I could give you a more appropriate welcome," she said with a note of sadness in her voice.

"It's alright, Iridaan. Susan has told me about the negs and what they are doing. I would like to help if I can," Seb said resolutely. He spoke clearly and without fear. Somewhere in the warmth of Iridaan's embrace, he had lost any hesitation or fear that he had first had.

"Yes," Susan added." We both want to help. Please tell us what we can do."

"Dear children, what I need you to do is to come to the coast with me and help to defend the coastal border. You will be in no danger."

"Let's go as soon as possible," Susan said, anxious to spare the faeries any more casualties than necessary.

"Hawthorne, take command in my absence. Watch all the battlefronts. We are sustaining casualties in all areas," Iridaan said with authority.

"Rest assured that I will do all in my power, dear queen," he said reassuringly.

With that, Hawthorne discarded his cloak, unfurled his wings, and, in a second, took to the air with a whoosh of beating wings.

"What about his cloak?" Susan asked, thinking that he might get cold and need it.

Iridaan smiled. "The cloaks are for your benefit my sweet ones. We do not, as a rule, wear them. They impede our flight. It is rare that we have such direct encounters with mortals as we are having with you. We wear our cloaks to prevent you from being shocked by our winged appearance."

"Why?" Seb asked earnestly. "It is quite the opposite. You look fantastic! Your wings are absolutely brilliant."

"Yes, I can feel from your vibration that you would love to have such wings," Iridaan said with an amused smile playing around her gentle lips. "Now, are you both ready to fly with me?" she asked, already sensing their answer.

"Oh, yes!" exclaimed Susan and Seb in unison.

Iridaan cast off her cloak and unfurled her magnificent wings; they were bigger and more iridescent than Hawthorne's. The children watched in awe as they saw how far her wings spanned. She began to beat her wings slowly and lifted herself slightly off the ground. Gently, she gathered the two children up, one in each arm. They felt no discomfort at being lifted in this way. In fact, they felt as light as feathers themselves. After a few more beats of her wings, the three of them were airborne and moving quickly towards the coast.

"Are you comfortable?" asked Iridaan.

"I'll say," Seb said excitedly. "This is mega!"

"Oh, yes, yes!! This is the most brilliant thing I've ever done in my life!" answered Susan enraptured.

The children felt very safe in Iridaan's arms. They marvelled at her strength. To look at her, she didn't appear strong enough to carry the two of them in flight, but there was no denying the strength that was emanating from Iridaan's body. There was no sign of strain on her face, only a benign look of concentration.

"Is it very far?" enquired Susan.

"It is about fifteen of your minutes away," declared Iridaan. All too soon, the coast came into view. The two children had enjoyed their flight immensely and were not looking forward to encountering the negs.

"We are almost there, children," she informed them. "We will go to the beach and make ourselves comfortable there."

The rhythmic beating of Iridaan's wings began to slow

The Heart Stone

and they began to descend gently to the ground. They landed softly on the beach to the sound of pounding surf rolling onto the shore about a hundred feet from the sea. The smells and sounds of the ocean flooded their senses and they could feel the warmth of the morning sun on their faces.

The sea was an unusually vibrant blue and the waves that were cresting on the shore looked pristinely white. The sky above was a shade darker than the sea, dotted with wispy, lazy-looking clouds that were in no hurry to go anywhere in particular. The sun shone majestically above the beautiful scene, almost as if it were the proud parent of the beautiful seascape below. Birds abounded and their joyous cries mingled with the sound of the ocean, creating the familiar sound of a day at the sea.

This is like Earth's seaside, but ten times more intense, thought Susan, who passionately loved the sea.

"Oh!" she exclaimed. "This is so beautiful! Please don't say that the negs can take this away from you."

"That is what we are here to prevent," answered Iridaan resolutely.

As they gathered themselves together, the children became aware of other sounds emanating from the ocean. "That sounds like whales and dolphins," Seb said informatively.

"Yes, it does, and they are getting closer too by the sound of it," Susan replied.

"You are correct, children. That is the sound of the whales and dolphins and some other sea creatures too," confirmed Iridaan.

Their sounds became louder and louder. But it was not a cacophony of random sounds. Their voices seemed to join in harmonious unison with the sea bird's song and the pounding of the waves on the shore. It was as if a massive orchestra was playing a magnificent symphony.

"I've never heard anything as fantastic as this," Seb said, looking questioningly at Iridaan.

"It is indeed a most wonderful experience to hear the song of the sea and all of its creatures," said Iridaan with a far away look on her face.

"Why is it getting so loud?" asked Susan.

"They sense my presence. They come to greet me and await my greeting," she answered with warmness in her voice.

"Oh! That is so impressive," Susan said in awe of the whole event.

"Mmmm, yep," Seb said, unable to speak very coherently for the wonder of it all.

"Children, I must answer my loved ones. Do not be afraid of the sounds that you will hear," Iridaan said gently. She threw back her head and let forth an indescribable sound of such purity that it brought tears rushing to the children's eyes. It started softly on a very high note vibrating gently into the air and slowly increased in volume. As it did so, it seemed as if her voice became a choir of voices, with every range and pitch that could be imagined blending in perfect harmony.

The children were transfixed with the beauty of the sound. They felt it vibrate through their whole being and touch some hidden part of them that resonated with pure love. Seb reached out and took Susan's hand and it was as if the joining of their hands amplified the wonder of all that was taking place.

"I'm not at all afraid," Susan whispered, enjoying the feel of Seb's hand holding hers. It felt so natural and right.

"No, neither am I. This is unbelievable. I feel as though I'm dreaming," Seb replied, enjoying the closeness of Susan and the pleasure of feeling her hand tightening around his.

"Look," Seb said, pointing out to sea, "There are lots of fish and things leaping out of the water."

Susan turned her gaze to the ocean and marvelled at the myriad species of fish and mammals that were leaping out of the water with pure joy and excitement. They were

The Heart Stone

reacting to Iridaan's greeting and, in seconds, they began emitting a chorus of sounds that blended in perfect harmony with that of Iridaan's. The children were transfixed with the sights and sounds that they were experiencing. All too soon, the magnificent chorus reached a crescendo and slowly ebbed away. Iridaan looked out to the horizon and her vibrant features began to cloud a little.

"What is it?" enquired Susan, seeing the change in Iridaan's demeanour and sensing the apprehension rising in her.

"It is the negs. They are approaching us," she replied, regaining her composure and taking a strong stance as if to do battle. "They want to take our beautiful ocean and annihilate the wonderful creatures that live within her."

"We're here to help you, Iridaan, and we're not going to let that happen," Seb said resolutely.

"My brave one, your courage inspires me, as does dear Susan's. We will make a stand here today for as long as we are able. If we become overwhelmed there are other faeries close by who will fly you back to safety, so do not fear my little ones."

As she spoke, there came a darkness on the horizon that spread menacingly across the whole breadth of the land and then slowly rose into the sky, issuing an aura of cold and deathly emptiness. Susan recoiled a little, knowing that what she saw was the enemy of the Faerie Realm, the relentless and ever-growing negs.

Seb stood his ground, not wishing to seem afraid in front of Susan and the stalwart queen. His heart was racing, and he could feel the negativity contained in the shadowy, cloudlike formations that were manifesting themselves, ever closer, in the sky. Slowly, the negs were obliterating the vibrant, blue of the sky and the shining, crystal waters of the sea.

"What shall we do, Iridaan?" Seb asked, anxious to provide whatever service he was able.

"We stand a little longer until we see the extent of their numbers and then we strike!" she answered with passion.

"What are we to do?" asked Susan wishing to be prepared for the onslaught that she knew would ensue.

"On my command, I want you and Sebastian to take my hands and form a circle. I would like both of you to concentrate very hard and think about the beauty that is all around you here. Imagine that there is nothing that can take away what you have seen and if you feel love for this place let it flow from your heart like a mighty river," she said gently and yet with a passion that could not be restrained.

"That's all?" queried Seb. "I can envision this place in my mind so easily and to love it is even easier."

"Yes, me too," interrupted Susan. "But will that really drive these monstrous negs away?"

"Yes, my dear ones. You have no idea of the strength that you posses within your minds. No matter what you hear or see, do not stop believing and projecting your images and your love of this place outwards," Iridaan said solemnly.

As she stopped speaking it seemed as if every beautiful thing in the place had become overshadowed with a soulless darkness that chilled to the bone. Iridaan strode to the ocean's edge and intoned the most beautiful sound that could be imagined. It seemed to echo and ring from every rock, pebble, and shell that was strewn about the beach. Indeed, it seemed as if every grain of sand rang with the resonance of her cry. Within seconds, an almighty sound arose from the ocean as thousands of sea creatures came to the surface and began to intone a harmonious accompaniment to Iridaan's cry. It was a sound that moved both Susan and Seb to tears. It was different from the harmonious symphony that had taken place earlier in response to Iridaan's greeting. These sounds seemed to clutch at the children's very heart and speak to the depths of their soul with love and compassion.

The children were entranced by the exquisite melody that

was becoming louder and louder. They felt as though their souls were joining in this overture of passion. It was as if they were experiencing some long forgotten rhapsody that spoke to something deep inside of them. Their eyes were slowly drawn to the sky where the negs had revealed the extent of their might. They saw that the army of voices from the sea was having a weakening effect on the negs. The darkness was dissipating from the sky. The children felt hopeful.

"They're weakening," Seb cried in delight.

"It is not yet over," said Iridaan gently. "The children of the sea cannot sustain their voices for much longer," she said with much seriousness. "Now is the time for us to act. Take my hands," she commanded the children.

"Remember all that I told you to do."

"Yes, we will," replied the two children in unison as they stretched out their eager hands to help her.

As they clasped their hands to Iridaan's, they felt her power flowing into and through them. It felt magical, like a thousand butterfly wings brushing against their skin and yet empowering them immeasurably.

Immediately, the two children closed their eyes and imagined that everything around them was impermeable. That nothing could destroy the beauty and grace of this land. As they did so, they sent waves of love out to the sea, the sea creatures, the birds and all the land that surrounded them. As they used their mental abilities in this way, they heard the cries of the ocean dwellers become louder and more powerful. Through their closed lids, the children could tell that the sky was becoming lighter again which seemed to give them even more power to project.

Susan and Seb felt a rapport between them that was indescribable. It was as if they were aware of the power that lay within each of them. They could feel each cell vibrate in harmony with each others and experienced the joy of being human and projected it outwards to help save the beloved land of the faeries.

Iridaan, aware that the foe had been vanquished, took a moment to look at the faces of the children still so intent on their imagining and projecting. Their small frames were emanating a brilliant glow all around them and their faces were shining with a radiance of true endeavour. Her kind heart was touched at this scene, and a small tear of joy slid silently down her cheek. "It's over children," she whispered to them as the voices from the sea slowly ebbed away.

"Oh, that was so unbelievable," said Susan opening her eyes. "I've never felt like that in my life."

"You did well, children. We have vanquished the negs."

"You mean what we did actually helped?" Seb asked in awe.

"Yes, without your help, victory would not be ours today," she said smiling fondly at the children.

"But it didn't seem as if we were doing anything. It felt as if we were being given something," Susan said as Seb nodded in agreement.

Iridaan smiled enchantingly as she whispered, "Love has untold power and can break down the greatest of fortresses. When we use our mind with love, we become invincible."

The two children looked at each other, still able to feel the power that coursed through them during the battle, and, intuitively, understood the words that Iridaan spoke. It was as if she had imparted, in each of them, wisdom far beyond their years whilst still allowing their youth its innocence.

"How were we able to defeat the negs?" asked Seb, full of curiosity and wonder at what had taken place.

"When we do battle with such vile creatures as the negs, we project love outwards. We envisage all the things that we hold dear and wish to protect and keep them firmly in our minds. When we were doing battle, I thought about my lovely creatures in the sea and their beauty and their love of life. I thought about this magnificent land and how well it sustains us. In short, everything that lives and breathes in this place was in my mind," Iridaan concluded with a gentle smile.

"Why did we have to come here with you, Iridaan?" asked Susan. "I thought that you were not to do battle until the last stand?"

"That is my observant girl," said Iridaan, her smile increasing. "The reason that the three of us are here is because the ocean is vast and there are countless life forms within it. None of my faeries have enough knowledge of all the sea creatures to be able to hold them in their minds and protect them. Even though I know each sea creature by name, I do not have enough power of projection to defeat the negs alone. It was your projections that made the difference. You two are both creative and untouched by the power of the negs in your own world. When you bring all that here, you bring untold power with you. Within both of you, resides great love for humanity. That is why we need you and those like you to overcome the negs."

"So," said Susan, feeling pride at being called Iridaan's observant, girl, "when the negs attack we are fighting them with love?" she queried.

"Yes, that is largely true, but you must understand that it is not the negs that we are giving love to, for they are unable to accept it; we project the love that we have for others and our realm outwards. In that way, we are constantly creating what we want to happen. If we do not project in this way we cannot protect ourselves and we are in the gravest danger. If we allow ourselves to lose hope the negs will overpower us easily. For they immediately sense negativity and can align themselves with it and so amplify the deep melancholic misery and lethargy that spawns their vile forms. As they become more powerful, they need to constantly feed upon the beautiful creations of nature to satisfy their voracious appetites and spread their negativity.

"Once they were relatively harmless, little more than a void, which imaginative souls would fill with creative endeavours. At some point, however, the negs developed a crude consciousness which is fueled by unrelenting greed. Now with the many children who no longer use their imaginations and creativity, everything has got out of balance and the negs have proliferated and we have this battle on our hands with these hideous, unnatural creatures," Iridaan sighed.

The Heart Stone

"Why was it so important for us to fight here rather than at the front where all the other faeries are fighting?" asked Seb.

"That is an excellent question, young man," responded Iridaan. "Had the negs gained a foothold here, they would have been able to penetrate deep into our realm."

"How is that possible?" interjected Seb.

"Well, dear one, if you think about all the many rivers and streams that flow into the ocean, you can see that if a neg got a foothold here, very soon they would sail up the rivers and streams into our lands on so many fronts that we would be unable to defend our land."

"Oh!" said Susan and Seb together. They were both trying hard to understand all the information that Iridaan had imparted. She sensed the air of overwhelming fatigue and confusion that the children were feeling and immediately began to change the subject away from the negs.

"Today, my dear ones, you have done magnificently!" she cried. "And I believe that you deserve a reward. Are you hungry?"

"Oh yes!" they cried again in unison.

Chapter 11
A Food Reward for a Strategic Victory

It seemed like a very long time since Susan and Seb had eaten breakfast and the time spent in projection had caused them to feel the need for sustenance.

"I shall take you to a place that makes the most wonderful food that you can imagine," she said, scooping them up in her arms and launching once more into flight.

The thought of food and drink had raised the spirits of the children, along with the victory that had just been achieved with their help.

"This flying stuff is great, isn't it, Susan?" Seb asked, obviously thrilled by their flight.

"I'll say," Susan replied with enthusiasm. "I wonder where Iridaan is taking us?"

"Don't know, but I bet it'll be good!" said Seb enthusiastically.

Iridaan's flight took them in a different direction from which they had come. The scenery was just as breathtaking. It seemed to them that everywhere they looked was a paradise to behold. Looking ahead in the direction that they were flying, Susan could make out a conglomeration of tall buildings with vivid colours that shone serenely in the midday sun.

"Wow! Look at those buildings up ahead, Susan," Seb said.

"Yes, aren't they lovely looking?" she responded enthusiastically.

"Do you like them?" enquired Iridaan smilingly.

"Oh yes!" chorused the two children in unison.

"That is where we live. Those are our homes," Iridaan

said with pride.

As they neared the beautiful buildings the children could see that no two houses were the same. Each one had its own unique character. The buildings were set out in their own little plots with no real boundaries other than where one faerie's garden ended and another one's began. Each one had a distinctly different style that they had used to plant out their garden. The houses were as unique as the gardens, each house being of a different shape and colour.

"You don't seem to have any streets in your town, Iridaan," Seb observed.

"We do not really need any, as we do not need transportation in the same way that you do. But for convenience we do have one central street called Main Street where communal supplies are located. In fact, that is where we are going now," she concluded with a smile.

As Iridaan spoke, her large wings slowed their rhythmical beat and they began to descend to the ground. Iridaan set the children down gently on the ground and took them over to what looked like a restaurant. There were very high tables set both inside and outside of the large castle shaped building that was a brilliant yellow and white colour.

The chairs that were set around the high tables were of a rather strange shape. They looked like a normal dining chair except the backs curved sharply and had two large, cushioned semi-circles carved out on either side. Seeing the children looking curiously at the chairs, Iridaan smiled.

"The chairs and tables are very high to allow for the drop of our wings when we sit to eat. Here, let me demonstrate." She walked up to a chair and, using a small stool (one was set at each table), hopped up on the chair and leaned back, allowing her large wings to fall behind the chair. They rested comfortably on the two, cushioned semi-circles on the back. She leaned forward, putting her elbows on the table showing the children how comfortable she was. "Do you see why we need specially designed chairs and tables now children?" Iridaan said with a smile.

"That's really neat," Seb said admiringly.

"Yes, it is," agreed Susan, "but how are we going to manage?"

"That is no problem," Iridaan said, closing her eyes briefly and projecting forth a normal sized round table with two chairs for the children.

"Oh! I had forgotten about projecting," Susan said with a quick smile.

"Before you children sit down, perhaps you would like to come and look at the food that we have to offer today?"

During their flight to the town, Iridaan had taken the precaution of peeking into the children's minds in order to ascertain their favourite foods. She projected the information to the faeries that were preparing the food that day.

Iridaan led the children to the centre of the very large dining area and to a circular, glass room with the most delicately woven lace curtains that the children had ever seen. The curtains draped decoratively from the ceiling in scalloped shapes. Inside this room, the children beheld the most beautifully presented food they had ever seen. It was laid out on a large, round buffet table in the most appetizing way.

"Oh! This is magnificent," cried Susan in wonderment.

"Wow!" was all that Seb could muster as his eyes took in the many varieties of pizza and pasta dishes that lay in front of them.

"This must be very expensive," Susan said. "Are you sure that you want to spend so much on food for us?"

Iridaan threw back her head and roared with laughter. "My dear children, first of all, I would willingly spend any amount of money on you brave children but that is not needed here. We faeries have no need for money."

"Well, who pays for all of this?" interjected Susan gesturing towards the food and lovely restaurant. "Who pays for the food and for the people that work here?"

"Oh Susan, Hawthorne was right about you and your two questions at once! First of all, nobody pays for the food; we can either grow it or project it. In this case, the food has been lovingly grown and prepared by your friends the Catkin twins who are waiting to see you in the restaurant. The faeries that work in this restaurant do so because they want to. Sometimes, nobody works here because no one has the wish to do so. When this is the case, we simply project our food and enjoy the company of others while having a pleasant rest. Sadly, most of us are engaged at the battlefront and have no time to enjoy the community of spirit in the restaurant. But to ensure that you have a lovely time here, the Catkin twins asked to be here and spend time with you!" Iridaan concluded merrily.

As Iridaan stopped speaking, the children could hear the tinkling chimes of the Catkin twins approaching them. Tina May and Laura June approached the room where Iridaan and the children were viewing the delicious food.

"We hope that the food pleases you!" they chimed in unison.

"Oh, it's lovely! I can't wait to eat it!" Susan exclaimed.

"Mmmm, me too," agreed Seb.

"Well, help yourselves. Take as much as you would like," the twins chorused.

Iridaan waited until the children had filled their plates and were sitting down at the table before telling them that she needed to leave them for a little while.

"The twins will look after you now, as I must go. Please enjoy yourselves," Iridaan said and took her leave.

The twins sat on a nearby table, perched with their wings resting on the chair backs and their elbows on the tables with their pretty faces cupped in their hands watching the children eat their food. Once the children had finished their food, the twins projected all the dirty dishes away from the table and projected in their place a selection of delicious desserts of which the twins, themselves, partook. The twins seemed to have a million and one questions to ask of the children and the children of the twins. They discovered much about one another and alternately roared with laughter or listened intently as the occasion demanded. All in all, the four of them had a fine time together and it seemed as if no time had passed at all until Iridaan returned.

"I see you children have been having a wonderful time!" she said with a warm smile.

"Oh yes!" cried the four of them.

"Well, as much as I would like you to be able to spend more time together, it is time for Susan and Sebastian to go back home."

"Awwww!" the four of them said in disappointment.

"Come along Susan and Sebastian," Iridaan said firmly. "You two need to get back to Earth before the time differential becomes apparent."

Taking their hands she said, "You know what to do now."

"Yes, we do," Susan said closing her eyes to begin the inward journey home.

Iridaan checked to see that Seb's eyes were closed and that his thought patterns were locked into an enjoyable occasion before she gently let go of their hands and allowed them to slip back into their space and time.

"We had such lovely time with the Earth children," said Laura June wistfully. "I wish we did not have this horrible Neg War going on and we could spend lots of time with them."

"I know how hard it is to part from such lovable Earthlings, especially as those are the kind of children that we are born to work with. We help to make their imaginative dreams become an Earthly reality," Iridaan replied with a sad smile.

"Why are there so few children like them?" enquired Tina May.

"Because, dear one, they are losing the battle with the negs too. The negs, have caused an air of negativity to descend upon the Earth children and only the very strong can hold out against their influence. Susan is exceptional in her inner strength and creativity; she simply will not be influenced by the negative words and deeds of others. Sebastian, is almost as strong and if he continues to be in Susan's company he has the potential to be her equal and may even surpass her if he stays focused," she responded affirmatively.

"Will there ever be a time when all of the Earth children will be able to withstand the influence of the negs?" Tina May asked.

"It is possible, but there needs to be a shift of consciousness among the Earthlings. They must start believing that their dreams can become a reality. They must understand that there is not one of them who is better, or cleverer, or more important, than the other. They must also learn to share the bounty of their Earth with one another. Only when they have made those changes will we hear the strong call of the Earth children again. Then we will be able to work with their fertile minds and help them make their dreams become a reality as we did eons ago."

"Oh! It would be so nice if that happened!" said Tina May with enthusiasm.

"Yes, it surely would," said the queen. "But first we have a battle to win! Join me in focusing on the battlefront. I need to see how our troops are faring."

The twins looked at each other with a touch of sadness, sorry to leave the pleasant memories of their time with Susan and Sebastian. They closed their eyes and joined their minds to Iridaan's and began to scan the battlefronts to see what was taking place there.

The scene before, Iridaan's, closed eyes was not pleasing to her. Her brave warriors were making numerous stands on many fronts, holding back the ever encroaching negs. She saw many of the faeries fighting until they could hold on no longer. Their ability to project and hold onto their land was draining from them under the oppressive dark power of the negs. The queen saw her valiant troops falling to the ground, sometimes in exhaustion, sometimes in death. Her heart broke for their sacrifice and courage. Despite knowing that she must reserve her energies for the last stand against the negs, she sent forth some of her energy to the troops.

The twins, sensing what she had done, sent a thought message of gentle reprimand to their queen, telling her that she must reserve her energies to the last. She responded by acknowledging their concern and explaining that things were becoming critical now and time short.

She told them of her hope that Susan and Seb would return with as many of the Earth children that they could as soon as possible. She reassured them that Hawthorne had returned to Earth in preparation for helping the other children on their first journey to the Faerie Realm.

"How is it possible that we will be able to defeat the negs with just ten children?" enquired Laura June.

"Because you and your sister are very young, you have never encountered the call of a child's mind and felt its incredible power. When you first hear the call of an Earth child's mind, you will be amazed at its imaginative and creative power. Even the children themselves are unaware of how powerful and creative their minds can be. When they allow us to work with them, their power is enhanced further and we become great, creative, allies. This is a power that the negs are unable to defeat. We do not need many Earth children, just ones that are able to focus and believe in what they can accomplish," Iridaan said in reply.

"I can't wait until I can hear the call of a child's mind," interjected Laura June.

"I know, my dear, for that is our prime purpose in life, a purpose we chose whilst we were still essence, before we ever entered this realm," said Iridaan kindly.

The Heart Stone

"I do not remember when I was essence," Laura June responded in confusion.

"No, few of us ever do, but the way we can know that we are following what we planned when we were in essence, is through our emotions. They tell us that we are following the right path," Iridaan informed her.

"I am still not sure that I understand," persisted Laura June.

"Well, let me explain more clearly. You said to me just now, that you could not wait to hear the call of a child's mind. That is your emotion guiding you. You feel the joy of anticipation, the real desire to interact with an Earth child. In this way, you know that you are following a true path. If, for instance, you felt unease or a dread of something, you should be cautious. It could be an indication that you are on the wrong path," Iridaan explained.

"What if I follow a path that does not feel good?"

"Well, that will not be a good path for you to follow, but it will serve to show you that it is something that you ultimately do not want."

"How will I know that I do not want it? Laura June queried further.

"Because you will not feel joyful and happy," said the queen with a smile.

"Is it really that simple? I can know my true path by understanding that when I feel happy, I am on my true path and if I feel unhappy, I am not on the right path?" marvelled Laura June.

"Yes, my little one, it is that simple. The only worry that I have, is that there are fewer and fewer Earth children calling to us, and you lovely girls may never have the opportunity to fulfil your true calling," responded Iridaan with a gentle sigh.

"I refuse to believe that we will never have that chance!" said Tina May fiercely.

"Excellent my child! That is exactly the kind of spirit

that will help win this battle and attract the very thing that you and all of us want. It is that same spirit that Susan has. No matter how bad things are going for her, she never gives up. She just believes that she can overcome any obstacle. Susan's belief has served her well. There have been many times when she could have given in to the bullies at school that tormented her, but she did not. In the beginning, it took her all her courage to stand her ground but, as time passed by, it got easier. Susan does not enjoy the continuous torments that the bullies inflict upon her but she knows that she can manage and that one day they will be gone," explained Iridaan.

"Why do Earth children do that to each other? I do not understand," cried Tina May in alarm.

"No, child, you cannot understand because your life has been one where you feel secure and loved. Your world, until now, has been a happy one, free from war and want. The Earth children's world has not evolved as ours has. They have not, yet, learned the futility of trying to dominate others. They do not understand that we must all allow others the freedom to express themselves as they wish to. They do not understand that they are all, truly, equal and that no one deserves to have more than another. They do not realize that when they begin to respect each other and share all of Earth's resources they will be empowered to develop in ways that they cannot imagine right now. When they see that there is more than enough of the Earth's resources and enough love for everyone they will not want to push and bully others. They will, instead, learn to fully develop their minds and be able to do many of the things that we do here in the Realm of Faeries," said the queen wistfully.

"It seems so obvious what they must do. Can't we just tell them?" asked Tina May.

"Ah, we have tried, many, many times over the centuries. We have whispered in the ears of many sleeping Earth children, but to no avail. That was a lesson for us to learn, we cannot interfere. We must allow the Earth children to develop at their own speed. What we can do dear, Tina May, is to continue to believe that they will soon learn new ways. In that way, you send out a positive vibration into the universe which helps to bring about change for the good," offered the queen.

"Then we will believe with all our heart that they will soon understand and that they will change things on Earth!" cried the twins, allowing their tinkling voices to be audible rather than telepathic.

"Good girls! Now, I must fly! There is a meeting of the elders about to start to discuss the placing of the stones!"

With a whoosh of wings Iridaan was gone and the twins were left to ponder the wisdom that their queen had imparted to them.

Chapter 12
Peace with Gran and Ten Go to the Faerie Realm

Susan and Seb found themselves back at the same spot that they had left after what had seemed like several hours.

"Wow! Susan, that was an incredible experience," Seb said, somewhat overwhelmed by all that had transpired.

"Yes, it was. I'm still trying to come to grips with it all myself," she responded cheerily.

"Oh, heck, what time is it?" asked Seb. He had forgotten to put on his watch in his haste to meet Susan. "I said that I'd do some shopping for my mum at eleven o' clock and she's not going to be happy about me being late!" he moaned.

"I'm not sure," said Susan. "Let me have a look." She checked her watch and stared in amazement at what her watch was telling her. "I can never get used to this," she cried. "It's just half past nine. Hawthorne told me that time passes differently in their realm, and when we seem to have been gone for hours it's only just minutes."

"Phew! That's a relief," exclaimed Seb. "Mum would have been in a real mood if I'd been late." At that moment Hawthorne appeared, jumping down from the Horse Chestnut Tree as he had done before.

"Children, you did a great service for us today, well done!" he congratulated them. "But we still have work to do if we are to beat these negs. I need you to gather together as many of the children that you believe will be able to help us. When you all meet and explain what is required of them, I will be close by listening to their thoughts to see if they are suitable to undertake the task."

"We can do that, Hawthorne, but I am concerned about the little ones. I don't think that they'll be able to understand what we're asking them," Susan said with concern.

"Susan, you would be surprised to have a glimpse into the minds of the young ones. They understand things of this nature far easier than older children," Hawthorne said sagely.

"How can they?" Seb asked condescendingly. "They have no logic and haven't learned about how things are in this world, never mind yours."

"Um, that's where you would be wrong, Master Sebastian. The little ones have not been versed in the way of your world long enough to erase their instinctual knowledge. It is their instinctual knowledge that will serve them better in our realm than logic will, young man," Hawthorne replied.

"Well, how do they know their own minds at that age?" Seb inquired.

"Let me explain, dear boy," Hawthorne said imperiously. "When you children come into being you originate from a very strong Source Of Energy. While you are with Source, you express your desires to that Source so that you may come into the world and experience certain things. Then Source, with great love, grants you your wish and you come forth into your world as a mortal individual. It is often the case, that most individuals forget their connection with the Source as they become integrated into Earth's system. The young children are, therefore, closer to the Source and still remember, in a natural way, the things that they wish to experience. Thus, when you speak to the younger children of coming to our realm I will glimpse into their minds to ensure that what we ask of them is compatible with their Source intentions. Do you see, dear boy?" Hawthorne asked, setting his chin upon his curled fingers.

Seb was speechless. In hearing Hawthorne's words, he felt the truth of them. It was as if there had been a curtain lifted from his mind. Somehow, he knew that he too, had set forth into the world with a strong intention so he might experience something wonderful. Moreover, he was fairly sure that taking part in this endeavour with Susan was a big part of it. He looked over at Susan who was also looking very introspective.

Susan had experienced a deep awakening at Hawthorne's words. She felt that everything that he had said made perfect sense. She also realized why she never felt entirely alone and deserted during the times that she had been tormented by the bullies at school. She instinctively knew that the Source was with her, giving her the courage she needed to withstand the verbal lashings that came her way.

"I understand better now, Hawthorne. I'm quite happy to talk to the younger children about this," Seb said with a new reverence for Hawthorne.

"Me too," agreed Susan.

"Then let us be on our way to contact the others!" Hawthorne said with enthusiasm.

"Will you be—?" Susan hadn't finished her question to Hawthorne before he answered her.

"I will meet you in the Pine Woods," he said, disappearing into the Horse Chestnut Tree.

"Shall we go to Aliya's house first and see what we can arrange?" Susan asked Seb.

"Yes, I think that would be best. We could just arrange to meet at the Pine Woods for a larp game and then when everyone gets there we can explain the situation," Seb answered with a new sense of purpose.

The two children carried out their plans and Aliya said she'd tell her cousins and friends about the larp game in the Pine Woods. They agreed to meet at two o'clock, Susan and Seb left Aliya's house pleased with their progress so far.

"Let's phone George now" Seb suggested.

"That's a good idea," Susan said. George readily agreed to meet them at two o'clock, delighted that he'd finally found some friends to spend the summer holidays with.

"Would you like to go and have a cola or something at Hattie's Café? It'll be my treat," asked Seb. He had been saving his pocket money for a while and felt that there was nothing better that he would like to spend it on than Susan, especially now, as he felt so close to her after the bonding experience they had shared on the beach in the Realm of Faeries.

"Ooh! That would be really nice!" she exclaimed happily. "Are you sure you can afford it? It's a bit pricey,"

"No problem," Seb said, feeling rather grand at being able to impress Susan with his generous offer.

"Just let me phone my gran and tell her that I'll be home for lunch," Susan said remembering her promise.

Her gran seemed a little less hostile this time when she spoke to her. Susan just hoped that it would last until lunchtime!

The two children went to Hattie's and were shown to a nice table on the corner next to the large plate glass windows.

"This is lovely," Susan said appreciatively. "They've given us a window table. They usually save those for the posh people!"

"Yes, it's a bit swish," agreed Seb.

They ordered their drinks from their waitress, who was immaculately dressed in the Hattie's traditional outfit of black and white and began reflecting on their adventures so far. Time seemed to speed by and before they knew it, it was time for Seb to go and do the shopping for his mother. Susan agreed to accompany him before returning home for her lunch.

"I'm home," Susan yelled to her gran.

"Been up to no good, I'll be bound. I suppose you'll be wanting your lunch now," replied her gran in her usual grumpy manner.

"Yes, I'm really hungry," Susan admitted, actually

looking forward to her gran's tasteless offerings.

"Well, I don't know if you're going to like it, but I've followed a recipe from the TV. It's a bean casserole with cheese scones," she replied warily.

"Well, something smells really good, Gran. Let's see if it's as good as it smells!" Susan answered, feeling rather pleased that her gran had made a special effort for her. The food was duly served and proved to be equally as good as it smelled.

"Ooh! Gran this bean casserole is delicious and the cheese scones are just brilliant!" Susan enthused.

Her gran seemed to swell with pride at Susan's words. She was delighted to be able to do something to please her granddaughter. She knew Susan was a good girl, but never seemed to be able to find a way of pleasing her.

Susan's gran had been brought up in a large family where money was tightly controlled and discipline had been the norm. She really didn't know how to show affection to Susan any more than she had to her own daughters. She didn't really approve of the displays of affection that were allowed in Susan's home. She couldn't understand what benefit all the hugs and reassurances of love would have. Susan's gran thought that every child should know his and her place and should be seen and rarely heard.

Susan, spontaneously, jumped up from the lunch table, put her arms around her gran, and told her how nice the lunch was.

"Gran, it's so nice of you to make this food for me. It's lovely and so are you!" she said with enthusiasm.

Her gran was taken aback. She didn't know how to respond to this over-enthusiastic girl, but she did feel a rush of love towards her and began to have an inkling of why hugs might be a good thing.

"Well, young lady, it is a pleasure. I must say that I enjoyed it too," Gran said, disentangling herself from Susan's embrace and patting her on the back to indicate that she had been hugged enough. "We'll have to see if these TV chefs have any more recipes that we can try."

"That would be excellent," Susan said, fervently hoping that such cuisine might be repeated.

Susan helped her gran clean up the dishes and then took herself upstairs to her room to plan for the afternoon's expedition. She was wondering how she would explain things to the older children. Hawthorne had said that the younger children would likely understand easily, but Aliya, Omar, and George might be quite another thing. Before she knew it, the time had come for her to set off to meet the others at the Pine Woods.

"I'm going to meet my friends now, Gran. I've got my phone with me and I won't be late," she informed her grandmother.

"Well, you have a nice time and be careful," her gran said in a pleasant tone.

Susan was pleased to hear Gran speaking in such a kind way to her rather than in the disapproving tones that she usually used. She began to feel a warmth towards her that she had never experienced before. *Perhaps, my gran isn't such a dragon after all!* she thought.

Seb was already waiting in the Pine Woods when Susan arrived. They never went too deeply into the woods, but stayed around the top end where there was plenty of light and enough trees to make playing larp an adventure. They spent the first few minutes reviewing their situation and wondering how best to tell the others about the plight of the faeries.

"I think that we should just say it straight out," Seb said. "They'll either think that we're bonkers or they'll be prepared to listen."

"Yes, I think you're right and, besides, we'll have Hawthorne to give evidence of what we've been through," Susan said in agreement.

"Look! Here come Aliya, Omar, and George now!"

exclaimed Seb.

"Hiya!" shouted Susan and Seb in unison.

"Hiya!" responded the other three with a cheery wave of greeting.

"What's going on?" Omar asked inquisitively. "Have we got a plan for this afternoon's game?"

"We certainly have a plan," said Susan cautiously. "But where are the little ones?"

"Oh, Omar and I have to go and get them at three o'clock. One of them is at the dentist," Aliya told them.

"Ah! Perhaps that's a good thing," Seb said, sounding rather mysterious. Susan nodded her agreement.

"So what's up then?" George chipped in.

"Well," Susan said, equally mysterious. "Something happened and we need to tell you about it. It's something very strange and difficult to believe."

"Well, get on with it," Omar said impatiently. He was eager to hear what was causing all the mystery.

"Look guys," interspersed Seb, something happened to Susan that is incredible and I could hardly believe it until I experienced it too."

"Well, here goes," Susan said, launching into the lengthy explanation of the events of the past twenty four hours. Susan and Seb told the story between them. Aliya, Omar, and George listened with incredulity to their story with many questions and explanations being required.

"So there it is," Susan said with an almost apologetic voice.

"Wow!" said George enthusiastically. "If what you say is true, then you can count me in!"

"Yeah, me too," said Omar. "What about you, Aliya?" he asked with a winning smile.

"It all sounds amazing, but I'm concerned about the little ones," she replied looking at Omar with large melting eyes. At that exact moment there was a loud rustling in the tree branches above them and the diminutive form of Hawthorne sprang into view.

"Aliya, please do not fear for the little ones, they will come to no harm. We have already reassured Susan of this. Furthermore, I will not allow any one of them to accompany us unless they truly wish to. Every possible measure will be taken to ensure the safety of all of you," he explained with a sweeping gesture.

Aliya, Omar and George were astounded at seeing Hawthorne's elfin like form and realized that all that Susan and Seb had told them was obviously true.

"Oh, Mr. Hawthorne, thank you for reassuring me about the little ones. If they'll be perfectly safe, I have no objections at all to helping you. In fact, I'd be delighted to!" she said with enthusiasm.

"That's the spirit, dear Aliya. And it's just Hawthorne; we faeries have no need of titles and formalities."

The five of them continued to have an exciting conversation with Hawthorne, eagerly awaiting the time when the little ones would arrive and their journey to the Faerie Realm would begin.

Aliya and Omar left the others at quarter to three to fetch the little ones and returned promptly at ten past three. Susan spoke gently to them, telling them that there was a magical adventure that they could choose to go on if they wished. She spoke of the faeries, of Hawthorne, and of the great battle with the negs.

None of the five little ones showed any kind of surprise at her story. They were aged between six and eight. Three of them were Aliya's cousins on her father's side. Her uncle had married an English girl of Russian descent and these three were their children. The two boys Justin and Jake were seven years old and were twins who favoured their mother, having straight, dark blonde hair and skin the colour of a Café Latte. Their eyes, however, were dark with long sweeping lashes like their fathers. All in all, they promised to be a handsome pair.

Their sister, Mischka, was a little cutie, with blonde curls, the same colour skin as her brothers and large blue eyes. She had small cherubic proportions that gave her the appearance of a doll. She was younger than her brothers by a year and they took great pains to take care of her, fearing that such a doll-like figure could easily break. However, Mischka was made of sterner stuff, but so enjoyed the attention that her brothers gave her that she played along with the role of delicate doll!

The other two little ones were cousins on Aliya's mother's side of the family. Her auntie had married an Englishman and again the resulting children were delightful. Zoe was the same age as Mischka and they were firm friends.

Zoe was tall for her age taking after her father. She had long Gazelle–like limbs and an innate grace that seemed to make her float as she walked and ran about. Her long straight hair and luminous eyes were dark like her mother and she had an elegant straight nose with a sweetly curved mouth that seemed to be ever smiling. Her brother Rolf, who was eight years old, looked like a male version of Aliya, except that he was heavier set and didn't have the same timidity about him that Aliya did. He was a well-built, rough and tumble boy who could hold his own in any playground dispute.

Hawthorne appeared again at this point, with a large grin upon his face. "Greetings children! It is so nice to encounter such vibrant minds!" he exclaimed.

The little ones weren't quite sure what he was saying, but showed no surprise whatsoever at the sight of him.

"Are you sure that you would like to come with us on this journey today?" he asked the little one's with great solemnity.

"Mmmm, yes, we'd like to," answered Rolf on behalf of all the little ones in a very matter of fact voice.

Hawthorne looked at each one of them in turn and asked if they were entirely sure. The twins nodded and Mischka

The Heart Stone

smiled at him engagingly saying, "yes" with a bit of a lisp. Hawthorne afforded her a smile in return, obviously captivated by the little moppet. Zoe responded with a broad, somewhat boyish grin and a nod.

Having ascertained their agreement, Hawthorne began his explanation of how they would reach the Realm of Faeries. After establishing that they all understood what would take place, he held out both of his hands on either side of him and told them to hold his hands and form a circle. With a great whoosh the ten of them arrived in the Faerie Realm flushed with excitement and amazement at their swift journey. Susan and Seb saw the familiar majestic figure of Iridaan waiting to greet them by the changing tree that was currently portrayed as an Oak Tree.

"Welcome, welcome, my dear children!" she cried, holding her arms out towards them.

The little ones ran spontaneously towards her and were enveloped in her warm embrace.

"My name is Iridaan and I am so happy to see you all!" she said in an elated voice.

After releasing the little ones, she went over to Aliya, Omar, and George, giving a reassuring hug and kiss to each one of them. When she came to George she seemed to look intently at him with what looked like approval in her eyes and gave him a gentle caress on his cheek. Turning swiftly to Susan and Seb, she praised them, saying how well they had done to bring the others back with them.

Hawthorne had undergone his usual transformation into a tall and gallant warrior, much to the approval of the newly arrived children. They all had so many questions to ask that it resulted in a loud, indiscernible babble of voices.

"Children, there will be time for questions when this battle is over, but now we desperately need your help. The negs are gaining ground and we are losing our faeries all the time. We must place the stones as soon as possible!" she said with great urgency.

Hearing the alarm in the queen's voice, the children were immediately silent.

"I am assigning four faeries to each of you children for your safety and protection. They will fly you to your designated area of this realm to place your stone. They will help you with anything that you need, or anything that you do not understand," Iridaan told them in a hushed and serious tone. "Are all of you entirely sure that you wish to do this task for us faeries?"

A unanimous chorus of "yes" rang out from the children. They had no doubt in their minds at all that they wanted to help these beautiful individuals.

"Then let us begin," she said with relief in her voice. Iridaan closed her eyes and summoned the faeries that were to be the guides and protectors of the children.

Within seconds, a whooshing of wings announced the

arrival of a host of faeries. Some were obviously straight from the battlefield as evidenced by their armour with their coloured plumes denoting the house to which they belonged. Others were dressed in leggings and tunics and soft, high, boots. Susan and Seb were delighted to see that Tina May and Laura June were amongst the throng. The two faeries waved in greeting, making the children feel rather important and experienced in faerie ways. The others noted the greeting and looked suitably impressed.

Susan was wondering whether Tina May or Laura June would be assigned to her when she heard Hawthorne's voice in her mind, telling her that this would not be the case. Tina May and Laura June had been assigned to Mischka, along with her other faerie guards, he told her. "Although, my dear Susan," continued Hawthorne telepathically, "You will be having three of my relatives from the House of Hawthorne to protect you," he said with pride in his voice, "and the other will be from the highly esteemed House of Rose. And, by the way, your telepathic powers are developing wonderfully!"

Susan turned to Hawthorne and saw that he was smiling fondly at her.

With the arrival of the faeries, the queen reached inside her cloak and brought out a large green velvet bag and took out its contents. "These, dear children, are the stones that you will place for us," she said with seriousness. The stones were circular and about an inch in diameter and shone with an iridescent, pearly glow.

"They are very small and pretty, but will they be able to do the trick?" asked Mischka in an equally serious manner.

"They may be small, but they are very powerful. Just think of a little acorn that is given sun and water and then grows into a huge Oak Tree. Or even think of yourself, my little one, everyone thinks that you are such a pretty and delicate little creature but, in fact, you know that you are very, very strong," Iridaan said with a smile.

"Yes, I understand that," Mischka responded, surprised that the queen realized that she wasn't just a little doll, but had plenty of inner-strength and was not a timid child.

"It's important that each of you should carry your stone during your flight. In this way, the stone will attune itself to your essence and be ready to do its job when it is placed. Each of you will fly for about thirty minutes each in a different direction. It is crucial that we place the stones in sequence, starting from the oldest child and ending with the youngest child. So it will begin with you, George, and end with you, Mischka. Again, I ask you, are you willing to carry and place the stones for us?"

"Yes," was the immediate and rowdy chorus.

Iridaan allocated a stone to each child and spoke a word that none of the children had ever heard as she passed it to them. Susan heard Hawthorne's voice in her head again. "She is adding a little of her power to each stone and blessing it."

"Is everyone ready?" Iridaan asked.

"Yes!" they all chorused.

The queen joined Tina May, Laura June, and the other two faeries, who were from the House of Cedar. With an elegant, sweeping wave of departure to the others, she took Mischka into her strong arms and lifted to the skies, flanked by the four other faeries. In the same manner, each of the other children was swooped up by a faerie and encircled by the other three, keeping the children in a protective circle as they flew. George was entranced at the sight of the four faeries that were assigned to him. He noted that they all wore the same colours and looked very similar to each other, two of them were female and two were male.

"Do you all come from the same house?" George asked timidly, rather in awe of the magnificent creatures that were encircling him.

"Yes," replied the taller of the two males. "We are from

the House of Heather. My name is Blaze and I am the oldest male of our house."

"Oh! You don't appear to be very old," George responded. He thought Blaze looked no older than twenty.

Blaze smiled. "Our time here passes in a very different way than yours does on Earth, but I assure you that I am, indeed, old by your standards. On my last Birth Remembrance Day I was five hundred and sixty years old," he told George with a large, friendly grin.

Seeing Blaze's wide, friendly grin made George think of his grandfather for a fleeting moment. His grandfather had always been a jovial and enthusiastic character. He had spent many happy hours with him. George had been inconsolable when he died and he still missed him terribly.

Sensing George's sad memory of his grandfather, Blaze continued to speak, distracting George's thoughts to other things. "Can you see that distant spire?" Blaze asked.

"Yes," responded George.

"That is where we are heading; it is where the first stone must be placed."

"Why is it so important that the stones be placed in a certain order?" enquired George.

"Because when the stones are placed, they are said to activate dormant power reserves in our realm. They need a certain sequence to allow the process to begin. The reserves can only be activated in times of critical danger. And they can only be activated by, willing, Earth children," Blaze informed him.

"Why can't you activate them yourselves?" asked George rather puzzled.

"Because we do not have the power. Our very reason for being alive is to enable Earth children to fulfill their dreams. With so many negs being created by Earth children now, we are overwhelmed and have little energy left. It was decreed eons ago that if our realm was ever compromised, our last hope would be to use the stones," Blaze stated with a note of sadness in his voice.

"How awful!" exclaimed George "How could we ever want your beautiful realm to disappear?"

"You do not mean to do it," Blaze replied. "But Earth children are not dreaming anymore and they are not believing that their dreams can come true. The magic has gone out of their lives; they believe that science and technology will deliver them all that they desire. Unfortunately, most of you do not even know what you truly desire any more. You listen to adverts on a television screen that dictate to you what you should want instead of listening to your inner being. No one can tell another what it is that they want, every individual has different desires and dreams that are exactly right for them. But, you have forgotten how to desire and dream about the things that you really want. As a result, you have no need for us and the negs have gained a strong foothold in our realm. So we are counting on you and your friends to help us in this time of desperation," concluded Blaze.

"It's a sad state of affairs," George said, feeling more than a little shame for what had been created on Earth through lack of imagination and enthusiasm. "I'm sure that if other children knew of your existence and the danger that you face from the negs, they would rally round and help you."

"That could be true, dear George, but sadly the children are so much in the thrall of the negs that they are powerless," Blaze said sadly.

"Why are the ten of us not affected by the negs?" enquired George.

"You and your friends are not afraid to be different. You have no need of the latest fashion clothes, nor do you need a TV or PC screen to keep you amused, you have the courage to stand alone and be individuals. All that you need is an outlet for your imaginations. We knew you, before you came here. We are the ones that listened to your dreams and wishes and put in place the opportunities for you to be creative. You are the remnant of a time when we were wanted and loved by many children. Now they scoff and ridicule us. The negs have corrupted their imaginations to such an extent that children would rather occupy their time indulging in barbaric violence on their PCs rather than create a thing of beauty from their imaginations," Blaze said sadly.

"Can this state of affairs ever change?" asked George.

"If we find a way to defeat and eradicate the negs, we stand a chance," Blaze said with a little hope rising in his voice.

"Look, we are nearly at our destination," cried Blaze. The four faeries circled over a beautiful garden close to the spire that they had seen in the distance earlier. With a whooshing of wings they lowered slowly to the ground keeping George in the centre of them the whole time. Blaze indicated an object that resembled a small bejewelled egg-cup. "That is where you must place the stone," he said solemnly.

"Well, here goes!" said George with excitement at placing the first stone.

As George set the stone into its ornate holder, an intense beam of light shot out from the stone that exploded into what looked like a million stars cascading in every direction. After the initial surge, the stars became fixed in the air and began spinning in their own small orbit, shining with every colour of the rainbow and amazingly even a few more. It was a wondrous spectacle to behold. Even the faeries were captivated by the sheer beauty and wonder of it as none of them had ever seen this sight before.

George was transfixed by the scene he was beholding, unable to speak for several moments. When he found his voice he asked Blaze what the function of the stars was.

"The stars set up a vibrational field that is impermeable to negative energy. If the negs try to pass this field they will be unable penetrate it. Their dark energy will be dissipated,"

Blaze told George with a look of satisfaction and new hope beginning to burn in his eyes.

"That is so cool, so mega!" responded George with enthusiasm.

"Come, let's go to the Reflecteum we can watch the other stars take their place," Blaze said with great energy.

Blaze picked George up and swooped high into the sky in sheer ecstasy. He felt some release from the curse of the negs, as did the other three faeries. At least the first stone had worked and they would have some respite to gather their resources and re-evaluate their position. They began to believe that this war could be at an end if all the other stones worked their magic too.

Blaze descended from his swoop of joy next to the beautiful spire that he had pointed out to George earlier. On approaching it, George, could see that it was the towering glory of a majestic building that was as big as some of the largest Cathedrals in England. The outside of the building shone with the same translucent, mother of pearl iridescence as the wings of the faeries. It seemed, from the outside, to have no windows yet the whole building gave the appearance of softly, shimmering light.

"Oh, wow!" exclaimed George.

"This is our Reflecteum, it is where we come to reflect upon our lives and the things which we have created in the Earth Realm with you children," announced Blaze with pride.

"Oh, it's so lovely. I cannot find words to describe how beautiful it is," George uttered in amazement.

"Come, let us go inside. If we go up to the tower, we will be able to watch the other stars from the best vantage point," Blaze said.

The small party entered the Reflecteum and George was equally awed by its interior. From the inside, the whole place was completely transparent and he could see the view outside from every direction he looked. Its interior glowed with softly diffusing lights of every shade and hue that could be imagined. The lights took on different shapes similar to that of a kaleidoscope, shifting and changing endlessly in design and complexity. In the centre of the Reflecteum there was a large, round, elevated disc with a large circular hole in the middle of it that seemed to hover in the air about six feet off the ground. Looking upwards, George saw the ceiling rise up into a majestic dome with a magnificently cut, exquisite, jewel rotating within the dome. From this jewel seemed to emanate all the light within the Reflecteum.

"What a fabulous jewel!" exclaimed George in wonder. "What is it? What is it made of?"

"That is our Heart Stone; no one knows what it is made of. It is very old, older than anyone remembers. Not even Iridaan remembers when it was put here. The Reflecteum is also ancient, and again, no one knows when it was built," answered Blaze.

"That disc below it, what is that for?" George asked.

"That is where we sit and commune with Krailaan. He is our soul searcher who helps us to keep our intentions focused," said Blaze.

"Erm, what does that mean?" George asked, baffled by Blaze's statement.

"Oh, well our intentions are the ideas that we are born into the world with. When we were in spirit form we decided on certain courses of action that we believed to be beneficial to us. Krailaan ensures that we are still keeping our intentions in our minds and also suggests other possible courses of action that might be appropriate for us," Blaze responded.

"So is he a kind of priest then?" asked George.

"Not really. He never imposes his beliefs or his will upon us; he is a very gentle guide. He is one of the elders, like Iridaan, and has a wealth of knowledge and wisdom. We treasure the time he gives us," said Blaze with obvious affection in his voice. "Look, you can see for yourself. He approaches us now."

From, seemingly out of nowhere, a tall, elegant faerie appeared before them. His hair was like shimmering gold that was shot with silvery-white streaks that fell to his shoulders. His skin was pale and luminous but his eyes blazed like burnished bronze. His nose was straight and slim set above a mouth that appeared to be smiling although it was only gently set together in repose. His face was long and oval with sharply defined cheekbones. About him there was an aura of peace and tranquillity that intensified as he drew nearer to them. George was both intrigued and slightly afraid of this majestic being.

Krailaan spoke in deep, rich tones that seemed to strike a beautiful chord within George. "Welcome child, you are a true blessing to us this day. Let us go to the tower and watch the progress of the other stones," he said gently.

George felt all fear leave him as Krailaan spoke. Indeed, he felt himself resonate with a feeling of anticipation, as if something good was about to happen. He could not explain it. It just felt a little bit like Christmas Eve when he was younger. The small party went to the far end of the room where a large, shining, crystalline staircase spiralled upwards.

"Why do you have a staircase to the tower when you could easily fly up there?" George enquired, thinking that it was a very intelligent question to ask.

"Because we like to use all our limbs equally. Our wings have no priority over our arms or legs and besides the staircase is such a beautiful piece of architecture it would be a shame just to have a hole in the ceiling for us to fly through."

"Oh, yes, yes, of course," replied George now feeling that his question was incredibly stupid.

They ascended to the tower which looked out, for as far as the eye could see, in every direction. From this vantage

The Heart Stone

point they watched as stone after stone was placed and the magnificent spectacle of the stars shone forth and took their place in the skies throughout the Faerie Realm. Just as the last stone was being placed, they saw the formidable shape of a huge neg rushing to intercept Iridaan, Mischka, and the other faeries.

Iridaan was well aware of the danger in placing the last stone. It was the most vulnerable time. If the negs prevented the placing of the last stone, it would invalidate all the others and the Faerie Realm would be left entirely at the negs mercy.

The stones had never been called upon in all of faerie history. Even Iridaan was unsure of what the outcome would be. She knew that if it stopped the negs and they were unable to penetrate the force field it would buy them time, but if it neutralized them, then the negs would be defeated.

Iridaan, carrying Mischka, landed gently on the spot where the final stone would be placed, flanked by the two empaths and the three faeries from the House of Cedar. She then explained to Mischka the importance of the last stone.

"I chose you, Mischka, to place the last stone because you are the youngest and are still, closely and consciously, connected to the Source so your energy will be the strongest of all the children. Besides, you are a very strong character indeed!" she said with a smile and a small chuckle of affection. "I do not want you to worry about your safety, we have the strongest faeries in the realm with us and Tina May and Laura June will be able to predict anything that threatens our safety," she concluded.

No sooner were the words out of Iridaan's mouth than Laura June uttered a warning to them.

"There is a massive neg travelling towards us at great speed. We must place the stone with all haste!" she said in a calm but assertive tone.

"Let it be done!" cried Iridaan.

"I'm not afraid!" We'll finish these negs!" Mischka said with great courage for a little girl.

The four faeries cheered at her words and encircled her, as a deep, cold darkness bore down upon them. The stone in Mischka's hand began to glow with a brilliant intensity as if seeking its place in the skies with the other stone's starbursts.

The silence of the neg seemed to screech louder than any battle cry. Its penetrating emptiness and impending doom began to touch Mischka's tiny heart as if to freeze it of any emotion. Immediately, the two empaths closed in around Mischka and set up a vibrational field with their beautiful, tinkling voices. As they did so, a brilliant light shone forth from them, encircling Mischka in its warmth and suffusing her tiny frame in its glow. This, immediately eradicated any coldness that she had experienced from the approaching neg.

The empaths led Mischka to the place where the stone was to be placed. The neg was almost upon them, at this point, seeming to grow larger and larger by the second.

"Do not fear, little one! Place the stone now," said Iridaan warmly.

"I will," she responded, looking defiantly at the neg. "Now leave and never come back!" Mischka shouted bravely to the ugly, towering, form of the neg.

Mischka placed the stone, which was glowing and vibrating in anticipation of its task, firmly in its holder, and within an instant it sent forth its shower of golden stars into the skies.

The faeries and Mischka stood their ground bravely as they watched the formidable neg surge forward to challenge the shimmering veil of stars that had emerged from the stone. However, in seconds, their demeanour changed to one of awe and elation as they watched the dark foe that was the neg, disintegrate as it touched the golden light of

The Heart Stone

the stars from the stone.

"This is a great day!" proclaimed Iridaan loudly. "The negs are vanquished!"

"Are they gone forever?" asked Mischka with a large grin forming on her lips.

"Yes, my sweet child. You children have freed us. Thank you for your great courage. We owe you a debt of gratitude!" Iridaan said with great feeling. "Let us fly to the village and join the others. Today we will celebrate!" With a whoosh of wings they took to the skies and headed for the village.

Krailaan, George, and his accompanying faeries watched as this spectacle unfolded before their eyes.

"This is better than we had dared hope for. It appears that the negs are defeated," said Krailaan, jubilation evident in his voice.

"This is amazing!" cried George.

"There has been great work done here today," proclaimed Krailaan. "We owe you children a debt of gratitude. You have been courageous and generous and deserve to be honoured."

Krailaan's words touched George so strongly that he felt as though he had been awarded the medal of valour. When Krailaan spoke, it was as if he touched a part of him that had been long forgotten. A part that had once screamed to be heard but could not find the voice to communicate with. Here, with Krailaan, he was beginning to feel, again, that part of him he didn't understand. George looked at Krailaan with incredulity as he began communicating telepathically with him as easily as he was able to speak. Krailaan was telling him things that he could scarcely believe. George's mind was straining to comprehend his words.

"What I tell you is correct," spoke Krailaan into George's mind. "Do not fear this. I believe it to be a blessing for you," George looked around at the four faeries that were now gazing intently at him and smiling warmly.

"Do you mean that these faeries are related to me somehow?" vigorous nodding from the four smiling faeries of the House of Heather reinforced Krailaan's words.

"How is this possible?" asked George.

"Let us fly to the town. All of the others will be there. It is right that Iridaan should be present at this time of revelation for you. We have much to celebrate," Krailaan said happily.

Chapter 13
Victory and George's Incredible Story

George, Krailaan, and the four faeries of the House of Heather flew swiftly and joyfully to the centre of the town where the vibrant throng of human children and faeries were united in their successful mission to stop the advance of the negs. They were gathered in the restaurant where Susan and Seb had eaten their delicious meal with Tina May and Laura June earlier.

Iridaan immediately drew close to Krailaan and George, knowing instinctively about the revelation that George was about to have.

"Greetings George, Krailaan, and all my brave Heather faeries!" Iridaan looked directly at George as she spoke with a warm and welcoming smile on her beautiful face.

Susan, observant as ever, noted that the energy of the group had now turned toward George. Her recent success with telepathy told her that George was able to communicate in this way too, and that there was some mystery afoot.

"George, you're able to communicate telepathically," she thought to him.

"Yes, it's amazing. I feel so different here. It seems that I have a connection here and they're going to tell me all about it," he transmitted back with ease.

"Will we all hear about it?" Susan asked.

"Only when we have spoken to George alone and he agrees to share the information," Iridaan stated firmly.

"No, it's okay, Iridaan. They're all my friends and I trust them. I have an inkling as to what's going on, and if it is true I'll be proud to share the information with my friends," George responded telepathically.

"As you wish, dear George. I can guarantee that these children are truly your friends or should I say our friends?" she said with a smile.

"Oh, do tell us everything!" exclaimed Susan.

"Well, gather around everyone, and I will tell you a very special and interesting story,"

Faeries and children gathered around Iridaan in great curiosity.

"You faeries are aware of the story of Richard Slater," she began. "This is his great, great, great, grandson George," she said with solemnity.

A gasp of disbelief went through the faerie ranks, followed by warm, friendly smiles directed at George. Susan and the other children were entranced at this mystery, and couldn't wait for Iridaan to continue.

"A time ago when, Richard, George's ancestor, was young, he managed to find his way to our realm on his own. It is a remarkable thing to be able to do. But then, Richard was a very special young man, full of dreams and enterprise. His family was quite well off and he had been lucky enough to travel around the world and even explore unknown parts of it. However, his quest for adventure could never quite be satisfied no matter how hard he tried to fulfill it. He delved into all sorts of things—he painted, he wrote a book, and he even tried his hand at sculpting. But, somehow, Richard could never quite find his niche. He could never find the thing that he most sought in the world. One night, he was having trouble getting to sleep and started reminiscing about all the wonderful journeys he had undertaken and the magical childhood that his loving parents had given him when, all of a sudden, he appeared in our realm. We were instantly aware of his arrival and I rushed to greet him to ensure that he was not afraid or confused. However, on greeting him, he was anything but distraught; Richard was looking about him in amazement taking in everything. When he saw me he was ecstatic. *Yes,*

yes! he cried. *This is what I've been looking for.* Then he spoke to me and introduced himself, saying that he was an explorer and that this was the discovery that he had been hoping to make; a discovery of a different realm that existed in a different dimension. His time with us brought him great happiness and as he learned more about us, he didn't want to leave. Fortunately, time passes differently here and his absence from Earth was not initially noted. In order to stay longer, he returned to the Earth Realm and told his parents and friends that he was undertaking another journey abroad and would contact them when he arrived there. They didn't think this strange, as Richard was in the habit of going off on expeditions on a whim with no forwarding address. His parents were very liberal and allowed him his freedom with little question. When Richard returned to us, he learned our ways and became one of us. He was able to do everything that we can do, such as projecting and telepathy. He could do everything except fly," Iridaan said with a chuckle of remembrance. "He spent time with as many faeries as he could, learning the traditions associated with their Houses and their abilities. All faeries have a special power associated with their House," Iridaan emphasised. "After some time, many of us noticed that he had begun to spend much of his time at the House of Heather and with one beautiful faerie in particular, named Azure (for the intensity of her blue eyes). Very soon it became obvious to all of us that Richard and Azure had fallen in love. Richard came to me and asked if it would be possible for him and Azure to marry. I told him that it was a very unusual request, but not one that was unknown. In the past there had been the occasional marriage between human and faerie. But, without exception, the human was of a calibre that exceeded the usual. Given that Richard was, indeed, a remarkable man whom we all trusted, I agreed to their wedding. It was a wonderful affair with celebrations lasting for days. Richard and Azure began their idyllic life together. They had so much in common with one another. They spent their days discussing classical works, from paintings to literature and creating new inventions of every imagination. They were truly soul mates and were unbelievably happy. To add to their joy, Azure became pregnant with Richard's baby within the year. This gave rise to even more celebrations. A human/faerie child is a very rare thing and everyone was both delighted and intrigued at the news. Then the bad news came. Richard (who used to look in on his parents secretly every now and then) discovered on a night time visit to them that his father had suddenly become seriously ill and was asking for him. Richard explained to Azure what had transpired and said that he and Azure must discuss what they would do next. After long hours of discussion, Richard and Azure came to tell us of their decision. They said that they had made the decision to return to the Earth Realm so that they could help Richard's mother, who would be left with no close family to help her run the family business, during her husband's illness."

"Oh!" exclaimed Susan unable to contain herself. "But what about Azure? Wouldn't she become tiny and be looked upon as different? What about her wings?"

"Three questions at once this time!" muttered Hawthorne under his breath.

"Yes, Susan. That was what we were all concerned about," Iridaan replied. "A strange thing happened when Richard and Azure returned to Earth for a trial run. They found that Azure was able to maintain a size that was compatible with that of humans. She was a little on the petite side, around 4 feet, 11 inches, but still quite normal. As for her wings, she was able to use her powers of projection to make them disappear."

"Oh, how wonderful! How did that happen?" Susan asked, clapping her hands in delight.

"We were to find out later through our empathic investigators that her ability to maintain mortal form was

The Heart Stone

due to her being pregnant. Her half-human baby's blood mingled with that of Azure's. It gave her the physiological capability of maintaining human form. Now to continue with the story. Richard explained to his parents that he had met and fallen in love with Azure in a distant land and had married and stayed with her. While being quite shocked at first by the news, they were so impressed with the beautiful Azure that he was soon forgiven. His parents insisted on having another wedding ceremony for them. Many guests were invited and Azure was welcomed into the community. Unfortunately, shortly after the wedding, Richard's father died and Richard took over the running of the family business. Very soon after that, Azure and Richard's baby was born, a beautiful baby girl that stole the hearts of everyone that saw her. They named her Heather, after Azure's House. She was mortal in appearance, but as with all descendants of the faeries, she carried faerie blood. Richard and Azure inherited all the wealth of the family and did many good things for the community and especially for the workers in Richard's factories. They were much loved by all," Iridaan looked warmly at George and said, "I think that you probably know the rest of this story, but for the others I will just add that Azure was not able to bear any more children.

"When Richard died, Heather took over the running of the family business. During this time, the First World War broke out and everything was chaotic. Heather sold off much of the family's holdings and distributed the money to those who were in need. She then left for the battlefront to care for the sick and dying soldiers. It was there that she met and very soon after married your great, great, great grandfather," she said, looking warmly at George. "Any child carrying faerie blood has always been told of this when they reach the age of twenty one. So, George, you are ahead of the game!"

All the mortal children gasped at hearing that George

was the descendant of a faerie and looked at him with new admiration.

George looked at Iridaan with questioning eyes and said out loud for the benefit of those who had not yet learned to converse telepathically. "Iridaan, you didn't mention what happened to Azure."

"Indeed, I did not," she said with feeling. "That is because Azure was not subject to aging the same way that mortals are, so after Richard's death and after Heather became old enough to manage the family affairs, Azure went for a voyage abroad. Once there, she took measures to ensure that it was reported that she had died while overseas. But, of course, she did not die, and if you will turn around you will see the lovely Azure waiting to embrace you and welcome you into your faerie family," she said motioning towards a magnificent looking faerie who looked to be about twenty-five years old.

Azure stood before George with her arms outstretched towards him. Her golden hair cascaded down her back in shimmering rivers of light, her blue eyes shone like a sleepy ocean reflecting the sun, and her smiling mouth spoke George's name like a chord of beautiful music. George walked into her arms and was overcome with the joy and emotion of the greeting.

"You resemble my Richard so much, dear child. I am so happy to meet you at last. Many are the nights that I have peeped into your room as you slept and tried to speak kind words to you in your dreams. I did this with all my descendants, but you are the first to come here to me in such a way and I am so delighted!"

A spontaneous cheer went up from the Earth children, closely followed by whoops of delight from the faeries.

"I always felt so different from other children and now I know why," George said in both relief and delight.

"I proclaim this as a day of remembrance and celebration!" Iridaan cried in elation.

Chapter 14
Susan, Aliya, and the Voice of Nature

The throng of faeries and Earth children celebrated the defeat of the negs and George's reunion with his faerie family long into the night with singing, dancing and, tales of brave deeds done by ancient faeries. Eventually, a calm overtook them and the children were despatched to a dormitory to rest and get some sleep. It was decided that the children's absence would not be noticed on Earth due to the time differential between the two worlds and that the children should relax before their return to Earth. A guard of twenty faeries stood around the children's sleeping quarters.

The next morning, the children woke after a sound sleep full of magical dreams, still wearing the clothes of the previous day. Aliya stretched and looked around her as the happy memory of the day before flooded into her mind. She looked over at the waking Susan with happiness shining in her eyes. "Susan, what a wonderful day it was yesterday! I can hardly believe what we all did," she said excitedly.

"Mmmm, yup. It was amazing," replied Susan sleepily.

"Can we go and explore, do you think? The others are still fast asleep," Aliya asked, feeling particularly adventurous and brave after yesterday's victory.

Susan looked around and saw that the boys' dorm room was still shut and all the little children were still sleeping.

"I don't see why not. We could ask the faeries that are outside guarding our dorm if it would be alright," Susan responded brightly. "Actually, I can do better than that. I can ask them telepathically," she volunteered remembering her new skills in the faerie realm.

No sooner than the words were out of her mouth, she was replying to Aliya telling her that they could go out exploring, but only if they kept in telepathic contact with an assigned faerie. The girls agreed to report in every thirty minutes with one of their faerie guards named Castano. He was from the House of Horse Chestnut and was a strong, well built faerie that looked as though he would be well suited to playing vigorous sports such as rugby. He was rough and tumble looking with dark brown curls that flopped over his eyes and skin the colour of dark mahogany. His deep, brown eyes reminded the girls of melting chocolate and his slightly crooked nose only added to the roguish charm of his appearance. His mouth was even and manly looking. The girls thought him to be very handsome indeed! They had a few girlish giggles about what a "dish" he was after they had taken their leave of him.

Susan checked that her watch was working and the two girls set off walking in the direction of a small thicket of woods that was near the dorm and decided that they would begin exploring there. As they neared their destination, Aliya shouted, "Look, look! There's a beautiful little faun just by the trees."

"Yes! Yes! I see it!" Susan replied with equal enthusiasm.

"I hope it won't run away before we get closer," Aliya said hopefully.

"I believe it's actually walking towards us," Susan said incredulously.

"Oh, yes it is!" said Aliya, trying to contain her excitement.

"We better not rush," cautioned Susan. "It might think that we're going to harm it."

"Yes, you're right," Aliya agreed, calming herself for fear of frightening the beautiful creature.

As the children walked gently towards the faun, they found that it was drawing ever closer to them, showing no sign of fear.

"Let's just stand still and see what happens," Aliya said, hoping to make contact with the faun.

"Okay," agreed Susan, who was thinking similar thoughts.

The two girls stood very still and waited. Within seconds, the little faun was prancing towards them with the same confidence as a young puppy.

"Oh, it's actually going to come to us," Aliya gasped, holding out her hand toward the approaching faun.

"I wish we had some food to give it," Susan said.

Then to Susan's surprise, she heard a little voice in her head saying that it didn't want any food, only to come and greet them. Susan gasped in surprise and told Aliya what had happened.

"I wish that I could do telepathy," Aliya sighed.

"You can, you know," Susan said encouragingly. "Here in this realm, all sorts of things are possible. You just have to believe that you can and that's all there is to it!" she concluded with confidence.

Aliya was so determined to have mental contact with this lovely creature that she sent her thoughts out towards it so forcefully that the little faun stopped in its tracks, unaccustomed to the strong mental contact. Then, to Aliya's delight, she heard the gentle voice of the faun in her mind asking her what her name was.

"It's Aliya," she said, hardly daring to whisper with her mind's voice for fear of frightening the little faun again.

"Well Aliya, I am so pleased to meet you. It was your hope of meeting a woodland creature that drew me towards you," it said gently.

"Oh, I'm so pleased to meet you," she cried in excitement. "I didn't know that animals could actually speak, so this is very surprising to me."

Susan, who had been able to listen telepathically to this conversation, had decided to sit down on the lush, verdant grass and watch and listen to the entrancing spectacle that was unfolding in front of her eyes.

"Animals do speak, but not with the words that you are accustomed to," said the little faun. "We are born with an affinity for nature and ability to converse with it. Indeed, we are nature!"

"How are you able to speak to me so well then?" Aliya enquired.

"It is because you are in tune with nature. Your vibration matches mine and the communication that we are having is an exchange of vibrations rather than words. It is only your human brain that is changing the vibration into words so that you can better understand what I say," concluded the little faun.

"Does that mean you're not actually speaking to us in words?" Susan chipped in, unable to refrain from speaking any longer.

"Yes, that is right. I speak to you with the innate voice of nature that is older and wiser than anything you see about you, from the smallest blade of grass to the tallest mountain."

"Do you mean to tell me that even a blade of grass can communicate?" Susan asked in astonishment.

"Yes, for if it did not, then how could nature possibly know what it needed? Whether it needed water or sunshine, whether it needed nourishment from the soil, or whether it was at the beginning or the end of its life cycle, nature must constantly keep her balance so as to keep order in the realm," the little faun explained.

"So, we're not just talking to you," Aliya said, reflectively, to the faun, "We're speaking to nature herself?"

"That is correct, little one," the faun answered.

"Oh, I wish it was like this on Earth," Susan said with sadness in her voice.

"Once, it was that way on Earth, but man has become

The Heart Stone

greedy and has upset the balance of nature. Now, nature has to make harsh adjustments to maintain any sort of balance at all. This wreaks havoc in your realm and causes disasters and death. That was never the way it was supposed to be," lamented nature's voice.

"Can't we stop it?" Aliya cried in alarm and sadness over what had been done on Earth.

"Only if all of the world will agree to stop abusing the animals and the land," nature's voice informed them.

"Can this be done?" Susan said seriously.

"It can be done if there are more children like you that allow themselves to listen to their inner-voice; the voice that guides them towards the benefit of all, rather than the benefit of themselves. It is my hope that you children, on your return to Earth, will be instrumental in influencing the beliefs of other children for the better."

"We'll do anything!" Aliya cried without any hesitation.

"Yes, we will," Susan said thoughtfully. "I'm not sure that any of them will listen to us."

"There are ways," said nature's voice gently. "Ways that you may not realize. You will have all been strengthened greatly by coming to this realm. Your capacity to dream will be greater than others on Earth and it is in this medium that you can do the most good. You will find that your dreams are more lucid, that you are able to be quite conscious of your actions in your dreams. It is in this manner that you will be able to speak to other children. You can suggest the idea of a better, healthier, world whilst they are sleeping. You can ask them to speak to their parents about the way that they abuse the Earth and ask them to stop. Remind them that there will be nothing left for them and their children if they do not stop abusing the Earth now. When they awaken, it is quite possible that many of the children will feel the urge to create a better world for the future."

"We'll do that!" Aliya and Susan exclaimed in one voice.

"Then I will leave you now to spend time with Rastus, my little faun, who will still be able to communicate with you but perhaps not in such a serious way," concluded nature's voice.

Rastus, the little faun, drew close to the children and plopped down beside them on the grass, nuzzling his head into their arms. Aliya tried out her new skill of telepathy again and asked Rastus what he would like them to do.

"I would like to have the back of my ears scratched," came the prompt reply.

Immediately, the two girls began scratching Rastus in the designated spot and he closed his eyes in bliss at their gentle touch. The two girls were lost in the wonder and enchantment of their morning with Rastus and their conversation with nature's voice. They were solemnly discussing this when a voice boomed out behind them.

"It would appear that you two are not very good at time-keeping," remarked Castano, pointing to where a watch would be worn on his arm.

"Oh! Oh! Are we late? We forgot to report in. I am so, so sorry!" exclaimed Susan feeling very guilty. Aliya nodded her apologies too.

"Don't worry too much, children. I was listening to your thoughts and heard your conversation with nature and decided that you would be better served listening to her than to me interrupting such a wonderful exchange," he said beaming at them.

Susan looked at her watch and according to faerie time, they had been speaking with the voice of nature for some two hours.

"It only felt like minutes since we left the dorm," Susan explained.

"Yes, that is the thing with wonderful exchanges, you never feel as though time is passing. The wonder and enchantment of the moment seems to exist beyond time," he agreed. "Anyway, the other children have been up for hours and are asking for you. Perhaps, we should go and join them," he invited.

Eager to tell the others of their encounter with the voice of nature and, Rastus the faun, the girls hurried to Castano's side.

"Walk or fly?" he asked the two girls.

"Oh, fly please," chorused the two, never wanting to pass up the chance to fly in the arms of the magnificent faeries.

Castano flew the girls to the village where the other children had joined some of the younger faeries. They found them all laughing and chattering in the restaurant, munching on all kinds of delights that the Earth children had convinced the young faeries to project for them. Susan and Aliya hadn't seen any of the younger faeries and were astonished to see that they were of the same size, shape, and colour as the different races of children on Earth.

Hearing Susan's thoughts of astonishment, Castano spoke to the two girls and explained that in order for the young faeries to learn, they must first empathise with the children of Earth and learn how it feels to be a particular size, shape, or colour. When the faeries become older, they return to their traditional appearance.

Susan and Aliya thought this to be an excellent thing. However, seeing the abundant spread of delicious food, they realized that they were very hungry and soon got stuck into the appetizing fare before them. Soon after, Iridaan appeared striding purposefully into the large room.

"Hmmmm! I am not sure that this is the kind of food that your parents would approve of," she chastised, eyeing the enormous pies and cakes that were strewn amongst heaping piles of chocolate sandwiches made with white bread among many other delicacies that required the inclusion of refined white flour.

"Faeries, you should know better than to feed our honoured guests this kind of food," she chastised.

"Oh, but that is what they wanted," lamented a sweet

looking, young faerie.

"Yes, but you know that there is very little here that will actually sustain them," Iridaan continued.

"But," interjected the little faerie.

"No buts! You must not do this again!" Iridaan said sharply. "However, as this is a time of celebration, I will allow it on this occasion," she concluded, her face relenting into a warm smile.

A loud cheer went up from both mortal and faerie children.

Chapter 15
The Return of the Negs

The extended feast continued with Iridaan supervising her young, errant faeries. Their laughter and joviality seemed to permeate the whole village. The Earth children were beginning to get the hang of projecting and some hilarious concoctions of food were being manifested! Everyone who popped in to see the impromptu party found a reason to stay and join in the fun.

It was to this scene that Tina May and Laura June flew, breathlessly, into the building.

"Iridaan, we must talk to you in private, immediately," they said, trying not to look as alarmed as they felt for the sake of the children.

"Come, let us go outside," Iridaan responded, sensing the agitation in their voices.

"What is it? Why did you not speak to me telepathically?"

"Most of the children have learned to use their telepathic abilities and we could not be sure that they would not hear our thoughts to you. The news that we bring is not good and we wanted you to decide how it is given to the others," Tina May said.

"Tell me," said Iridaan patiently.

"Oh, dear Queen," spoke Laura June sadly. "It is the worst news that we bring. We have detected the negs returning. We witnessed their attempts to breach the star field and it is no longer neutralizing them as before. We fear that they may have found a way to breach our defenses."

"You were right to come to me this way. This news is serious. Call all the elders to meet me in the Reflecteum as soon as possible and call the entire House of Cedar to encircle and guard the restaurant where the little ones are," the queen said purposefully.

The two girls closed their eyes and sent out telepathic messages to all the elders in the realm and to the strong and courageous men and women of the House of Cedar.

Iridaan returned to the children who were still enjoying a riotous time with the young faeries and told them that she would be leaving for a while but she would be sending for some of her faeries to watch over them in case they got too carried away with their projecting. She didn't want to alarm any of either the Earth children or the young faeries before it was necessary. She knew that they would be safe with their guards from the House of Cedar. She had also called Hawthorne telepathically and told him to join the children in the restaurant, and if there was a hint of danger to them he must return with them to Earth immediately. With one last wistful look at the rejoicing children she took to the skies to meet the other elders at the Reflecteum.

"We will speak with our voices in this meeting lest any of the children should happen to hear our thoughts," she informed the assembly of thirty elders who were gathered in the Reflecteum. The queen continued to tell them of the grim news regarding the negs return.

"We must consult every book that has been written about the negs and see what can be done. Any of you who have any knowledge of how we might defend ourselves, please speak."

She looked into the eyes of each elder imploring them for direction and help.

The elders were a magnificent sight to behold. Each one seemed to have an aura that emanated a power and majesty. Together, their combined energy seemed almost too much for the Reflecteum to contain. Their appearance was similarly striking. They bore the same white flashes in their hair that both Iridaan and Krailaan possessed and they were taller than the majority of the faeries. Both men and women elders could be described as handsome; their age was not apparent to the beholder. They seemed to have an air of

The Heart Stone

timelessness about them. When they walked it was like a slow ballet, each foot carefully and purposefully following the other in long measured strides that spanned a meter and a half at a time. Everything about them seemed to be measured and calculated. Indeed, over the many millennia that they had existed, they had learned that in times of dire threat, impetuous behaviour would not bring solutions. Steady, calm thought would be their best ally.

Krailaan was the first to speak. "It is, indeed, ill news that reaches us. It is clear that there has been an imbalance somewhere. It should not have been possible for the negs to survive the star field. The fact that they are surviving contact with it is not rational. We must search our minds and our souls to find a solution. The answers will not be in our great books, for I have read them all many times and there is no mention of the negs being able to withstand our star field. However, we must remember that the situation is unique. Never in the whole of faerie history has there been a time when the negs have managed to get such a foothold as this. In the past, they have been dispersed with moderate projection. Never have we had the need to call upon the stones, much less the dear Earth children. The fact that the stones are failing, indicates to me that there is an imbalance between the power of the negs and the processes that we have used to eradicate them. It is my opinion, that we should look inward upon this subject with all haste," concluded Krailaan sagely.

The queen was silent for a moment while she digested the unspoken complexity of what Krailaan had said. "I agree. We must look inward upon this subject. Let us use the Reflecteum to aid our thoughts," she said determinedly.

At the queen's words, the congregated elders simultaneously looked upwards to the Heart Stone that rotated and shone brilliantly above them. As they linked their minds to the Heart Stone its intense beams of light flooded down upon each of them. As this mind link took place, they closed their eyes and looked inwards for a solution to their terrible dilemma.

Back in the village there was still merriment taking place among the children and young faeries. However, the older faeries that had been rejoicing with them had begun to leave, sensing an imbalance occurring in the realm. They took to the village street and sought out the two empaths, instinctively knowing that they had news for them. Slowly, they began returning to their homes looking for their loved ones and preparing for what might be their last battle.

Susan and Aliya had noticed that Castano was outside again and called to him to join them. "Oh, do come and join us! We're having such a lovely time," pleaded the girls.

Castano shook his head, sadly, knowing of the return of the negs. "I have my orders to stay here and I must not disobey."

"Oh, but it's a day of celebration. I'm sure it won't matter," chirped Aliya.

Castano shook his head firmly and his demeanour told them that to plead with him would be useless. Susan felt a change in the air, as if their merriment was somehow at odds with what was happening elsewhere.

"Can you feel that?" Susan asked Aliya.

"Feel what?" queried Aliya, still immersed in the merriment of the moment.

"Something has changed, I can feel it," Susan said, her senses alerting her to the change of atmosphere.

Aliya began to sense the change too and as they looked around they saw that the others, both faerie and Earth children, had begun to cease their merrymaking and were becoming silent.

Castano saw the children's joyfulness begin to subside and quickly sent a telepathic message to Iridaan to inform her of the change of mood within the youngsters. Iridaan replied to him saying that he should instruct Hawthorne to go to the village and explain to the children that the negs had returned and that they must return home for their own safety.

Upon hearing Castano's telepathic communication, Hawthorne immediately flew to the, now sombre, restaurant with a flourish, bestowing a warm smile upon all the gathered children. "Children, of the two realms Earth and Faerie, I come to you with urgent news from Iridaan. The news, I am sorry to say, is not good," he said, reluctant to be the bearer of such bad news.

Susan interrupted his eloquent flow of words. "Hawthorne, something terrible has happened hasn't it? We can all feel it."

"Yes, dear girl, although it is a great delight to me in this hour of sadness that all of you children have availed yourself of your intuitive powers. You have equalled yourselves with the younger faeries of the realm. Well done, to you all," he opined.

Seb stood forward and spoke in a manner that brooked no more prevarication. "What's happened, Hawthorne? We can all feel the encroaching danger, we need to know."

"It is the negs, they have overcome the power of the star field and it is no longer neutralizing them. It is only a matter of time before they breach the star field and consume the rest of our realm," Hawthorne said sadly.

An audible gasp went around the room as the impact of the negs return sunk in.

"It is my task to ensure that you children return to Earth safely. We must leave at once," he said with authority.

"What will happen to all of you and our new friends?" Susan asked, gesturing to the little moppet faeries that they had been sharing the morning with.

"As ever, Susan, two questions at once!" chided Hawthorne with a sad smile. "Unfortunately, the answer is the same for all of us in the Faerie Realm, we will fight to the death to protect our realm. Even the little ones will stand and give battle for they have strong powers of projection.

In the final hour we will call upon the Source to accept our spirits speedily and bid farewell to what remains of our beautiful realm before it is annihilated by the negs," he concluded, unable to prevent a tear welling up in his eye.

"What if we don't go back to Earth? Is there some way that we could help? Susan asked, sensing the mood of the others who, like her, were horrified that the faeries wouldn't survive this onslaught by the negs.

"Dear child, children, all you could do is give us a little more time as the negs would not be able to destroy you, but it is not permitted for you to stay. It is the queen's decision. I cannot disobey this," Hawthorne said kindly.

Susan looked at her nine friends and said, "Who is for staying?"

A unanimous chorus went up. "Me!"

"There, it's decided," Susan said defiantly to Hawthorne.

"We will see," said Hawthorne. "I will send word to the queen of your stubbornness and see what her decision is."

In seconds Hawthorne had related the children's decision to the queen and she had given her answer.

Hawthorne cleared his throat and gave the children the news from the queen, "Iridaan is touched by your courage and is, indeed, most grateful. She acknowledges that your wish to stay comes from a deep love of our land and of us faeries. She took much time to come to this decision. She took it outside of regular time, which means—"

"Hawthorne, just tell us what Iridaan has decided," George interrupted, unable to wait for Hawthorne to finish his eloquent offering.

"You may stay," he said, feeling somewhat miffed at George's untimely interruption. "Iridaan is still in counsel with the elders, but she sends her warmest regards."

The children and faeries sent out a loud cheer and the atmosphere in the restaurant became tangibly lighter.

In the Reflecteum, the gathered elders had been

The Heart Stone

discussing the results of their inner-mind searching, which had been greatly empowered by the Heart Stone.

Valdaan, a beautiful looking female elder began to speak. "It is true what Krailaan says. It is the balance that must be restored. When we made the decision to allow the children to use the stones to activate the star field, we thought that it would be enough. There were ten children, a perfect number to represent balance one and zero, positive and negative. However, the negs have never before been so powerful. Their strength has outweighed the children's spirit and capacity for creation. What is required is an additional child to face the negs. But this child must be one that is in the thrall of the enemy but can be brought into the light and willingly break free from their power." Valdaan paused to gather her thoughts.

The assembled elders noted that, as Valdaan spoke, a golden glow began to emanate around her frame, a sure sign that a truth was being spoken. Valdaan continued, the golden light turning her deep auburn hair to the colour of burnished gold, streaked with rivulets of wheaten sunshine. Her face too, was lit with the magical glow, softening her beautiful features to a golden haze.

"If one of the children here would agree to return and seek out such a child, then I believe that our realm, and ultimately that of Earth, may be saved. However, it will come at a great price, for we must entrust the child with our Heart Stone. The child will have to take our Heart Stone from here to the battle front and hurl it into the midst of the negs. If the child succeeds, we will be able to retrieve the Heart Stone but if the child is not sincere in their intent, then all will be totally lost. You all are aware of the cost to all of us faeries when the Heart Stone is removed from the Reflecteum?" she asked of them.

Each of the elders nodded in sadness, knowing that once the Heart Stone was removed from the Reflecteum then the power would begin to drain from their bodies. They would weaken in the very hour when they would need their strength the most.

"That completes the knowledge that has been given to me through the inner-self and the Heart Stone," she concluded, bowing her head to the others with the intensity of the golden light shining even more brilliantly about her.

"Thank you, Valdaan, for bringing us this truth. Are we all agreed that this is the course of action that must be taken?" Iridaan asked of the gathering of elders.

"Aye," said each elder sagely.

With that, Iridaan took her leave of them and flew straight back to where the children were gathered. She was both surprised and pleased to see that merriment had again broken out among the children and young faeries. Smiling, she addressed them. "I see the news of the negs return has not dampened your spirits."

"It did for a little while," said Susan. "But it felt so much better when we were cheerful again that we just continued. There's no point in being miserable before we have to."

"Words of truth, indeed, my little one," Iridaan said. "Now I must speak to all of you Earth children, so please gather around."

The children obediently gathered around her, eager to hear what she had to say to them.

"The elders have decided that, in order to defeat the negs, we need to bring one more child to our realm. This child will not be as all of you are; the child will be one that is in the power of the negs' force. It is hoped that this child will be persuaded to change their ways. My request is that one of you might agree to return to Earth and try to encourage such a child to return here with you."

Without a moment's hesitation, Susan spoke up. "I'll go," she volunteered purposefully.

"Thank you, Susan. You are perhaps the best suited to this task, as you are more familiar than the others with the journey to and from our realm," said the queen.

The Heart Stone

"I'll go with Susan," Seb volunteered, wanting to both be with and protect Susan.

"That is a kind offer," said the queen, "but, in truth, we would welcome your energy here with us. We will need to keep the negs at bay until Susan's return. The negs are impeded by children of your calibre who have never succumbed to their influence. In a way, you act as a force field that they cannot penetrate. So with each one of you assigned to a squadron of faeries at strategic positions, we will be able to hold our position longer. Of course, the decision is yours to make. We accept whatever you say."

Seb thought deeply for a moment. "I'll stay. I want to be of the greatest use that I can to you," he said earnestly.

Turning to Susan he continued. "Will you be alright on your own?"

"Of course I will," she responded kindly, happy that Seb had wanted to go with her.

"Susan, you must go with all haste. The danger is very close for us here. Hawthorne, will accompany you and aid you in your task," Iridaan said.

"I'm ready to go now," said Susan, happy that dear Hawthorne would be with her.

In seconds, Hawthorne had taken Susan's hand and they were zooming back to the Earth realm.

Chapter 16
Susan Returns to Earth to Ask a Neg Child for Help

They returned to a quiet neighbourhood street near where Susan lived. The sun was shining brightly in the warm August sunshine and she heard the church bells begin to chime. She counted the chimes.

"It's four o'clock," she said to Hawthorne. "Is that four o' clock on the same day as we left?"

"It is indeed, my dear child," he responded grandly, knowing that Susan was marvelling at the time differential between the two realms.

"But we have slept a whole night in your realm," she said incredulously.

"Yes, and you are communicating with me telepathically here on Earth, is that not also a wonder to you?" Hawthorne responded, with a chuckle.

"Oh, I hadn't realized that I was doing that," she said, amazed at how her abilities had grown.

"Well, child, it is rather a good thing. It will allow us to keep in constant communication when I am not able to be with you. I will return to the Pine Woods now, but with your consent, I will maintain a constant mind-link with you. If there is danger, I can be with you in an instant," he said with seriousness.

"Yes, I'd like that," Susan said, happy for Hawthorne to be close at hand.

"Then I'll take my leave now and let you do your work," Hawthorne said cheerfully.

Susan was sad to have Hawthorne leave her but knew that his presence would cause a stir if he were spotted. Her mind began to race trying to think of a child that was affected by the negs, yet who might be amenable to change their ways. Susan was aware of the need for haste and began walking in the direction she was facing with no particular plan in mind. She hadn't gone more than a few steps when she heard a familiar voice behind her.

"Yoo-hoo! Susan! Can you wait a minute?" shouted the voice.

Turning around, Susan saw Mrs. Robinson running towards her, rather out of breath, with Rocky straining at the leash to get to Susan. Susan wanted to continue with her mission, but couldn't ignore her.

"Hello, Mrs. Robinson!" she said, kneeling down to let Rocky greet her.

"I'm glad I was able to catch you. Your gran said that you might be round and about. I was wondering if you could look after Rocky for me. I have to do some shopping and Rocky hates to be tied up outside the shops," she said, still a bit out of breath.

Susan heard Hawthorne's familiar voice in her head telling her to take Rocky and continue with her task.

"Don't worry, Mrs. Robinson. I'll look after Rocky," she said smiling, and also rather pleased to have the happy excited puppy with her.

"Well, I'll be about an hour, but you can keep Rocky for as long as you want. I know how much you like him," said Mrs. Robinson, handing over Rocky's leash to Susan. "Have fun," she said, with a wave of her hand, as she walked off, her plump frame waddling ever so slightly as she went.

Susan petted Rocky for a minute or so and continued walking on with no particular destination in mind and started to talk to Rocky. "Rocky, I don't know where to begin. Who shall I choose to talk to?" she lamented.

Rocky, impervious to Susan's words, was pulling her onwards in an excited manner, happy to be with her. Suddenly, Rocky caught sight of a cat, and with a great lunge, dragged Susan round the corner of the street. Spying the cat again, Rocky became even more excited and frantic. Susan tightened the leash to restrain the puppy but Rocky wouldn't give way. The puppy was determined to get to the cat, but the leash was restraining him. His paws were going twenty to the dozen, but not actually getting him anywhere because of Susan's hold on the leash. It was during this tug of war that Susan heard another familiar voice behind her. This time, it wasn't a welcome voice.

"Little Miss Prissy, got herself a puppy has she?" came the mocking voice of Kerry Boswell.

Susan turned around, her face clouding as she saw Kerry standing behind her, dressed up to the nines. "So what?" said Susan crossly, not wanting to waste time trading insults with Kerry at this important time.

"Oh, getting brave are we?" mocked Kerry.

"I've never been afraid of you, Kerry Boswell. You're shallow, you have no interests, and your friends are all the same way," Susan said venomously.

As Susan heard herself speak, a realization came upon her. Kerry was exactly what she was looking for. She was a child that wasn't interested in anything other than appearance and superficial things. Her time was often spent watching frivolous television programmes or playing mindless computer games. She was fascinated by the latest fads and fancies in clothes and hair, to the exclusion of adventure and fun. Kerry was indeed the candidate Susan was looking for. The realization that Kerry had been captivated by the negs allowed Susan to interact more kindly with her.

Susan looked at Rocky, who was still lunging forward trying to reach the evasive cat that had perched itself, tantalizingly, on a nearby wall that was too high for him to reach. The cat was sat smugly, aware that it had the advantage of the high ground and continued to sit there, glaring defiantly at Rocky.

The Heart Stone

"Do you like puppies?" Susan asked Kerry sweetly.

"They're alright, I suppose," Kerry said dismissively.

"Would you like to stroke Rocky?" Susan asked.

"I suppose so," Kerry said, relenting a little. She bent down to stroke Rocky and was immediately assaulted by numerous licks to her face and neck. Rocky put his paws on her shoulders in order to have a firm platform to plant the necessary licks upon her face.

"Steady on, Rocky!" chided Susan, knowing that Mrs. Robinson was trying to stop Rocky from jumping up at everyone.

"He's alright, don't worry," Kerry said, enjoying the unrestrained attention that she was getting from Rocky. It felt good to have a creature show her this amount of affection without her having to pose and pout for it. She felt a sense of liberation at having such unconditional affection given to her.

"I'm going to take him for a walk to the Pine Woods. Do you want to come with us?" asked Susan, taking a huge chance in asking Kerry to accompany her.

Usually, Kerry would never be seen dead with the likes of Susan; she only mixed with the "perfects."

"Yeah, why not?" said Kerry, to Susan's great surprise.

"Do you want to hold his leash?" offered Susan.

"Okay," responded Kerry coolly, not wanting Susan to see how much she really wanted to.

The two girls set off towards the Pine Woods at a steady pace, Rocky trotting happily between them. They made some stilted conversation about the new schools that they would be going to after the school holidays. Kerry said that she would be going to the same school as Susan, but most of her friends would be going elsewhere due to a change in school catchment areas.

"Never mind. I'm sure that you'll make some more friends at the new school," Susan said, glad that she had both Aliya and Seb going to her new school.

"Yeah," Kerry said unconvinced. Lately, she had begun to feel that her world was crumbling around her. Her mother was planning to get married again and her friends were leaving her. Even her little brother didn't want to have much to do with her. He was far more interested in pursuing his sporting hobbies. She was actually quite glad that Susan had come along with Rocky.

Kerry pulled some chewing gum out of her tight jeans pocket and offered some to Susan.

"Want some of this?" she offered sticking a brightly coloured packet of gum in front of Susan. "Its sugar free."

Susan didn't really care whether it was sugar free or not, as she was not over-keen on gum because it made her burp a lot. However, she decided to take it, not wanting to do anything to interrupt the flow of goodwill that was beginning between the two girls.

"Great. Thanks," Susan said, stuffing it gingerly into the side of her mouth.

"Have you ever read any faerie stories?" asked Susan, wanting to get to the point of her mission as soon as possible.

"Um, yeah. When I was little I did. My mum used to read them to my brother and me," Kerry said in reply.

"Did you ever believe that they were real when you were little?" Susan inquired.

Kerry thought for a moment and said, "Yep, I think that I did."

"What would you say if I told you that they're real?" Susan asked, going out on a limb, aware that time was of the essence.

Kerry turned to Susan, and looked at her as if she were insane.

"Look, it's been fun walking the dog and all that but I think I'd better be off," Kerry said, wishing to distance herself from Susan's stupidity.

"No, Kerry. Please don't go. I can show you something

that will prove I'm right," Susan said as they neared the entrance to the Pine Woods.

Kerry shrugged her shoulders. "This better be good!" she said.

Susan led Kerry to the base of a Weeping Willow Tree that afforded them privacy from public view. She mentally called to Hawthorne who appeared, with a loud rustling sound, from the branches of the willow tree in which he had been ensconced.

"Is this good enough for you?" enquired Susan, with a hint of triumph in her voice.

Kerry's jaw dropped open at the sight of Hawthorne. For once she was speechless and totally out of her depth. She had turned quite pale and sounded very breathless when she finally spoke.

"What are you?" Kerry asked of the diminutive Hawthorne, incredulously. Her eyes unable to comprehend what she was seeing.

"May I introduce myself to you, dear child? My name is Hawthorne, and I am from the Realm of Faeries. I am delighted to make your acquaintance. Although, I must confess, that it is not the first time I have done so. When you were a small child you had a very active imagination and you were one of the children assigned to me for the purposes of dream fulfilment," concluded Hawthorne, rather grandly.

Kerry was both confused and amused at Hawthorne's greeting. She had no idea of how he would have any knowledge of meeting her previously. She did, however, consider him to have a very endearing way of speaking that allayed any fears that she had of meeting such a creature.

"I'm sure that I would have remembered meeting you before, but I am pleased to meet you now," Kerry said, finding her ground. She even extended her hand to shake his.

"Enchanted, my dear Kerry," Hawthorne said, bowing

slightly and giving her hand a mock kiss in the manner of a chivalrous knight.

Susan was rather miffed at the attention that Hawthorne was giving to Kerry, especially as Kerry was a neg child.

Hawthorne was quick to respond telepathically to Susan. "Do not fret, Susan, I must put Kerry at her ease if we are to obtain her help. I have looked into her mind to find the most comforting and interesting way of portraying myself to her. Remember, we are desperate for help and her cooperation is vital. I do not want to run her off at first contact. I would also caution you to use the utmost tact when speaking to her."

Susan was immediately ashamed of her jealous thoughts and told Hawthorne telepathically that she was willing to do anything to help the situation. Kerry was exceedingly flattered and touched by Hawthorne's chivalric attentions and was fascinated to hear more about him and the faerie realm.

"Do you mean to tell me there's a realm where all faeries live?" Kerry asked, smiling beguilingly.

"Yes, indeed there is, dear child," Hawthorne responded with a wide smile.

"Where is it?" she enquired, while enjoying being referred to as "dear child."

It seemed like such a long time since she had felt like a child or even been treated as one. It had fallen to Kerry to look after her young brother since she was about eight years old when their father had left them, and her mother had to go and work as a bar-maid. She looked after him through all his childhood illnesses and helped him with his schoolwork. She slept in the same room as he did, comforting him when he had nightmares. Her mother was always so tired from the long hours she worked that Kerry tried never to disturb her sleep or bother her with anything that was not urgent. So, in many ways, Kerry, had become a parent to her brother.

The Heart Stone

When her brother began to stand on his own feet, she decided that she was never going to look after anyone again. She would live for herself and make up for all the good times that she had missed. Unfortunately, this attitude made her selfish and thoughtless. She also envied children like Susan, Aliya, and Seb who still enjoyed a happy childhood and had a childlike quality about them. She felt that they represented the childhood that she had lost through having to take care of her brother and assume such a responsibility at such a young age. Now, hearing Hawthorne speaking to her as if she were still a child gave her a warm feeling.

"My realm is closer than you would imagine, dear Kerry. Indeed, Susan and some of her friends have already travelled there," Hawthorne informed her.

Kerry was instantly jealous that Susan and her cronies had already travelled to the Faerie Realm. However, she swallowed her gall and asked pleasantly whether she might be allowed to visit too.

"You would be most welcome to come. It is what we were hoping you would want to do, for we are in dire need of your help in my realm," Hawthorne said with great seriousness.

"What help could I possibly give you?" Kerry asked, beginning to feel that she might be put upon to do things that she did not want to do.

"I sense your reluctance, dear child, but rest assured that the help that you can give will not be of a tiresome or prolonged nature. I will try to explain."

Hawthorne told Kerry about the negs and how they were engulfing the Faerie Realm. He explained how many of Earth's children were in the thrall of the negs and carefully explained to Kerry that she was also captivated by the negs.

"Do you mean to tell me that I'm being influenced in the things that I do by these neg things?" asked Kerry, with slight alarm rising in her voice.

"Sadly, dear child, that is the truth. However, now that you are aware of it, you can begin work to rid yourself of their influence," Hawthorne replied sympathetically.

"How can I do that?" Kerry asked, anxious to begin the process.

"The first step is to examine yourself and see if you like the person that you are. If you do not, you must ask yourself why. The second step is to try and be creative. All of you Earth children have the capacity to create great things, be it in the world of arts, nature, the sciences, or business. You can all bring something good to those fields. In doing that, you begin to feel fulfilled, to truly feel the reason that you came into the world," Hawthorne informed her, with enthusiasm. "Indeed, dear Kerry, if you truly wish to be a more positive and creative person, you can have the help of the faeries, for that is what their role is–to help humans fulfill their dreams and be more creative."

"I'd like that," Kerry said without hesitation. She knew without any self-examination that she didn't like the person that she had become and desperately wanted to change.

"Will you come with us to the Faerie Realm and help us defeat the negs?" Hawthorne asked with great seriousness.

Kerry wanted to have the help of the faeries and knew that she must do everything that she could to save them so that she, herself, could be saved from the negs power. Lately, a depression had come upon her that she could not shake. She felt like a prisoner in her own body, her moods were dark and she had lost sight of happiness. She was willing to do anything to feel normal again.

"Yes, I'll come," responded Kerry without hesitation.

"Then we must make haste," Hawthorne said. "Kerry, the journey that you are about to undertake will not be as easy for you as it has been for the others, but Susan and I will be right beside you holding your hands all the time."

Hawthorne knew that Kerry had experienced very few happy times to help her take the inner journey to the

Faerie Realm and as a consequence, she would experience turbulence on her journey.

Kerry looked uncertainly at Hawthorne. "Do not fear, child, no harm will befall you. I only wish you to be prepared for a few bumps along the way. Try to focus on the happiest memory that you have," he told her with a warm smile.

At that point, Rocky let out a little whimper to remind them that he was not getting any attention.

"Oh goodness, I had forgotten all about Rocky. He's been so quiet. I'm supposed to be looking after him for Mrs. Robinson. What am I to do?" Susan asked in alarm.

"Do not worry, Rocky knows the way to our realm and can come with us. Animals never lose their ability to make inner journeys and can cope with it very well. Mrs. Robinson will not notice your absence or Rocky's," Hawthorne said.

With that, Susan, took hold of Rocky's lead in one hand and Kerry's hand in the other. Hawthorne took hold of both girls' hands and their journey began.

Chapter 17
Susan and Hawthorne Take the Neg Child to the Realm of Faeries

True to Hawthorne's word, the journey wasn't a smooth one. Susan was used to having a smooth transition and didn't enjoy the bumpy ride. However, Hawthorne was communicating telepathically with her the whole time and explaining that Kerry needed lots of help because she had lost the child inside her and had very few happy memories to fuel her journey.

Kerry was holding tightly to both of their hands, completely at a loss for words about what was happening. She tried with all her might to hold onto the memory of her mother and father and herself, as a very young child, enjoying a picnic on The Stray.

Eventually, the three of them arrived with a thump in the Realm of Faeries, finding Iridaan waiting to greet them. Susan was horrified by the damage that had occurred whilst she had been gone. The sky was becoming overshadowed and dark great swathes of land had lost its vibrancy and there was a coldness permeating the air.

"Where are the others?" asked Susan of Iridaan telepathically, concerned about her friends.

"They are helping us at the battlefront," responded Iridaan, speedily turning her attention to Kerry.

"Kerry, we are so glad that you have agreed to help us," she said with a warm smile. "There is no time to spare, we need you to perform a deed for us that will stop these monstrous negs from their deadly quest. Are you willing to do that?"

The Heart Stone

"Yes, I am," Kerry replied, looking in wonder at the beautiful Faerie Queen. She was amazed at the transformation that had taken place in Hawthorne, who now stood before her as a tall, handsome faerie.

In an instant, Iridaan had gathered Kerry into her arms and had taken to the skies. Hawthorne lifted Susan and Rocky up and followed closely behind Iridaan, his large wings beating at great speed as he assimilated the telepathic information of what had occurred in their absence.

As they flew, the scene beneath them was one of devastation. There was little left to show the beauty that had been there before. All that was left were ashes and smouldering forms of buildings and trees. In the distance they could see the remnants of the faerie land that had not yet been decimated. It was there that the faeries were making their last stand.

Hawthorne spoke to Susan telepathically, telling her that there had been many faerie casualties and that the negs had become ever stronger. Unless intervention came soon, all would be lost and their realm would no longer exist. Iridaan and Hawthorne, carrying their charges, arrived at the battlefront. Susan immediately looked for her friends.

"Don't worry, they are safe. I will take you to them," Hawthorne said, reading her mind.

He led Susan to a long, low, white building that housed strangely shaped beds containing injured faeries. It was the Community Hall that had been hastily converted into an infirmary. Susan saw her friends tending to the wounded and helping the physicians to do their work. Iridaan and Kerry had stopped for a little while to speak to one of the elders at the battlefront, but were now entering the building.

Susan saw Aliya and ran to her, throwing her arms around her. "This is terrible!" Susan said.

"Dreadful things have happened to the faeries while you were away," said Aliya, with tears stinging her eyes. "I'm so happy to see you," she continued, hugging Susan even tighter.

Susan could see all the little ones, but not Seb, George, or Omar. "Where are the others?" Susan asked, alarm rising in her voice.

"They're still at the battlefronts assigned to faerie squadrons. They sent me and the little ones back because it was so terrifying for us," Aliya sobbed. "You cannot imagine the horror. The negs have evolved; they're no longer just like horrible clouds. Now they're able to take on any form that they want."

"Are Seb, Omar and George in any danger?" asked Susan worriedly.

"To some extent they are. The faeries tried to encourage them to return here with us, but the boys flatly refused. The faeries are not permitted to force any human to do anything that is against their wishes so they had to let them stay and fight the negs. Iridaan has assigned four faeries to each of the boys to protect them," Aliya said shakily.

"Are the boys doing any good at the front?" enquired Susan.

"Yes, yes, that's the good thing. It seems that the boys' presence gives the faeries that they are with extra powers of resistance from the negs. It's very unlikely that the negs can harm the boys because they've never been influenced by them in their lives," said Aliya reassuringly.

Susan's thoughts went out to all the three boys, but especially so, to Seb. She felt a very close bond with him and couldn't bear the thought of him being in danger. She just wished that she could be at the front with them.

No sooner had the thought come into her mind, than she heard Hawthorne speaking into her mind telling her that it would be advantageous if she could accompany them to the front. It would be a reassurance for Kerry, as she would be facing the negs for the first time, he told her.

Susan readily agreed to this as she wanted to see Seb and

the others, and to have this devastating war over with.

Iridaan had been conversing with the other members of the faerie counsel who were also gathered there helping the wounded. Valdaan told her that after speaking with Kerry, she believed her to be an ideal candidate to carry the Heart Stone and throw it in the midst of the negs.

"Then we must make haste," Iridaan said, feeling hope rising within her, "Kerry, I must ask you at this critical moment whether you sincerely and freely wish to help us defeat the negs," added Iridaan, with seriousness.

"Oh, I do," Kerry said without hesitation. She was both amazed at the beauty of the faeries and what remained of their land and shocked at the devastation that the negs had wreaked upon them. She truly wanted to help them.

"I know that you are a strong girl Kerry, but you must prepare yourself for the horror of the negs," Iridaan turned to Susan and added, "Susan, you must also prepare yourself for what you are about to see. The negs have become more grotesque. They have taken on a more physical appearance and this may shock you."

"Don't worry, Iridaan. I'll be more than ready when the time comes," Susan said bravely.

"Me too," said Kerry.

"Then let us fly to the Reflecteum to collect the Heart Stone. Hawthorne, you take Susan," Iridaan said with authority.

Aliya ran to Susan, knowing what horror she would encounter at the battlefront and hugged her tightly. "Good luck, come back safe!"

Susan hugged her tightly and told her that all would be well and handed Rocky over for safe keeping, knowing that his warm comforting presence would be of help. With that, Hawthorne swooped Susan up and followed Iridaan and Kerry to the Reflecteum.

Taking a zigzag route to the Reflecteum, they once again encountered faerie land that had not yet been destroyed by the negs. The Reflecteum, containing the Heart Stone with its enormous store of positive energy, was still intact. It was a difficult target for the negs, as its power served to repel the darkness of the negs.

Krailaan was there to greet them and take them to the Heart Stone. He spoke telepathically with Iridaan and told her that she should prepare all the faeries for a weakening of their power once the Heart Stone was removed from its place.

Immediately, Iridaan called to all the faeries in the realm to warn them of the impending danger. She told them that they must expect a lessening of their vital energy. They walked to where the Heart Stone was located and Krailaan flew up to it, his wings feathering rapidly as he hovered abreast of it. Taking it in his hands, he spoke some words that Susan and Kerry were unable to understand.

Hawthorne spoke into Susan's mind, telling her that Krailaan was speaking directly to the stone in the ancient faerie tongue and asking it to work with Kerry to defeat the negs.

As Krailaan lifted the stone from its rightful setting, the whole of the Reflecteum dimmed. The beautiful dancing lights that the Heart Stone created ceased to shine and play upon its walls. A dull, greyness took its place. Krailaan, Iridaan, and Hawthorne immediately reeled backwards as if they had been punched in the stomach. An ashen greyness overcame them too. Susan was alarmed at the immediate alteration of their appearance.

"Are you alright?" she asked of them in a concerned manner.

"Do not be alarmed, Susan," said Iridaan. "We still have power and energy within us and if we can finish this battle soon all will be well."

"I'm ready," Kerry said, equally concerned about the deathly pale colour that had overtaken the faeries.

"Kerry, this Heart Stone is heavy, but you must carry it

The Heart Stone

in order to allow it to absorb your intentions. Iridaan will take your weight as you fly to the battlefront, but you must reserve your strength to hurl the Heart Stone into the midst of the negs. Is this acceptable to you?" Krailaan asked with a weakening voice.

"Yes, yes. I'll do anything I can to help," she responded eagerly.

Krailaan presented the Heart Stone ceremoniously to Kerry. She held out her two hands to receive it. The moment it touched her hands, she felt an immense energy run through her. She felt incredibly strong. Her whole being was pulsating with energy. An aura of pure gold shone around her whole body giving her a magical appearance.

Krailaan looked at Kerry solemnly. "We are entrusting you with the spirit of all the faeries as you take this stone. Be strong and may the Source of all be with you," he kissed her on the cheek and withdrew.

Iridaan was able to gain some reflected energy from Kerry as she took to the skies and headed to the battlefront. Hawthorne, however, was struggling. Every beat of his wings was causing him pain. Faeries rarely experienced pain so it was an unaccustomed handicap.

Chapter 18
The Heart Stone and the Neg Child

They arrived at the battlefront to the sounds of mournful howls coming from the attacking negs. The faeries were gathered in a horseshoe formation and were protecting the last vestiges of their land. Some hovered above the ground, others stood on the ground trying to gain some advantage over the ever encroaching horror of the negs. All of them were now weakening and their skins had taken on the sickly, ashen grey, hue.

Susan jerked as she saw the new forms that the negs had taken. They were truly repulsive; they stood like towering giants of darkness, their faces contorting into grotesque grimaces as they consumed the energy of the faerie's land. Their fat bellies becoming engorged as they fed upon the beauty and majesty of the land, turning light into darkness and beauty into desolation and exhaling a foul smoky fog that hung in their wake.

"Courage, Susan," spoke Hawthorne into her mind.

She immediately gritted her teeth together and prepared herself for whatever should come her way. Susan looked over at Kerry who was already standing on the ground holding the Heart Stone and asked her how she was feeling.

Kerry had been appalled at the sight of the negs but the enormous strength that was surging through her stopped her from being afraid. "I'm feeling alright Susan. I wasn't prepared to see anything as disgusting as those things," she said, indicating towards the towering negs that were drawing considerably closer.

With diminishing strength, Iridaan gathered the two girls

The Heart Stone

together and told them that they must walk to the front lines and wait until the negs were close enough that Kerry could throw the Heart Stone into their midst.

With laboured steps, Iridaan and Hawthorne led Kerry and Susan through the ranks of weakening faeries. As they passed, each faerie cried out to Kerry with the words "Rei Meiti."

Hawthorne told them that it was an ancient faerie blessing for one going into battle to do a heroic thing meaning "let your belief be strong."

As they passed through the ranks they saw more and more dead and dying faeries. The removal of the Heart Stone had been too much for many of the battle weary faeries to withstand. To Susan's horror, she saw some of the child faeries that she had played with earlier lying lifeless among the dead and wounded.

With Hawthorne and Iridaan beginning to stagger, they arrived at the front line.

The sight of the Heart Stone initially repulsed the advancing negs, but they regrouped and conversed in undecipherable baleful utterances. They had observed how the faeries had suddenly weakened and believed that now would be the time to make a concerted strike upon them. The Heart Stone, they knew, would impede them, but they recognized Kerry as one who had once been in their thrall and believed that they could still influence her. They reckoned that their chances were good to make a final coup and take the realm completely.

A loud, earth shuddering, vibration emitted from the negs as they made a swift advance toward the battlefront. Their whole compliment was united in this foray.

Iridaan sent word to the dragons to fly to the front to help the weakening faeries and allow those helping the wounded to take them to a place where they could receive help. The dragons had not suffered, as the faeries had, through the removal of the Heart Stone. They existed in the faerie realm because of a divine edict. Iridaan had interceded for their right to exist after Toby Allium had inadvertently projected them into being. That right had been granted and, as such, they were not subject to the same laws and influences that governed the faeries.

Within seconds the dragons appeared in the darkening skies, their silvery bodies shining in what remained of the dwindling light. They flew straight and swift into the midst of the negs, their fiery breath aimed at the heads and hearts of the vile negs. Initially, they were able to repulse the negs, impeding their advance. But soon the negs were able to transform themselves into horribly distorted versions of dragons and they took to the skies to fight them head on. The faeries' dragons held their own for some time but this was not to last. One by one the dragons were being forced downwards to the ground where the negs could consume them along with the land. Iridaan immediately ordered the dragons to withdraw. This wasn't to the dragons liking, as they wanted to fight to the death to defend their beloved faeries and their land, but they were bound to obey Iridaan.

All of the dragons except one managed to retreat successfully, the last one was being attacked both at the front and at the rear by the dragon negs. Iridaan didn't have any forces left that were capable of bringing the last dragon home, his name was Raedo. He fought bravely, swirling around unleashing his fiery breath on the ugly dragon negs. However, despite the courageous fight, his strength was beginning to fail him and, slowly, he began his fall to the ground with the two dragon negs bearing down upon him.

All those gathered were horrified at the sight. No faerie or dragon had been taken by the negs. All the dead and wounded had been rapidly transported away from the ravening negs. Now Raedo was about to be consumed by these monsters.

Susan couldn't stop herself from crying out. "No!" she

wailed pitifully as she watched Raedo falling, his back almost on the ground.

All eyes had been on the skies and no one had noticed that Rocky had escaped from the infirmary where Aliya was concentrating on tending the ever increasing amount of wounded.

Initially, Rocky was looking for Susan and had just been able to detect her scent in close proximity and heard her sad cry. He was heading for her when he saw the spectacle of the dragon negs trying to kill Raedo. With great speed, Rocky ran through the lines to where Raedo was being mercilessly attacked and in an instant was circling Raedo in a protective manner, snarling and barking at the negs. The negs were astounded at this strange creature that was attacking them and drew backwards in surprise.

This respite was sufficient for the other dragons to fly in and rescue Raedo and swoop Rocky up with their large feet and bring them both to safety. A loud cheer went up as this minor victory was won over the negs. It served to hearten all of the faeries and children.

Once Rocky had been released by the dragon who had rescued him, he shook himself vigorously as if to shake off the darkness of the negs and started sniffing the ground to try and pick up Susan's scent.

"Rocky! Rocky! I'm over here!" Susan cried, sensing his need to find her.

Sprinting smartly between the columns of faeries that had lined up to congratulate him for his valour, he heard Susan's call and ran towards her, his head held high in the air.

"You're such a magnificent and brave dog Rocky!" exclaimed Susan, vigorously patting him and scratching the fur round his neck with her fingertips. She was immensely proud that he had performed such a courageous feat. Rocky accepted his reward of affection eagerly. He had followed his instinct to protect those he felt safe and secure with and that, he thought, was well worthwhile!

Susan took Rocky back to the relative safety of the nearby infirmary and asked that everyone keep an eye on him. She didn't want to risk his safety any more than necessary. The news of Rocky's heroism had already, telepathically, reached the infirmary and there was no shortage of volunteers to watch over him, despite the increasing casualty load. Once Rocky was settled, Susan returned to Iridaan and the others at the battlefront. She was distressed to see how all the faeries were losing their power. It was as if the light was going out within them. Nonetheless, they were not faltering in their stance. They were holding the battle lines preparing for the next neg onslaught.

The weary warriors regrouped and sounded their battle cry; now the once strong and rousing cry had diminished in sound but the intention behind it was strong. The faeries would defend their realm or die trying. There was no other way!

"Iridaan, if things get really bad here and the negs overpower us, would it be possible for all of you to come to Earth and live there?" asked Susan. "Hawthorne has made the journey and so did Azure. Couldn't you? Then you wouldn't have to die," Susan said hopefully.

"No, dear one, that is not possible for us. Our realm is part of us, like our arms or our body. When it dies, we die. We cannot separate ourselves from it. Without the land to sustain us, we cannot do our work with Earth children. We love our land as dearly as we love each other. It is our creation," Iridaan said with great emotion. "Even if we were in the Earth realm we would still die."

"Oh," said Susan forlornly, her last ditch plan in ruins.

"Do not be sad Susan, for we still have hope. Kerry is going to help us and, if all goes well, we will win the day," Iridaan replied brightly.

Susan's spirits lifted a little as she looked over to Kerry

who was nodding in agreement that she would be giving her help.

At that point, Hawthorne's voice rose above the others, shouting in alarm. "The negs are approaching fast in a C formation!"

Immediately, Iridaan asked Kerry to position herself in the centre of the faeries and prepare to hurl the Heart Stone into the midst of the negs. Iridaan spoke both telepathically and vocally to everyone assembled. "I want all Earth children to gather before me as soon as possible. I want all faeries to take their battle positions. Those in the Infirmary and in supply contingents must come to the battlefront and be prepared to defend our realm. If things do not go our way today, our first duty is to ensure the Earth children are returned to their realm.

I entrust this duty to Hawthorne and Castano. With that, I bid you all, Rei Meiti! And know that we shall be together again within the Source."

The faeries all responded to Iridaan with a united cry of "Rei Meiti!" and began assembling themselves at the battlefront. Castano flew to Hawthorne's side and gave a greeting to Susan. She was shocked to see how his wonderfully strong, brown, body had weakened and become a sickly ashen colour. The negs were approaching at an alarmingly rapid speed; they would be upon them in minutes.

Kerry, flanked by Castano, Hawthorne, and Iridaan, reached the centre of the battlefront. Susan was to the rear of them, surrounded by four of the stronger looking warrior faeries. All the Earth children had begun to gather together, the faeries directing them to Iridaan's position.

In one horrifyingly swift motion the negs were upon them. A cold desolation overcame the whole gathering as the negs mournful howling battle cry assaulted their ears. Susan found it very hard to keep her nerve as the terrifying sound, sight, and feel of the negs bore down upon them.

She looked around for her friends, desperately wanting their comfort at this moment.

Ensuring that Kerry had the most advantageous position to hurl the Heart Stone at the negs, Iridaan cried, "Kerry, you must throw the Heart Stone now as hard as you can into the midst of the negs!"

Kerry felt the enormous strength that she was getting from the Heart Stone begin to increase as all the faeries sent the last ounce of their strength to empower it to its full extent. She felt enormously strong; as if she could accomplish anything she wanted, including killing these vile creatures that were beginning to surround her. She raised the stone above her head and decided upon the direction of her aim.

In that moment, Seb, who was arriving from an easterly direction, caught sight of Susan looking pale and lost. In a second, he was by her side. They instinctively threw their arms around each other and clung on to each other tightly, happy to be reunited and feel the comfort of one another. The negs, who were wary of the Heart Stone, seized this moment to exert their influence upon Kerry. They knew her weakness to be jealousy and used the spectacle of Susan and Seb embracing to fuel the fire of jealousy that had started to burn within her. In that instant, Kerry felt uncontrollable rage rip through her as the negs played maliciously upon her weakness. All the power that she had gained through the Heart Stone was now channelled into her jealous rage. Without conscious knowledge of what she was doing, she turned and hurled the Heart Stone onto a nearby rock splitting it into two pieces. A cry of horror went up from all who were gathered there as the negs moved in for the kill.

The faeries, in a united throng, dropped to one knee and bowed their heads to prepare for death.

Hawthorne and Castano, with sorrowful faces, gathered the Earth children together for a rapid return before they too would return and meet their death.

Kerry, coming to her senses, realized with horror what she had just done and was filled with overwhelming remorse. Without a thought for her safety she ran headlong into the horde of negs to try and stop their merciless advance. Iridaan tried to go after her, but her strength was almost gone and as she started to run she fell onto the ground, reaching out toward Kerry, unable to move further.

The Earth children were huddled together holding onto each other in sheer terror of what was taking place. Only George was missing. He had been fighting with the faeries from the House of Heather to which he belonged. He had decided to stand with them to the last and give his life too. Azure was at his side, holding him tightly in this terrible moment, unable to send him back with the others because it was his will to stay.

George had never been happy on Earth because of the cruel taunts and jibes that other children levelled at him because of his quiet, gentle way. He would rather die here among those who accepted him unconditionally, than return to a world that did not accept him.

Kerry sped into the midst of the negs, still feeling the power of the Heart Stone within her body. However, as the negs drew her into their midst the power rapidly began to drain from her. Her nerve began to falter and she started to be afraid. As the horror of the situation unfolded around them the Earth children were confused. They wanted to stay and help the faeries. They also wanted to help Kerry to free herself from the negs but knew that they must return home. Hawthorne and Castano linked hands with the children and told them to prepare for their return.

Chapter 19
The Arrival of the Slegna

"No wait!" cried Susan spotting a brilliant light shining through the darkness. "What's that?" she asked of Hawthorne in a loud voice.

Turning his sorrowful eyes to the skies he began to brighten. In an instant, all the faeries had begun to look towards the sky. The light was shining directly into the midst of the negs to where Kerry was held captive. As the light fell upon her, all fear subsided within her. She felt warm and comforted. The negs didn't frighten her any more. She knew that all would be well with her. If she had to die, she could do so peacefully, knowing that she had given her all to save the beautiful faeries.

As the light shone on Kerry, the negs surrounding her began to fade and the light became stronger and stronger.

Iridaan pulled herself, painfully, to her feet and cried, "It is the Slegna, we are saved!"

Slowly the faeries began to regain their strength again. Those who were wounded, or drawing their last breath, returned to health taking large, gulping, breaths of air. The light of the Slegna began to spread over the land, and as it did so, the monstrous negs began to disintegrate unable to withstand the purity of the brilliant light.

Kerry found herself able to walk away from where the negs had held her and join the others.

Susan ran and embraced her. "You were so brave Kerry! We thought we had lost you. I'm so glad that you're back here with us!" she said with joy flooding into her heart.

"So am I!" said Kerry. "It was the most terrifying thing being amongst those negs. I never imagined that I'd be saying that you're the most welcome sight in the world!"

All the Earth children and the recovering faeries crowded

The Heart Stone

around Kerry to congratulate her and ensure that she was well. As the congratulations subsided, they began to notice that within the light of the Slegna, shapes of beings were forming and they could hear the most beautiful music approaching.

"What is happening? Who are they?" Susan asked Hawthorne.

"Dear Susan, as always, your two questions at once," he said with a warm smile, his strength almost entirely restored to him. "The truth is, dear one, I do not know. I know that they are the Slegna, who are higher beings, and have been known to intervene in other realms at times of extreme crisis. Only Iridaan knows the whole story. She encountered them many years ago."

Susan and the others ran to where Iridaan was standing. Her strength was totally restored and she looked truly majestic, standing tall, with her eyes fixed upon the approaching Slegna. She turned and smiled at the group of Earth children and faeries who were gathering about her. "I know you want to know who the Slegna are. They are the higher beings; they have the greatest power of all the winged beings. On extremely rare occasions, they will intercede on behalf of a Realm that is at war. Their intercession is usually triggered by acts of extreme bravery and sacrifice. I believe that in this case, it is because of Kerry's brave and selfless action that they have come." Turning to Kerry she said, "It was a courageous act indeed, but never do I want to hear of you risking your life in a reckless manner again."

"No, I never will Iridaan. I've learned my lesson. I've never been so afraid in my life and I never want to be again," she said emphatically.

At this point the forms in the sky were beginning to take shape. The music was getting louder and sweeter as they approached. All of a sudden, a huge and brilliant-white winged unicorn stallion came into view; his long, snowy-white mane and tail flowing in the breeze like a million silken threads. Wide feathered wings propelled him through the air as accurately as those of an eagle. Within seconds, the magnificent beast touched the ground and reared up onto its hind legs whinnying a greeting to the assembled crowd of children and faeries.

Iridaan strode purposefully over to the shining creature and spoke some words that the children did not understand. "She is speaking in the ancient language of the Slegna," explained Hawthorne. "She is welcoming him. His name is Pax."

"Can he understand Iridaan?" asked Susan.

"Yes, he can and he can communicate too. He sends a picture into your mind to tell you what he is saying," Hawthorne said in reply.

The music became even sweeter as four other forms began to appear clearly in the sky. The light around the Slegna was at its most brilliant, it was emanating from their bodies. They were dressed in white tunics, not unlike those of the warrior faeries. Their breastplates were of burnished gold and shone forth as brightly as the sun. Their legs were bare except for golden sandals with thongs of gold that criss-crossed around their lower legs and tied behind their knees.

As they neared the ground, those watching could see that the Slegna were enormous in stature, each one standing about twenty feet tall. They were muscular in build and evenly proportioned. The first of them had dark copper-coloured skin and hair the colour of ebony that fell in tight ringlets to the shoulder. The second one, had pearly, white skin and silken, black, shoulder length hair that shone like a raven's wing in the wind. The third one had brilliant red wavy hair that fell to the shoulders which looked like a fiery flame as the wind blew through it. This Slegna's skin glowed with a snowy radiance. The fourth one had very long pale blonde hair shot with silver streaks and a light golden skin that was etched with fine lines and looked older than the other three.

As they descended upon the ground, the music ceased and the one with very long hair began to walk towards Iridaan. As they approached, Iridaan fell to one knee and bowed her head.

Susan and the others were awed by the sight of these magnificent beings. Their eyes were transfixed upon them. Unusually, Susan was left speechless at the sight of them. All she could do was to gaze upon them and think how wonderful they were and how they made her whole body seem to vibrate with a magical feeling. Looking at the others, she knew that they were all feeling the same way.

The oldest of the Slegna dropped down onto one knee and extended his hand to help Iridaan to her feet. They exchanged some words that the children could hear faintly but not understand. With that, Iridaan led them to the children who were waiting with great anticipation.

Iridaan introduced the Slegna to the children. "This is Libro, the Keeper of the Word. He records the deeds of extraordinary bravery in the Book of Time. He is the oldest of the Slegna, his gift is knowledge." Libro bowed his head in a serious, fatherly manner to the gathered children.

The children bowed in response to Libro and were both awed and curious about this magnificent being whose deep blue eyes seemed to hold a million secrets. They were kind eyes, not frightening; there was a twinkle in them when he looked at the children. He had a straight, thin nose and thinnish lips that smiled gently at the children as they exchanged greetings. His face was long and very handsome and he appeared to be about fifty-five years old.

"These are his helpers," Iridaan said, pointing first to the two with dark hair. "On the right, is Chrystal, she has the gift of clarity and can see clearly the intentions of any being and know if they are good or destructive,"

Chrystal afforded the children a bright smile that touched

their hearts with pure joy. She was the one with the silken black hair. She had a round face and beautiful jet coloured eyes that were oriental in shape. Her beauty shone from her like a beacon. Her nose was small and straight and her lips were full and well defined. Despite her muscular frame, she looked entirely feminine.

The children felt completely at ease with Chrystal as she exuded a sense of joy and fun that felt very childlike to them. Chrystal gave them a little curtsy and a playful smile. The girls attempted to curtsy back to her but fell into fits of giggles as they wobbled and fell over. The boys bowed their heads to her.

Iridaan continued with the introductions, pointing to the one with the beautiful copper-coloured skin, she smiled and said, "This is Heb, his gift is that of love."

Heb smiled warmly at the children. His eyes, the colour of honey, shone with a love so pure that it could melt a heart of stone. His elegant, slightly hooked nose gave him a roguish look and his eager smile revealed teeth that shone like pearls. His copper coloured oval shaped face was entirely charming and handsome. He blew a kiss to the children and they responded in kind.

Iridaan gestured towards the red-haired Slegna. "This is Spera, and his gift is hope."

Spera's square shaped face lit up with a brilliant smile, his green eyes alight with enthusiasm. His nose was medium sized and slightly upturned and his smiling lips were even and well defined. Like all the other Slegna, he was very good looking.

"Spera also has the gift of music," concluded Iridaan.

Demonstrating this to the children, he opened his arms wide with his palms upwards and opened his mouth and a few bars of most enchanting music burst forth. The children loved this display. They were all so full of questions, but it was Susan who was able to summon up her courage the quickest and asked Libro the first question.

"Libro, how is it that you were able to defeat the negs. The faeries couldn't defeat them with their powers of projection and you don't even have any weapons?"

Libro took a moment to respond as Earth language was not his first tongue. He seemed to withdraw into himself and then nod as if he had just located the exact thing that he was searching for.

"To answer your question, child," he said in a very serious voice, "We came here, not to battle with a sword, but to restore balance. This can never be done with violence," he paused to look at all the children who were listening with rapt attention to his every word. "First, we come in peace, which is the job of Pax."

Pax trotted over to where the children were standing and bent down upon his knees and bowed his head. Libro stroked him and he indicated for the children to do the same.

"After we come in peace," continued Libro, "we bring wisdom to the negotiation." he closed his eyes as if to acknowledge his own gift.

"Then comes clarity," he nodded towards Chrystal. "With that, we can see where solutions lie. All this is done with love," he smiled in Heb's direction. "Then finally, we spread hope for the future that resonates like a beautiful symphony," he nodded appreciatively at Spera. "Then everyone wins," concluded Libro.

Susan was extremely impressed with what Libro had said but she was still not clear how they had defeated the negs.

Sensing her confusion, Hawthorne spoke gently into her mind. "Susan, dear child, the power of the Slegna is immense; they are the highest of beings before The Source. They defeated the negs through their ability to dispel darkness and despair. They bring wisdom, clarity, love and hope in such abundance that no force can withstand them. In short, the negs were powerless against such purity and light and they ceased to exist because they had no ability to negotiate. The negs are the lowest of beings who cannot evolve into anything more because they have no positive intent. They are a dark presence created through negative energy that has no true form."

Susan understood better with Hawthorne's explanation and so did the other children. In Susan's absence, they had all learned how to communicate telepathically. It had been a necessity when they stood with the faeries in battle.

After these rather lengthy explanations from Libro and Hawthorne the children's attention became focused upon Pax, who was enjoying the attention that he was receiving from them. He seldom came into contact with children and he loved their spontaneity.

Libro started to speak again. "All of you children have been extremely courageous and we salute you. Because of your bravery, it has been decided that we will delegate a task for you to do."

Chrystal flew over to where the Heart Stone had been broken in two and brought the two pieces back and set them at Libro's feet. He raised his right hand in the air and spoke a few words over them. To everyone's amazement the two halves of the Heart Stone increased in size and became two separate complete stones in their own right.

"With your consent, children," continued Libro, "we ask you to take one of these new Heart Stones back with you to Earth and keep it in a very secure location. Once on Earth, it will enable those with good intentions and creative ability to project their gifts for the good of the Earth and for the good of you all. What do you say?"

In a united voice the children wholeheartedly agreed.

"But where shall we keep it?" asked Aliya, worried that they might not find a safe enough place to conceal it.

"Iridaan can help you with that, for it is now time for us to leave," he said solemnly.

The children were disappointed that these wonderful beings had to leave so soon. Susan had particularly wanted to talk to Chrystal, thinking her the most lovely and friendly of beings. As if sensing this, Chrystal looked over at her and gave her a warm smile and a little wink. With that, the four Slegna began to beat their massive wings in preparation for flight. All the faeries dropped to one knee and bowed their heads as the Slegna took flight into the blue sky. As they flew, the land beneath them vibrated and shook and glowed with a thousand rainbow colours and was restored to its former beauty. A loud gasp came from those who beheld this wonderful sight and then a loud cheer went up.

Then Iridaan's voice rang out like a bell. "Look! Look!" she exclaimed pointing to where the Slegna had just passed over. "It is Laurelei! And, with him, are all of our brothers and sisters that we thought dead! The Slegna have interceded and returned them to us!" Iridaan, with others who had lost their family members in battle, ran to greet them. There was such happiness in that moment, words could not describe it.

Susan and the other Earth children were overwhelmed with joy at this spectacle. They hugged each other in sheer delight. "Oh, this is better than I could ever have wished for," said Susan to Seb. "I'm so glad that we were able to help and that Kerry was so brave."

"Yes, it is unbelievable and so are you Susan Grey. Will you please be my girlfriend?" he asked, feeling great emotion for this plucky girl with a heart as big as a lion's.

Susan didn't hesitate "Yes I will, Sebastian Alameda, with great pleasure.

They hugged each other warmly and Seb ventured to plant a kiss on Susan's cheek making her blush the colour of Claret wine.

Kerry watched the two of them, but this time, she smiled in warm affection. She would never let jealousy rule her heart again. She had seen the dreadful destruction that it could bring.

"You children ought to be getting on your way home

very soon," Hawthorne said with a warm smile.

George stood forward and started to speak. "The faeries already know this," he said looking at all his mortal friends, "but I want to let you know that I've decided to stay here."

The children all looked very surprised as they were all beginning to have pleasant thoughts of going home to their parents.

"Why aren't you coming back with us?" Seb asked, astonished.

"I belong here, Seb. On Earth I'm a misfit. You've seen how the other boys torment me. My life is a misery there. But here, I'm loved, accepted, and I feel very, very happy," he said, smiling at his faerie brethren.

"But what about your parents?" persisted Seb.

"My parents will understand. My mother is the one that passed on the faerie blood to me so she won't be distressed at my decision to stay here. Azure told me that my father knows about the faerie blood so he will understand too. Besides, they can always come here to visit me," concluded George.

"Why don't you just return with us to say goodbye to them?" asked Susan.

"It'll be very difficult for me to return because when I was on the battlefront, I thought I was going to die. If I was to die, I knew that I wanted to die a faerie so I took the oath," George said.

"What do you mean, George? What oath?" Susan persisted.

"Those like me that have faerie blood may swear an oath that allows us to develop fully into a faerie, but to do this I had to renounce my mortal side. The oath gives me the power to project wings and be able to fly. I will study with the elders and learn all the faerie ways. If I return to Earth, I won't be as I am now. I'll be very small like Hawthorne was when he was there. So, you see, it's better if I remain here. But I would ask that you and Seb go and tell my parents what has happened," he said, smiling at Susan and Seb. They nodded their agreement.

Iridaan strode over to the children, her face alight with happiness. "Children, children, this is a momentous day! We are so proud of you and what you have accomplished here. To have the honour of a visitation from the Slegna is unbelievable. It is such a rare occurrence."

"Oh, do tell us more about the Slegna," pleaded Aliya, who was enjoying having Omar's arm around her shoulders.

"The Slegna are the highest beings before the Source. They are the guardians of all our souls and are full of wisdom and joy."

"Are they guardians of Earth children's souls?" asked Susan.

"Indeed they are. You see there are many realms that the Source has created and the Slegna work with all of them," Iridaan replied.

"When the Slegna arrived, Hawthorne said that you had met them a long time ago. Please tell us about it," Susan asked enthusiastically.

"Well, it is a very long time ago, perhaps ten thousand in your years."

"You can't be that old!" Susan exclaimed, with all the other children nodding their agreement.

"Dear ones, I am, indeed, that old and more!" she said laughing at their astonishment. "The memories that I have of them were of a time when there was a great sorrow in the land. People from another realm, called the Kroyeen, had invaded ours and wanted to take our great books of wisdom. They were a greedy people who did not respect the possessions of others. However, they were very powerful with weapons that wreaked devastation upon our land. At that time we still used weapons to defend ourselves, killing sticks of every kind; we had not learned the sacred nature of life then. We lost many, many faerie warriors in that war. Our hope was at an end. It was then that the Slegna appeared. They came and made peace between us and the Kroyeen, and they became our friends. The Slegna stayed with us for some length of time and taught us their language and gave us some books of wisdom, most importantly, they taught us the futility of taking the life of another. How you can never really eradicate another person in that way." Iridaan's eyes took on a misty demeanour as she seemed to reflect on a past sorrow.

Susan wanted to make Iridaan think of something less sad and interjected, "Have you still got the Slegna books of wisdom?"

"Yes, dear," answered Iridaan, immediately brightening.

"Oh, can we see them and perhaps read them?" asked Susan excitedly.

"You can all see them, dear children, if you wish, however, you will not be able to read them as they are written in the script of the Slegna, which is very different to your written word."

"Wow, we'd love to see them," said Omar. "What kind of language do they use?"

"They use symbols rather than words. It is rather complicated; it took me many years to understand it properly. The symbols are called Mandalas and are made up of strings of letters that wind into complex shapes and patterns that then fit inside the Mandalas. The Mandalas are tablet shaped, rather like the Egyptian hieroglyphics."

"Oh, that sounds fabulous!" said Omar. "Did the Slegna ever visit Earth and leave any of their books there?"

"As a matter of fact they did," Iridaan said, pleased to see the children's obvious interest in the Slegna scripts. "Unfortunately, they were discovered at a time of degeneration in your time. There were once very wise beings that lived upon Earth who were able to understand the Slegna Scrolls. However, they were slaughtered by savage warriors who had no respect for culture and many of the Scripts got destroyed. When they were eventually discovered, it was by those who did not have the intellect to decipher them. Indeed, many of the scripts have been read backwards. Those on Earth, at that time, even thought the Slegna to be winged warriors that would wreak destruction upon mankind. They did not realize that the Slegna are gentle beings that protect and love others. I believe that now there has been progress made amongst archaeologists and scientists in deciphering some of the Ancient Slegna Scripts and they are beginning to understand your history in a very different way."

"Can we see the Slegna books now, please?" asked little Mischka, impatient to finish the long explanations and actually see the books.

"I will take you there now. It is not far," Iridaan smiled indulgently at the impatient little moppet.

Iridaan took the children to a beautiful building that had intricate designs all around it. It was made of white and gold marble and sparkled in the newly bright sunlight. Inside there were thousands of books that were all in beautiful condition, despite looking very old. She led them to a large glass case which sat atop a solid golden base. Very carefully, she lifted one of the magnificent books out. The outside of the books were bound with deep purple velvet, with silver and gold scrolling work on them. Slowly, she opened the book to reveal pages of tablet shaped symbols filled with intricate patterns and designs.

"The patterns inside the Mandalas are called Cordellas," Iridaan said, pointing to the swirling print. The Cordellas are the Slegna's alphabet."

"Oh! They're magnificent," said Aliya with all the other children nodding their agreement.

The children were allowed to spend a little time looking around the faeries' library. It was one of their most revered and respected places and the children felt very honoured to be allowed to be there.

"Now children, it is high time that you returned to your homes. I want to speak to you about the Heart Stone before you leave though."

"Yes," said Susan. "We had been thinking about that. It's quite big and none of us have a place where we could hide it."

"The Slegna knew that you would have a problem concealing it. That is why they asked me to speak to you about it," responded Iridaan. "I want you to take it to George's parents' house. They will know of its importance and be able to conceal it. It is very important that the Heart Stone stay in good hands; for if it fell into the hands of those with bad intentions, they would be able to use its power to enhance their ill deeds."

"Oh," Susan said, a little disappointed. "I thought that it only gave good positive energy out."

"Unfortunately, the Heart Stone aligns itself to the hearts of people who are using it," Iridaan said regretfully. "However, the Slegna were so impressed by your courage and dedication to the Realm of Faeries that they have entrusted you with this stone. Now, you must all remember, it is not enough that you merely carry this stone to Earth; you must spend time with it and imbue it with your energies. This will make it harder for anyone to steal it. Once you are aligned with the stone, you will receive great energy from it and will know that something is amiss if you do not feel its energy."

The children all felt a sense of great responsibility for the Heart Stone, but still wanted to take it to Earth. Sensing this, Hawthorne chipped in. "Don't worry, children. We too, will be keeping an eye on your Heart Stone for it is the sister of our Heart Stone and, to some extent, they will share their energies. We will alert you if anything threatens our lovely Heart Stone," he said with a smile.

"Children, you must be on your way now for the time differential between our two worlds is becoming critical

The Heart Stone

and your absence may be noted if you stay longer," said Iridaan with a note of sadness. She would have loved to keep these lovely children in her realm, but she knew that she must let them return.

"Will we see you again?" cried Mischka, alarm rising in her voice.

"Yes, you will. It is easy for all of you to return here now. You have a positive connection with our realm. If, at night, you tell yourselves that you wish to visit us in your dreams, you will be able to come here in the dream state. You can also return in the way that Hawthorne has taught you all. So this is not goodbye forever, it is adieu until you choose to return," concluded Iridaan, scarcely able to conceal the tears in her eyes.

All the faeries and George had gathered around to see the children leave. Those faeries that were not in close proximity, hovered in the sky to bid the children farewell. They blew them kisses and spoke kind words of thanks into their minds and asked that they soon return. Tina May and Laura June came, especially, to say goodbye to Susan. Speaking to her one more time in their lovely tinkling voices that they knew Susan loved. "Remember us and the lovely times we've spent together and please come back soon!" they cried in unison.

Mischka threw herself into Iridaan's arms and cried, "I love you! You're the most beautiful person in the world."

Hugging her tightly Iridaan said softly, "And I love you too, little one. I love you all."

With that, Hawthorne instructed Susan to carry the Heart Stone and take up a position in the centre of the children. He then asked the other children to lay their hands upon it and then to link hands and make a circle around her. With Seb holding Rocky on his lead, they were all set for their journey back to Earth.

"Susan, my dear, the Heart Stone will begin bonding with your energy and that of the other children. It will make our journey to Earth even swifter and energise you all," said Hawthorne taking off his billowing cloak. "Here Susan, take my cloak to wrap the Heart Stone in. It is important that it stay concealed from view once you are on Earth."

Hawthorne told them all to imagine themselves back in the Pine Woods and within an instant they were there.

Chapter 20
The Children Carry the Heart Stone to Earth

Susan and Seb were the first of the children to recover their senses as they had both made the journey there and back before. Hawthorne ensured that all of the children were safe and sound before he started to take his leave of them.

"It has been an honour to have met all of you children. You are most courageous and have shown yourselves to be exceptional individuals." Turning to Kerry he said, "You, young lady, have made great progress. You made the ultimate sacrifice to save us and for that, we will be eternally grateful. You turned from the negative side, which was a great challenge for you. Now you must work to keep yourself free of neg pollution, for although they are gone from our realm, they are still within yours," he said on a cautionary note.

"Don't worry, I'll never allow myself to be drawn into that kind of life again. Besides," she said turning to the other children, "I have my new friends to keep me on the right path," she said smiling.

The others smiled and nodded at her to affirm their friendship for her. Hawthorne, then, solemnly, took Kerry's hand and planted a gentle kiss upon it.

Turning to Susan he said, "My dear Susan, without you, our realm would have been lost. You are a most "extraordinary" child with great potential. Your creativity is already beyond compare and your imagination knows no bounds. You have excelled yourself in helping us; the Faerie Realm will be always in your debt!"

Susan's heart sang with joy! Finally, she had excelled

at something; she wasn't just "ordinary" any more. She felt very proud of herself and knew that her parents would be overjoyed if she was able to tell them. However, she knew that it would be very difficult to explain to them and decided that she wouldn't even try.

"Go swiftly now to George's parents house for it is not safe for you to be so exposed carrying the Heart Stone."

Finally, giving Rocky a good pat, to show his appreciation for the courageous deed the little puppy had done, he waved to all the children and was gone. The children stood silent for a time, Kerry nursing her kissed hand as if it were a precious jewel.

Seb looked at Susan and said, "We had better go now."

"Susan, wait!" cried Kerry. "After you have taken the Heart Stone to George's house, may I please have Hawthorne's cloak as a souvenir?"

"Is that okay with everyone?" asked Susan. They all nodded their agreement "Yes, you may keep it. I'll bring it to you tomorrow," Susan said, smiling.

Turning to the other children, Susan told them how much she appreciated their help in coming to the Faerie Realm. The little ones all said it was a great adventure and they wanted to go again. She hugged Aliya tightly whilst Seb punched Omar on the arm in brotherly affection and they took their leave.

Turning to Susan, Seb said, "George gave me his address. It's on the West side of town."

The two of them set off, with Rocky trotting proudly at their side, anxious to deliver the Heart Stone to a safe place but less anxious to tell them of George's decision not to return. It took them a good twenty minutes, walking at a fast pace, to get to George's parents' house. They were surprised when they saw his house. It was large, very grand and very different from their modest houses.

"Wow!" said Seb. "I bet this place cost a million pounds."

"Yes, it's very grand," agreed Susan.

They walked up the long driveway and used the large brass knocker to knock on the door, as they couldn't see a bell to ring. Within seconds, the door opened and a beautiful looking woman stood there. She looked to be in her early thirties and closely resembled Azure in features and stature.

"Come in children, my name is Esther," she said smiling brightly at them while patting Rocky "I've had a visit from Azure and know the reason for your visit here." Susan and Seb exchanged glances, unsure whether she knew about George's decision to stay in the Faerie Realm.

Sensing their hesitance, she told them, "Don't be concerned, children, I know of George's decision to stay in the Faerie Realm and in many ways, my husband and I are glad for him. He has suffered badly in the Earth realm, more than any of our predecessors with faerie blood have. The neg influence has never been as great as it is now here on Earth. It is driving children to do dreadful things. Things that were unthinkable even when I was a child. George is safe and happy and that is what counts. We shall miss him, but we can visit him whenever we want."

Susan and Seb were relieved not to have to break this news to Esther.

Esther smiled at them and continued. "You have the new Heart Stone with you, Susan; we must take it to a place of safety immediately."

Esther led them towards a large library containing hundreds of beautifully bound books. She walked purposefully over the shiny marble floor to the centre of the room. There she aimed a small torch-like object at the enormous glittering chandelier that hung above them. The torch-like object sent out a beam of blue light towards the chandelier which then emitted a long slow pulsating sound that increased in intensity. At peak intensity, it shot a beam of light down directly beneath it and in the centre of the marble floor a square opening appeared with steps leading downwards.

"Follow me," instructed Esther. The children followed, amazed at what they had just witnessed and marvelled at the beautiful room that was coming into view beneath them. It shone with a soft glow from every façade. In the centre of the room stood a square display case encrusted with crystal. At its centre was a cup shaped receptacle.

"This for the Heart Stone," Esther said, gesturing towards the cup. "Azure helped me to project it into being a short while ago. The Heart Stone will be safe here. It will be protected by a strong electro-magnetic force that has been programmed to accept the vibration of all the children that visited the Faerie Realm with you. That will allow all of you to have access to it. Now you must place it in its receptacle."

Susan stepped forward very solemnly, knowing the importance of her mission. Very gently, she placed the Heart Stone in its receptacle and as she did so, it immediately shone forth with myriad shapes and colours as the one in the Realm of Faeries had. The room became suffused with brilliant light and colours and a strong positive vibration emanated all around it.

"Oh!" cried Susan and Seb in one voice. They were lost for words at the transformation of the room. The room filled them with such strength and happiness they felt as if they never wanted to leave it.

"Can we really come here and be with the Heart Stone?" asked Susan thinking that this was such a grand house that Esther and her husband might not really want them visiting.

"Yes," replied Esther. "Of course you can. You and the others must consider this your home. It's very important that the Heart Stone be visited by all of you. For the qualities that you possess will help the Heart Stone to function well. As the Slegna told you, the Heart Stone will reinforce the intentions of all those on Earth who wish to be creative and work for the good of the people and the Earth. Your creativity and imagination is like food for the Heart Stone because it has bonded with you. In return it will empower you and give you advantages over others as long as your intentions are good."

"Wow," said Susan and Seb as one voice.

"Of course, if you don't agree to this, there's no pressure upon you to do it."

"No, no," said Susan. "I want to do it. It is fabulous and I want to help."

"Me too, me too!" echoed Seb.

"Always remember, that the door to this house will always be open to you and the other children," Esther concluded with a warm smile.

George's father appeared; a tall, handsome man with delicate, elf-like features yet with an aristocratic bearing. It was from him that George got his refined features and gentle look.

"Hello children, welcome. It is an honour to make your acquaintance my name is Patrick," he said, extending his hand for them to shake. "Everything that Esther has said, I echo. You must consider this house to be your home."

"Thank you," said the two children, both thinking that George's father had an "other worldly" look about him too.

"I think that we should be getting home now," said Seb thinking that their absence would have been missed.

"Don't worry," said Patrick. "In Earth time you'll find that you have been away only two hours. When you return home, it'll be just about time for tea," he said with a wide cheeky grin.

Susan, Seb, and Rocky took their leave of George's parents, chattering none stop about all of their adventures. Seb walked Susan to her house and reluctantly they parted. Seb headed off home and, like Susan, tried very hard to settle back into a normal routine.

That afternoon while Susan had been away, Mrs. Robinson had visited Sylvia, Susan's mum, and asked whether Susan would like to have Rocky, as he only seemed to behave properly when he was with her. After consulting Susan's dad, it was agreed that Rocky would, to Susan's delight, come and live with them. He became her loyal pet and slept at her bedside at night to protect her.

All of the children met together once more before the school holidays finished and went to George's house to visit the Heart Stone. The children found that they had a strong bond between them that united them in a special and magical way. They were still able to communicate telepathically and were having some success with their powers of projection on Earth. Susan had managed to retain the height that she projected for herself in the Faerie Realm. Her mother told her that she had "shot up over the holidays and was growing like a weed!"

The children somehow knew that the things that they had experienced were of the utmost importance and they could feel the magic and strength of the Heart Stone coursing through their veins. They had changed, their wisdom had grown, and the older ones, Susan, Seb, Aliya and Omar all felt ready to take on the demands of moving on to their new Secondary School.

On September 5th, the first term began in the new school. Susan, Omar, Aliya, and Seb were walking to the bus stop to catch the bus to their new school when they were hailed by a familiar voice. It was Kerry, dressed modestly, in her new uniform. Her skirt was worn at knee length and she had sensible shoes on her feet and her hair was no longer highlighted. It was a lovely shade of strawberry blonde.

"Hiya guys," she said cheerily. "Can I walk with you?"

"Of course you can," Aliya said, linking arms with her.

"You know, you look really nice," Seb said, linking arms with Susan.

The Heart Stone

"Thanks, Seb," Kerry replied, wishing that she could find a boyfriend as loyal and suited to her as Seb was to Susan.

Together, they set off happily to their new school ready to meet new friends. On their way there, they were approached by a good-looking, blonde haired boy of their own age with impish, good-looks who was wearing the same school uniform as them.

Addressing Susan he said, "I believe that you're Susan Grey. I've been asked to give you this letter."

"How do you know who I am?" said Susan, curiosity mounting in her voice.

"The person that gave the letter to me pointed you out. She's over there," he said, pointing to the opposite side of the road.

The children all turned to look, but all they saw was the fleeting flash of a hooded figure disappearing into the distance.

"May I walk with you please? I'm new here and I don't know anyone. My name is Robert Sherwood, but you can call me Robbie," he said with a roguish smile.

They all nodded and happily made space for him in their small group.

Susan was curious about who could have sent her a letter in such a strange manner, so she asked Robbie to give her the letter. Handing it over to her, she noted the shiny, pearl coloured envelope and read the golden script upon it. It was addressed to "The Extraordinary Susan Grey and her Friends."

Definitions of Neg and Faerie

Definition Of A Neg

Negs are a product of the idle minds of many Earth people.

They are composed of negative energy.

They have evolved over hundreds of years.

They now strongly influence children's minds negatively.

They are growing stronger and stronger through the negativity produced by Earth's children.

They are attacking the Realm of Faeries to try and stop the faeries from protecting Earth children.

In the Earth Realm they are invisible.

In the Faerie Realm they have evolved to become visible, grotesque apparitions.

Their attack on the faerie's is directed at their minds. They plant sinister images in the faeries minds, which disorient them.

Their master plan is to spread negativity. They consume positive energy and turn it into negativity. They want to destroy the Faerie Realm and the faeries and then take over Earth by controlling people's minds through negative thought. They will then use Earth as a base to infiltrate other worlds.

Definition Of A Faerie

Faeries are kind, benevolent beings whose mission in life is to work with nature to nurture children's imagination and help their dreams come true.

They are tall and elegant in stature in their own realm.

In Earth Realm they appear small as they are subject to the electro-magnetic forces on Earth that prevent them from projecting their appearance normally.

The negs are attacking the faeries because they are trying to protect the children of Earth from the negs' influence.

Lightning Source UK Ltd.
Milton Keynes UK
22 October 2009
145284UK00001BA/208/P